The Conjunction

Taryn East

ISBN 978-1-922888-01-3 / First, paperback

NATIONAL
LIBRARY
OF AUSTRALIA

A catalogue record for this
book is available from the
National Library of Australia

For my dad, my first fan.
I hope to continue giving you Hope. ♥

CONTENTS

1 - The little fish

HOPE

Hope slipped through the crowd like a tiny fish, intent on her target. She loved this part. Poised, ready and waiting for the right time to strike, to steal the food straight out of her prey's mouth.

Glittering shoals of entertainers, vendors, and society ladies drifted around her, their conversation as bright as the overhead bulbs, a desperately happy tinge to the sound. Time was rolling on, and this party wouldn't last forever.

Keeping sight of her target was challenging in this crowd, but Hope had an edge that was hard to beat. She followed the internal tug infallibly despite the contrary surge and wash of the people around her.

The target was dressed in plain, dark work clothes; a strong contrast to the vivid rainbow of the heaving masses – each one competing in a display of flamboyance. Lekking birds of paradise strutting their wares. And yet their over-saturated efforts resulted in displays so similar that they blended together into a wash of colour.

By comparison, Hope's prey was a drab pigeon, a professional courier with clothing calculated not to stand out. She carried a stack of parcels that seemed too heavy for her athletic frame. Hope, however, spotted the gleam of steel that hinted at body augmentation. Arm upgrades were common among bonded couriers. The best let a slim person lift half a truck, but the basic model still upgraded you to weightlifter standard without putting on the requisite bulk.

The courier pushed through and between the bright swathes, her drabness causing the drifting party crowd to overlook her as she

1

passed. Just another service worker fading into the background.

A band of gaudy revellers stumbled across her path, slurring their way through a bawdy song. A woman in canary-yellow silk, interwoven with LEDs, veered sideways – waving a flame-red handbag.

The courier stepped back in haste, narrowly avoiding being brained, only to trip over the next reveller's articulated prehensile tail. Overburdened with packages, she stumbled and fell, knees cracking as they hit the concrete and packages tumbling into the crowd.

Hope struck. "Oh my. Are you all right?" she bubbled, her voice thick with concern. "Here, let me help you." She grabbed at the tumbled parcels that had scattered around the woman.

The party goers lurched around them, yelling, "Get off the footpath," as Hope and the courier fumbled for the parcels, trying to retrieve them before the surrounding crowd could damage them.

"I'm all right!" the woman snapped, ignoring Hope's outstretched hand and heaving herself to her feet. She huffed as she realised Hope hadn't left and had, in fact, collected her property, holding it out to her with one raised eyebrow.

The courier snatched the packages. She rapidly inspected each one, tutting over the torn and dirty paper. Then she froze, her gaze skittering wildly, hunting for her misplaced property.

Hope was still smiling. "Here, are you looking for this one?"

The pigeon's gaze zoomed in on the black document case Hope held out to her. The woman sighed with relief and snatched it back, cradling it to her chest.

"Thank you," she grated out, then turned away from Hope, rebalancing her pile of packages to check her watch.

Hope slipped back into the stream of people around them. Through a lull in the hubbub, she heard the tiny *SNICK-CLUNK* of the case being opened.

She upped her pace.

The yelling began immediately.

Hope walked as fast as she could without breaking into a run. Too attention grabbing. As was the way she was clutching the other black leather document case to her chest. There was no way she'd be as sloppy with it as the other woman had been. Now that it was hers, she wouldn't let it out of her grasp, even if she were to trip and fall.

Hope dove deeper into the press of people, and the furore she'd caused drifted further behind. She breathed deep once more. She knew how hard it was to chase somebody through this crowd. Without a tracker, it'd be near impossible.

But then she heard a roar like a cresting wave bearing down on her. She picked up her feet once again.

Dare she look behind? Sliding to the edge of the street, she scooted in close to a shopfront that had a large picture window. She ducked around the proprietor, who was standing on the stoop and reaching out to draw in prospective buyers. Instead, she studied the reflection as she walked by, trying to catch a view of what was happening behind her as she slid past.

Her drab pigeon was chasing close behind. Now package free and a tower of rage, heaving pedestrians left and right to get herself through.

To get to Hope.

Ok, might need a bit more speed.

She abandoned the pretence of being an idle shopper and broke into a run. The crowd pressed close. She pushed when she had to, ducked through gaps and dodged past overhanging display cases heavy with merchandise. Hope nipped through a side alley, into a parallel street. She must've given her pursuer the slip by now. She doubled back, turning randomly through the maze of streets and shops. You can never be too careful.

Once again, she blessed this rabbit warren of a shanty town, a temporary market thrown together to milk the gullible of their credits, taking advantage of the feverish hype over the upcoming Conjunction event. It was a sprawling temple to money and desperation, and a godsend for her and her profession. An entire miniature city built to draw in an ocean of easy targets. A plentiful feeding ground, no matter whether you were a shark or a minnow.

Hope slowed to a brisk walk and reintegrated with the crowd. She ducked into an alley and sat there, watching the people drift by and ensuring she wasn't being followed. The pigeon would've found it difficult, but not impossible, to keep up with her, and it always paid to be careful.

A few minutes of quiet time had her satisfied. She stood and crept deeper in, finding a nook out of the way. She sat again and rested the case on her lap. Then pulled a knife out of a hidden jacket pocket and used it to pry up the latches. They squeaked in protest, then popped open, and she was free to inspect her winnings for the day.

Her eyes widened as she gazed at what lay inside.

This wasn't what she'd expected.

The case was heavy. When she'd seen company goons handing it to the bonded courier, she'd speculated that it might be full of blueprints: plans for alchemical processes or designs for mechanical wonders. Instead, she found a single, thin box – not much wider than a heavy pamphlet, but as large as the case itself.

Could it be?

Her hands shaking, she lifted the box, set it atop the case on her lap, and paused for a moment. She breathed in, deep, then out. Then she edged her thumbs under the flap of card holding the box shut, and lifted.

She saw black, curved lines etched into heavy parchment. They flowed and curled around each other, surrounded by esoteric script and strange symbols.

She smiled.

Fantastic!

She looked closer and smiled again. This was superlative! She'd hoped for a simple conjuration matrix, but this looked next level. Professional; high grade; expensive work.

But what made her breath catch in her throat and her eyes widen was what lay in the centre – a palm-sized, perfect circle of glittering metal attached to the paper by delicate golden threads. It was a single slice of the purest dream steel.

It drew her gaze in. The noises around her quieted, and her senses all rearranged themselves to focus on this. Only this. She felt herself tracing the whorls of patterning with her eyes, drawing them down into the centre of the design.

A deep part of her mind protested.

She wasn't safe. This wasn't what she wanted... and yet it really was. She could gaze into this cool, glittering circle and be lost to its wonder forever.

Slowly, she became aware of another sound coming from beyond the edges of the circle. Her mind tried to push it away, to get back to her gazing. The sound wasn't important.

And yet her deeper survival instincts rebelled. They were yelling at her to pay attention. Instincts honed from years of surviving on the streets were demanding her attention, and she'd learnt the hard way that you ignored them at your peril.

She dragged her reluctant mind out of the pull of the dream steel–induced trance and back into the present.

A deep reverberation echoed through the air overhead, and suddenly every sense was on high alert. She knew that sound. A noise to strike fear into the heart of any would-be *"entrepreneur"* in this town.

She leaped up, trying to locate the origin of the heavy-engine noise, and now she could see the armoured zeppelin, only a few streets over and pulling hard towards where she was hiding. Men lined the edges of the canopy, guns and spotlights trained on the streets around her, searching.

How did they find me?

She wondered for just a second. Then she regrouped.

Not the time to wonder. Time to go.

She leapt towards the alley entrance, only to pull up short. It was blocked, and by none other than the original, drab pigeon. She was out of breath, her chest heaving. She dragged a hand across her brow, wiping the dripping sweat out of her eyes so she could inspect the read-out gleaming from a large, flashing device in her hands.

Damn! She's a tracker too!

Hope stood.

Seeing the movement, her pigeon looked up. She yelled incoherently and launched into motion.

Hope spun and sprinted in the other direction.

How's she tracking me?

She dove back into the crowd, paused, and smacked herself on the forehead.

Not me, the case!

She pushed her way through another gap, trying to angle away from the oncoming zeppelin. Stuffing the conjuration matrix down the front of her shirt, she transferred the case to her other hand. She stumbled through the edge of the crowd and into a vehicular clearway.

"Move it!" a red-faced man yelled as he pedalled his bicycle around her.

Bikes, velocipedes, and other mechanical contraptions rolled past at a rapid clip, bells ringing and curses thrown her way. An articulated centipede loaded with suitcases undulated past, pushing its own way through the press of wheeled contrivances. As it bore down on Hope, she dodged it and dumped the case on top of the pile it carried. She spun and ran in the opposite direction, sparing a glance back through the crowd.

The pigeon was gaining on her, her eyes glued to the device in her hand. But she stopped, confused, at the edge of the street. Then she turned, racing after the centipede at top speed.

Hope took off in the other direction, aiming to put some distance between them.

But before taking another step, she froze, suddenly caught in a blinding beam of light, brighter than the cloud-filtered sunlight.

The noise of the surrounding crowd dimmed into static.

"Halt, in the name of the Imperium!" a tinny voice blared from above.

Hope couldn't see up – the light was too bright, outshining the grey-filtered day.

In the distance, her pigeon spun around at the sound and gaped at her. The courier's face twisted with rage as she began pushing her way back through the crowd towards Hope.

Hope was torn. Should she run? Should she hide?

Rope ladders rattled, dropping over the side of the zeppelin and unrolling around her. A pair of uniformed men climbed down them towards her, while above, another pair trained guns and spotlights at both her and the crowds that were reluctantly parting around her, melting away from the harsh lights.

If she ran, they could shoot her before she made it to safety.

The raging pigeon pushed her way back through the heaving crowds, her eyes blazing with determination. Her movement hampered by the flows away from her and the incoming police, but she ruthlessly shoved both aside, continuing forward.

Hope could stay and be caught or run and have a chance. She'd get no quarter if she was captured, so she might as well try it. Fortune favours the bold.

< < < BOOM > > >

Hope was on her back, her ears ringing.

The wall of the building two doors down was gone, replaced by huge billowing clouds of acrid, green smoke.

Green? Why green? Weird.

She tried to reassemble her thoughts into a coherent whole. Her head was buzzing and she was… where? On the ground? Still in the street? Which way was up?

Overhead, the zeppelin rocked in the aftershocks, the attached ladders swinging wildly. The vessel's basket creaked and swayed in the roiling updraft. The two police officers desperately clung halfway down the writhing rope.

Sounds began to return to her. Screams and shrieks. Pain and terror.

Hope turned to look at the destroyed building and saw something moving, undulating like a wave. The surrounding crowd looked dazed, but as the wave advanced, they shrieked and ran.

She couldn't see what it was – and then she could.

Is that what I think it is?

Spiders! Giant spiders swarming out of the hole!

The crowd was running, fear glinting in their eyes. Escaping every which way – as long as it was *away*.

If Hope stayed still, she'd be crushed. She hauled herself to her feet and staggered as the crowd pushed and shoved around her. She lurched away from the smoking hole and the stream of unnatural spiders.

Are they real? Am I hallucinating?

She blinked, but they were still there. Leaping on bystanders, swarming and biting. Dragging one person down, kicking and screaming. More spiders leaped up, climbing the ropes up to the zeppelin.

Hope tripped, staggering to her knees. In that second, she glanced through the sea of pounding legs and saw her drab pigeon lying sprawled on the ground. Head bloodied, eyes glazed and fixed. Hope hauled herself back to her feet, surging up to rejoin the stampeding mob. Better to run with them than be dragged under.

The police on the zeppelin were yelling and firing into the heaving mass of spiders. Those still caught on the swinging ladders hauled themselves back up to safety.

Heavy engine vibrations rumbled through Hope's body as the wildly rocking zeppelin simultaneously tried to compensate for the wake of the explosion, and to back away from the leaping spiders. The spotlights were off Hope and were instead fixed on a lone, masked figure, cackling madly after having pulled himself from the wreckage of the explosion. He stood among the teeming wave of spiders, apparently immune. He jammed a top hat on his head, then turned and fled as the zeppelin's heavy engines cranked up to follow him.

Hope saw her chance and took it. She let the diverging crowds pull her away from the fiasco.

There was one thing you could depend on in this strange, artificial reef – a bigger fish was always just around the corner. And sometimes, that worked in your favour.

2 - The score

Hope pushed her way through the crowds until they thinned. She left the mad thoroughfare and headed into the Crossways – the byways and connecting roads that held the industrial zones and the darker underbelly of the city.

The bright surface lights barely reached down here, into the guts that fed the beast and kept it ticking along. There was a light-industrial factory, churning out clothing printed with sparkling depictions of the coming Conjunction. Here was a café filled with tired workers grabbing a bite to eat before heading back on shift – a greasy spoon she wouldn't trust her stomach to.

She walked past several hole-in-the-wall shopfronts selling basics, and through the back-alley doors of a darkened shop. Its front windows opened onto one of the brighter streets, with trinkets and tools of various trades on display for the general public. But the bulk of the shop's trade was undertaken out the back, in the dark, and that's how Hope liked it.

She stepped through the low doorway, pushed past overcrowded benches covered in heavy equipment, and ducked under a set of mechanical legs sticking out into the narrow path through to the crowded back room. Cupboards and shelving overflowed with random equipment, strange instruments, and jars and pots full of unusual elements, all poorly labelled with inscrutable symbology.

She could hear murmuring voices coming from the small office that lay deep inside the building. She slipped past a well-oiled wooden counter, ducked under another low-hanging mechanical monstrosity, and knocked sharply on the door.

"Be with ya in a minute, love," a familiar voice called from inside.

Hope raised an eyebrow. Henry was with another client this early in the day? She'd hoped to get in before his usual line-up of shady characters. She hopped up on the counter and settled in to wait.

She wasn't *trying* to eavesdrop, but the voice coming from inside was strong and resonant – it carried so well.

"You said you could get it for me. I paid you an enormous sum of money for it, and now it's being held ransom!"

Curious, Hope leaned closer to the doorway so she could hear Henry's reply.

"You paid me to hook you up with a legit dealer, and I did that. They don't come cheap. After that, you made your own arrangement with them for goods and transport, and from what you're telling me now, they came through. Despite the inherent difficulties, I might add. So if you're wondering, that's what you paid me for and that's what you got. I did my part, so there ain't no use whingeing about it. What more do you want from me?"

"I want the dream steel I paid for," the voice insisted, sounding a little desperate, "not excuses and weasel words!"

"You tell me it's held up by Customs. That's not my department, mate. What do you want me to do about it? I can't go up against Customs and Excise. Have you seen their gunships? They're the bloody Imperium, they are, and they've got a hotline right to the Imperial Guard. Ain't no way I'm gonna get on their bad side. Have you considered just paying them off?"

"It's extortion!" came the voice, frustration leaking through the words.

"Of course it is!" Henry chuckled. "A bit of bribery on the side's all part of business."

There was a loud thump that sounded like a fist slamming on the table.

"Hey, settle down!" Henry urged.

"I will not settle down. I paid for this merchandise, and the transportation costs. I even paid extra to make sure the papers were in order before shipment. And they're saying we haven't even sent them yet. But I checked with the vendor, he said they sent the paperwork last week. They have no reason to hold my goods up now – especially for such an outrageously high fee. It's robbery!"

Henry made some soothing noises. "I dunno, mate. Maybe the paperwork got held up or got lost in filing or something. It's sitting on some overworked secretary's desk under a coffee mug. The vendor can re-send the documents, I'm sure, and that'll sort it all out."

"Don't patronise me. You assured me this would all go smoothly. I demand you make good on your promise."

Henry sucked a breath through his teeth. "I'll see what I can do, mate, but I just can't guarantee you any traction. I'm sure they'll get all the paperwork eventually, but if you want to be sure it'll happen soon, you might just have to pay the piper to look the other way. Know what I mean?"

The other man huffed in exasperation.

"You know how this town operates, I'm sure," Henry added, "what with your... *profession* and all."

There was a moment of silence, followed by a hissed response. "Exactly what do you mean by that?"

"Well, I'm sure you need to get some somewhat... less-than-salubrious items past Customs all the time."

"How dare you?" the man spat. "I am a surgeon!"

Hope heard the man leap to his feet, and something heavy clattering to the floor. She had only a moment to lunge away from the door before it burst open and a tall man came charging through – right into the overhanging equipment. He fell to the floor with a clatter.

As he grunted in pain, she briefly glimpsed warm, hazel eyes, dark hair and high cheekbones before he put a hand to his damaged forehead. He stumbled over the scattered detritus, a long ponytail swinging wildly as he nearly fell.

Hope reached out to catch him, but he glared in her direction, righted himself, and rushed out the door. He slammed his wiry frame against the back door making it crash into the alley wall, and he disappeared.

Hope stared, slightly dazed, as the door slammed back into place. She shook her head, shrugged, and turned back to the inner door that led to Henry's office. Inside, she could hear him grumpily muttering to himself.

Darn. She'd been hoping he'd be in a good mood. Better for negotiations. She paused for a moment before knocking.

"You'd better not be another bloody necromancer!" Henry yelled.

She grinned as she let herself in. "Not last time I checked."

Henry stared for a moment, then barked a laugh. "I guess not." He turned to retrieve the upset chair from the floor. He placed it near her and gestured for her to have a seat. "Sit yourself down, love, if you're gonna." He sighed as he squeezed himself around the small desk and resettled himself in his chair.

Hope side-eyed him as she pulled the chair back and slouched in it.

"What?" He squinted at her. "Were you eavesdropping?"

"Of course," she replied, a smile playing on her lips. "You should lock your door if you don't want to be overheard."

He huffed and turned up a corner of his mouth. "Well, he got exactly what he paid for, and no more."

"Artificially increased prices to max out his pocketbook, you mean?"

He grinned smugly. "As much as he can pay, and no more."

"Aaand… you wouldn't happen to know who might've tipped off Customs about an incoming shipment of previously unaccounted-for dream steel, now, would you?" The sarcasm was dripping off her.

He raised his eyebrows and drew himself up with mock dignity. "It'd only be my civic duty to inform our friends at Excise of a transfer of unaccounted-for expensive luxury items now, wouldn't it?"

"Ha! 'civic duty', hey? And you gained nothing from this 'civic duty', hmm?"

"Not a penny!" he insisted, hand on heart.

She raised an eyebrow.

"Of course," he continued, smiling, "it always helps for Customs to owe me a favour or two…" But then his smile dropped away. "That said, I don't think the necromancer's got any more funds to pay them, so that favour mightn't be as big as all that."

She rolled her eyes. "What a sad day. When you've milked your mark so badly, you can't squeeze another drop of blood from that stone for your friends."

He shrugged and sighed. Then looked at her more clearly. "So, what can I help you with today, love? You got something for me to look over?"

Hope smiled at him and pulled out the thin but heavy package she'd been carting around in her shirtfront. She stroked it gently and smiled wider, looking up at Henry through her long eyelashes. "I have something special for you today," she purred.

He raised a sceptical eyebrow, but smiled back at her. "You certainly seem to think so, but I'll believe it when I see it." However, he couldn't hide the fact that he was eyeing up the package with intense curiosity.

Hope lifted the flap, keeping her eyes firmly on Henry, determined not to let herself be sucked into the mind-bending effects of the dream steel again.

Henry smirked at her playful reveal.

She spun the box dramatically to face him. She enjoyed the split second of shock that rippled across his face before he slammed down his professional mask once more.

She was on to him, though. His feigned disinterest was betrayed by the glimmer in his eyes. They flicked over the beautiful parchment laid out before him, and the whorl of magnificent dream steel at its centre. Which, she noticed, he didn't allow himself to fall into. And yet she could see he was hooked.

He slid the heavy parchment towards himself, examining it carefully for any flaws. "We'll figure out the dream steel by weight, of course." He shifted his gaze to the surrounding brushwork. "But I'll give you two hundred credits for the matrix itself."

Hope snorted. "This is high-quality work, not just some mass-produced corporate junk. It's worth three hundred at least."

He shook his head, smiling. "You don't actually know what it does, do you, love?"

Hope's smile twisted into a frown, and she tried to hide her chagrin.

"Thought not." He smirked again. "Two twenty-five."

"Doesn't matter what it does. It'll only cost you ten creds to run it by some shady spell-scribe to identify it, and then you can sell it for five times what you're paying me. Especially with the current market so hot. Two seventy-five."

Henry sucked air through his teeth. "You should know every spell-scribe worth his salt is over-burdened with work requests right now, especially the shady ones. It'll cost more than ten creds to bump this up the queue, and I don't want to pay those rates or share profit with the Help."

Hope sighed in frustration. "Maybe you don't need to. I could tell you who I knocked it off, and you could sell it back to the morons who let it slip from their grasp. That way you wouldn't have to care what it does."

He guffawed, his eyes twinkling. "That's brilliant. Ah, you're a woman after my own heart. Look, I'll tell you what. I'll do it for two fifty, and you consider a job I have going."

She squinted at him warily. "What job?"

Henry didn't answer, instead he glanced up at her, mouth set in a smile and parroting her own eyelash-batting attempt at beguilement. Then he stretched out behind him, rummaging through a small pile of parchment on a shelf. He took out a single sheet, inspected it, and put it back. He chose another, weighing it in his hand, and handed it to her.

Hope took it without speaking and examined it. A standard, heavy-weight matrix blank. It bore two faint imprints of perfect circles in pale ink. One stretched nearly to the edges of the page, while another nestled in the centre, roughly the same size as the circle of dream steel in the completed matrix she'd brought with her. She looked up at Henry and saw he'd produced a set of fine, well-used digital scales.

"Are you satisfied it matches?" he asked her.

She raised an eyebrow. "I'll need to compare like for like."

He grimaced, but it was an acceptable request. He reached back into the cupboard behind him to rummage around some more.

Hope lifted the edge of the completed matrix, comparing the weight of the parchment to that of the blank. Henry was mostly honourable, but he'd get away with skimming off the top if she'd let him. She wouldn't put it past him to use a heavier parchment for comparison, so he could cheat her of a few precious grams of dream steel. When it came to this stuff, every milligram counted. She wouldn't let him get away with that, and thankfully there was already a "Best Practice for Keeping Things Honest" in these kinds of trades. She was going to follow it to the letter.

He turned back around and handed over a large, heavy paper punch. "Don't clip the matrix, just the edges," he warned.

Hope rolled her eyes at him. "And ruin the merchandise? I'm not stupid."

She punched a circle of parchment from the corner of the matrix blank, and then carefully, from her own complete matrix. The corners were devoid of the special markings that made up the body of the work. She used the proffered scales to weigh each tiny circle of paper and ensure they each weighed the same. Then, she pulled a tiny box from an inner pocket of her jacket, producing a set of small squares of lead – each marked with the Imperial imprint.

Hope cleared the tiny circles of paper off the scales and set her tiny weights on, one by one, checking the numbers went up appropriately.

Henry watched her and sighed, as though long-suffering.

Hope grinned at his theatrics. This was standard operating practice, and they both knew it. Neither one wanted the hassle of being accused of cheating, and this little ritual ensured it was all as aboveboard as a back-alley exchange could be. Even the official dream-steel traders went through a similar ritual to ensure their buyers couldn't accuse them of cheating. Legal fights were expensive and a waste of both time and resources – better for each party to know that the other had done their best.

When Hope was satisfied, she set the matrix blank on the scales and tared it. She replaced it with her own parchment. They both leaned in to examine the number.

Her heart fluttered. The figure was a lot higher than she'd expected.

Henry marked it down. "We'll use the standard measure for ink and gold weight, eh?"

Her heart dropped a little. *Darn.* She'd forgotten to take off that weight, but it was still more than she'd expected to score this time around. Maybe even enough to set all her plans in motion. She allowed herself to hope. At least it'd be enough for her to get a good way towards her goal.

Henry tapped the numbers out on his calculator. Hope watched carefully while doing some mental estimates to ensure the final figure matched her expectations. Finally, she stared at it, wide-eyed, as Henry read it off.

"Two thousand, eight hundred and twenty-six credits for the dream steel." Henry read off.

Hope's eyes glittered. It was enough.

Finally.

"Plus the standard hundred for the gold weight and… Did we say two twenty-five for the matrix workings?"

She glanced up and narrowed her eyes. "You said two fifty."

He raised an eyebrow and smiled pleasantly. "I said two fifty if you take the job."

"You said two fifty if I *considered* taking it. Well, I'm considering, but I can't consider it properly if you haven't told me what the job is."

Henry spread his hands wide, a predatory grin on his face. "Well… It just so happens I know of a shipment of dream steel just sitting around at the sky docks, waiting around for somebody to claim it…"

Hope stared at him, then barked a laugh. "You sly dog. I'm impressed. You have endless ways to make money on the same shipment, haven't you?"

He smiled more broadly and shrugged. "What can I say? We all have our special talents. Are you interested?"

"I'm intrigued, but not convinced yet. Can you tell me more? But do it while you're fetching my three thousand, one hundred and seventy-six credits, will you?"

He huffed a laugh and began counting out credit chits. "I don't know how much you overheard. The shipment's at the sky docks, but it's been *'conveniently mis-labelled'* by my mate in Customs to pull off the paperwork dodge."

She snorted at the word *'conveniently'*. "So, does that mean it's not in the high-end lockup?"

"That's right. It's been labelled 'Machine parts' and dumped in general storage. In fact, from what I can tell, the only person who even knows it's there is my Customs buddy – and they only know 'cos I tipped them off." He grinned, pleased at his deception. "And from what I know of that one, it's unlikely they'll be sharing with the rest of the crew, which means it won't be heavily guarded." He frowned. "Unfortunately, it also means it's in one of dozens of giant warehouses stacked to the rafters with other boxes also labelled 'Machine parts', and the little shit deliberately didn't tell me where they put it."

"So you have no idea where it is." Then it dawned on her. "You've already tried to find it."

Henry's eyes flashed with irritation. "Yeah. The scout I sent in spent nearly all night scrabbling 'round, without any luck. Then, the moron managed to get caught and spent a night in lock-up, for trespass. I haven't heard from him since."

She raised an eyebrow. "Could your scout've made off with the goods?"

Henry's eyes flashed again, this time with something darker. Then he shook his head. "Not this one. He's one of my best clients. I keep a close eye on him." He grinned at her sharply.

Hope shivered; she didn't see that predatory look often, but she knew what it meant. Whoever this poor sap was, he was deep in debt to Henry – not a safe place to be. She raised an eyebrow once more. "How large a score are we talking?"

He grinned and handed over the shining pile of credit chits. "Let's just say your share would put this pile to shame."

Hope frowned. She double checked the number of credits and shuffled them into her purse, which she stuffed away into an inner pocket. "My share?"

"Yeah, split four ways with the team, after my commission, of course."

She glared at him. "You know I work alone."

"Yeah, yeah, I know you've got 'trust issues'." He made *finger*

16

quotes! "But this is a big job – lots of moving parts. I can't risk it all on a single operator…" He watched her expression darken even more.

"No," Hope said firmly. She pushed the chair back and stood.

Henry looked up at the stubborn set of her jaw and sighed. "I need you, Hope… to find it for me. That place is a rabbit warren, and I need to find that stuff before the Conjunction makes it all worthless again."

She glared down at him and snarled, "You need me to be your bloodhound."

"Of course," he replied. "You already know you're only an average thief, but with your ability… It's unique and it's useful – especially for this job."

Hope sighed and closed her eyes. She re-opened them and gazed into his. "I told you already, Henry, I'm done being your dog." She patted her inner pocket. "And I no longer need to be."

Henry's eyes flashed again, but they both knew he no longer held anything over her. He hadn't for a long time.

She smiled. "Thanks for the offer. I considered it, but I've chosen to decline."

She spun on her heel and walked out.

3 - At home

By the time Hope arrived home, her irritation had faded and been replaced by a bubbly feeling fizzing through her veins. It wasn't a feeling she was familiar with, but she belatedly recognised it as anticipation and hope for the future.

I have enough!

She was so excited that she took a few moments to get the key in the door, giggling at her trembling hands. Once she'd unlocked it, she pushed her way past the overflowing side table and hung her coat on one of the three hooks mounted next to the door. She sat on the little stool and set her boots beside the wall, eyeing up the pile that was scattered across the hallway and was threatening to trip any would-be intruders (or guests, if there ever were any).

"I'm home!" she shouted, "and I'm flush. Lunch is on me today."

"On you?" came a voice from deep in the living room. "I'll take that!"

"Hooray!" came another, followed by a small head popping around the edge of a bedroom door. A lanky child shot out towards Hope, little legs pumping and long hair flying, and nearly bowled her over as they threw their arms around her.

Hope grunted from the impact and staggered backwards a step.

They bounced energetically, bumping against Hope's constraining arms. "Aunty Hope! You have to see! I finished my painting! Come see! Come see!" they said.

"Hi, Sam," she replied, once able to fit a word in edgewise. "I'd love to see your picture."

They bounced even faster, nearly vibrating with happiness. "I painted a rainbow lion! It's growling, but it's not scary. It's a friendly lion, but it's totally majestic!"

"Do you want to show me while I'm changing for lunch?"

"Yes!" Sam replied, bouncing off towards the bedroom they shared with Hope's sister Felicity.

Sam was wearing pants today but had become equally comfortable wearing a dress. When they were born, Felicity had thought they were female, but a few years earlier, Sam had expressed discomfort with that restrictive designation. The previous year, Sam had finally asked everyone to use "them" instead of "her", and specifically asked Hope to call them "nibling" instead of "niece". And the happiness they now felt at being their authentic self was palpable.

Hope smiled at the departing figure and headed to her room to hunt down some cleaner clothes. She was slipping into a nice top and skirt when Felicity appeared at the door.

Felicity stood next to the dressing table while Hope dressed. "What happened with you? Did you get yourself a new job?"

Hope grinned as she popped her head through the shirt. "I scored big time. Check it out." She thrust her chin towards the purse on her dresser, pushed her arms through the armholes and settled the fabric.

Felicity weighed up the purse appreciatively before taking a peek inside. She froze. "Holy shit, Hope! That's a lot of cash."

"I know, right?" Hope burbled happily. But when she turned to look, Felicity wasn't looking pleased. In fact, she was frowning. Hope's emotions deflated. She frowned in response and opened her mouth to speak, but, before she could ask what was troubling her sister, Sam burst in bearing a huge stretch of heavy paper covered in coloured paint.

Hope cleared a spot on her bed and Sam laid the paper on it reverently.

It was beautiful. The swirls of colour somehow meshed harmoniously, despite every colour being used at once. "You're really talented at this, Sam."

Sam blushed, uncomfortable with the praise. "I made it for you."

Hope turned back to the painting to take it all in. By applying a few rough strokes, Sam had portrayed the majesty and grace of a lion gazing across a grassy savannah, his mane ruffled by a breeze that Hope could practically feel moving across her skin. "I like it."

"Would you like it up on your wall?" Sam's voice was small and timid.

"That would be the perfect place!" Hope replied. She found some fixings, and she and Sam lifted the paper up to hang above Hope's bed. When it was secure, they stood back to admire it together. "May I hug you?" Hope asked Sam.

Sam nodded.

Hope hugged them gently. When she released them, they ran off to their bedroom.

Felicity called after them, "get your coat and shoes on if we're going out!" Then she eyed the purse again and turned her gaze on Hope. "Do we need to talk about where this came from?"

Hope glowered, her happy feelings evaporating. She tossed her hair over her shoulder, then straightened up. Trying to keep a lid on her bad mood, she faced her sister. "There's nothing to talk about."

Felicity glowered back at her, scepticism and concern chasing each other across her face. "Are you..." She paused, licking her lips. "Are *we* in danger from this?"

Hope huffed in exasperation. "Damn it, can't we just enjoy this for once? I have money! We can pay rent and buy groceries, and I'll still have plenty left over for my savings plans. Let's just go out, eat some good food and enjoy it instead of fighting about it again."

Felicity put her hands on her hips and glowered at Hope more fiercely. "Are we in danger?" she reiterated, her voice stronger, more insistent.

Hope set her jaw. "Don't you go into mother mode with me, little sister. I'm the one who looked after you when we were still on the street; I kept us fed, clothed, and with a roof over our heads, remember?"

Felicity folded her arms and shook her head. "Oh, I remember. But that was a long time ago, Hope, and I'm not your baby sister any more; I can see you for what you are now."

Hope was taken aback. "And what exactly *am* I, apart from the chief breadwinner around here, huh?"

"Don't throw that in my face like I'm contributing nothing, Hope. I have an income, too."

"We'd barely cover the bills with your income!"

"At least it's a good, steady, respectable job. An honest job. One I can be proud of. One we can depend on. The way you pull in jobs whenever you can find them, we never know if we can feed ourselves or make rent. We're always feast or famine with you."

"Well, today we're feasting!"

Felicity snorted. "Until next time. And what happens when the money runs out again, hmm? How long until you're back in debt to that awful man?"

Hope stood in shock. "That is not fair! We were only ever in debt to him to get us out of the gutter, and I worked my arse off to get free and clear of Henry and you know it."

"But you're still pulling jobs for him, aren't you?" Felicity glanced at the heavy purse. "There's no way you'd get paid this much for a normal job."

Hope felt the cut of that, and it stung. She frowned. "Once upon a time, you were happy with me pulling this kind of cash."

"Once upon a time I was young and stupid, and anything seemed better than living on the street. But I have Sam now, and they depend on me and my steady income. Don't you understand? I can't afford to be as reckless as we used to be when it was just us. Besides, I understand the risks a lot better now than I did when I was a kid. I know what we stand to lose and how close we came to losing it."

Hope went quiet, her mouth open in shock as her sister's words poured over her, her thoughts and emotions tumbling wildly.

Felicity continued. "You can do what you like with your own life, Hope, but what happens to *us* if you fall foul of Henry again, and one of those shady 'friends' of yours brings the underworld home to us? Have you even thought about that possibility? At least my job doesn't get us into trouble with the law, or with any of the dozens of your dangerous 'acquaintances'."

Hope gritted her teeth and lifted her head. "Fine then. I was planning on telling you over lunch anyway, but I finally have enough now. I'm moving out." She looked away.

Felicity's face fell.

"I have enough for tuition and the first six months of lodging. After that, I'll see what I can get to keep me going. Maybe even get a 'real job'."

Hope sneered at the last part. "I'm sure I'll be transcribing matrices for some boring mid-level corporation in no time, and you won't have to worry about me and my 'risky behaviour' any more. I'll be out of your hair forever."

She pushed her way past Felicity into the hallway.

Then stopped short.

Sam was cowering in the hall, curled in a little ball with their hands over their ears, tears pouring down their face.

Hope sighed, hung her head, and covered her own face with her hands.

Felicity stepped up to the doorway to see what the hold-up had been.

Hope was already moving, crouching down beside Sam. "I'm so sorry, Sam." She reached her hands towards them, offering a hug.

Sam shrank away from her.

Hope let out another sigh, dejected.

"You were both yelling so loud." Sam moved their hands away from their ears.

"I'm sorry for yelling. I'll try to do better."

Sam nodded and looked away from her.

"Would you still like to go out for lunch with me today?"

Sam's wide eyes wandered the hallway, avoiding Hope's gaze. "Will there be ice-cream?"

Hope's mouth turned up at the corner. "I think we can arrange that."

Sam smiled up at her through their tear-streaked face, and nodded.

Hope smiled back. "Okay then, let's go get our coats."

* * * * *

Hope was still simmering with pent-up emotion when the three of them arrived at her favourite café on the plaza. She perked up a bit when the waitress seated them at one of the nicer outdoor tables, and by the time her pasta arrived, she was feeling much better.

She loved her sister, she really did, but sometimes their relationship grated. Still, she was always happy to spend time with Sam. Her nibling was excitedly explaining all the intricate details of the plans for their next painting project. They always had a new one on the go. Sam came alive whenever they talked about painting, and Hope loved to see the zest for life burning within them – especially after today's argument.

Felicity was unusually quiet and reserved, picking at her food and gazing out over the busy traffic. Hope assumed she was still stewing over the showdown, but when Hope raised an eyebrow in her direction, Felicity responded with a wide, if strained, smile. It didn't completely reach the sadness in her eyes. When Sam jumped up and declared their intention to hunt down the bathroom, Hope braced herself for a continuation of the earlier confrontation.

"Hope?" Felicity began, her voice quiet and nervous.

Hope avoided her gaze and looked out over the street. Some kind of parade was approaching. Scientifically-engineered hybrid animals – an academic research demonstration by the local university. It was an excellent diversion, and she sat entranced. Unwieldy animals coaxed into motion by stressed trainers, surrounded by hordes of fascinated onlookers. The animals looked like somebody had pulled apart their zoo toys and stuck all the heads and limbs back on the wrong bodies – monkeys, camels, elephants and lions all mixed up.

"What are the scienticians getting up to these days?" she said.

Felicity looked, and her eyes widened.

The noise coming from that direction was cacophonous. Hooting and shrieking and the tramping of many unusual feet (and a few pseudopods). The animals seemed jumpy, rolling their eyes at the pressing crowds, and the trainers and carnival hands were having a hard time pushing people back behind the inadequate rope fences. Small children snuck through their legs to approach the giant beasts before being captured and manhandled back to their parents.

Hope pointed. "Look at the tentacles on that thing!"

"Are those gorilla centaurs?" Felicity said, pointing out the next pair.

Hope laughed. "That's awesome. Is that a camelopard?"

"Those are just giraffes," Felicity replied, her tone disparaging, but looking fascinated all the same.

The two of them sat in silence, watching the flow of strange-looking creatures approach and drift past.

Felicity broke the silence. "Hope, I need to say something."

Hope sighed, turning to face her. "Haven't we said enough already?"

Felicity looked stung, but didn't deny it. Instead, she reached out and took Hope's hand.

Hope looked up, surprised by the affectionate gesture. Weren't they still cross at each other?

Looking deeply into Hope's eyes, Felicity said, "I'm sorry."

Hope was even more surprised now.

"I know you were just trying to share some good fortune, and I'm sorry to have dragged it down. I just..." She turned to the street to watch a pair of zebras with striping that looked more like a tiger's than the standard black and white – they even looked furred. "I just worry about you. You know I care about you, right?"

Hope smiled and put her hand on top of Felicity's. "I'm doing the best I can to get out of old habits, you know?"

Felicity turned back to her and returned her smile. "I know you are, and I know that's difficult, and you've come so far and worked so hard, and..." Her eyes spoke volumes of the love they held for each other. "I worry you'll get dragged right back into the thick of it and I'll lose you. I don't think I could bear that." Her eyes glittered with unspent tears.

"Neither could I," came a voice from behind her.

Hope spun around to see Sam hovering in the open doorway behind her chair.

"How long have you been eavesdropping on us, hey?" She gently drew Sam into a hug. "You take after your Aunty Hope, you know," she muttered into Sam's hair, smiling.

Sam hugged her back. "Long enough. Though it's *really* hard to eavesdrop over the noise of all those animals. What is that? Some kind of elephant octopus – an elephant-opus? And is that thing on top a flying monkey? It's blue!"

"It has wings," Felicity replied, "but I don't see it flying around – some flying monkey that turns out to be."

"I think it looks too heavy to fly on those tiny wings," Sam said.

Hope giggled as they bantered about the parade. "Maybe you could paint one of those next." She gave Sam another reassuring hug, then stood. "I should go pay for all this. I'll be back in a second."

"I'll keep gathering imagery for my paintings!" Sam said, walking to the edge of the balcony to get a better view of the goings-on.

Hope smiled and headed into the darker recesses of the café. At the far end, she saw a countertop with a till. As she approached, she heard the volume of the cacophony rise behind her. A sharp chittering, followed by a thunderous trumpeting. She heard the crowd "Ooh!" and "Ahh!", the pitch and volume of which quickly rose to yelling. Then she heard a wet, splattering sound that raised her hackles.

She spun around in time to see a tight ball, covered in blue fur, flying towards the front of the café. It crashed through the outside tables and thumped hard against the plate-glass window, spider webbing the glass. Patrons shrieked and ran in all directions to avoid flying tables, flying glass and one angry flying monkey.

But Hope's attention centred on what was coming up behind, and at a steady clip: the massive elephant-opus – giant and grey, with a face full of angry writhing tentacles. It was trumpeting at top volume and barrelling directly towards the fallen monkey, trailing a heavy lead-rope with a desperate human hanging on for dear life.

The blue monkey had righted itself and was chittering at top volume, throwing fallen tableware in the general direction of the elephant-opus. It was taunting the giant thing, which was trumpeting louder and swinging its pseudopods around as it charged even faster. Which didn't bode well for anyone in the creature's path.

The monkey clambered up and over the awning, to the second level, using its ineffective wings for balance. It climbed rapidly away from the oncoming giant, whose enormous feet were drumming the ground until she could feel the earth shaking her bones.

People scattered from its path, but Hope could see it was bearing down on two figures. Felicity, who was desperately tugging at a curled-up ball – Sam.

At the last second, Felicity curled her body over her child, shielding them and pressing them into the ground.

Hope leaped forward, trying to reach them, but in vain. She watched the beast's foreleg connect with her sister's body.

Hope shrieked, and time slowed to a crawl as the elephant-opus's great, grey leg lifted Felicity off the ground. It tossed her to one side, her body flew into the railing surrounding the café and disappeared from sight.

Hope ran towards where she'd last seen Sam, angling around where she thought the elephant-opus was heading. But the beast was enormous, and as it approached, it darkened the whole shop-front.

It arrived, slamming its great feet on the balcony, mashing the tables, plate glass, railings, and people. Debris flew everywhere – glass, wood, cutlery, tableware – a storm of detritus.

Something struck Hope in the head, and everything went dark.

4 - The hospital

White.

White ceiling and walls and sheets.

A low burble of noise in the distance.

A high-pitched twittering followed by a rumbling voice – familiar.

Hope pulled herself back to consciousness. Her head ached, throbbing behind her eyes. Her eyelids were gummy and crusted shut. She pulled them open and saw white again. Had she already looked at this or imagined it? White walls and white ceiling; a white curtain on a railing curled around her bed.

Slowly, the rumbling and twittering resolved themselves into two voices that ebbed and faded. Both seemed familiar, but she was still too floaty to place them. She couldn't pick out any words she could understand. Her thoughts drifted away from her again, skittering around her like swirls of breeze in the mist. She couldn't quite grasp them and pull herself back into focus...

But then she heard a sound she recognised.

Somebody was crying, somebody nearby, and her heart ached.

So she tried again, pulling hard at her scattered thoughts, until... POP ...one caught.

Her sister! She could hear Felicity crying.

Hope struggled to lift her head. To tell Felicity there was no need to cry – that she'd be okay – but the mist closed over her again, and she was drifting...

When it cleared again, the voices had gone. But she remembered the crying, and the thoughts began to catch and tumble back into her mind. She remembered the restaurant; the elephant-opus; the crashing tables and flying debris... and the heavy leg crashing into her sister. She remembered her body flying through the air and landing with a heavy crunch.

Fear rolled through her, and adrenaline followed. Her thoughts cleared as though dawn had rolled across a misty field, stabbing bright rays into the fog. She struggled harder, yanking against the constricting blankets.

She sat up. Then she moaned as her stomach roiled and her head pounded. She gagged and tried her best to hold down her lunch.

The curtains were torn aside, and in bustled a white-clad woman, her voice washing over Hope. "Now, you shouldn't be sitting up just yet, dear. You've had a nasty bump on your head, you have. Ten stitches in it, you know! Just lie back, now, and rest up till the doctor can have another look at you. There you go. Do you need a sick bowl? No? Another pillow then, perhaps? Here you are. There you go, lie back and relax. I'll just stuff it down here, behind your neck – that'll help you feel more comfortable. I'll get you a glass of water."

Hope tried to get a word in, but the woman's voice rolled over her like a tidal wave, smothering any responses beyond a nod or two. Hope submitted to the nurse's will. Lying back, not because she wanted to but because she had no energy to fight the woman's mothering. Pulling herself conscious and lifting her head had taken every ounce of will she had. But she kept her eyes open, fighting her body's wish to drop back into sleep again, and scanned the room for her sister.

She wasn't there, but Hope could've sworn she'd heard her speaking right next to her. Perhaps she'd been dreaming?

The nurse held a glass of cool water up to her mouth, thankfully with a straw. She sipped at it eagerly. Her mouth was dry as sandpaper and tasted awful.

"There's a good girl, have some lovely water – that'll help you feel a bit better."

Hope released the straw and lay back down.

"You lost a good bit of blood, I hear. Head wounds. Tch. Even a tiny one like yours always bleeds a torrent. Like a stuck pig." She touched Hope's forehead. Gently moved her chin this way and that and looked into her eyes. "Should be good, though. Doctor said it's probably just concussion – a bit of a bump, but no internal bleeding or bruising, thank goodness. Lucky thing it wasn't two inches to the right or you might've lost an eye! Instead, you just got a few stitches, and it'll be right as rain. One of the doctors will be back to check you out, in case he missed anything. You've been drifting in and out for a while. You got a right knock when that blasted beast knocked a hole in that café. People've been coming in all afternoon from that, filling our beds. Like we don't have enough going on without rampaging abominations to deal with. Damn scienticians are always messing about with what they don't understand. It's good enough when they're inventing new medicines but they always manage to take it too far, and then people end up hurt, or dead – or both."

The nurse kept talking while bustling around the room, checking on the other patients and setting things right. There were three other beds, all occupied.

An older woman ignored the nurse's ministrations. Her bed was tilted up so she could sit, intent on her knitting, as the nurse poked and prodded her, replaced her pillows, and checked the bruising on her legs.

Another patient watched the nurse's every movement; sitting up, bright eyed and with an enormous smile, nodding happily as the nurse spoke, but never replying.

The third patient glowered at her once, rolled over, and pulled the blankets over his head.

Hope tried to speak but only a mild, wet squeak emerged. She cleared her throat and tried again. "Excuse me," she croaked.

The nurse spun around, apparently astonished at being actually addressed. "Yes, dear?"

"Did a small child come in? Brown hair, grey eyes? Name of Sam. About eight years old? With their mother, Felicity?"

The nurse's eyes dimmed for a moment. She quickly recovered her professional demeanour, but Hope had seen the woman's sorrow, and now fear caught in her throat.

"Are you a relative, dear?" the nurse asked gently.

"Yes!" Hope croaked. "She's my sister. Please tell me they aren't… are they all right?" Her stomach roiled again, and her head resumed its throbbing, but she struggled to sit, to better see the nurse's reaction.

"Oh now, dear, don't sit up – really! I don't exactly know how they are, and it's not my place to give you a prognosis when I barely know myself. But I can find your sister and her doctor, and we'll see what we can find out. You just stay right here and don't try to get up, okay? I'll be as quick as I can." The nurse trundled out of the room, leaving Hope panting on the bed after her mild exertion.

Fear rolled across her in waves, making her skin prickle. What had happened to her sister that made the nurse so sad?

"Oh dear, I'm so sorry," came a croaky voice from across the room.

Hope pulled her eyes open again. Had she drifted off? She focused on the woman, who'd put her knitting down and was now staring at her intently. "I'm sorry – what did you say?"

The woman cackled. "Yes, that's what I said."

The woman's mouth was empty. Hope glanced down at a glass by the bedside table. Plastic teeth floated in the water. They looked enormous.

Hope was drifting again. She pulled herself back together, focusing on the woman's face once more. "Why are you sorry?"

The woman grinned. She didn't look sorry at all. "About your sister; I'm sorry to say I don't think she'll make it."

Hope was fully awake now, her skin cold and her stomach once again doing somersaults. "Why? Did you see her? What do you know?"

The woman grinned again, her eyes glittering. "Oh yes. I saw them take her in on a gurney. The sheets were red and dripping with blood. She was in a terrible way, screaming in pain! I think she must be dead by now!"

"Shut up, you old crone!" cut in a new voice.

The woman went back to her knitting, cackling to herself.

The patient in the middle bed joined in the cackling, eyes sparkling but empty of understanding.

"Stop scaring the poor woman. It's not kind," the grumpy-looking man in the corner said. He glared at the knitting woman in disgust, then turned to Hope. "We did see your sister go through to surgery. She was hurt bad, but I heard the doctor talking. She's not dead, at least as far as we know."

Hope took a breath, surprised to realise she'd been holding it. She nodded to herself. Her mouth was dry again, her heart was beating fast. She took a few more deep breaths as her heartbeat slowed its pace. She took one more deep breath and held it. Then she pulled the sheet down and swung her legs over the edge of the bed.

She paused. Her head was aching once more, the room was spinning, and her stomach continued its rebellion. She eyed up the sick bowl left on the side table. None of it felt any good, but she didn't seem in imminent danger of retching.

"He-he-he, you don't look so good, lovey," the old woman called out to her in apparent glee.

Hope glared back at her.

The old woman giggled. "As green as an apple in spring. Are you going to throw up all over the nice, clean floor? The nurse'll be so cross!"

The bright-eyed person giggled along with the woman.

Hope did her best to ignore them both, as well as the slow tumble in her stomach. She decided to try fetching her glass of water – it would be a good starting mission. Her mouth was parched, and the water might calm her stomach again. She dry swallowed, trying to push down the gorge rising in her throat. After a few deep breaths, she leaned over, reaching for her glass. The room spun again, and she leaned against the bed to steady herself. She had the glass in hand now and tentatively took a sip. The water was cool and refreshing.

She felt better, although wasn't yet sure whether she could trust her stomach to stay put if she tried to stand. She reached one foot towards the floor and had enough time to register just how cold it was, when the door burst open again and the nurse came bustling back in.

"Oh, dear! Oh, no, you shouldn't be up and about just yet. Now, you get back in bed, and rest." She came towards Hope, her arms reaching out to herd her back into the bed.

Hope set her jaw and interrupted her. "No! I want to see my sister!"

The nurse froze, and her face softened. "I know, dear, but she's in surgery right now, I'm afraid. You couldn't see her even if you were able to walk."

"Is she... Did you find out whether she's going to be okay?" Hope asked, her voice trembling.

The nurse dropped her eyes to the bed and helped Hope tuck her legs back in under the sheets. "I can't rightly say, dear. She was badly hurt by that great, lumbering abomination. But I don't know the full extent of it. You'll have to ask the doctors when they're done."

Hope's face crumpled, and she turned away to hide the tears that threatened to spill.

The nurse patted Hope's arm. "I *can* say she's in with our best surgical team, and if anyone can help her, they can."

Hope nodded. "Thanks," she croaked, trying a watery smile.

The nurse smiled back, gentle and sympathetic, but it didn't reach the sad corners of her eyes. "Now here, the doctor's coming to check whether you're all right."

A slim, dark woman in scrubs walked into the ward. She took Hope's temperature and pulse, shone a torch in her eyes and checked the response, and asked her a few questions to gauge her wellbeing.

"Well, you clearly have a concussion. As to treatment, I now have to ask you the, uh... delicate question?" The doctor was looking at her expectantly.

Hope looked at her blankly, her brain unable to make the leap necessary for guessing the context that the doctor was assuming existed. "Um... Concussion, yeah? My brain's too dumb to guess what you're asking. Can you just spell it out?"

"Oh," she replied, blushing slightly. "Sorry. I have a lot of patients who prefer us to be less direct."

"She wants to know how much you can pay, lovey!" the old woman yelled across the ward. "Are you skint or loaded?"

The doctor looked flustered. "Um, yes. I'm asking whether you have enough means to pay for the more intensive treatments. If your means are more limited, you might prefer to undertake the remainder of your healing in the old-fashioned way."

Cottoning on, Hope chuckled and replied gently, "You seem new to this."

The doctor flushed more. "Yes."

"It's okay," Hope assured her. "I don't offend easily."

The doctor sighed. "Five years of medical school, and they teach you everything you need to know about the healing arts. But then you hit the hospital and they expect you to act as a salesperson and financial counsellor to the patients. Plus, I have to tell some patients the bad news that they can't afford the treatment that might save their lives – or their children." She frowned, her eyes filled with a deep sorrow. Then she caught herself. "I'm so sorry, I'm rambling."

"Oh, dearie," the knitting lady said loudly, scorn dripping from her, "if you can't cope with giving bad news, you might be in the wrong profession. Maybe you should go off and marry somebody rich and have lots of babies instead."

Hope glared at the woman, and the doctor looked shocked.

"Gods damnit, woman, do you never shut your hole?" yelled the surly man, nodding at the doctor but directing his words to the knitting woman. "Good doctoring's a different skill set from bilking patients of their hard-earned. The good doc here hates the latter, for which she has risen in my admiration. So you can stop pestering her."

The old woman glared at him, and he glared right back. The patient in the middle bed smiled broadly at both of them.

Hope stifled a giggle as she turned back to the doctor, who seemed to have completely lost her tongue. "How much does the treatment cost and what exactly am I buying?"

The doctor blinked rapidly, then shook herself off. "Oh. Yes. For a concussion like yours, we have an alchemical tonic. Part physical medicine, part healing magic. You wouldn't need much to give you a significant and rapid improvement in your circumstance. You'd be out of here inside of an hour." She went on to explain the costs, including the cost of her stay on the ward.

Knowing she had cash, Hope decided it was worth the money to get back on her feet straight away.

The nurse bustled out again to fetch the tonic for her.

The doctor moved to stand, and Hope reached out to catch the woman's hand to stop her from leaving. "My sister, Felicity, and her child, Sam, came in with me. I'm told Felicity is badly hurt. I'll need to pay for both of them too."

"Oh," the doctor said. "I haven't been on shift long, so I don't know what they are being treated for, but I'll find out and charge their treatment to your account as well."

"I'm told my sister is in surgery. Perhaps Sam is on a ward or in a waiting room nearby? I was hoping I could see them if they're about."

"Of course," the doctor replied with a smile. "I'll find them and ask whether it's okay for you to visit."

"Thanks," Hope said. "They're probably worried about their mother."

"No problem. After you've drunk your tonic, it will take only a few minutes to work through you. You'll need to stick around for a little while, for observation, but you should be up to visiting in no time. After that, you'll be free to leave at your leisure – after settling up, of course. Don't forget to stop by Accounts on your way out." She stood and headed off to her next patient.

Hope looked thoughtful as the doctor closed the door behind her.

"Don't think you can get away with doing a runner," the old woman chimed in.

"Hey?" Hope said. "Why would you think…"

"You look the sort," the woman interrupted, her lips pursed and eyes narrowed. "Up to no good."

Hope glared at her once more.

"In case you were thinking of skipping out on paying, they've stuck a tracker on you already." She held up her wrist and shook it.

Hope lifted her wrist and examined it. A temporary but relatively potent tracker matrix had been inked on her skin. She studied the working. It had an embedded charge of magic and it was being used to continually communicate with at least three or four nearby targets. Some kind of reverse-monitoring at those stations would work to triangulate each matrix's current location.

That was new! They hadn't had that the last time she'd hit the ER – admittedly some time ago. Last time it'd just been proximity-sensors and boundary wards, but those were notoriously finicky. Prone to both false positives and negatives. This new system was impressive. Great for quickly hunting down anyone who'd failed to cough up, and even for locating a patient who'd wandered off and gotten lost in the hospital warren.

Of course, Hope could easily disable the working if she wanted to, even though it had elements intended to detect that kind of tampering. She might not have studied thaumaturgy at university level, and high-level conjuration matrices were beyond her ability to replicate, but she'd read everything available to read for free at the local library, and she was self-taught in the skills used to keep herself alive on the streets.

Tracking was her particular forte, and she knew intimately how these matrices worked. She wasn't as strong in other fields of magic, although she'd familiarised herself with an odd smattering of matrices she'd come across while practising her profession. Also, she had a good working knowledge of magical security systems – having had to work her way past too many of them not to have picked up the basics. She'd become more than passable at identifying and bypassing them.

She was still staring deeply into the intricate design, puzzling out the details, when the nurse reappeared carrying a small bottle. Hope started, feeling guilty. She'd let Sam and Felicity fall out of her mind again as she'd drifted off into her own world. Damnit. She needed that tonic to clear her head and keep her in the game.

She reached for the bottle, but the nurse pulled it back out of her grasp.

"Uh-uh dear, just give me a moment to pour it and let it settle." She fetched a tumbler from the cabinet in the corner and carefully poured out the drink. It was a fizzing and swirling purple liquid that gave off a faint pink mist. She held it a moment and swirled it in her hand. "You don't want to drink it too soon," she said with a chuckle. She waited until the froth had settled, then handed the tumbler to Hope. "It'll give you awful gas. Just leave the glass here when you're done." She wandered away.

Hope downed the tonic, coughing as the froth tickled her nose. It was saccharine sweet over an awful, bitter base – and was anise flavoured. She gagged. Not her favourite flavour (and that was an understatement). Her stomach rebelled once again. She drank the rest of her glass of water to wash away the horrible taste before she brought it all up again.

A few minutes later, she felt her head clearing like the fog burning off on a sunny day. Suddenly, everything was clear. She felt around her skin. Even her bumps and bruises were a lot better and the smaller scratches were gone entirely. She checked the gash on her head. It was tender but had already begun to close over. She could probably get the stitches out before she left.

She shook her head in awe. Modern medicinal magic. The great wonder of the modern age.

Hope slid out of bed, collected her few belongings, and made for the door. Just as she stepped up to it, it opened, and in walked the doctor, nearly running her over.

"Oh!" the doctor said. "I'm so sorry, I didn't see you there." She looked Hope up and down with a critical eye. "Looks like the tonic worked well. Are you satisfied, or do you want some more?" She stepped closer to Hope and inspected the gash on her head. "One more would completely heal this wound – though you'd have to take it easy for a day or so, to recover from the after-effects of the magic fatigue."

Hope shook her head and then paused, wincing – expecting it to start pounding and throbbing again. She was delighted to find it felt normal once more. "Thanks, but this one's fine. I'm happy to let that last one heal up by itself from here."

The doctor smiled and nodded.

"Um... did you manage to find out about my sister?"

"Oh," the doctor replied, "yes. Ward 7B; it's right next door. But you might need to be quiet; most of the ward is sleeping."

Hope nodded and thanked the doctor, who returned the nod, then excused herself, turning to the knitting woman. "Now, Mrs Copeland, it's time I re-examined your leg wound."

Hope tuned out the resulting complaints and the doctor's inspection, slipped out the door, and padded down the corridor to the next door along. It was clearly marked with a large "7B".

She quietly opened the door and peeked in. Four beds, just like her ward – but unlike hers, each bed was laid flat and contained four quiet, white forms tucked into their sheets. From where she was standing, she couldn't see who was whom and was about to take a step further in, when her attention was caught by the clack of a door closing behind her.

She spun around and looked down the length of the corridor to a pair of double doors labelled "SURGICAL UNIT". Through two tall, glass windows, she could see a woman in scrubs exiting a room and carrying a heavy enamel basin covered with green surgical cloth.

The woman's face caught Hope's attention. It was drawn, and her eyes looked ready to spill over with tears. She stood outside what must've been one of the operating rooms, catching her breath, tipping her head back and fighting off tears. The woman turned in Hope's direction and started when she saw her watching. She blinked rapidly as she pulled on her professional mask, like slipping a hand into a glove. She turned away from Hope and carried her heavy dish out of sight, around a distant bend in the corridor.

Hope looked around to check whether anyone else was watching and then snuck forward. Poking her head around the corner of the corridor, she saw that a sole woman was staffing the nurses' station. She seemed to be consumed by a mountain of paperwork, too busy to notice as Hope crept across the last bend of the corridor and through the double doors. As they closed, Hope caught them behind her so they wouldn't make a sound.

She crept up to the operating-room door and peeked through the narrow window.

Beyond it, a small team of people in scrubs were working methodically on a prone form on the table. A large woman had her back to Hope, so she couldn't see much past her. What she could see was that the woman and another surgeon were working in tandem to sew a flap of skin and flesh over what must've been the amputated stump of an arm.

A small arm.

Hope was fascinated, transfixed, and a little horrified at what she was witnessing.

The large woman shifted sideways to select a new instrument.

In that moment, Hope saw two things.

One: The person on the table was not her sister Felicity; it was Sam.

And Two: The surgeon at the far side of the table was looking right at her – just as he had been that morning.

She blinked, frozen in the moment. How could he be here?

He opened his mouth but before he could yell at her, she ran. She burst through the double doors and skidded towards Ward 7B.

"Hey!" the station nurse shouted as she zipped past. "You weren't allowed in there!"

Hope ducked inside the ward and scanned the faces of the sleepers. She recognised Felicity instantly, rushed over to her, and scanned her for injuries.

Felicity groaned and opened her eyes. "Hope?" Her voice was thick and groggy.

The nurse burst into the room and hissed at Hope, "You can't just go wandering around wherever you like – we've got protocols to ensure everyone's safety and health!"

"I'm not. I swear I'm not! I was just trying to find my sister, and..." Hope burst into tears. "Oh, Felicity!"

The nurse relaxed, and her face fell in sympathy.

Felicity tried to sit and winced. Her cheeks looked scoured, her eyes red from crying. She clung to Hope's hand, and whimpered, then winced again in pain.

The nurse sighed deeply, came over to Felicity, using her hand to check her patient's forehead. "Is this woman okay to visit with you?"

Felicity nodded. "She's my sister."

The nurse nodded in return and turned to leave.

"Wait!" Hope called, and then put a hand over her mouth, having glanced at the sleeping patients. She dropped her volume. "Has Felicity been given healing tonic?"

The nurse shook her head.

"Hope," Felicity began, "we can't afford..."

"Nonsense!" Hope interjected. "I have enough money for this." She addressed the nurse. "Can you please bring one that's suitable for her wounds?"

The nurse raised her eyebrows but nodded and left the room.

Hope and Felicity shared a long look that was filled with fear and pain.

"Sam..." Hope began.

Felicity shook her head, her eyes spilling more tears. She drew in a shuddering breath. "The doctor said they'll lose the hand." She spoke fast, trying to get it out before the emotions overwhelmed her. "It stepped on Sam's hand, Hope – a fucking elephant on their tiny hand! There was too much damage. They can't heal it before it goes necrotic! I don't even... Even the surgery's so expensive. The simplest prosthetic would cost all the money you've just earned – but how will Sam paint with that?" She burst into a deep, aching sob.

Hope's heart ached for her sister. Felicity looked drained, beaten. Hope held her gently, her own tears disappearing into Felicity's hair. "We'll figure it out," she said at last, offering reassurance she knew was based on bravado more than fact.

But she would find a way. She promised herself, and she promised Sam.

She would find a way.

5 - The sky docks

Hope glanced over the top of her book and out the window beyond her table. A fresh cup of coffee steamed beside her, untouched. She'd already drunk three and her heart would leap out of her chest if she drank another, but it stood as cover – allowing her to sit here, endlessly watching the unfolding drama.

The roads around the block were cordoned off, and few people were allowed through even this far. So the café staff, who'd usually be eyeing up her seat by now, were happy to host her, even if she wasn't ordering heavily.

Beyond the window stood a row of heavy-set people, their arms linked and glowering at anybody who approached the hastily erected barricade.

The stevedores' guild was on strike today.

Hope cursed her luck. This was a complication she had not anticipated when she'd planned this foray.

Beyond the picket line lay several acres of docklands, half filled with warehouses and administration buildings; the rest with flat, open fields sporting landing towers and mooring points – all of which were currently occupied.

Overhead floated several cargo balloons and heavy zeppelins, ready to unload – all heavily laden and trying to stay abreast of the strong updraft coming off the baking soil. Their crew yelled down at the stone-faced dock workers that stood, shaking their heads at them and wiping their sweaty brows.

Even more heated arguments raged around the few craft that had managed to secure a mooring. Most crews were used to only light work – keeping a zeppelin flying. Now they were having to unload their own heavy cargo in the oppressive heat, with no help from the usual cranes and lifters. Tempers were riding high, and arguments were brewing, especially when the crews had to leave their goods lying on the tarmac. Any attempt to cart the goods off to the warehouses met with a wall of silent bodies, all bio-enhanced muscle and steel.

Some crews took off, leaving their boxes on the tarmac. Most of the moored ships stayed put, protecting either their goods or their spot in line for whenever the strike eventually lifted. The result was a steadily growing overhead flotilla – all impatient to land and get on with their overdue schedules.

One altercation had already come to blows. The crew had sallied forth and stormed the warehouses to fetch some portion of their own expected cargo. They'd gotten it aboard their ship and raced to take off. The dock workers had swarmed the mooring lines as the engines spooled up, hanging on to disallow the exit.

Hope had watched in fascination as the crew hacked off their own lines and dumped the ballast to ensure a quick escape, dropping several bellowing dockers onto the ground below. Most of them had walked (or at least crawled) away. Two steadfast workers had hung on, hand-over-handing their way up to the basket, only to be met by armed crew.

Their bodies landed hard, and they hadn't moved again.

Hope hissed in frustration. This should've been a simple job: sneak in; find the goods; sneak out. Most of the dock workers would be too busy working and too thinly spread out to spot one wayward thief, and there were usually plenty of off-site workers coming on to the lot for her to hide among.

A strike, though? They must've called in every shift. The place was crawling with pissed-off dockers on the lookout for outsiders, and they were none too gentle about turfing them back out again.

The stevedores' guild was a tightly knit crew. Everyone knew everyone else – at least in passing, and they looked after their own. Even if she could somehow sneak past the primary picket line, how was she supposed to get to the warehouse and back without somebody spotting her and hauling her back out?

She'd been watching this scene all morning, and hadn't spotted an opening yet. Once again, she huffed in frustration and debated whether to give in, return to Henry's and accept his offer of a team. He had contacts within the guild, although maybe even they weren't good enough to get a team across this picket line. These dockers were dead serious about their cause, whatever it was, as evidenced by the bodies lying unmoving on the fields.

Still, Henry certainly had more resources at his disposal than one lonesome thief. Perhaps he could bribe their way in.

She looked at the bodies again and shook her head. Nope, that wouldn't work, not for this guild. It was impossible to corrupt – a rarity in this city, especially during the crazy Conjunction fever that had the place in its thrall.

No doubt this strike was some attempt by the city to squeeze the guild, and they weren't taking it lying down. However, the guild held the power right now, and they knew it. The city knew it too, and would no doubt eventually cave to whatever the demands were. Though, who knew how long that would take?

Hope sighed again. She did not want to return to Henry – not for anything. And besides, it'd be harder for a team to slip across the lines. She'd have better luck staying small and relying only on herself. Henry would have to cope with her bringing in the goods for sale instead. She was sure he'd make enough on his commission and resale profits for him not to care who did the deed – and if he wasn't happy with the arrangement, she'd find herself another fence.

After all Henry had done, he deserved to have his precious dream steel stolen out from underneath him. He'd already made enough profit on this shipment – several times over – and she didn't want to share the proceeds four ways with a team she'd have to carry along with her. Besides, she needed the entire amount if she was going to buy Sam a high-quality prosthetic arm as well as keep enough to put her own plans back on the table.

That still left her original problem. How to get past that picket line without arousing suspicion (or worse, ire).

She needed to think. Despite Henry's commentary on her skills, she was good at this, and not being noticed was her speciality. Nobody gave a damn about a small fish like her.

She closed her eyes and rubbed her temples, hoping to push inspiration in. She sighed again, picked up her coffee, and gulped down a large mouthful. It was hot enough to scald her throat and made her insides even hotter. A ridiculous drink for the season, but damned if she was going to waste it, regardless of the weather.

It was the end of summer, and the sun was giving the city one last kick in the teeth. Sweat rolled down her back. She grimaced.

Her stomach was growling; lunchtime had almost come around,

and she needed to pee. She couldn't keep sitting here in the blistering sun forever.

And then she realised how she could get in.

6 - Break-in

Twenty-odd hard-bitten faces turned towards her as she approached the picket line, dragging her cart behind her.

The sun beat down, scorching her back and making her squint. Sweat trickled down her back in an irritating, near-constant stream, and her armpits felt like a swamp. She scrunched her face at the itchy sensation, doing her best to ignore it.

The folks in front of her looked hot too, and irritable – they'd been standing in the sun all morning. Their faces dripped with sweat, and they looked at her hard, annoyed at her intrusion; yet some of them were already gazing at her cart with longing in their eyes.

She smiled back at them, sliding a false mask of confidence over her face, and said, "Hi."

"Off with ya!" growled a man nearby. The grimmest and most determined of the lot, he was huge – his arms bulged with artificially enhanced muscle. The sun glittered off external steel prosthetics that supported his massive frame. He was literally built for heavy lifting.

Hope didn't drop her smile, instead she re-oriented herself to point it at him.

"Go'orn! Git outta here!" he continued. "We won't let ya profit off a strike, ya scab!"

The people eyeing her up changed their gazes from longing to regret. Many averted their eyes, and some glared at her.

Hope made herself look shocked and a little insulted. "Profiting? Oh, no – you have it all wrong!" She burbled happily and shifted over to stand in front of the man who'd outed himself as their leader. "This is a gift!"

The man looked sceptical, and the others returned to staring hungrily at her cart.

"From the catering branch of the hospitality guild, in support of your strike action today." She felt the weight of the man's stare pressing down on her, and fought hard not to visibly tremble.

"Hospitality said they weren't gonna join this strike. They're making too much profit to stop trade."

Hope's eyebrow went up. "Oh, well, that's the official line from the main guild, sure. But the catering branch is still supportive of your cause; it's just... you know... politics." She waved her hands. "And *some* of us don't agree with those politics, so I'm here *unofficially* to help out in my own way." She beamed at them all, hoping they'd swallow the waffle. She had no idea what this strike was about, let alone what inter-factional bullshit had caused a rift between the city's two strongest guilds. But whenever two people came together, there were politics involved, so the tactic was worth a shot.

The leader glared at her even harder.

Sweat dripped down her back, this time not all of it from the sun.

"C'mon, man!" one of the strikers pleaded.

"A gift you say?" he grated, dubiously eyeing her cart.

She beamed once more, dug out a box, and handed it over. "Yes!" she nodded, trying to keep her nervous energy in check – damn those four coffees. "Totally free, to help you guys cope with this weather! There's plenty here for your picket line, and heaps left over for your hard-working folks in the field as well." She fished out another couple of boxes and handed them out to the overheating picket liners.

They eagerly tore into the boxes and handed around the spoils. One of them handed a packet to the leader.

The man tore into it and pulled out a half-melted ice cream that proceeded to drip down his enormous arm. He glared at Hope a bit more, for good measure, as though weighing up her soul via her eyeballs. Then he nodded sharply and announced, "this one's all right!" He turned to his line-up, all of whom were slurping up their own ice cream before they turned into puddles. "Take enough for us, then let her through to the field."

Hope smiled again and breathed a sigh of relief. She handed out another two boxes and then closed the cart. With one last smile for the dockers, she squeezed through a gap in the wall of human flesh. She headed across the fields, towards the warehouses on the far side, the ones she'd been eyeing all morning, from the safety of the café.

"Hey, you!" came the leader's voice from behind her.

She froze.

"Wass yer name?"

She turned, readying herself to run. She gave a smile, hoping it didn't look quite like the painted rictus it felt like from the inside.

However, the big man didn't make a move, and his question trickled through her sun-addled brain. "Ummm... I'm Hope."

He nodded back at her. "Nice to meet ya, Hope. I'm Timmo. Thanks for the ice-creams – you're a lifesaver. It's a damn hot day today."

She gave another smile, and this time it was genuine.

The man raised a fist, pumped it in the air, and bumped it against his chest twice.

Hope copied the gesture and declared, "Solidarity."

The man smiled back for the first time. "Solidarity, sister." He turned back to resume his watch on the street.

Hope turned and continued on her way.

The crowd of dock workers filled the field in front of her but they thinned out up ahead, towards the buildings.

She made her way through the groups of people, avoiding the moorings and associated aircrews. She handed out boxes of ice creams to the grateful, overheated people along the way, edging ever closer to her intended destination.

When the boxes ran low, she asked where she might find a bathroom. They pointed to somewhere between the buildings and gave her some directions, which she filed away for later use. The directions led her away from the strike action and through the warehouses she was intending to search first. She ducked through a narrow access way, eyeing up her first target. There, tucked in between two of the bigger buildings, she wasn't out of sight, but nobody was walking around the area, and with all attention on either the picket line or the air ships she was unlikely to be spotted, at least for now.

She looked in through the dirty windows. Inside, she saw rows and rows of shelving, stacked floor to ceiling with boxes – the excess flow of goods demanded by the Conjunction-mad citizens, and the industry supporting their wild parties. Now add the overflow caused by the strike action, and you had warehouses filled beyond capacity.

They would be a nightmare to search. She now understood Henry's eagerness to pull her on to the team. They wouldn't be able to locate just one important shipment in that mountain. Thank goodness she had an edge over them.

She sat down on some steps and pulled out an ice cream for herself. While enjoying its cool taste, she snuck a look at the newly re-modified tracking matrix on her wrist, checking that her excessive sweating hadn't compromised it. She could've built her own matrix, but why waste resources you'd gotten for free?

She dug a tiny baggie out of an inner pocket and extracted a tiny shaving of dream steel she'd snuck off her previous find.

Looking around, she scanned the protest nearby. Nobody seemed to be keeping tabs on her, and she was out of the main sight-lines. She'd be spotted if she did anything dumb enough to draw attention, but sitting in a cool spot to eat an ice cream, out of the scorching sun, was harmless enough that it didn't raise anyone's notice – especially with everything else that was going on out there.

After popping her ice-cream wrapper away in the cart, she lay back and put her wrist behind the cart, out of view. She touched the dream steel to the centre of the matrix, and muttered a short incantation to attach it as the signifier for the new target. "Like calls to like," she muttered to herself, as the matrix glowed a neon blue.

She glanced up again and scanned for watchers, but the glow was hardly noticeable in the bright midday sun. Nobody seemed to have perked up at the flash of magic, either. Trackers used only a little magic – more of a slow trickle; however, it was something a competent magic user could sense, even at such a distance. Still, stevedores weren't exactly well known for being practitioners, and anybody who had latent talent was a little preoccupied.

After a moment, the glow faded, and the ink rippled like smoke over her skin, resettling in a new configuration. She immediately felt a slight but distinct tug towards the warehouse located opposite to where she was sitting. She felt a lot of other little tugs as well – in all directions across the city, but her unique talent lay in being able to sift through and ignore the overwhelming number of incoming signals and pinpoint the most relevant one. And that one was pulling her directly towards the building in front of her.

She double checked for watchers and headed down the alley, looking for an easy way inside. There was a door nearby, just before the alley opened up on to a street that led to the administration buildings. A few people were hurrying back and forth along there, but it was quiet enough to take a closer look without being disturbed.

She nearly giggled out loud when she spotted the side door had been chocked open with half a brick – the time-honoured tradition of leaving an easy way in and out for a quick smoko break.

She listened at the door and couldn't hear any sounds of a patrol or work happening inside. Internal security was a bit light on today, with the warehouses off limits. All eyes were up front at the picket line, or on the busy airfields.

She glanced around once again to check whether anybody was watching, and then slunk inside. She carried the heavy cart up the step so it didn't bump and make a sound. It was awkward as hell, but there was no use leaving it outside to announce where she'd gone. She left it just inside the door, covering it with a canvas tarp to make it less conspicuous.

Inside was a massive warehouse with shelving reaching up multiple storeys above her head. Pallets were packed full of boxes, then covered in cling wrap to keep them from falling apart, then piled up on the shelving all the way up to the roof. They were just as she'd seen them from outside, only stretching on through a gargantuan space. Each stack was like an impenetrable medieval wall of boxes. It'd take very tall forklifts to get to those pallets. An inkling of concern tingled through her. Would she even be able to get at the box she needed once she found it?

She sighed and shrugged.

That's why they pay me the big bucks.

She had to at least try. There were always the forklifts.

She closed her eyes and concentrated on the tiny tug that the tracker made within her, letting it guide her forward through the giant stacks. It led her deeper into the labyrinth of box canyons, and she walked in and out of the aisles to get a sense of how deep within she needed to be. The tug grew stronger and more insistent. She was closing in on her target.

Then she heard a whisper-light sound, high above her, hidden behind the upper rows of the shelving. She froze, listening.

She couldn't place it, but it didn't matter. Ducking under a shelf, she squeezed herself in between a metal shelving rail and the sharp corners of a stack of narrow boxes. She waited there, bent unnaturally and with a corner sticking into her ribs.

She couldn't hear a thing. Perhaps she'd imagined it? Well, nobody in her line of work lost out by being over-cautious. She waited another few breaths before she began to uncurl.

And then she heard it again: a faint fluttering; a whirr on the wind.

She froze again, trying to look up through the narrow gap between the boxes above her and the gridded metal shelving holding them up.

Then she spotted it. Tiny and far above. Near invisible against the mottled grey metal of the ceiling far above; some kind of winged surveillance drone. It looked a bit like a tiny dragonfly sporting a bulbous black head. It flew along the aisle two beyond hers, parallel to the one she was hiding in, moving fast enough to get a good coverage of the aisle below but slow enough to have spotted her in an instant as something that doesn't belong.

She'd come across these things before in her line of work. A kind of automated watch dog. It'd investigate and record video of anything interesting it spotted, but it wouldn't bother recording if all it saw was business as usual. If she stayed quiet and out of shot, it wouldn't even know she was there.

It passed overhead again, now following the aisle next to hers. She had a moment to move, to double-check that her hiding spot was out of sight before it swung around the corner and into her aisle.

If she could see it, then it could see her; plus, she was super-uncomfortable, so she wriggled in deeper.

The whirring sound approached the corner of her aisle.

Her body was tucked in behind a low-rise box that sat next to her on the back of the pallet. She lifted her leg up into place. It scraped on a burr on the edge of the metal shelf, tearing into her skin. She gasped and jumped in shock, and her leg clanged against the shelf above.

She bit down on a curse and tried to stay still.

The whine of the drone stuttered, then grew in sound.

Shit… it was coming down to look. She'd be exposed!

She raised her head to see whether she could slip over the back and into the gap between pallets. But the gap was too small. She had no time. Pulling out her knife, she sliced through the tape on the box in front of her. The front flap lifted to fill the gap between her and the shelf above, and she held it in place with her finger, trying not to tremble. Between her and the drone was just a flimsy bit of cardboard, three millimetres thick at most. She held her breath, not daring to twitch a muscle.

The whirr was loud now, and she felt the air lightly buffet around her. She hoped it wouldn't flutter the cardboard flap too much – the movement would betray her hiding spot.

If the drone was being operated by an intelligent person, it'd see through her flimsy attempt at hiding, duck around the sides, and spot her immediately. If it was on autopilot, though… She wished as hard as she could that nobody was staffing the vid panels today.

The drone hovered, swaying to and fro. She heard it turn. Her heart pounded. She waited.

The whirr lifted – up and away, returning up above the stacked pallets to look down on them once more. It resumed its slow progress down the aisle.

Hope let her breath ease out and waited while her racing heart slowed back to normal.

The drone retreated out of her hearing range. She'd have to keep an ear out for that thing – it'd come back this way soon enough.

She took advantage of the brief window of opportunity as quickly as possible. Tumbling out of her hiding spot and doing her best to stay silent, she followed the now more persistent tug towards the target. She skittered up one aisle, keeping an ear out for any more drones above her. Thankfully, there seemed to be only the one, and she was heading further away from it as it continued its slow search pattern, aisle by aisle, in the other direction.

Her tracker dragged her all the way through the warehouse, to the very back, which meant moving away from the furore happening outside. Unfortunately, the further inwards she moved, the further upwards the tracker seemed to tug her, until at last she stood looking straight up towards the pallets stacked way up on the top shelves.

She sighed.

Of course. It couldn't have been on the bottom shelf, could it?

She understood why, of course. All the better to hide the dream steel from anyone deliberately looking for it, as well as it being practically impossible for somebody to stumble across it by accident. But still…

She grimaced and began to climb.

The shelves were never intended to have humans scale them. She'd spotted the industrial forklifts, all parked over by the front doors. They were super-tall to reach the pallets at the top of the stacks – at least three storeys high – and bring them safely down to ground level. Each shelf was the height of a fully loaded pallet, which meant every "step" was nearly as high as she was tall.

She hauled herself up the vertical side rails, scrabbling for purchase and hand-over-handing up the metal bars. She tried to find intermediary footholds on the stacks of packed boxes while trying her best to remain silent. The worst part was that the shelves were so tightly packed she had to lean out over the edge and crawl up the outside like a rat climbing a drainpipe.

She sincerely hoped the shelves were well secured to each other and solidly bolted on to the floor. The last thing she needed was to tip one of these things over.

She banished thoughts of the shelving toppling like dominoes around her, and focused on following the tug that was now yanking her upwards.

The pallet she wanted was second from the top. She clung to the vertical rails lining the edge of the shelf, hanging out over the aisle. She felt the uncomfortable tug from her tracker aiming in towards the middle of the pallet in front of her. The tracker had, by now, outstayed its welcome. She disabled it and relaxed as its pressure disappeared, along with the continual drain on her magic.

The dream steel was close enough now that she could feel the magical radiation coming off it – its own brand of magic. She'd become familiar with the sensation from her previous heist – she'd recognise it anywhere. And it was pouring out of the deepest part of this pallet.

Damn. Still making it hard for me. Couldn't have been an easily accessible outside box, could it?

However, she was smiling to herself as well. Whoever had hidden this had done their best, but they couldn't have anticipated her abilities.

She took a moment to search for the drone and guesstimate how long she'd have before it headed back her way. It seemed to have nearly completed its run at the end of the warehouse.

As she watched, though, instead of turning around and working its way back along the aisles, it stopped and turned at the centre aisle and headed straight back down it, bee lining to the other end of the warehouse. Maybe it'd re-start its circuit there – but the problem was, the pallet she was on was so close to the centre aisle, and here she was hanging off the shelving. She'd be spotted for sure!

She was too far up the shelves. There was no time to climb down again. Even jumping quickly down the shelves would be super-*loud*. She was too high to jump straight to the ground. That'd be a quick way to two broken legs and a jail cell.

She looked across the aisle and spotted a bigger gap between the two pallets.

The drone was zipping towards her. There was no time!

No! Am I really doing this?

Oh, yes, she really was.

She took a deep breath and leaped!

Her feet landed against the cardboard and cling wrap with a soft *THWUCK*.

She scrabbled for the shelf and grabbed hold of the vertical bar, sliding down it. Her hands bit down on the shelf edge. She stifled a cry – that hurt!

She hauled herself up over the top of the boxes, wincing at her bruised fingers, and squeezed herself in between the surrounding boxes, just as the whirring sound buzzed past the edge of the aisle.

It paused.

She imagined the drone spinning towards her. Had she made too much sound?

It couldn't see her from the centre aisle, but she wasn't actually hidden, just squeezed into the gap between two stacks of boxes. If it came to look this time, it would see her easily.

She held her breath.

The whine didn't increase, and after a moment, it resumed its flight back towards the far end of the warehouse.

Ow! That hurt.

She breathed out again and let herself feel the pain while rubbing the newly formed bruises.

Then she set herself to planning as she looked back across the aisle at the target pallet. There wasn't enough room for her to hide there. Maybe she could climb down and back, but she wouldn't have much time to do anything useful before the drone was back again, covering this aisle. She'd be better off waiting it out until it passed by her again.

She checked her watch. Too much time had been spent just finding the right pallet and then hiding from the drone flyover – both times. She really didn't want to spend fifteen more minutes sitting still, but nor did she want to chance being exposed when the drone came through one more time.

Some minor sounds coming from her were one thing, but if it caught her messing around with the pallets, that'd be significantly worse. It would most likely trigger some kind of alarm system, and that would bring everyone running. Her new and tenuous friendship with the guild wouldn't stand up for a second if they caught her here red-handed.

She was cursing her luck when she heard a faint KACHUNK.

Hope listened hard but heard nothing else. Was it a door closing? She couldn't hear any footsteps.

She leaned forward tentatively, doing her best to stay inside her new and not-so-effective hiding place. Just the top of her head was poking out from between the pallets.

She saw nothing moving. She couldn't hear anything, either.

Wait.

She couldn't see *anything* moving. Where was the drone?

She scanned the far end of the warehouse for the tiny form, listening out for the telltale whirr.

Then she spotted it and had to stifle a laugh. It was sitting on a charging station high above the warehouse, a light on its back slowly fading in and out. What a stroke of luck! Assuming it took several minutes to recharge, she had more time than she'd expected, and she decided not to waste it.

She slid down the shelving's vertical rails and climbed back up the other side. No way was she going to jump that aisle again – ow!

She paused when she reached the target pallet once more. How was she going to get into it to get the package she wanted? It was buried deep within the centre of the pile.

She pulled her knife back out of an ankle holder and slid it through the surrounding cling wrap, pulling a flap down and away. The boxes on top were light enough that she could push them aside to make a gap. It wasn't much, but was wide enough for her to peer in between the boxes.

She felt the dream steel deep inside, pulsing in time with her heartbeat. She could see a metal surface – scratched red paint and a clip. Perhaps a toolbox? It was buried deep within the stack. She could see it but couldn't quite get to it.

She pulled a few boxes out further. One of the outer ones turned in place, leaving a gap, but the deeper layers wouldn't budge without her removing some to make more room. She pulled out the first one, balancing it in one hand while hanging on, and then lifted it up above her head to slide it in next to the pallet on the shelf above. Then she inspected the hole she'd made.

She could reach the target now. It was definitely a toolbox, but it was still stuck behind another couple of boxes.

The next box was even bigger. She grabbed one corner of it and pulled it towards herself. It was also heavier than the first. She chocked it underneath her jaw, balancing it on her sternum, and re-adjusted her grip underneath so she could lift it up.

She pushed it up above her head, ready to slip it above the previous one. But just as she had it aligned with the gap above her, something rolled inside it. The box tipped back over her head and slipped off her fingers. She fought the instinct to let go with her other hand and grab at it.

It tumbled down to the floor below and landed with a heavy *CLONK.*

She paused as she heard the *KACHUNK* sound that meant the drone was off its charger and whizzing her way.

No use being careful now! She plunged her hand deep into the remaining stack of boxes and yanked hard on the toolbox. The other boxes gave way, some scattering to join those on the floor below, but that didn't matter now.

The toolbox was heavy! She had to re-adjust her grip on the vertical rail. She was going to have to climb down one-handed, but at least she didn't have to be as quiet now.

She slid down each level, hooking her other elbow around the upright as she transferred her free hand to the level below, all the while listening to the oncoming whirr above. It must've been programmed to keep to the aisles, because it was coming down the centre instead of flying right over the top of the stacks. That gave her an extra few seconds. She jumped the last shelf, landing on the light boxes she'd dropped earlier, crushing them and whatever contents were inside.

She ran – as fast as she could. Sprinting for the end of the aisle and ducking around it just as the drone spun around the corner.

She didn't stop. The whirr behind her slid over to hover above the boxes she'd knocked down. She had only a few moments of grace left, so she ran flat out. She thanked her soft-soled sneakers for keeping her footsteps quiet. The drone would have to hunt for her.

With the toolbox clutched against her chest, she bolted for the side door and her hidden cart. The heavy toolbox slowed her down. It felt like she was carrying a lead brick inside a steel case. But she wasn't letting it go for anything.

The cart was just up ahead. Once outside, she'd hide the toolbox in it and slink away. She was nearly there when the lights suddenly turned red and an alarm sounded – a rising shriek blaring from loudspeakers throughout the building.

"Intruder detected!" sounded a loud but tinny voice coming from the drone above and behind Hope. It was approaching fast down the centre aisle.

Hope grabbed the cart's handle. A loud *CLUNK* sounded from every doorway in the warehouse, including the one right beside her.

No!

"All doors and exits are sealed!" echoed the voice from the approaching drone. "Please give yourself up; you are locked in!"

Hope's heart sank as she spun around to look at the door, then soared again, and she stifled a giggle.

Thank the gods for half a brick!

The locks had engaged, but had met only empty air.

She pushed her way through the chocked-open door, backing out while pulling the cart behind her. Then yanked the door shut in front of her, to block the drone's view, just before it pulled level with her and recorded her leaving.

She spun around… right into a wall of bio-enhanced muscle and steel.

7 - Foiled!

Her heart dropped. They'd caught up with her. There was no escape from so deep in their domain. She looked up into a grimacing face. Two steel-reinforced arms grabbed her upper arms and lifted her on to her toes, where she teetered.

"Well, well, what have we got here?" a voice nearby crooned.

Hope craned her neck to look around beyond the wall of muscle holding her. A wiry man sporting a buzz-cut slunk around the giant woman who was holding Hope tight. Beyond Buzz-cut, Hope spotted another man – tall and athletic; keeping watch on the goings-on in the airfields.

Why would they need to keep watch?

She mentally smacked her forehead. "You're not dock workers!"

"Nope," the wiry man replied. "Neither are you, though, are you? Found you right where I expected you, too."

She scrunched her forehead in confusion.

Why were they expecting me? HOW were they expecting me? WHO was expecting me?

"She's got the goods, Buzz," called the watcher. "I can feel it in that toolbox."

"Ah, I'll just help you with that," the wiry man, 'Buzz', replied. He took the heavy toolbox by the handle and yanked at it.

Hope yanked back. "That's mine!"

"Tink?" Buzz said, and the woman in front of Hope squeezed her arm, hard.

Hope wriggled, but the woman's hands didn't budge. Buzz pulled the toolbox out of her loosened grip and she squeaked in pain. "That doesn't belong to you. I worked hard for that. Give it back!"

Buzz tutted. "But it's not yours either, is it? And it's in my hands now – possession is nine-tenths of the law, and all that." He looked her up and down, assessing her figure.

"We've got what we need," Tink said to him. "Let's get going."

"Put me down, you big lout!" Hope demanded, lifting her legs and kicking hard at the woman's stomach.

It was hard as rock! Her feet bounced off, and hurt! She could swear she'd heard them go *CLANG* when they connected, too. She whimpered a little.

Tink chuckled. "That won't work on me, sweets."

"Keep it down, you lot!" the man on watch hissed.

Hope's eyes narrowed. She drew a deep breath. "Oi! What were you doing in that warehouse?" she yelled as loudly as she could. "What are you doing? Help! Thieves! Put me down! Help!"

The woman holding her was staring at her, open jawed.

Buzz widened his eyes. He spun around and looked out at the field that lay beyond the alleyway. Several workers had turned in their direction, trying to figure out what the ruckus was all about.

"Thieves!" Hope yelled again.

The dockers started running towards them.

"Shit!" Buzz hissed. "Time to go, Dodge!"

The lookout nodded and ran up the alley, checking the street at the far end.

"Tink, put her down – hard," Buzz instructed the woman. "Then get moving." He turned and ran off after Dodge, carrying Hope's hard-earned dream steel with him.

Tink grinned and lifted Hope, drawing a hand back for the world's most telegraphed punch.

Hope gritted her teeth and drew deep on her magic. No time for finesse. She curled the raw magic into a ball and slammed it right into Tink's face – hard enough to feel the crunch.

Tink shrieked and dropped Hope, but her fist was still travelling, at speed.

It struck Hope, a glancing blow on her side. She spun away, landing hard against the building. Whipping her head around, she saw Tink clutch her bleeding face and lurch off after her companions.

Hope's lungs hurt. She concentrated hard on pulling in a breath as the pain pounded through her. She took another breath, letting the pain ease to a dull ache.

Heavy feet bounded past her, and people called out as they ran down the alleyway and beyond. Voices yelled in the distance, followed by the distinct sound of an engine gunning it.

She was more concerned about the footsteps approaching her. She cringed.

"You all right, mate?" came a gentle voice above her. One of the dockers was standing over her.

She nodded tentatively. "Yeah, man, just a little winded – that lady packed a punch."

He held out a hand to her. She took it and was grateful when the man pulled her back to her feet.

Several more people ran past, chasing the now long departed thieves. The man glanced at them. "Can ya tell us what happened here? We didn't get to see much."

Hope blew her breath out and took a deep one, to give herself a second to spin her tale. "I was sitting here eating an ice cream when I saw those people running out of this door." She shrugged. "They were carrying something and acting fishy, so I stood up to see what they were doing, but they grabbed me. So I yelled."

The docker nodded. "Thanks, mate. We saw their faces. We'll catch them, or..." He paused.

A heavy *THWUP-THWUP-THWUP* echoed above the noise of the airfields.

Hope froze. She wasn't the only one. "Shit. It's the Imperium."

"Strike-breakers," the man whispered, scanning the sky and looking past the nearer flotilla for the incoming heavy zeppelins. The men on the airfields were running; swarming like a kicked anthill.

"How do I get out of here?" Hope asked urgently.

"They're not here for you." The man's eyes glinted as he scowled up at the skies.

Hope sighed. "I can't afford to sit in a holding cell for a couple of days while they figure that out."

The man refocused on her, and understanding flooded through his eyes. He nodded once and took a hold of her arm. She winced as he grasped the spot Tink had bruised.

"Oh, sorry, mate," he whispered, loosening his grip. "C'mon, we've gotta go this way." He gestured for her to follow him. "Leave your cart – it'll be safe. You can come back for it later."

She nodded and leaned it against the wall. She wouldn't return for it. It had served its purpose.

The heavy engine noises were louder, echoing through the walls. The Imperial gunships were closing in overhead. They ran across the backstreet to the alley tucked in behind the administration buildings.

A series of thuds landed behind her, and she jumped back as a set of heavy canvas bags dropped at her feet, splitting and throwing sand in all directions. She looked up and saw the flotilla of waiting balloons and zeppelins dropping their heavy ballast and taking off. Some were gushing steam as they cranked up their engines and tried their best to get away as fast as they could fly. Nobody wanted to be caught in a firefight between the Guild and the Imperium.

And they were coming up fast. A small battalion of heavy gunships rolled up like a storm. The forward ships were already dropping large canisters. They hissed angrily and gushed choking clouds of smoke across the fields, scattering the dock workers and sending any remaining aircrews scrambling back to their ships. Masked drop troops were manning the ropes. The armoured zeppelins came abreast of the moorings, and the heavy troops rappelled down to land on the airfields, stirring whirlwinds in the smoke clouds.

Hope tore her eyes away as they ran around a corner of the alley and hit a dead end.

She pulled up short. "We're stuck! Where now?" Her voice bled desperation.

But the man in front of her grinned and heaved a heavy red skip bin away from the wall, to reveal the double doors of an old coal chute, long out of use. "In here! It's dark, but mostly level, and it leads straight out into the canal on broadside."

Hope's eyes glittered. "Thank you!"

"Solidarity, sister" he declared, and pumped his fist against his chest twice.

She repeated the gesture, then ducked into the coal chute, landing hard on a dirt floor.

The man replaced the doors with a clang, cutting out the growing levels of smoke but also covering her in darkness. She listened and heard the heavy scrape of the skip bin being moved back into place, followed by the man's footsteps as he ran back into the field.

Beyond, she could hear a lot of yelling and tramping of feet. She listened out for the telltale rattle of gunfire... but it didn't come. The dock workers were smart enough not to fight back. She started looking about, satisfied that her newfound acquaintances were at least not getting wiped out.

As her eyes adjusted to the dark, she made out the outlines of an archway and, beyond it, the deeper darkness of a tunnel heading down.

She closed her eyes and felt within herself. She'd used up most of her magic in blasting Tink, but thankfully it took only a tiny trickle to light up a fingertip. Pretty pitiful for a werelight, but enough to keep her from stumbling as she made her way down and out.

When she got out of here, though, she'd track down those rotten thieves and get back her hard-stolen dream steel.

This was her catch, and if she was going to get her pay day, she'd have to fight for what was rightly hers.

* * * * *

Hope trudged down the tunnel, following her tiny werelight and paying little attention to her surroundings. Instead, she was planning what she'd like to do next.

She could try tracking the dream steel again but that seemed a tall order. At any other time, it might be simple in a city this large. The material was rare. Vanishingly so. But here? Now? In this town? It held the largest conglomeration of dream steel ever seen since... well, since the previous Conjunction, over two hundred years earlier.

The fact was that the material was the most effective conduit for the bizarre and powerful energies that were now beginning to flow from the rare and celebrated event. Every power-hungry tin-pot practitioner with a half-baked idea for self-empowerment was scrabbling for their share of the mind-warping stuff.

She knew she could set the tracker running again – no problem. But without at least a vague idea of where the thieves might've taken the loot, the working would trigger a signal for every matrix and dream-steel stockpile within a hundred clicks of her... which she reckoned would be quite a lot.

She was an expert at sifting through them for the relevant one, but now she couldn't use proximity to filter out the noise. She'd be stuck with a brute force search, and that meant looking at all of them. Each one took some time to look at and potentially discard. Without something to help narrow down the search space, she'd be here until next year hunting for the same one again.

Not that she'd complain about replacing one high-value target for another; it was just that she'd already witnessed firsthand how strongly most practitioners defended their personal stash – even a small one. Anyone with enough credit to buy such a stinking great pile of the most valuable *mineral-du-jour* no doubt also had the cash to front a sizeable protective service aimed specifically at keeping out predators such as herself.

After all, that's what'd made this particular haul so deliciously appealing: it was almost unguarded. All it had was security through obscurity, plus the unexpected protection that the somewhat intimidating, but not impregnable, Stevedores' Guild afforded it.

Hope's heart drooped.

She'd come so close! Held the box in her hands – felt its weight. A veritable fortune in metal! It'd been hers… and then…

She kicked a rock in frustration. It bounced away down the tunnel with a satisfying clatter. She kicked another one, for good measure. She snorted at the irony of thieves stealing from a thief.

"No honour among thieves," she growled, and rolled her eyes at the idea. "How did they gods damned know I was going to be there, anyway?"

Then she froze and slapped her own forehead.

"Henry!" she hissed through gritted teeth and continued on down the tunnel.

Of *course* it was Henry. The whole damned thing had his stink about it. Knowing him, he'd set it up from the beginning, from when she'd overheard the conversation. Henry knew she worked alone and that she'd likely turn him down when he offered her the team job – or at least he wouldn't have minded her answer either way. After she'd turned him down, he'd probably set the thieves to watch for when she showed up, with instructions to wait while she did the hard part – the finding and the fetching. Then to nick the dream steel when she got out.

He'd used her. Even more so than usual.

He'd set her up to do the hard yards and to take the fall if things went south. That was one way to get out of paying for her services and her rightful share of the loot.

Well, the joke was on him. She was determined to find those double-crossing thieves and claw back her pay day. All she had to do was narrow down the search space more effectively.

Did she have anything of theirs? She thought back over the few minutes she'd spent in their company. Then she smiled and grimaced as she examined her hand; the one she'd used to smash a ball of half-baked magic into Tink's very deserving face.

Guess she wouldn't be washing the blood off that hand any time soon.

8 - Watch and learn

Hope stalked across another rooftop, approaching the target slowly and carefully. She'd been led a merry chase as the thieves returned to their lair – or wherever it was they liked to hang out when they weren't lying in wait to doublecross innocent, hard-working thieves like herself.

The tug on her magic was grating after such a long haul across the city, but the outbound flow was decreasing now that she was so close to her target.

She was tiring, and her magic capacity was bottoming out. It hadn't fully recovered from the burst she'd used to escape from Tink's clutches. However, she knew she was getting close now; to both the dream steel and Tink, thanks to whatever mix of blood and nasal secretions left on her hand after she'd used it to smack the woman.

Following two targets drained her guttering magic levels so much that she'd been tempted to drop one of the channels. But she didn't want to lose sight of either her precious dream steel or the location of the one-woman mountain, so she gritted her teeth, dug deep, and bore the strain for a little longer.

Although she was now quite certain that the thieves had come to a stop, Hope kept moving to make herself into a less obvious watcher, and also to triangulate the thieves' position. She walked around the block, trying to blend in with the pedestrians. Fitting in was harder than usual because this suburb was far from the centre of town, and the local crowd comprised cheap labourers and less than savoury types scraping out a living. Hope might be one of them by profession, but she dressed up to fit in with the needs of her job. To blend in with her marks, rather than her peers.

The feel of this suburb was far less affluent than her usual stalking-grounds. Still, she knew how to fit in when necessary. Affecting a slouch and a defeated attitude got her a long way there, and she drifted around the target buildings without attracting too many funny looks.

They actually weren't that far from the sky docks. The thieves had done a run-around trying to lose the stevedores, who had managed to follow them for a good while. She was doubly glad she hadn't run afoul of the dockers now she'd seen half-a-dozen of them running nearly as fast as the motorised skimmers the thieves had been riding.

The dockers had chased the skimmers most of the way across the city. She'd never have gotten away from them as fast if she'd been in their cross-hairs. She'd stayed well clear until the stevedores had lost their heart for the chase and turned back; only then had she begun zeroing in on the thieves herself. No way was she going to let the stevedores associate her with the thieves – she certainly didn't want to be a target of that guild.

And now she circled a small number of broken-down tenements that bordered the light-industrial zone. Checking her tracking matrix, it looked like the thieves had gone to ground in the workshop backing on to this block of apartments. She climbed onto a roof across from the block to get a better look.

She needed to scope out the hideout before she went barging in. Sure, she might take them unawares, but there were three of them. She'd barely escaped last time, and she hadn't even tangled with the practitioner yet. He might be as low powered as the average street mage – all smoke and no mirrors – but you never knew what surprises he might have up his sleeves. Also, she had no idea what Buzz's speciality might be, apart from sleaze and theft.

She'd take the cautious approach, thanks.

She took a moment to concentrate on the one matrix she always had available to her, muttering a few arcane words to activate the hideaway conjuration she had tattooed on her back.

A tingling sensation slipped over her body, like being dipped naked in an icy lake. She shivered.

The drain on her magic increased, and she shook her head to clear a sudden wave of dizziness. But it was worth the effort. She wasn't as adept at hideaways as she was with trackers – she couldn't build them on the fly. Being tattooed on made hers unalterable, but she always had it on hand, which made it invaluable for slipping away after a job. It only worked on people, and not brilliantly well, but it made anyone who was looking at her less interested in seeing her.

Not invisible.

That took way more magical energy than she had to spend and a level of skill with matrices that was beyond her own meagre self-taught abilities. But it made her harder to spot at a casual glance, which was enough to keep her hidden while she scoped the joint.

The thieves didn't seem to have moved since they arrived here. At first, she'd been worried they might head straight to Henry with their loot. She'd been ready in case she needed to jump on any opening with alacrity, or even barge in and bluff her way into her rightful share. But these guys steered a wide berth around Henry's back-alley trading post. They had something else going on, and that meant she had an opportunity to reclaim her rightfully stolen loot.

She'd take it if she could.

The warehouse had an industrial-size roller door beside a more human-size front door. High up in the wall, a set of windows let in the afternoon sunlight, and more windows wrapped around it into the side alley; maybe for offices. But nothing looked out onto the street. In theory, anyone inside wouldn't be able to spot her watching the place from across the road, especially with an active hideaway. So she could watch safely from here.

Nobody went in or out, and she heard nothing above the regular hum of the city. It looked like a good time to sneak up and take a closer look.

Hope paused as she reached the front fence and felt for any defensive wards. Nothing there. Up ahead, though, she sensed the familiar tickle that warned of some kind of perimeter, but it wasn't particularly strong. A trip-wire ward, most likely. They were pretty common in these circumstances, and any street practitioner would be familiar enough with the basics.

She squeezed through the gate and approached the front of the building. She felt around the edges of the ward, searching for a weakness. It clung tightly to the building, which was nice. Likely, the thieves didn't want to be disturbed by a courier dropping a parcel on their doorstep, so they hadn't extended the ward to the fence line. She hopped over the fence, keeping to one edge, to avoid anyone who might be looking out the office window. Pressing herself up against the building's blank wall, she sensed the edges of the trip-wire, confirming her suspicions. If she entered the building, it'd fire a warning – very loudly.

She crept down the side alley. It was barely arms-breadth wide and led to a tiny back courtyard filled with rubbish bins. About halfway along, she spotted a tiny window in the wall below the row of office windows. It wasn't open wide enough to climb in, but she might get eyes and ears inside while she was still outside the trip-wire boundary.

Hope pulled a milk crate from the pile of rubbish out the back and placed it under the window. She stood on it to peer inside.

She gagged as the stench of an infrequently cleaned urinal washed over her. She turned her head to catch a few breaths before she faced the smell again, and looked down through the window into a tiny, grubby bathroom. Thankfully, currently unoccupied.

The door beyond opened on to the back portion of a large room; one she imagined filled most of the internal space. She couldn't see much more than the last few metres of it – giant industrial lights; a cheap wooden table sporting white, plastic dining chairs; and the back wall of the workshop, lined with a large cabinet.

No people, but on that wall she spied a set of shadows, cast by the sunlight streaming in from the high windows on the front of the building. And those shadows looked familiar. The low voices she heard confirmed their identities; recognisable although indistinct from this distance.

The bathroom she was looking into seemed to be stuck behind a set of metal stairs that were coming down from somewhere above and angled towards the back wall. They had a solid metal safety fence she couldn't see past. About half of the table, and just the legs of the chairs, were in view.

As was at least one familiar person lounging on one of those chairs.

Tink.

The chair's legs bowed out under the weight of her heavily muscled body. She had her back towards Hope, and she'd propped her legs up on the tabletop.

Hope swallowed her fear and leaned in to better listen. But of course, that was when they fell silent. She pressed herself against the wall, hoping to hear them when they began speaking again. But she had to be careful to keep her head out of the window so as not to cross the boundary of the perimeter ward.

Most simple perimeter alarms were pretty dumb magic – they had to be, or the magic drain would be too much for only one practitioner to uphold for long. They worked by noticing sudden changes to the local environment. Anyone new set them off. But stick around nearby for long enough, and they'd eventually treat you like part of the furniture. So Hope leaned up against the wall, listening... and waited.

At some point she'd have to make her move, but would it be better to jump in, all metaphorical guns blazing, or would she be able to sneak in, unheard and unseen? How much time did she have? Surely they had a buyer for their goods and was that buyer on the way? They didn't seem to already be present.

She was still contemplating her options when a small, refrigerated truck pulled up and parked opposite the building. She leaned out to peer down the alleyway, trying to get a better view. This must be their buyer.

A man hopped out, his back to her. He walked around his truck and she ducked back into hiding. When he turned his back to her, she popped back out again. She caught no more than a glimpse of him before he opened up the truck's back door and climbed inside. He reappeared holding a large black bag, and this time she realised he was an unexpected, yet familiar figure wearing scrubs. That doctor sure got around!

The thieves must've decided to cut out the middleman. Smart on the surface, but if Henry found out they'd deliberately cut him out, they'd have to leave the city to escape his wrath.

Hope recognised that her own situation was similar, but she hadn't been officially hired by him, so she'd probably get away with trying to edge back into the job. She was even less worried about Henry's wrath, given he'd anticipated her enough to send these goons after her.

She hopped down and squashed herself flat against the wall, hiding behind the drainpipe as the doctor reappeared and approached the building. It wasn't much of a hiding spot, and wouldn't have fooled anyone if she hadn't been covered by her hideaway. But it was good enough for now.

She watched as the doctor hesitated at the front gate. As he looked up at the roller door, she squashed herself even flatter against the wall. But he didn't look her way, even once. He opened the latch and approached the front door.

Before she climbed back up onto her milk crate, she re-assessed her options.

It was likely they'd be distracted by the doctor's arrival, which meant this was her best shot at sneaking in unnoticed. The doctor didn't seem to have set off any obvious traps at the front door. Could she slip in as he entered? Was the trip-wire simple enough to register two incoming people as one?

She didn't like her chances.

The trip-wire was still acclimatising to her, but before too long, she'd be able to slip in undetected. She just had to hope the doctor would keep them talking long enough for that to happen.

She pressed herself up to the window once more.

Inside, she heard voices.

As the doctor knocked on the front door, she felt a ripple run through the trip-wire ward. It hadn't triggered the full alarm – this was clearly an expected visitor.

Buzz's voice rang out. "Dodge, get the door, will ya? I think the good doctor's here with the cash."

Tink chuckled.

Hope watched Buzz's feet appear on the metal stairs as they clanged down to the ground level. He pulled out a chair next to Tink and sat down facing the front door. Hope could see him from the waist down.

Then she heard the scrape of a lock in the front door, some muttered greetings, and the door being locked again – a door that sounded pretty solid. Good thing she hadn't tried to barge through it.

Footsteps approached the table, but the doctor and Dodge were just out of her line of vision. That was annoying. She looked about to see whether she could get a better view. In the wall above her was another larger window, and it was partially open! However, to get up there, she'd have to scale the drainpipe and hand-over-hand along a narrow ledge, and that might set off the trip-wire. She'd wait a bit longer to get a better view.

"Hello, doctor!" Buzz called, his voice tinged with a distinct sneer. "Did you bring the cash?" He spoke as he would to a wayward child.

"In your message, you said you recovered my package," the doctor replied, deep and loud. He was clearly ignoring the attempt at mockery. "I'd like to see it first."

"All in good time."

"I've had no end of trouble with this package," the doctor cut across Buzz, "so if you don't mind, I'd like to make sure I'm not wasting any more of my time on this. Please show me that you have my package, as you stated, or I'll leave."

Buzz sighed and gestured to Tink, who pushed herself to her feet and walked over to the cabinet. She pulled it open and fetched out a battered and very familiar-looking toolbox. She carried it back to the table and dropped it with a heavy metallic *THUNK*. Her hands stayed firmly upon it.

Hope felt the tug on her tracker targets, and they were both aiming at the same spot. Tink had the goods.

The doctor appeared nearby, or at least the part of him from the chest down. He approached the table to inspect the toolbox.

"We've got it," Tink said, tipping the toolbox back and forth, and Hope heard something large and metallic rolling inside. Tink picked up the toolbox again and cradled it in her arms.

"Satisfied?" Buzz asked.

The doctor didn't reply, but Hope guessed he must've nodded, because Buzz continued. "Good, good. I'm glad because, you see, we ran into a bit of unintended extra trouble, getting this out for you. You might've heard of the stevedores' strike at the sky docks today?" He paused, as though waiting for an answer.

Hope didn't hear one.

Buzz continued. "Well anyway, we fell afoul of a few of the dock workers, who took it amiss that we were extracting a package over the picket line. We took some unexpected damage to our vehicles. Costly repairs, you see. So the price," he sucked some air through his teeth. "Well, it's gonna be a bit more expensive than we first quoted you."

Hope couldn't see the doctor's face, just his chest, so she had to imagine the look he had on it – gobsmacked, if she guessed correctly, followed quickly by that scowl she'd seen earlier when he'd flown out of Henry's office – the one with the little crinkle between his flashing eyes.

She saw when he shifted his stance, and his hands – one curled into a fist and the other white-knuckled, gripping the black leather case.

Buzz moved back a step, and she guessed that her imagination wasn't quite living up to the angry reality.

"You have *got* to be kidding!" the doctor growled.

"Now, now," Buzz responded.

The doctor overrode him. "Do you expect me to be paying more at this juncture? You have no idea how much this has already cost me!"

Tink leaned in to stand in the gap between Buzz and the doctor and then leaned an arm on the table – not quite menacing, but making her presence felt.

Dodge moved up silently behind the doctor, who if he'd noticed he'd become hemmed in didn't give any indication.

Hope leaned in a little closer. This situation could get very dangerous, very quickly, and the doctor didn't seem to have realised it.

"Hey," Buzz began, "no need for all this anger! Look, I know it's not what you wanted to hear, and not what we originally planned for, but I can't be held responsible for unanticipated events. Our services are always charged out on a 'cost plus expenses' basis, and you know, sometimes those expenses blow out."

"I don't care what your expenses are. We negotiated a price. You did not discuss expenses at the time, so I do not recognise them as legitimate. Your repairs are just a cost of your doing business." The doctor emphasised his words by stabbing with his index finger.

Buzz sounded irritated. "Well, we might've negotiated a price, but as I said, it's standard practice for us to run a job at 'cost plus expenses'."

Dodge, standing behind the doctor, had his hands on his hips, and they were awfully close to his well-stocked tool belt.

Tink just stood by; her arms folded and her body relaxed.

The doctor was riling them up, and he was not on an even footing with them.

Does he have any idea how much danger he's in? Probably not – stupid, naïve, little innocent...

She shook her head. Something nasty was about to go down. She could sense it coming, but she couldn't see well enough to decide what she was going to do about it.

Whether she was going to do something about it, she reminded herself. She didn't know this guy. This wasn't any business of hers, if he got himself into trouble he couldn't handle.

Still, she looked all around her. There was that drainpipe up to the window on the next floor. Could she climb up without them hearing her do it? Maybe she could get a better view inside – it'd at least be a better vantage point than looking in through a bathroom and stairs. Had the perimeter alarm acclimatised enough to her presence by now? Would it let her through?

She took another look in through the bathroom window. The doctor had been saying something scathing, but she hadn't caught the words, only the tone. He was treading on thin ice, and it was melting under his feet.

She decided to risk climbing up; she had to get a better view.

The drainpipe led to an open office window.

She couldn't see a thing from here; it was worse than the bathroom below.

She took a deep breath. Could she stand by and let the doctor get taken down? She wasn't sure, but she knew that from here she wouldn't be close enough to do anything to help, and besides, if she got closer, she'd be in position in to take advantage of an opening for her to grab the toolbox and make a break for it. The doctor was certainly an excellent distraction; now all she had to do was get past the perimeter alarm.

She decided to chance it. She heaved herself up and in through the window, wincing in preparation in case she had to run.

No perimeter alarm, at least. Phew!

She dropped to the floor and crept along the dirty carpet, staying low. The stairs turned into a walkway, which spanned the workshop's entire top section like a small verandah. She stayed below the top edge of the safety fence to keep out of direct sight. Her hideaway should cover any slight movements in the gaps.

She crept up to the edge, peered out of a gap between the fence and the floor, and looked down at the small gathering below. All present were still standing where she'd expected them to be, but she could see their faces now.

Buzz was grinning, but although his words were honeyed, his smile was full of teeth.

Tink was hovering beside him, a smug smile on her lips. A bruise spilled over her right cheek and nose, from where Hope had whammied her earlier.

Dodge was scowling at the doctor, who was still blithely standing in front of him. He had his hands poised to pull out a weapon as soon as Buzz gave the word.

The doctor was red-faced and trembling, and she caught the last of what he was saying: "… So I just can't afford any more than we agreed on, and to be frank, I don't see why I should be liable for any more. I can pay what we agreed on and that's it. Take it or leave it."

"Can you pay right now?" Buzz asked casually.

No, no, no, no, don't answer that! Don't answer that!

Hope never wished for telepathy more than right now. Sadly…

"Of course I can pay right now!" the doctor asserted, lifting his leather bag. "I came here expecting to make this deal with you."

Hope closed her eyes and sighed. She had to visualise slapping her own forehead. This guy was green as grass. He might as well have had a sign over his head that read 'GULLIBLE MARK' in flashing neon letters.

Buzz grinned. "So you've got the payment right here, then?"

The doctor dropped the bag onto the table with a satisfying thump. "I've held up my end of this deal; now it's your turn to honour yours." He kept one hand on the bag while facing Buzz, who laughed as though he were humouring the doctor.

Tink dropped the toolbox back onto the table, beside the bag.

Buzz grabbed the lid of the toolbox and flung it open like a showman, keeping his eyes firmly on the doctor, who unfortunately looked right in.

Hope watched as his eyes glazed and his face softened into a relaxed smile. Fully entranced, he didn't notice when Buzz's smile turned predatory or when Dodge stepped up behind him and clasped a heavy metal ring around his neck.

9 - The scuffle

His eyes widened. He opened his mouth to scream, but nothing came out. He staggered to the side and caught himself on the table, breathing heavily.

"Sorry, mate," Buzz said, with a smile that belied the intent of his words. "Just business – no hard feelings."

Tink stepped around Buzz to catch the doctor before he fell, and eased him to the floor.

"Wha?" the doctor slurred. "Wha you done t'me?" He lifted his wide eyes to Buzz, who was leaning down over him.

Buzz grinned back. "Just a neural clamp, buddy – not to worry."

The doctor made a clumsy grab for him but missed, swinging wildly. His face was pale and frowning. His eyes darted between Buzz and Dodge.

"It cuts down on your frontal-lobe neural activity; it's a bit like being drunk. But it's not permanent," Buzz reassured him with a grin.

Hope watched on in horror. Those things were heavy-duty illegal. She'd never seen a neural clamp in the flesh before.

Buzz patted the doctor on the head. "Don't worry, dear doctor. You won't be upset about it for long. We'll let you go after we sell the dream steel to our other buyer."

The doctor eyed him warily while ineffectually grappling with the clasp on the neck brace.

"Or maybe we'll let the drone-slavers take you," Dodge said from behind him.

Buzz grinned wider. "Depends how I'm feeling about you, hmm? So be a good boy and behave, okay?"

The doctor's eyes widened further, and his jaw dropped. His face had gone grey.

"Oh, dear," Dodge chuckled, "I think he's gonna cry."

From her hiding place, Hope gritted her teeth. Tears were dripping down the doctor's face. But what could she do? There were three of them, and they weren't distracted anymore. She'd missed her opening.

Tink had left the toolbox on the table and was lounging on her plastic chair again.

Dodge inspected the contents of the doctor's leather bag.

Buzz cocked his head.

Dodge nodded at him and closed the bag again.

"Why?" the doctor asked.

"Why?" Dodge repeated in a sing-song voice. He laughed and glanced up at his two companions.

Buzz returned the laugh.

Tink grimaced and turned away.

"Just doing business, mate," Buzz replied, "nothing personal."

Hope watched on, horrified but hoping for another opening. Her eyes flitted between the people below and the toolbox that was her real target. There were too many people to take on with a frontal assault. Plus, that wasn't really her speciality. This was meant to be a stealth mission: snatch the dream steel and get out.

This doctor complicated everything. Maybe she could –

WEEE-OOO WEEE-OOO

Shit! The perimeter alarm! How did I set it off?

Hope cringed and slunk backwards into the office behind her. She yanked at her thigh pocket and pulled a grey orb from the emergency stash she had in there. A magical flash-bang. She had not intended to use this on live targets tonight. These were effective, but worked better on the unsuspecting. A distraction instead of an offensive weapon.

She held it securely and spun around to face the room, ready to throw the orb at the first person to climb those stairs…

But the folks below weren't running; they weren't even looking in her direction.

Hope forced her muscles to relax and crept forward once more to peek through the gap below the banister.

Tink and Dodge had moved to cover the front door.

It gave her time to mentally kick herself. She'd only brought the one stunner for keeping them distracted while she took off with the goods.

This was supposed to be a simple smash-and-grab. Simple and

easy… but noooo. This stupid mark had to get himself in the way, and now she had to do something about it.

She crept down the staircase, keeping her movements slow and her body hidden well below the edge of the banister. Her hideaway kept her hidden from any casual glance, but wasn't proof against any sounds she made. These people might investigate any strange noises and if they looked at her directly, she'd be exposed. Thankfully, the stairs led down towards the back of the building, which was opposite where everyone was looking.

Hope peeked around the edge of the banister again. Tink was holding the front door open as two enormous figures entered, followed by a smaller one. She saw Tink tense up and begin cursing. Then Dodge unhooked some kind of weapon and aimed it at the newcomers, who paused.

She heard a low growl from one newcomer, but Tink and Dodge were blocking her view. The smaller person put his hands up.

"Calm down, guys! Settle!" Buzz said, not looking at all calm but holding out a placating hand. "It's our buyer, Mr Green. Here with the goods, I hope. We were expecting him, if not his… companions."

Hope lifted her head to get a better look, and her jaw dropped. The man in the middle seemed relatively normal, if a little tall and sporting a grey top hat. But the two creatures flanking him, well, they were something else. They looked like they'd just stepped out of yesterday's zoological parade – huge; heavily muscled; each filling out a big, shapeless coat. They could almost have passed for men, except that instead of a human head, each had a dog's head. They weren't even slightly human – more like somebody had chopped the heads off two German shepherds and sewed them on to a pair of massively muscled people. And they were both growling with a deep, "You're in the shit now!" rumble.

"Of course I have the goods," came Mr Green's smooth reply.

Buzz eyed up the dog-headed goons, keeping well back. "You've got the cash, then?"

"I do, but I want to see the merchandise first."

"You show me yours; I'll show you mine."

Mr Green smiled and gestured at one of his goons, who opened a case for Buzz while standing well back.

Hope was debating her next move, and how best to position herself to get in and out fast, when she glanced down… right at the doctor… who was openly gaping at her.

Shit!

She put her finger to her lips, but too late.

Buzz, his back to her, looked down at the doctor and then spun around.

Shit! Shit! No time! Act!

She chucked the stunner orb over Buzz, aiming it at the middle of the team, then closed her eyes and put her hands over her ears.

The light flashed against her eyelids and the sound thumped through her body.

Her ears rang in the aftermath, but she was expecting that. She was up and about quicker than the others, running while they were still reeling.

Buzz was hunched over, holding his head. She kicked him solidly in the crotch, and he dropped.

Mr Green was staggering to his feet, and his mouth was moving, shouting.

All she could hear was the ringing.

One dog-headed goon rolled on the ground near Tink, both of them stunned.

The other leaped at Dodge, who grabbed Mr Green's case and began weaving some kind of spell. His hand was dripping with blue flame, but the magic kept slipping out of his grasp.

Mr Green was trying to get around him, aiming for the case.

Hope ignored them and grabbed at the toolbox. A hand grabbed her ankle. The doctor was on the floor, staring up at her with big puppy eyes.

She swung the toolbox up above her head and brought it down as hard as she could.

His eyes went wide.

The box connected with the ring around his throat. She heard the clang as the shackle broke – the first genuine sound she'd heard besides the incessant ringing in her ears.

She heard other sounds now, too – dogs howling, and yelps and groans from Dodge and Buzz.

The doctor grappled with the brace ineffectually, and she grabbed hold of it and yanked it hard, pulling him along the floor until it let him go. He scrambled to his feet.

Hope turned for the stairs, only to jerk backwards as a hand clamped around her arm.

"I'll take that!" yelled somebody nearby.

She spun. It was Mr Green talking, but the arm holding her steady belonged to one of the dog-headed goons. She looked down to see a decidedly non-human hand wrapped around her arm, dwarfing it by comparison. The arm was heavy and black and was covered in thick fur. It looked exactly how she'd expect the arm of a gorilla to look – straight out of the jungle books at the library. The only difference was that the arm was painted with silver ink. It looked like matrix calligraphy, covering the arm and disappearing up into the creature's sleeve.

Mr Green held out his hand and looked pointedly down at the toolbox.

Glancing around the room, Hope saw that Buzz was still rolling around on the ground, clearly in pain, but that the others had been busy while she was freeing the doctor.

Tink was laid out on the floor, unconscious – whether from her flash-bang or the gorilla-dog, Hope didn't know.

Dodge was conscious but had several hundred kilos of gorilla-dog of his own sitting on his chest.

Mr Green lifted his eyebrows in anticipation. He reached out and took hold of the handle of the toolbox alongside Hope's hand. He nodded at the gorilla-dog, who squeezed her arm.

She yelped and dropped the handle of the toolbox, which swung towards the creature.

It tossed the box to Mr Green.

He caught it and grinned. "Thank you kindly, madam."

The gorilla-dog released Hope's arm, and she pulled away, rubbing at it.

Mr Green turned to walk away.

"No!" the doctor yelled. "That doesn't belong to you!" He lunged for the toolbox, yanking Mr Green back a step.

Mr Green scowled at him. "I beg to differ, good sir."

"I *need* it!" the doctor exclaimed, pulling on the handle.

"*I* need it. I'm paying for it, and I'm holding it in my hand." Mr Green yanked back, hard, tearing it from the doctor's grasp.

The doctor stumbled, pulling them both down.

Hope leaped back from the tussle.

"Please!" the doctor begged. "I need it to save my brother!" He pulled himself to his feet once more.

"I need it!" Mr Green replied, his voice dripping with irritation. "I need it so I can save humanity!"

Out of the corner of her eye, Hope sensed movement.

Buzz raised a weapon at the two men.

She didn't think. She leaped.

Time slowed. There was a bang. She was falling.

She landed, the doctor beneath her, grabbing her arms to slow her fall.

He looked at her in shock.

Rolling off him onto the floor, she struggled to rise. She slipped. She was moving slow, unsteady. Had she hit her head again?

Mr Green escaped through the front door, his gorilla-dogs following and Dodge in hot pursuit.

Buzz rounded the table and chased after him – or was he chasing the dream steel? Either way, he was gone; they both were.

The doctor climbed to his feet. He watched them go, a stricken look on his face. Then he sighed and his shoulders dropped. He gave one last, longing look towards the front door before turning back to Hope. He grabbed her around the waist and pulled her to him.

She squeaked with indignation as he lifted her, but stumbled against him, woozy.

Why am I so dizzy?

"We have to get you to a hospital!" the doctor said, pressing her against him, hard.

She looked down at where he was holding her, intending to pull his hands off. But she saw red. A lot of red. "No hospital," she croaked. "Too expensive; too risky."

He huffed in exasperation. "Here, press here." He moved her hand to push on the wound in her side. "Can you walk?"

She nodded, and he started walking for the both of them. She struggled to make her legs move, and he paused while she caught her breath. Hope looked around.

Tink was on the floor but lifting her head and looking about.

"We have to go. Now," Hope said.

"I know," he replied, grabbing the bag he'd brought earlier.

"Now! Tink is waking up!"

"Who?"

Hope vaguely gestured towards Tink, who was holding her head and shaking it to get the cobwebs out.

He nodded, lifting her up so she was leaning on him, and half carried her out.

"Hey!" she heard. Tink had spotted them!

The doctor picked up the pace and pushed them towards the front door.

Hope wasn't feeling good. In fact, she was feeling very *un*-good. She half walked and was half dragged out through the big roller door.

A frantic, scrambling sound came from behind them.

The doctor dragged her out towards the alley. By the time they reached the gate, the world was fading in and out.

The doctor cursed beside her. They jerked to the side and almost hit the fence.

Hope's head spun away from her. She watched Dodge playing with a dog in the street. That was funny. It leaped at him and licked his face.

Too big for a lap dog. Get down, puppy!

She giggled. Her feet were dragging across the gravel on the street. The dog was barking. There was yelling behind her.

Then, a heavy, thumping sound. That she knew! Engines in the sky!

She landed on her back, on a table. Couldn't see the sky. She needed to see the sky! And it was cold here. Freezing!

Then she was being tucked into bed, in the cold. The blanket was tight. Like being hugged all over. That was nice. A door slammed; then tyres screeched. The room bucked and shook. She spoke, but didn't know what she was saying, or to whom. The room lurched again, and the table slid to the side and slammed against the wall.

The jolt cleared her head a moment. They were driving! Was she stuck on a gurney?

Something… She faded again.

The doctor was here. She could talk to him. He was lying beside her in a box.

She asked his name, but he didn't answer.

He just lay there, quiet, staring. He was cold.

Was she cold too?

Maybe they were both dead!

The world went dark.

10 - The necromancer

The world phased in and out again.

There was a dazzling light.

Somebody was talking to her, but she couldn't figure out the words. Somebody was leaning over her. Or maybe it was two people?

She recognised only one of them.

Her mind was floaty and warm, but something sharp was biting her.

It was way… away in the distance.

Is there a bee sting? I need to do something with those…

Pull it out? Yes. We always pull out the bee sting. Or brush it off?

She needed to find it and brush it off, but couldn't quite make herself move.

Oh, and the cute-looking doctor was back!

I should do something about that bee. It hurts. Maybe the doctor can help me with it. He seems nice. But how can I ask? I have to say something nice first.

She looked up into his face.

He looked worried. She could see it because his eyes had that wrinkle between his eyes.

Cute concentration face. I should tell him that – that's a nice thing!

"Yer ver' cyoot," she mumbled.

The doctor looked up, astonished.

Her smile was lopsided, and she seemed to be drooling. She frowned.

*That's not supposed to happen. Drooling is **not** nice! He won't help me now!*

"You shouldn't be awake yet," he stammered, shaking his head as if to dislodge the astonishment. He was holding something long and sharp, but rather than be frightened, she was fascinated. It was shiny and red. Pretty.

He turned to the other person and loudly said, "Orderly, one more click of anaesthetic."

I can hear him. Why is he shouting at me?

The orderly turned away to a machine stationed behind the bed. There was something wrong with his head.

She heard a loud click.

The doctor looked at her, then at the machine. Then huffed. "Damnit, it's not working. No time. Have to get this done before the last of it wears off." He again shouted at the helper, "Orderly, pass me the forceps."

This other person must be a bit dim-witted. Maybe he just can't hear very well. Probably because he has no ears. Lots of stitches down and around his head.

She blinked. There were a lot of stitches... and there was something wrong with that. His mouth was shut with stitches, too.

How can he eat with his mouth all closed up like that?

Wait. Something's not right... he doesn't seem to have a neck at all. It's all shrivelled and loose. How will he swallow with a neck like that? How will he breathe?

She felt another tug on her hip.

Ow! That was not a bee sting! It hurt... a lot!

"Wha?" She tried to get her jaw working, shaking her head.

"Orderly, put your hands on her shoulders. Hold her still!"

The other person put their hands where they were told and pushed down.

She tried pushing up, but they were strong!

Her head was fuzzy but clearing, and she was distinctly not liking what was happening here, especially given the state of the person who was now leaning over her. Whoever they were, they were rake thin with loose skin over muscle. They made a peculiar, rattling sound in their throat, as if breathing were a strange and novel experience for them.

And the stink of it! Halitosis on steroids! She tried not to gag. Thankfully, they didn't breathe on her again... Then she belatedly realised that they didn't seem to be breathing at all.

Her eyes widened, and fear rolled over her in an icy wave.

The orderly was dead. She was sure of it.

The cold, grey skin; the dull eyes.

Definitely dead *and* still walking around.

That meant the doctor was exactly what Henry had accused him of. It wasn't just a slur. He really was a necromancer.

Damn. And he was so hot, too!

But worse, he was working on her.

Shit! What does he think he's doing without my consent? He could be doing anything! Necromancers are the scum of the magical world. Nobody sane would trust them to put you back together with all of your original pieces.

Hope pulled herself together and tried to roll off the table, legs first.

"Hey!" yelled the necromancer. "What are you doing?"

"Not lettin' yer tush me!" she slurred.

Her legs slid off the edge, but the necromancer pulled her back into place and tightened a strap around her hips. "Stop that! I'm trying to stitch you up!"

"Nooooo! Gerroff!" She tried pushing his hands away from her, but her control was all sloppy.

He's drugged me!

That was why her thoughts were all blurry. She tried to kick, but could barely lift a foot. She flailed at him instead.

He pulled his hands out of reach and hissed in frustration. "Orderly, hold her arms down!"

The creepy dead person leaned over her, grabbing her upper arms.

She cringed, cold shivers running down her spine.

The creature's throat was half torn out and restitched, and now loomed close to her face; its skin pale but mottled with unhealed bruising.

It really is a zombie!

Hope shrank away from it. She didn't like dead bodies at the best of times, but being pressed up against one, especially a reanimated one... she bit her tongue and tried not to scream.

A breath rattled through the undead creature's ruined throat, stinking of formaldehyde and rot.

She froze, paralysed with fear. Closing her eyes, she breathed deep to regain some composure. She had to think!

He was holding her too tight to wriggle free. Then, glancing lower, she noticed the graceful lines of conjuration runes painted all down its chest. The lines were faint but still visible – silver against the pale skin; swirling brushstrokes of ink that covered the orderly's chest and disappeared within its ragged shirt. For a moment, she forgot her fear as her curiosity led her to trace the lines, trying to divine their meaning.

The necromancer flicked her a quick look, then continued working on her side. "I'm almost done."

"Done wi' what?" she cried, her attention drawn back to what he was doing. "Wat yer doin' wif me?"

"Saving your life! That bullet travelled and nipped a minor artery. You'd have bled out internally. I'm just sewing you back up. Luckily for you, you got hurt while travelling with an excellent microsurgeon. And to be fair, I did not expect you to wake up in the middle, but I'm afraid my equipment is a bit on the dodgy side." He gave a weak half-smile.

She scowled.

The doctor frowned. "What can I say... budget cuts, hey? And my available medical team is... ah.. somewhat limited in skills." He flicked a glance at the dead orderly.

Hope glanced up at the zombie again, pushing away another wave of revulsion. Trying to ignore the feel of its clammy hands pressed against her shoulders.

She was regaining the use of her tongue, and her thoughts were clicking back into place. Just one fear held her tight. "You gonna turn me into one of 'em?" she whimpered.

He again looked astonished, and then several emotions chased themselves across his face – hurt and shame, settling on anger. "You're seriously being bigoted about my skill set now; when my arms are elbow deep in your abdomen trying to save your life?" He bit the words off.

Hope cringed some more, this time curling in shame. He was just doing his best to help her.

He pressed his mouth shut until his lips turned pale, and continued on with his work. "Thank you, Galen, for taking out the bullet pressing on my artery. Thank you, Galen, for sewing me back up. Thank you, Galen, for saving my life." He delivered the words in an angry, sing-song voice, and glared as he pulled his needle and thread, whipping them through the air.

"Thank you, Hope," she mimicked quietly, "for stepping in front of the bullet meant for me in the first place."

He paused, thread in the air, and his face softened. He glanced at her and continued his work a little more gently. "Thank you, Hope, for saving me first – which is another reason I'm keen not to see you die."

He sighed as he completed one more stitch, then put his tools down and inspected his work. "There. As good as I can do for now." He headed for the deep basin nearby. "Orderly, you can release her now."

Her arms free, she tried to lift herself up and turn on her side, but the tie down straps still held her securely across her hips.

The necromancer turned back to her and released the strap. "Be careful getting up. Don't want to blow those new stitches." He put his arms out to help her.

She batted them away, rolled on her side, and tried to push herself up.

The necromancer – Galen, watched helplessly as she flailed and heaved and finally got an arm underneath her body to push herself marginally upright.

Her head was spinning, so she paused a moment, breathing deep, and waited for the feeling to pass.

Galen turned back to the basin, evidently satisfied she wasn't likely to fall on the floor just yet, and began washing his hands and arms.

Hope's head cleared a little more, and she took a moment to inspect her wound. It was surprisingly small, bore a row of neat stitching, and seemed to be near the edge of her abdomen. She took that to be a good sign.

"The bullet didn't hit anything too vital. It cut through the muscle and into the pelvic bone but missed any organs." He watched her as he leaned against the basin and towel-dried his arms. "You'll be sore for a while, or you can get yourself a healing potion – though I'd wait a day or two for the wound to knit together; it's safer that way, especially so soon after you've already used one."

She looked up.

He raised his hands. "I recognise you – from the hospital yesterday, right?"

She nodded. "So, not going to turn into a zombie, then?" she asked with a raised eyebrow and a half-smile.

Galen snorted. "You'd have to die first for me to even attempt that, and you are demonstrably not dead right now."

She nodded again. "But it is something you could do if you wanted?" She glanced at the orderly.

It was now standing up against the wall and staring blankly into the distance, waiting. It looked like it would happily wait there until it fell apart.

"Yes," Galen mumbled, looking away, "I could if I wanted." He began clearing away his tools. "However, that takes time and energy I don't have to spare, and frankly, if I'd planned to turn you into a zombie, I wouldn't have tried as hard to stop you from dying, now, would I?" His voice was mildly acidic.

Looking at him, Hope noted the rings under his eyes and the way his shoulders sagged with exhaustion. She sighed. He was a bit of a puzzle, but it looked like he'd been working hard on her. "Thank you," she said, sincerely.

He turned around and looked at her.

"Thank you for saving my life... after I saved yours," she added with a smile.

He huffed a laugh and approached with his hand out to her.

She shied back.

His smile dropped, along with his hand. "You'll need to get down from there somehow – preferably without destroying all my hard work."

Hope looked down. She was sitting on a large metal table, and it was pretty high off the floor.

"Okay, suit yourself. But I'm not sure I have the energy to do another surgery right now – especially not to fix up stitches you pull out by being stubborn." He pulled a thin tube away from her shoulder and fiddled with the machine it was attached to. "Gods-damned cheap shit," he muttered, flicking the line, "stopping halfway through the surgery!"

The machine beeped forlornly. He switched it off and pushed it over to the far wall.

Hope sat up and waited as the world spun around her a bit more.

Galen returned and stood a step away from her. "Would you allow me to remove the IV shunt from your neck?" He pointed to where the tube had been attached to her.

She touched the place. It hurt a little. Something was stuck down with tape and it felt very uncomfortable. She nodded and held still as Galen approached.

He touched her gently as he removed the tape and shunt from her skin. His hands were soft and quick. "I have a couch in the next room, if you're ready."

She looked down at the ground. It was a long way away, and her head was still spinny. "In a minute. I'm just waiting for the room to slow down."

Galen nodded and stood awkwardly. "I, uh, feel like we got off on the wrong foot here." He stuck out his hand. "Hi, I'm Galen. Nice to meet you?"

Hope blinked at his hand a moment, then smiled and took it. "Hi, Galen. I'm Hope. It's nice to meet you, despite the unusual circumstances."

He smiled and gently shook her hand. His hand was warm. She didn't pull away.

After a few moments, he offered her his other hand.

She looked at it quizzically before realising he was offering to help her down from the operating table. She really wasn't firing on all cylinders. Knocked out twice in one week. That was probably not good for her – no wonder she was a bit brain dead. She took the outstretched hand.

He half lifted her down off the table.

She had a moment to admire his strength before collapsing in his arms.

"Damnit! Sorry. I shouldn't have had you move so soon." He held her up as her head spun.

He shifted his grip and lifted her into his arms.

She didn't have the mental strength to dissuade him as she faded in and out.

He carried her into the adjacent room, which was furnished with an assortment of old but comfortable-looking lounges.

"I'll put you over here," he said, placing her down in an armchair, and she sank gratefully into its plush cushions. "Here, this'll help the blood return to your head." He lifted her feet onto a footstool and tucked a cushion under them. He stood there a moment, looking down at her.

She blinked up at him, and the world regained some focus.

"I'll, uh, get you some soup or something," he said, and disappeared through a doorway before she could reply.

11 - Meeting Galen

With her eyes open, the room kept swooping and diving, but if she closed them, it was her stomach that rolled. So instead she kept her eyes fixed on the far wall and breathed deep and slow.

Eventually, she felt up to looking around. She seemed to be in some sort of staffroom which had been converted to an impromptu lounge. Bookshelves lined the walls, and they were filled with hundreds of books. They were stacked sideways, and in some places were two or three layers deep. There was the expected stash of medical and magical textbooks, but also an extensive selection of novels in a variety of genres.

If she could stand, she'd be up there running her fingers down the spines, simultaneously judging his taste in reading material and hunting for any titles of interest that she hadn't already read. That'd have to wait until the room stopped spinning.

Nearer to hand, there was a small array of mismatched armchairs surrounding a low coffee table. It, too, was covered in books, and sported several discarded and variously coloured mugs – and plonked right in the middle of it was the black leather bag he'd carried into the meeting with the thieves. She debated sitting up to take a peek, but the roll in her uncertain stomach won out against her curiosity.

Her stomach had settled slightly when Galen returned, bearing another mug, which he handed down to her. "It's just some chicken soup – warm, not hot. Too hot and you'll pass out again."

She sniffed at the soup gingerly, ready to push it away if her stomach protested, but it just growled appreciatively. It'd been a while since she'd had eaten more than a single, half-melted ice-cream. She slurped the soup. It was delicious.

"Thanks," she said, "for the stitching, as well as the soup."

Galen smiled down, looking pleased. He sat in another armchair, the one that looked the most worn in, and also the one that was closest to the pile of books on the coffee table.

"Can I ask… why were you there?" He looked at her expectantly. "Not that I'm not grateful for, you know, saving my life and all, but…"

Hope took another slurp of soup while she decided what she'd tell him. She didn't know this guy from a bar of soap. He seemed nice enough, but would he trust her once she'd told him the truth? She examined the room, searching for a clue as to how much she should divulge. The toolbox of great fortune was conspicuously absent. "I take it you didn't manage to get the dream steel out?"

He slumped his shoulders and his face fell. "No. I grabbed you instead – which I'm totally fine with. If I had to do it over, I'd obviously choose to save your life instead of my dream steel. It's just that… I wish I could've done both." He finished by looking into his empty hands.

Hope blinked. She wasn't sure she'd have made the same decision, given the circumstances. "Then I'm extra grateful. Thanks again."

She studied him with narrowed eyes.

What the hell. Let's see what happens. It's not like he hasn't already guessed what I am, anyway.

"I'm a… specialist retrieval agent," she said.

He raised an eyebrow at the euphemism, but said nothing.

"And I'm the one who retrieved your package out of the warehouse. But those thieves stole it from me. I tracked them down afterwards, and that's when I saw you get captured. I couldn't just stand by and watch." She took another sip of the soup, observing his reaction to what she'd shared so far.

"How did you hear about the dream steel?" Galen asked her, perplexed. "Do you work for Henry too?"

Hope frowned into her soup, pushing down the sudden burst of rage that welled up at the sound of Henry's name. "I used to, but not anymore – especially after this doublecross."

"So, I'm not sure I understand. Did Henry send you to fetch my dream steel back from the warehouse? It was you I saw at his shop, wasn't it?"

She nodded, then paused. Did she really want to keep telling him the truth? Could he handle it? She mentally shrugged, then nodded. "In answer to your question, no, and kind of yes. Henry didn't tell me to retrieve your stuff from the sky docks, but I think he set me up to overhear your conversation, and he knows me well enough that I'd try it – and probably succeed. But if I failed, he'd have plausible deniability, and I'd take the fall."

Galen snorted. "At least I'm not the only one he was screwing over, I guess." He turned thoughtful. "So, would you have brought it to me or sold it to the other guy who showed up?" His voice was tinged with a lurking anger.

"I had no idea about the other guy! From what I can tell, that was something the other team cooked up on their own. Ideally, I'd have tried to find you – cut out Henry as the middleman, if possible. But to be fair, I didn't have any way to contact you before now. I had been considering whether it was still worth bringing it in to Henry." She spat the name out with distaste. "He's one of the few options around for... uh... goods like this."

Galen looked at her hard. "You mean he's your fence, right? For stolen goods?"

"Hey, don't get too judgey." She eyed up the undead orderly, who was thankfully still in the operating room, standing silent against the wall; still staring and unmoving. It didn't seem to have breathed since she'd last looked at it.

"Hey," Galen replied, lowering his eyebrows, "what I do doesn't take from the hard-earned wealth other people have worked their arses off for."

"No, it just takes their actual arses and imbues them with creepy artificial life, until they rot off by themselves."

He glared at her, pointing at the orderly. "I'll have you know he donated his body to science." He huffed another breath and switched subjects. "So, you were just planning on selling the dream steel, then?"

She looked at him, a little confused.

"You had no plans to use it yourself?" He was gazing at her intently.

She blinked and shook her head. She hadn't even considered keeping any for her own purposes. "No, I can't..." She blushed. "There's no point. I'm not actually trained as a practitioner. I've never been able to afford university training and accreditation. All I've read is what I could borrow from the library." She looked away.

"Oh!" Galen exclaimed, looking genuinely surprised. "It's just that I saw the tracker matrix and assumed you'd built it."

She looked down at her arm. The matrix had stopped running again. Her magic had crashed when she fell unconscious. "Oh. It's not really mine – I mean I *can* write a basic tracker, but for this, I just modified the standard hospital tracker to take a new target – multiple targets, actually, as I wanted to keep an eye on Tink as well as the dream steel and…" She stopped.

Galen was looking at her, his face slack. "That's pretty impressive, you know."

She looked down, blushing again. "Well, maybe, but I can't build new matrices to do anything else. I need to use a library book even to interpret what any other kind of matrix does. I definitely don't understand the runes for directing flow through a dream-steel filter."

A small smile played over Galen's face – she'd call it a smirk but for the twinkle in his eyes that implied good intentions. "I wouldn't put yourself down for that. I *have* been to university, so I can tell you that most trained practitioners couldn't interpret a matrix straight up without a textbook to refer to, at least beyond their own specialised sub-domain. And material filters are damned tricky things. Most people use the pre-cut rune flows without even understanding how they work. And you both read *and* altered an in-place matrix to take extra parameters… on the fly." He nodded. "That's pretty cool."

Hope felt awkward – happy, but awkward. "Well, sure, Mister big-shot, university-trained necromancer. So, what did *you* have planned for the dream steel? Don't tell me it was to raise an army of the undead." She smiled.

He looked down at his hands.

She sat up straight. "Oh, my gods, it is, isn't it?" A note of genuine horror was creeping into her voice. "You do know it's highly illegal, right?"

He glared at her. "Illegal. Like thieving, right?"

She rolled her eyes. "Thieving is just plain illegal, but necromancy is, like, majorly illegal. The Imperium doesn't give two shits about what I do, besides slapping a fine on me. I'm practically in the 'regular means of income' column in their financial books. But this…" She hooked a thumb at the orderly. "This can get you shot, and if you're planning something that's big enough to use the amount of dream steel in that toolbox…" She eyed him up. "They'll send an army after you – and to be fair, it'll probably be justified."

He sat there looking back at her.

He didn't look like the mad-scientist type, not like the guy with the gorilla attack dogs and the top hat.

"So, are you planning on razing the city with an army of undead? Because if you are, please let me know so I can relocate to another continent."

He huffed. "No, nothing like that." He looked back down at his hands where they lay in his lap and muttered, "I'm not *really* a necromancer."

Hope raised her eyebrows and rolled her eyes at the orderly who was still standing facing the wall.

Galen blushed again. "Well, I am *able* to perform necromancy, but that doesn't define my skill set. I only picked that up recently, out of necessity." He opened his mouth to continue, but closed it again.

Hope watched a range of emotions flit across his face as he glanced at her, weighing up how much to tell her.

He straightened and asked, "How much do you know about necromancy?"

She silently raised an eyebrow.

"Of course. I understand, it's not common knowledge."

"That's an understatement," she muttered with a snort of amusement. "Sorry, please go on."

"Basic level raising the dead is, well… it's not easy, but it's the bread-and-butter." He gestured at his *friend* in the other room. "And, it doesn't last very long. The support matrices aren't all that efficient, and with the usual levels of preservation, they can only keep them going maybe a month, two at most, before their natural deterioration overcomes the self-repair capability. And they have pretty limited cognition, so they're kinda dumb and clumsy. And, well, the side effects aren't the best."

"Side effects?"

"Well, you know." He looked down at his hands, obviously embarrassed. "The rotting and the smell."

"Oh yeah, that. I thought that was part and parcel of the process."

"Well, it kinda is. But that's mostly a side effect of the initial preservation and restoration process." He gazed at his orderly, his eyes assessing. "Most damage occurs during the waking-up process – the transition. If the initial restoration of function isn't good, you need a lot of ongoing magical support to keep the body going. So the undead always depend wholly on the strength of the continuing self-repair matrices, and they all eventually fail at some point. However, with perfect initial preservation, and the highest-quality medical conjuration during the transition, a much greater level of restoration is possible – at least in theory. I found out only recently, after a lot of hard work and research, just what was possible to do, and I put it all together."

"Transition. Is that a euphemism?"

"I used to think so. We've all seen the war footage. Hordes of mindless zombies attacking anyone who comes close; the dead rising again to join the shambling horde. I always used to think that this," he pointed at the orderly, "this semblance of life was about as good as it got. But when I was properly motivated to go looking, I found there was a lot more to it. With enough energy in the right necromantic matrix, it should be possible to restore a well-preserved person to something very close to what they once were – a revenant rather than a zombie. And they can... well, I hope they can... live again for a long time."

He sighed and examined his hands once more. "But it takes a lot of energy to work, more than what one necromancer could provide on his own – even a team of necromancers, and I don't have that."

"So, like, Conjunction levels of energy."

"Exactly! And that means being prepared, and it means having a world-class conjuration matrix ready, and it means..."

"...it means having a metric shit tonne of dream steel."

"Yeah."

"Why would you go to all that effort? I mean, I get that you're keen to have a go, and all, but still... that's a fortune in dream steel, and from what I've seen, you seem to be skint. Are you that keen to make your mark on the world?"

He barked a laugh.

When she looked at him, his face had dropped, and he was frowning. And were there tears in his eyes? What had she said wrong?

"It's for my brother," he whispered.

She blinked. "Brother?"

"We saved up to buy this hospital together, you know?" He glanced around at the less-than-salubrious surroundings.

Hope stayed silent. He'd gone distant again, gazing into his past. Whatever this was, it was important to him.

"We saved for years after we made it through med school, and we planned it all out. My brother always wanted to be a world-class surgeon with his own team, running his own hospital, free to service any clients he chose. And me? Well, I told him that my dream was to have my own lab, where I'd be free to pursue my research and produce the next generation of medical miracles. Over time, though, I realised that was just a means to an end. I wanted to make enough money to run a free clinic – for refugees."

He gazed off into the middle distance. "We got as far as saving up the deposit and buying this place, but we couldn't agree what to do next; whether to follow my dream first, or his, so we argued… Right from the start, I wanted to make everything we did available to the less fortunate, but my brother, well, he was just as ambitious as a businessman as he was at getting us through university. He was the one who got us our scholarships and…" He glanced at Hope, who was listening politely. "Well, it doesn't matter now, anyway. It all came crashing down a year ago." He fell silent once more.

Hope debated whether to ask or wait, but he was staring silently for a long time. "What happened?"

Galen sighed. "Did you hear about the incident, about a year ago, with Professor Darke, who invented the flash-freeze gun?"

She was confused at the change of subject. She thought back. "Yeah, some guy invented what he thought was a revolutionary method for preserving food, but he went crazy and began freezing half the neighbourhood. I heard he went on a rampage through uptown – destroyed a bank; a school; a mall. I heard it ended in some kind of stand-off at a hospital…" She stopped, her eyes wide, and looked around her.

Galen looked up at her, his eyes brimming with tears.

"Oh," she whispered, "I'm so sorry."

He blinked and looked away, nodding. "Yeah. He always was a tad over-confident; had a bit of a hero complex – or maybe he just thought it would be good for business." He smiled ruefully at the memory. "My brother stood against him, alone in the street. He was such a charmer he even managed to talk the guy down and was about to take the gun off him when the Imperium showed up." His voice turned bitter. "The professor freaked out, and my brother was…" Another sigh. "One moment my hero – full of love and life, and the next minute… ice."

Hope reached out and put her hand on his arm.

He trembled as though deciding whether to pull away from it, but stayed put.

"I'm so sorry you lost your brother," she whispered, compelled to fill the silence. "I have a sister, and though she sometimes drives me crazy, I have no idea what I'd do if I lost her." She thought about their most recent fight, and how upset she was at herself; at how petty it all seemed, considering Sam's terrible injury. "My sister's child, Sam, was hurt really badly a few days ago. You were operating on them, so you might remember them; they lost their arm." She sat, quiet for a moment, thinking about how much she loved Sam and how much Sam had loved to paint with that arm.

"Is that why you took the job, to... ah... *retrieve* the dream steel?" he asked her, swallowing the croak in his voice.

"Yeah," she replied, the weight of her failure coming out in the tiredness of her voice. "I don't need to tell you how expensive prosthetics are, especially if you want a good-quality one. I spent all my college savings on the surgery to save Sam's life." The sorrow of that loss rolled through her, a wave of grief for the dream life she'd nearly held in her hands. Then she shook her head to clear it. Perhaps she wasn't that different from Galen after all – she'd always choose Sam's life over her own dreams. She wished she didn't have to, but she didn't regret the choice she'd made.

Galen had gone quiet again.

She looked up at him.

He was looking at her, but also through her.

She could see that the cogs were turning in his head, and turning fast. He was clearly plotting something. It was fascinating to watch from the outside. She waited while his thoughts ran their course. If he could come up with a plan, far be it for her to derail his train of thought.

Finally, his eyes focused back on her, and he smiled.

She raised her eyebrows.

"I have an idea. I think it will solve both our problems." He paused.

She drew her eyebrows together in puzzlement. "And?"

"Well, you might not like it, but please... just let me walk you through it before you decide." He looked at her intently, searching for something.

"No snap judgements. Got it," she said, staring back into his open face. She wasn't the best at reading faces, but he seemed earnest and, judging from his actions at the thieves' hangout, he seemed inclined to be overly trusting rather than the doublecrossing type. As long as he wasn't planning to make her into a zombie, she was willing to hear him out.

"I need the dream steel to revive my brother, and, well, I don't need to tell you I need your help if I'm to have any hope of getting it back," he declared ruefully.

Hope snorted and smiled, but nodded to him. "Go on."

He looked down at the leather bag he'd salvaged from the previous crisis. "I don't have a lot of cash. That's all I have left of our savings to start the hospital." He paused and smiled sadly. "But I'd be prepared to give it all to you if you can help me get that dream steel before the Conjunction. Now, I know it won't be enough for both a prosthetic and replacing your college savings, but it will be enough to get you one or the other."

Hope waited, seeing him shaking his head back and forth and jittering his feet. She could sense he was holding something back.

"Now, I don't expect you to trust my abilities right now, but if, by the end of this, you find you'd be a bit more willing to trust my more... unusual talents, I have an idea that might help your sister's child better than any prosthetic."

"No!" Hope barked.

"I understand you might be a bit reticent right now..."

"No!" she repeated, this time more strongly.

"You don't even know what I'm suggesting yet." He looked a little deflated.

"I don't care. Surgery, sure, but I will not let you get your dirty necromancer magic anywhere near Sam."

At the word *dirty*, his eyes flashed. The sadness turned to anger. He gritted his teeth and curled his hands into fists. "I would *never* harm a child! Or use any magic that would cause harm, either."

"I don't..."

"No, you listen now! I know I'm offering something unusual – experimental, but I'm offering something you can't get any other way."

"There is nothing we could want that..."

"I'm offering her own arm back!" he yelled, unable to contain himself.

Hope blinked, momentarily silenced.

Galen went on while he could. "Her original one, not a plastic or metal replacement. She's young. I think I can do it so her body will accept the native graft. It won't even need to contend with the body rejecting it as foreign tissue, because it's already from her original body. We just have to go get it before it's destroyed and then make sure it's present when I perform my conjuration. That should keep it alive long enough for it to heal fully, and afterwards, we can do the re-attachment surgery once she has fully recovered from her original injuries. It'll heal just as though it were a broken arm."

Hope sat stunned at what he was suggesting.

Would it really work? Could Sam have their real arm back, hale and whole again?

She tried to make her mouth move, to say no, but couldn't. It was tempting, and all she had to do was help this guy bring his dead brother back as a creepy zombie, and hope that the Imperium never got wind of it, otherwise it would be both their heads.

"I understand. It's a lot to take in. You don't need to decide right now. We can still get the dream steel and I can pay you, and you can use that money for a prosthetic. I can even recommend a good friend of mine who'll give you a solid discount. We've still got time to decide about your niece, Sam, later. Right up until the day of the Conjunction. That's when you will have to choose whether to go ahead with saving her real arm." He fell quiet and watched her as she thought it over.

She was tempted. Sorely tempted. Not only because he'd offered her a wildly optimistic scenario she hadn't considered possible for Sam, but because a selfish part of her realised that if he operated on Sam's arm for free, she could spend the money on her own schooling plans. However, she pushed that part of herself away and buried it. It was an enticing idea but shouldn't be the deciding point for this momentous choice. Instead, she should think about how he'd need to use necromancy on her sister's child. Hope suppressed a shiver, then closed her eyes.

Eventually, she spoke again. "Nibling," she said, and opened her eyes again to see Galen looking at her, confused. "Sam's not a 'she' but a 'they', so they're my nibling, not my niece." She monitored him carefully for a reaction.

"Oh," he replied. "Sorry. I didn't realise." He shook his head and looked deep into her eyes. "Will you at least consider it for them?"

She studied him closely. He seemed sincere. He was giving her the time she needed to think about it, and he hadn't even flinched over the pronoun change, just fixed the mistake and repeated the offer. She could tell he meant well – but were good intentions enough?

She thought about it some more and decided to tell him the truth. "I don't know."

His face dropped, and he nodded. "Okay. Okay. Let's go with Plan A." He made a move to stand up.

Hope laid a hand on his forearm, and he froze. "No, you don't understand. I haven't decided yet. I don't know. So, we'll go with Plan A, sure, but let's keep the possibility of Plan B open, just in case."

He blinked, and his eyes lit up. He hid the reaction quickly, but she'd seen his elation for a fraction of a second.

"Great!" he replied, and he had that twinkling half smirk again. "Great."

She wasn't sure whether it was the right decision. In fact, it wasn't really a decision at all, just the choice to postpone the decision. But it felt right, and she knew she shouldn't close off an option like this, no matter how creeped out she personally felt, until she'd talked it over it with Felicity and then with Sam. More than anything, they deserved the right to hear about this option and choose for themselves.

12 - Blood sample

Hope sat in the front seat of the truck and tried to keep her eyes open. It was dark out, and late. Any other city, that might mean a quiet, easy drive home, but not here, not now. An astonishing array of party hoppers, performers, and street walkers were parading past the slow-moving traffic. Alongside them were the panoply of vehicles supplying the bustling street-parties, bars, restaurants and late-night pleasure palaces all set up to service those here to celebrate the ever approaching Conjunction.

She looked out the front window. Two planets shone brightly, close to each other. She hunted round for the third planet, finding it not too far away from the other pair. The three of them remained a lopsided triangle, for now, but in a few short days, that third planet would edge closer to its partners. Then the moon would sweep into the frame. At which point the resonant energies from all four bodies would surge down through the crystalline matrices, laid down on the moon hundreds of years earlier, and the resultant flare of magic would rain down over the city like molten gold – with everyone holding up a metaphorical pan to capture it.

And here everyone was, swirling around them right now. Most of the people in these crowds weren't practitioners. They would come out of the woodwork at the Conjunction proper, but for now, they were all tucked away, adding the finishing touches to their conjurations. For every one of them, though, there were fifty more looky-loos who'd gathered to watch them display their skill – enjoy the shows put on for them while they waited, or hung around just 'to be seen to be seen' at the premier event of the century.

Normally, the sight of all these cashed-up marks would fill her with the joy of the potential score, but today, all she wanted to do was sleep, and these people were in her way.

"Damned traffic," Galen muttered beside her, and leaned on the horn.

Hope covered her ears and cringed. She may have even whimpered a little.

"Sorry," Galen said, noting her reaction. "Are you sure you don't want to stay at my hospital? It's closer to go back than to get through this crowd."

"No, thanks. I want to go to sleep in my own bed – plus, I need to check on Felicity and see how Sam is doing."

He nodded absently, his eyes scanning the endlessly moving crowds. "I'll leave some health tonic with you for the morning. You should wait until you wake up tomorrow if you want it to be the most effective."

She looked up at him, surprised at his generosity. Health tonics weren't cheap, and she already knew he wasn't exactly flush. "Thanks," she said warmly.

He glanced at her and smirked. "What, you think I'd leave you half-healed? Besides, I still need your help – you're no use to me at all if you're limping around half-dead."

"Ha. You don't care about my health; you just need me for my thieving skills!" She smiled mischievously.

"Mmm," he commented, his smirk growing, "totally using you for your thievery."

Hope observed the crowds and turned the problem over in her head. How *was* she going to find that mad dude with the gorilla-dogs and the top hat? "Did you get anything belonging to our Mr Green?"

"Anything like what?"

"Ideally, hair or blood, or anything? Did he hit you?"

But Galen was shaking his head. "No. You came closest when he grabbed that toolbox from you. Is this for a tracking matrix?"

"Yeah, I need something to target him. A signifier. Anything of his will work, even something small."

"What about the bullet? I still have that."

Hope shook her head. "That belonged to him, but it's not part of him. It would just lead me to the manufactory." She thought a while. "We could try to sneak back into the thieves' lair. There'd be lots of traces there. Unfortunately, we'd need to do it soon, before they're all cleaned up or contaminated – they degrade so quickly." She looked up at him.

He looked back at her, concern on his face. "You don't look like you're up to sneaking around that workshop again, and judging by what happened last time, I know I'm not up for the job!"

"I'd say it'd be our best chance, but I honestly think it might be our only chance. Can we do a drive-by and see what's going on?"

Galen glanced at her and sighed. "At least it will get us back out of these awful crowds." He muttered to himself under his breath, spun the wheel and turned them down a side street.

* * * * *

Even before they arrived, Hope knew they wouldn't be able to go back inside. Between the hard-eyed troops redirecting the traffic around the roped-off street, and the heavy patrol boat hovering in place, something just screamed 'KEEP OFF!' to her.

They circled the block, pulled into a side street, and settled in to wait. The workshop's lights were all on, and a small crowd was trooping around inside.

"Gods-damnit," Galen muttered. "This means no tracking signifier, doesn't it?"

"'Fraid so," she replied, studying the scene in front of them. They'd marked out a white-chalk outline on the street in front of the workshop. There was a lot of blood splattered around it.

"Was that Dodge?" she asked, nodding towards the blood.

"It was one of them, but they didn't tell me their names. Which one was Dodge?"

"The practitioner," she answered.

His eyes remained blank, as though he were searching his memory.

"Not the smug leader, or the augmented thug."

"Hmmm. It was all a bit of a blur, but I remember seeing those dog things attacking one of the shorter guys. I think I sensed him trying to pull some magic together before he got mauled – so, probably?"

She dug around in her pockets, assessing what she had on hand. "I'd really like to get some of that blood."

Galen snorted.

She blinked.

"And you think I'm the bloodthirsty one," he remarked.

"Hey! I never said you were bloodthirsty!"

"No. Just intimated I'm a body snatcher – and now here you are, thirsting for blood."

"I'm only after a sample of the blood left on the ground. It's not like

101

Dodge is using it anymore."

"My orderly wasn't using his body anymore either, and he, at least, voluntarily gave his body to me before he died." He was smirking at her, one eyebrow raised and his eyes glittering with unspent laughter.

She huffed, half in amusement but with a tinge of irritation, and continued rummaging around in her pockets, hunting for a suitable sample bag and a cotton earbud. When she found them, she leaned over and quietly unlatched the door of the truck.

"Hey, where are you going?" Galen asked her, a hint of panic in his voice. He reached out to her. "It's crawling with police."

"They're mostly all busy inside doing their jobs, which means they're distracted. They won't notice one lurker, as long as I'm quick."

"You're not planning on climbing in the side window again, are you? Surely you're not up to that!"

She smiled. "I appreciate the concern, but I was thinking you could distract the officer over there, while I slip by and pick up a sample or two from the blood out front."

Galen looked surprised. "Me? I'm not exactly skilled at this kind of thing. What do I say to him?"

"Anything you can think of. Ask him how to get to the sky docks, or where the nearest public lavatory is – heck, ask him for the time of day. It doesn't matter, as long as he's looking at you, not me, while you're approaching."

"While I'm approaching?" He squinted at her. "And where will you be?"

"Right beside you, but you won't see me. I'll activate my hideaway. There are cars and trees along here, so I should be good for a few minutes, as long as he's not looking right at me or scanning the road. I'll pop in, grab a quick sample and pop back out. I'll knock on the truck's roof when I'm done. You'll hear me – deal?"

He looked out at the officer lounging against a tree nearby, the street beside him cordoned off with tape. Galen's face had turned pale, and he was wriggling his fingers.

"You'll be fine," she said, taking hold of the fingers to still the wriggling.

He looked at her in surprise.

She dropped his hand and looked away. "Don't worry, just pretend to be confident and you'll do great."

She slipped out of the cab as silently as she could. Then, hidden from view inside the side alley, she activated the hideaway. Her magic was thin and sluggish – she'd used up so much today. But she could feel the slow drain and the tingling of the hideaway as it covered her, so she knew it was active.

Galen looked confused. He squinted at her with one of his eyes and then the other, then rubbed his temples as though he might be getting a headache. "That is super uncomfortable!"

"Stop trying to look at me. You'll get a nosebleed. Just go and be charming to that guy for a few minutes, and we'll get what we need to track down either Dodge or the weirdo gorilla-dogs."

"You think I'm charming?" he asked her, smirking again.

She opened her mouth to protest, but he was already hopping out his side of the cab. She crossed the street and watched from around the corner.

Galen approached the man leaning against the tree. The cop had become alert the moment he'd heard the truck door slam. He observed Galen walking towards him; his body language deliberately relaxed but ready for anything.

Galen wiped his hands on his pants as he closed in, but gave no other sign of nerves.

She waited until the officer was fully engaged and looking at Galen, then edged around the corner. She crept down the street, aiming to slide past the officer, behind the cars.

"Hi," said Galen. "I wonder whether you could help me?"

"Sorry mate," the officer replied; "you can't come through here." He stood up and held his hands up in front of Galen to block him. "Active crime scene – please keep behind the tape."

"Oh," Galen replied. "Sorry, I didn't know. I just wanted to ask…"

The officer suddenly spun around and faced Hope directly. "You too, ma'am."

She froze in surprise. The cop was looking right at her, squinting a little. She dropped the channel on the now clearly useless hideaway, pulled her face into a blank grin, and approached. "Of course, officer, I was just trying to get a better look." Galen's face was paling and his eyes darted about. She tried exuding an air of calm and easy confidence, hoping her companion would pick up on it. "Can you tell us what happened here?"

"I'm not at liberty to divulge specifics for an ongoing investigation," he replied, reciting the rote formula for the situation at hand.

Hope flicked her eyes to the spot behind him. One of the other officers was monitoring them from down the street but keeping her distance, poised to lend a hand, but only if needed. "Oh, of course. Sorry officer – I'm not trying to dig for detail. It's just I've heard talk of some kind of altercation here that involved an artificial chimera, and it so happens my companion is researching chimerae." She pointed at Galen.

Galen blinked in response.

The officer turned a flinty gaze towards him.

Hope raised her eyebrows and nodded encouragingly.

"Yes!" Galen agreed. "I'm studying their emotional responses in, ah... a non-native setting – specifically, the environmental triggers that can cause them to turn violent."

The cop looked sceptical.

Galen paled and dropped his voice to a mumble, but continued, "... in an attempt to stop that from, ah... happening?"

Hope smiled and took up the thread. "We're hoping this research will lead to biological solutions – biochemical calming-agents that'll then lead to a reduction in this type of violent crime. Which in turn will help local law-enforcement, such as yourself."

The cop looked interested, at least. "So, why were you trying to sneak into this crime scene?" He stared at her directly, his eyes hard. It was obviously his look for putting suspects on edge, hoping to spring information out of them.

The problem was that it was working. "Oh," Hope said, and paused, casting around for something she could tell him that wouldn't implicate herself and Galen in the greater crimes committed here.

"DNA!" Galen blurted.

The officer turned to face him again.

"We need DNA samples from known violent incidents to fine tune the biochemical calming-agents." He held up his hands and shrugged. "The samples change epigenetics after being exposed to the hormones present during violent incidents, and appropriate blood samples that contain both altered DNA and the hormones they were exposed to... well... they're a bit hard to come by – especially ones that are linked to a confirmed violent incident. Too many biological researchers cover up that stuff, so the most important samples have a nasty habit of being 'lost' before we can get our hands on them." He sighed. "Those that do make their way through the system usually take so long that the result is completely degraded." Galen's voice grew suitably bitter at the end of the spiel.

Hope was impressed. Maybe he had some talent for this kind of thing after all. "Sorry we tried to sneak in, officer," she added, filling her voice with chagrin. "We don't want to disturb your crime scene; we just want a tiny sample of the blood over there." She pointed to the chalk outline. "I figured you've already sent your forensics experts through and that soon it would all get washed away by the street cleaners, anyway."

"So why don't you wait till we've cleared the scene and take your samples then?" the officer replied. His voice was still laced with quite reasonable suspicion.

"Environmental degradation," Galen replied. "The longer the DNA is left open to the elements, the more degraded it becomes. Eventually, it's so degraded that accurately analysing it is impossible." He sighed deeply, "It's like what happened last week – the parade incident."

The officer's eyes flashed, but his gaze had turned inward.

"We're working hard to stop that kind of thing from occurring again," Galen added softly.

The officer nodded, still distant. He rubbed his chin and thought for a moment. "I'm really sorry, I just can't let you into the crime scene."

Hope's heart dropped. She nodded despondently.

Then the officer continued. "But if you wait here, I can take a sample for you – best I can do."

Hope raised her head, and her heart bloomed. "That would be just fine," she said with a smile of genuine gratitude.

"Do you have a sample kit?" he asked her.

She handed over the baggie.

The officer raised an eyebrow.

"It's a bit *ad hoc*, but it should do the trick. Dip this in the blood and swirl it around; then put it in here."

"Yes – thank you. I have done this before," the officer said, with a minor note of irritation. "You know that most of this blood is from the human victim, right?"

"That's okay," Galen replied. "we're used to separating out at least two discrete biological signatures. It's a chimera, yes? So, as long as at least some of it's from the animal, we'll be able to use it. Besides, human hormones differ from those of animals. They'll be straightforward to screen out."

"Just get a bit of blood from a variety of locations," Hope instructed him, "to maximise our chances of getting the chimera's multiple blood signatures."

The officer nodded and ducked under the tape. "You two stay

behind the tape, okay? My mates won't let you in, and I've got officers observing you from above." He pointed to the officers who were monitoring the other end of the street, and hooked a thumb at the hovering patrol ship. He picked his way carefully over to the chalk markings and started dipping the cotton bud into the various pools of blood.

As he had turned away, Hope had spotted an ear-bud in his ear. She suppressed a groan.

"Hmm?" Galen prodded.

"Oh, I'm just realising what a dumb-arse I've been."

Galen lifted an eyebrow. "You'll have to be more specific."

She glared at his smirk. "I mean about my hideaway. It was never going to work with crew up there monitoring us. You can't use a hideaway to fool electronic surveillance. I expected that the entire team would be down here, with nobody left up there to staff the scanners – they're usually too busy with their own scut work to bother watching an empty street. I guess it's so boring up there today that even a random showing up is worth observing."

"Maybe something about this case has them on edge."

She watched the officer drop the blood-soaked cotton bud into the plastic bag. "Good save, by the way. Perfect cover story for what we need."

He wiped his hands on his pants again while watching the officer return. "I wouldn't have called it perfect. I just blabbered out the first idea I could think of."

"Well, your first idea was perfect. Might make a good crook out of you yet," she whispered, ignoring his answering glare. She turned a grin to the returning officer. "Thank you very much," she said, accepting the offered baggie.

He also handed her a business card. "If you find anything useful, like who was responsible for this attack, get in touch." It wasn't phrased as a request.

"Will do, officer. Thanks again." Hope accepted the card and tucked it away in a pocket, fully intending never to call.

The officer nodded and kept his steel gaze on her as she and Galen returned to the truck and drove off into the night-time traffic.

13 - What's in the truck?

"Pull over here," Hope said, looking out the window to judge how much distance they'd put between themselves and the Imperium patrol ship.

Galen nodded and pulled the truck into a gap between the parked cars. Traffic wasn't as heavy out here, away from the dedicated party streets, but it was still present. At least there were fewer pedestrians about. This wasn't a destination – more of a through-place. The traffic mostly consisted of automated service vehicles trundling along – metal beasts of burden shunting raw resources in, and shunting fabricated goods out again. Working hard to move things between actual destinations. Grist for the ever-grinding mill.

Hope turned to Galen, silent beside her. He was staring out into the night, again wiping his hands on his pants. "Are you all right?" she asked him.

He jumped and turned to her. It took a moment for the cogs to engage, then his face lit up. "That was so cool! I mean, I just lied to an Imperium officer – to his face! I totally made up a story, and he didn't even bat an eye." A lopsided grin spread across his face. "I nearly wet myself in terror, of course." He gave half a giggle, half a cough. "Is it always this exciting? No wonder you do this kind of thing for a living – maybe I should take up crime for a living too."

Hope giggled. "Whoa there, big boy. Should I remind you of your previous brush with the life of crime only a few hours ago?"

His expression soured, and he started absently rubbing his neck. A bruise was forming there that hadn't been visible before.

"While you're rethinking your life choices, I'm going to activate the tracker matrix – get a sense of what's out there."

He nodded, watching her.

She looked out the front window at the people walking past. There weren't many, and most of them hurried by, eager to get to whatever their destination was. However, a few were ambling along lazily and looking in to see what the two occupants of the truck were up to. "I'd prefer a little privacy to do this part," she announced. "Can I hop in the back?"

Galen's eyes shied away. He opened his mouth and closed it again. "Do you have to?"

She drew her eyebrows together in puzzlement. "Is that a problem? I've been in there before."

He shrugged. "I know – it's just that... well... that was an emergency." He looked sheepish, gazing up at her through his eyelashes. "I don't normally let people inside my truck."

Hope smiled. "What, you have a secret sex dungeon stashed in there?" she teased. "I promise you aren't likely to have anything I've never seen before."

He looked at her wide eyed. "Keeping aside your clear familiarity with mobile sex dungeons – no, it's nothing like that. It's just..." He sighed; gave her one last, lingering look, then opened the door and hopped out.

Curious, she trailed after, following him around to the back of the truck.

He unlocked it and opened the door a crack. "Please," he implored her, "just be careful."

She rolled her eyes. He was being a bit precious about his truck. It's not like she'd care about whatever he has going on back...

She paused and looked.

She did *not* remember seeing all this last time.

"Come on, hop in. I've got to close the door before anyone else sees." He chivvied her towards the door, helping her up the steps and into the body of the truck.

It was cold in there; that much she remembered. The gurney was folded up and strapped against the right-hand wall.

As for all the rest...

She looked around, wide-eyed. The floor and walls were covered in the unmistakable silver ink of conjuration matrices – dozens of them. She had no idea what most of them did, although she caught a few, scattered references to magic supply, flow rates and oxygen partial pressure – some medical stuff she'd seen painted on herself when she was being patched up. However, a lot of it was foreign to her.

What she did know was that this truck represented many, many hours of painstaking work. No wonder Galen was being so protective.

She tiptoed around to a clear spot – a bench seat on the side opposite the gurney – and admired it all over again from the new vantage point. "What *are* these?" she asked in awe.

Galen looked at her sharply, a slightly haunted look on his face. He studied her to gauge her reaction to what was clearly his life's work. "It's the transition matrices," he breathed, with a depth of emotion she was barely brushing against. "Though it's mostly basic life support." He mumbled the words, pointing here and there. "It'll keep him alive and healthy during the transition, and for a while after, if it fails." He flicked a finger at something behind her.

She turned around and squeaked as she saw... him.

She looked closer. The bench seat wasn't a seat at all; it was some kind of freezer, with a small, frosted-glass window in the lid. She looked down into a very frozen and, by that point, very familiar-looking face. "You didn't mention he was your twin."

Galen raised an eyebrow. "Was it relevant?" He studied her while she gazed in wonder at his exact replica in the fridge below. His duplicate was suspended in some kind of clear, glittering liquid that was swirling over his frosty features.

She snorted. "Well, that explains part of what happened last time I was back here. I thought I must have been hallucinating, talking to you. I thought you were dead." She smiled as she said it. Just a funny dig.

Galen frowned and looked away.

Oops, that was a bit of a sore point.

"Sorry. It must still be very raw for you," she said gently.

He nodded, blinking rapidly.

"Wait. You drove this truck to the meet-and-greet today. You drive your dead brother around with you?"

He blushed, scowling at her. "Shall we get on with it, then?" He pointed at her tracking matrix.

"No, I really want to know why you're wandering the streets with a truck full of necromantic conjuration matrices and a dead body!"

"It's the only truck I have!" He waved his hands around. He breathed out hard, looking deflated – his shoulders falling. "I've spent all our money trying to get the dream steel. I have nothing left, and I'm already behind on mortgage and utilities. The bank sent a letter threatening to take away the hospital if I don't pay up soon. I'll probably have to sell it." His voice cracked.

She sympathised deeply. He was watching his dream life – the life he'd planned with his now-dead brother – crumble and vanish down the drain. She reached out to him and laid a hand on his arm.

He looked up at her, and the shadows in his eyes cleared a little. He drew in a deep breath and blew it out. "I don't know whether I can keep the hospital afloat – it might be taken away tomorrow. But if I can just keep the truck until the Conjunction, there's a chance I'll get my brother back."

Hope nodded. "Okay. Then let's start by trying to find those chimerae." She sat down. "Do you have some ink?"

He nodded and fetched a well-used kit from a box tucked away in a corner.

She spent a few minutes correcting and cleaning up the runes painted on her arm. She had already altered her matrix to accept two different signifiers, so it was now a simple task for her to adapt that to accept the mixed blood sample.

DNA was a great tracking signifier, as it uniquely specified the target. That made for a much easier search – very few extraneous targets interfering with the magical link. Having the matrix drawn directly on her own body strengthened the link with her magic, too. A little trick she'd figured out to improve her abilities. However, it came at the cost of the matrix degrading over time as the skin naturally shed the pigment.

Of course, there was one other downside of having the matrix drawn on her own body. You had to place the signifier directly on your skin. That wasn't such a problem with the tiny shaving of dream steel, but blood samples had a squick factor that was only overrun by the earlier blood-plus-snot she'd had to use for Tink. Ick.

Unfortunately for her, she'd lost that sample while she was unconscious – burned up at the same time her magic had burnt out. Not that she was complaining – she'd hunt Dodge over Tink any day of the week. Hopefully he was on his own. She did not want to go up against an augmented in addition to a practitioner.

"There. Ready," she said, looking up at Galen, who had been observing her closely.

He looked away, blushing.

She raised an eyebrow. "Hopefully, we have some blood from the gorilla-dog here. That'll be the best target to lead us to Mr Green. If it's just Dodge's blood, we'll have to scope out where he's holed up alone or with the others, and decide how to go in. As you said, neither of us is up for another rumble with their crew."

"Should we come back to him when we're more refreshed?"

"Maybe. But they'll be more refreshed, too, and less likely to be alone. We'll have to play it by ear. Either way, we can't decide until we have more intel."

Galen nodded.

Hope nodded back. Then retrieved the bloody ear bud from the baggie and, grimacing, dabbed a small amount on the centre of her matrix. She muttered her words and closed her eyes as the magic flowed through her and out into the world. It washed away from her like a small wave; a ripple reaching out across the city. After a moment, she sensed an echo rolling back, and felt the familiar tug forming in her belly. A few moments later, she felt another tug. Then, several smaller tugs joined the pile-on, but she discarded those – they felt weaker. She also discarded the bigger one that pulled straight back towards the thieves' lair. With the police keeping the thieves away, it was probably the pool of blood on the roadside.

She opened her eyes. "I have two strong targets. One is that way," she pointed, "quite a few kilometres away. The other is actually not far from here ...over there." She pointed in the opposite direction.

"That's back towards the workshop. Is it one of them, or just the bloodstains?"

Hope double-checked her magical link. "I don't think so. I can sense that blood pool too, but this one feels different – stronger."

"Maybe Dodge, holed up at a friend's place near their usual haunt?"

"That's possible. It could be a safe house. It'd be a heck of a coincidence if Mr Green had his headquarters anywhere near this district."

"Okay. Are you done with the visible portion of the tracking?"

She nodded. "Yes, all good. I suppose we should get going."

He helped her back into the front seat.

Her chest still ached, and she wished she could be done with the pain. "Do you have that healing potion on you?"

"I do, but I don't recommend taking it before tomorrow morning."

"Yeah, I know. I'll take it tomorrow if I can. It's in case of emergency. If we show up and find ourselves in the thick of it, I'd like to have it on hand. I could take it early to give myself a chance to run away."

He glanced at her, and she couldn't read his expression. "You know the risks. Either way, it's your choice." He nodded her way. "In the glove compartment."

Hope slid the potion into a pocket while he got the truck started.

"We need to go more that way," she directed.

"That's further away from the workshop," he said as he turned the wheel. "At least we're out of the Imperium spotlight – that's good, right?"

"Not if we're walking into Mr Green's mad scientist lair, or the thieves' well-protected emergency fallback position. Either way, there'll be some danger."

He thought for a moment. "Do you think we're walking into an ambush?"

She sensed the two tugs on her and tipped her head from side to side. "I can't really say. All I know for sure is we're getting closer to one. Can you pull over again?"

He found a spot in which to idle the truck.

She closed her eyes and felt down the connection. "Whoever it is, they're not moving."

"So they're not running away. That'll make it easier to catch up with them."

"Yes, but I don't think they're moving at all." She thought for a moment. "Both Dodge and the chimera were injured – badly, judging by the blood. Wherever they are, they're almost certainly holed up somewhere getting medical attention, or sleeping it off."

"Does that make it more or less likely to be an ambush?"

"I don't know. Let's approach slowly and scope it out."

14 - Tracking

They drove a wide ring around the location. There didn't seem to be any untoward activity nearby, at least no more than usual. The Imperium patrol ship was still hovering several blocks away, but hadn't moved in their direction. The ship's crew probably couldn't see them here as the streets were narrow, and the buildings several storeys tall – making it hard to see down to street level unless you were hovering directly overhead.

Galen reluctantly dropped Hope off so she wouldn't have to walk very far. "Don't move," he instructed her while taking off in search of a parking spot, "or I won't be able to find you."

"Too tired to go far," she replied as the truck departed.

The hour was late, and it had been a very busy day. She was exhausted.

She sat on the stoop of a crumbling apartment block and watched the regular procession of transport mechs trundle past, blowing steam or smoke, and sporting a variety of functional body shapes. Most of them were uncrewed and followed a pre-programmed route to drop off their load of cargo. A few had a single occupant hopped up on stims – eyes darting at her, through her, past her, and then gone.

She closed her eyes, hunting for a better sense of the distance between herself and her target, and found herself nodding off.

The jolt of waking tugged at her extremely painful side. She scowled at herself and began pacing, slowly, to keep herself awake until Galen returned.

This was no good. She wouldn't hold her own in a fight like this. Though she might get the drop on them if they were just as tired. A surprise attack could give her the edge she needed.

A few minutes later, Galen came trotting around the corner.

Watching him approach, she observed the bags beneath his eyes and the way he dragged his feet. He was exhausted too. She sighed. "We're both nearly dead. We only have one chance to surprise them, but I'm not sure either of us is up to it."

He nodded and rubbed his hands over his face, trying to wake himself up. "I have stimulants for myself, but you definitely shouldn't take any. They won't mix well with the tonic I gave you."

"Are you sure I can't have a little? How bad would it be for me?"

"Bad. Very bad."

"I mean, would it be wired-plus-tired bad, or puke-your-guts-up bad?"

"Destroy the lining of your damaged artery while it's still mending, so you bleed-out-and-die bad."

"Right! No stims for me!" She buried her disappointment under forced positivity and started walking.

Galen fell in step with her.

She angled them around the target, so they'd slowly circle in towards it, getting a good look at their surroundings on the way. They crossed over a busier street and entered the darker laneways.

These were quiet, narrow, and poorly lit. Dirty water dripped down mouldy walls into dank puddles filled with garbage. Abandoned places, ripe for dark deeds, or at least the plotting of them – and maybe for the cleaning up after and forgetting too.

She kept her head on a swivel.

As they passed apartment buildings, curtains twitched and closed. The occasional hooded lurker sat guard on a step – dark eyes following them.

"I feel like we're being watched," Galen muttered, shivering and hunching his shoulders.

"Most certainly we are. We just need to keep going about our business and hope we don't attract the wrong sort of attention."

He looked at her, a little wide-eyed. His eyes darted all around him.

"Relax. Your nervousness will draw even more attention."

"How can I relax?"

"Fake it. Your body language is screaming 'victim'. That will draw them in like flies. We belong here as much as they do – at least pretend to be confident." She stopped and looked at him, drew in a deep breath and let it go, modelling how to pretend to a state of calm she also didn't feel.

Galen repeated the gesture, and a little of the obvious tension left him. "At least the adrenaline will keep us awake."

As they circled closer to the target, it became clearer to Hope that they were aiming for the back alley between a pair of silent, empty-looking apartment buildings, their paint peeling, and several missing windows boarded over.

She paused at the corner to re-assess the pull of the tracker. Definitely between those buildings, not within them.

"In the alley," she said, closing her eyes. The target still hadn't moved. "We need to be careful. If it's Dodge, he might be passed out in there, or injured and bleeding out. He might even be dead."

Galen nodded; his eyes still wide, but he was doing his best to keep it together. "What do we do if he's dead?"

"Don't touch anything, and for goodness sake, leave nothing that Imperium trackers could get hold of." She checked for any visible watchers. None that she could see, which didn't mean there were none at all.

He nodded. "Treat it like a crime scene. Got it!"

"Familiar with crime scenes, are we?"

"Only from true-crime novels."

"I guess it'll do. We'll do a walk-by. Check the alley's empty before we go inside." She turned to go.

Galen stopped her. "What do we do if he's *not* dead?"

She looked at him. His concern was genuine. That might get in the way. They couldn't risk being merciful to a dangerous low-life like Dodge. Her eyes slid away. "Let's play that one by ear. Just be careful and stay close."

They walked past the alley, and she glanced in.

Empty. Well, apart from some piles of rubbish.

It was dark, but she didn't think there were any shelter-sized cardboard boxes or tents in there. No stoops or obvious doorways either. So, more likely Dodge was passed out – she didn't take him for the type to be living rough.

She walked them to the next corner, from where they surveyed the surrounding streets. A few randoms were hurrying down a side street, but otherwise the two interlopers were alone with the flickering street lights.

"I don't like this," Galen muttered.

"You and me both. That alley only has one way in and out."

He looked at her, then back towards the alley. "I didn't see anybody down there."

"Me either, and that's what worries me. Our chances of finding Dodge alive and in a fit state to answer questions are pretty low."

Galen's face paled. He opened his mouth, but closed it again. "I could..."

Hope spun around and looked at him.

He went silent once more.

"Don't even suggest it!" she hissed. "We're not so desperate that we need any of your *special* skills!"

Galen pressed his lips into a thin line but dropped the subject.

"Let's see what we have got." She turned them back towards the alley. "I'm going inside. You stand here and if anyone comes over, yell – do you hear me?"

He glared at her. "Are you leaving me on the sidelines?"

"I'm trusting you to watch my back. And I'm told I don't trust easily."

He looked a little mollified.

"I'll call you after I give it the once-over," she said, and entered the alley.

The tracker was tugging her hard now. It pulled her further in. It was dark, and she felt very alone. She flicked a glance back at Galen.

He had his back to her, and he was carefully looking down the street – one way and then the other.

This was weird. She hated relying on anyone else. You couldn't trust other people. She'd been doublecrossed too many times. Trusting only family was how she'd gotten herself and her sister through life so far, and she certainly didn't know Galen well enough to trust him long-term. But right here, right now? Well, it was nice to have somebody watching her back for once.

She peered into the shadows and took another step.

The breeze changed direction and she knew she didn't have to worry about whether Dodge was still alive.

The stench of death rolled over her.

She turned her head and gagged. Then she hurled up the soup she'd recently drunk and tried her best not to pop her stitches as spasms wracked her insides.

She felt hands holding her upright and keeping her hair back from her face.

When the retching calmed, Galen handed her a clean tissue and a bottle of water to clear her mouth.

She whimpered her thanks and stumbled back a few paces. She

blushed with shame. "Sorry," she said, turning her face away from the stench. "It just hit me all at once."

Galen looked at her with gentle concern. "It's okay. You should've seen me in my first year in med school – believe it or not, I used to faint at the sight of blood."

She looked up, her eyebrow raised sceptically.

"No, really," he said, laughing. "My brother always used to tease me about it…" He grimaced at the memory, and a fresh wave of grief rolled across his face. "Well," he continued, his voice catching a little, "let's just say it was a long road from there to what I can do now."

Hope smiled. "Maybe you can teach me how sometime." She glanced nervously at the piles of rubbish at the back of the alley. "I've seen a fair bit of blood in my time, but I'm really not okay with decay." She grimaced and fished around in her pockets for some handkerchiefs. She found two and tied them around her mouth. Breathing through the layers felt weird, but it was worth it for what they filtered out.

"You don't have to do this," Galen offered. "This is more my specialty than yours."

She considered it and flicked a longing gaze at the alley's mouth, before turning back to him. "Why don't we do it together?"

He nodded. Poking around in the garbage, he picked out a broken chair leg.

Together, they crept towards the pile that was still causing the tug on Hope's tracker.

It was dark back there.

She hunted around in her pockets, pulled out a tiny torch, and directed it towards the target. What she could see beyond the torchlight matched the stench.

They'd found their body, but it wasn't Dodge.

It was also no longer in one piece. The gorilla part and the dog head had separated. The stitches had torn through rotting flesh like paper; and heavy wires stuck out of the bones at odd angles. They must've once held those bones in place, but no longer.

"Why is it so rotted?" she asked. "It was running around only a few hours ago."

He snorted, inspecting the remains. "Look here." He pointed to the silver markings that were still visible on the gorilla's chest. "Do you remember I told you about the medical self-repair matrices keeping my zombie alive?"

She paled. "These chimerae are zombies?"

He half-shrugged. "Not exactly – but sort of."

She raised her eyebrows in query.

He huffed a laugh. "The line between necromancy and modern medical science isn't as clear as my university lecturers might like us to think."

Hope smirked. "Your lecturers told you not to study necromancy? I guess you don't do as you're told."

"I guess I didn't pay attention in that lecture," he said with a grin.

He poked around with the stick, exposing the gorilla's arm so he could examine the calligraphy. "This thing definitely seemed alive – but I recognise these markings. A matrix to oxygenate the blood is just a matrix to oxygenate the blood; it doesn't care whether the body's still being commanded by a living brain or one that's been switched off and then on again."

He studied the flow of calligraphy, tracing it with his eyes as he spoke. "I've come to believe that the difference between necromancy and the rest of medical science is negligible. People have all kinds of funny ideas about death, but a dead body is not significantly different from a live one, at least not at first. I've found that our standard medical treatments work just as well on a body that's recently died as on one that's still alive. We regularly bring back people from the brink of death who, once upon a time, would've been declared a lost cause. In fact, we keep pushing back the timeline we draw, over who is and isn't able to be resuscitated without being declared dead. I strongly believe that someday we'll push it back until there's no line at all."

"So," she began, half joking, "you're saying that necromancy is just a form of extreme resuscitation." But something turned over in her mind. "I guess I hadn't thought about it that way at all."

Now it was his turn to raise an eyebrow and a smile.

"This one's definitely beyond resuscitation, though, right?" she pressed.

He nodded and turned back to the body. "The rotting kind of gives it away." He sat back on his heels, thinking. "The biology of the two creatures here must be so different that some hefty ongoing self-repair support was required for the two halves to be kept alive and working together without succumbing to rejection. It's a pretty complex support system, and from what I can see of this work, well, let's say you wouldn't be getting an 'A' for this project. I'm not surprised it all fell apart so suddenly – look here."

He pointed to a red and blistered portion of the gorilla's chest. "These are burn marks, probably from Dodge's magic. They broke the conduit lines for some of the support functions. The gorilla wouldn't keel over straight away – it got the chance to run away before the rune flows failed – but this damage would inevitably lead to a catastrophic failure of the entire system, like a cascade."

He frowned and looked down at the body. "Poor thing. Looks like Mr Green left it behind to die alone." He looked up at her. "Is there anything you can use to track that guy down?"

Hope took the chair leg and eased the ratty clothing aside. "Not that I can see. Its pockets are empty. I don't expect that our Mr Green left this creature with anything incriminating." She sighed heavily, but regretted the gesture when the stench made her retch again. She stepped back, out of the smell's reach. "We've wasted our time here," she said, gloom filling her soul, and her eyes downcast.

She jerked up again when a scuffling sound caught her ears. She looked up to see that a trio of lanky teens had appeared at the end of the alleyway.

Hope grabbed Galen's arm.

He opened his mouth, but she squeezed the arm, hard. "Let me do the talking," she murmured, before he could say anything that got them into more trouble.

The young men ambled towards them. "Well, well, lads," said the one strutting out front, "what've we found? A pair of gutter rats picking around in the trash?"

The other two snickered.

"We were just leaving," Hope said with a scowl. She stepped sideways to put their backs against the alley's side wall.

One lad moved to intercept.

"We don't want any trouble here!" she said, putting up her hands. "Let us by and we'll be on our way."

The lads chuckled. "No trouble at all," one said, but they didn't step aside.

Hope couldn't remember which gang claimed this section of territory, or whether they were on friendly terms with Henry's crew. Some of the neighbouring gangs were known to keep the peace for Henry, but others would fight on the tiniest pretext.

"What were you digging for, little rat?" the one in front asked. "Anything you find in this area belongs to us."

"You're welcome to what we found," she replied with a forced grin.

"We weren't hunting a score, just tracking a body – which we found." She pointed back at the corpse. The stench would prove her statement for her. "It had nothing worth taking," she added ruefully.

The group leader nodded at one of his companions, who crept forward to look.

He stumbled back, gagging. "It stinks!" he complained.

The leader raised his eyebrows and emphatically gestured towards it. "Shit Theo. Check it out anyway, you wuss," he demanded, then turned back to Hope. "So, why were you after it?" he asked her, ambling closer.

"Tracking down another body who got away from us," she replied. "He set his goons on us, and we want payback."

Galen glanced at her nervously.

She put out a hand to him to reassure him.

The third thug stepped forward. He pulled a knife open with a SNICK.

Hope threw her hands up.

"Your boyfriend gonna make a scene?" he demanded, "'cos we can take you down."

"No," Galen blurted, "I'm not going to fight you! We just want to go about our business and let you go about yours – in peace!"

"She's right, Dig, there's nothin' here but some weird dead animals," Theo said, stepping back from the discarded chimera.

"Fine, well shit. Then we'll just have to take our score from you," said Dig, the smiling leader. "Empty your pockets and we'll let you live and leave!" The trio stepped forwards.

Hope's eyes flitted between the three. She did not want to hand over the spare kit she had on her. It was expensive and hard to replace. Of course, she also didn't want to die.

She backed up until she hit the wall. "Hey guys, you don't want to do this."

"Oh," Dig said, moving within reach, "I think we do." He let his eyes drift down her form and up again, taking it all in.

Beside her, Galen stiffened.

She squeezed his arm tight and whispered, "Don't react!"

"Bit old for my taste," Dig continued, licking his lips and letting his eyes drift over her chest again, "but I'll have a go anyway." He glanced back at the other two.

"Leave her alone," Galen grated. The threat in his voice was a surprise to her. As was the sensation of magic building within him.

Hope's eyes widened. This was not good. She had to get them out of here.

"Or what, Cupcake?" the closest thug crooned.

"Leave us alone!" Hope yelled, trying to take attention away from Galen. He had the combat awareness of a goldfish. If he tried to throw magic around, he'd just get them killed.

Hope concentrated, pulling together the remaining scraps of her own magic. It was hard work. She tried building something coherent for her hands to wield, but it sputtered limply and slipped out of her grasp. The busy day, full of heavy magic-use, and her injuries, had both taken a toll on her magic levels. She could barely raise a werelight, let alone spar with thugs.

"Watch out; he's a practitioner!" the third thug yelled, having finally noticed what Galen was doing.

Hope glanced down.

Galen's hands were glowing a deep ruby red.

Theo drew a gun and pointed it at them both. "Let go of your magic, or the girl gets it!"

She swore. This was escalating too quickly.

Galen was having trouble, too. Surprised at the gun pointed at his head, his magic was slipping away. "Damnit!" he muttered.

Dig's grin turned feral as the threat escalated. He clearly liked it that way. He stepped in towards Hope, put his knife to her neck, and hissed at Galen, "Go on, let's see if you're quicker than my knife and Theo's gun, hey?"

Hope looked Galen in the eye and gave a tiny shake of her head.

Dig cackled. "Looks like your girlfriend's tellin' you to back off."

Hope thought furiously, but they were outgunned. Her magic had run dry. She'd used her only flash-bang and hadn't re-stocked. What could she do?

Dig stepped closer and sniffed at her hair.

She went rigid. A shudder ran through her, and she couldn't keep the disgust off her face. Then she paused, listening. Her face lit up with a grin.

The thug lowered his eyebrows, scowling. "Orright? What've you got to smile about?"

She grinned wider and cocked her head to listen to the approaching voices she'd heard.

"This way, detective – it's close." The voice came from up the street.

The lads looked uneasy.

"That's an Imperium tracker, hunting down this body," she told them. "And maybe you missed it, but I know for a fact that an Imperium patrol ship is tethered less than five minutes' flight from here. So, you have a choice. If you tuck your gun away and leave now, you might just get away. But any other choice and this doesn't end well for you." She smiled her best smile and hoped against all hope they weren't the type to shoot out of pure spite.

Dig smiled at her, but she could see his grin was forced. He spun around. "Let's go!" he barked. His flunkies hid their weapons and scuttled after him.

Hope let out a shaky breath and sank to the ground.

Galen stepped close and knelt down on the dirty ground beside her, nervously hovering. "Are you... Okay?"

She nodded.

"I'm so sorry," he said. "I didn't know what to do!"

She looked up at him with a tired smile. "It's okay – 'nothing' was the right thing to do."

A moment later, an Imperium detective and two officers rounded the alley mouth.

"In here, detective!" one officer said, holding a glowing sheet of parchment.

Spotting Hope and Galen, the other officer speared their eyes with torchlight. "Who's there? Show your hands!"

Galen's hands shot into the air.

The tracker and the detective paused outside the alley. The tracker lowered his parchment. He put his hands to a weapon but didn't point it. That made a pleasant change.

"It's okay," Hope called out, raising her own hands. "We're the researchers from before."

Blank stares.

Torch-bearer looked familiar, although it was hard to see his face through the light. "We were at the scene earlier!" she explained, directing the remark at him. "We tracked the body here with the blood sample you gave us – same as you." She nodded at the tracker with the glowing parchment.

Torch-bearer squinted at them, then nodded at the detective.

"Do you know the people who just left the alley?" Asked the detective.

Hope shook her head. "No – just some street punks who tried to rob us. Lucky for us, you showed up in time." She smiled at them.

Torch-bearer pointed his torch in the direction of the departing thugs, but they must've already disappeared, as he made no move to follow.

The tracker crept past Hope, into the alley. He was made of sterner stuff than her, because when the stench hit him, he merely stiffened. "Found it!" he called out. "Blimey, it's pretty ripe!" He tucked his parchment away and stepped back.

The detective joined him and walked around the body, looking at it from various angles. "What are you doing out here all on your own at this time of night?" he asked, glancing up at them before continuing his own perusal.

"Same as you, detective," Hope answered, "hunting it down before the trail went cold." She looked up at Galen, held out a hand and asked him, "Can you help me up?"

Galen lost his stunned look and took her hand.

She groaned as he helped her back to her feet. She'd had enough adventure for one night.

"Did you disturb this crime scene?" the detective demanded peevishly.

She shook her head. "We looked, but we barely had time to do much more than gag at the smell."

"Did you touch anything?" he insisted.

"My partner poked it with a stick," she replied with a shrug and a point, "which is over there."

"Why on earth would you do that?" he demanded.

"I was checking the matrices on its skin," Galen said. "To see better, I had to move the clothes aside."

The detective turned a glare on him.

"I swear I didn't touch it myself." Galen protested.

The detective turned back to the body, grumbling under his breath. "Did you learn anything from your inspection?"

"Some kind of medical-support matrices," he replied. "It was all too degraded to tell much more."

Hope jumped in. "Look, officers, we don't know anything more than you, and we've just been nearly mugged. We're tired, this subject's too degraded to get a sample, so we got nothing from this hunt, and we just want to go home. Any chance of that happening soon?"

The detective picked his way back over to Galen. "You tracked the body here?"

Galen shook his head. "I'm the biologist; she's the tracker."

The detective nodded, pulling out a little notebook and taking notes. "And your names are?"

Hope was getting worried. Even fake names could land them in a lot of trouble. "Detective, are we being arrested for anything right now?"

"Not at all, miss...?" he asked, smiling pleasantly.

"Then we'd like to go home now, thanks," she insisted, ignoring the implicit question.

The officer and detective glanced at each other. "I'd like to ask you a few questions about how you're involved in this incident," continued the detective.

"And I'd like to get a good night's sleep," she countered.

"I'm afraid this is a murder investigation," he persisted, his voice hardening; "and we can compel you to answer our questions. If you choose not to answer, we can take you downtown."

The officer at the alley mouth had moved to block the way out. Hope's heart was dropping again.

Out of the frying pan and into the fire.

"A murder, you say?" Galen asked.

The detective turned his gaze on him. "And you were both found here with the body. Which makes you both persons of interest."

Galen smiled. "Oh, you mean this body?" He pointed. "Because from what I could see, this body doesn't belong to a person; it belongs to some kind of animal – well, two animals, actually." He turned to Hope. "Can animals be murdered?"

She smiled, her heart rising again. "No, they can't. It's a tragedy, for sure, but it means that no murder has been committed." She addressed the detective – "therefore, you have no mandate to hold us."

"I'd greatly appreciate it if you'd give us a statement about what happened here tonight," he said, a strained smile on his face.

Hope smiled. "Of course, detective. We'll try to swing by the precinct tomorrow." She turned to the police officer in the alley. "We'll be on our way, then."

The officer looked a question at the detective, who sighed and nodded. The officer stepped aside.

Hope did her best not to hobble too badly as she pulled Galen along with her.

"One moment!" the detective called out to them.

She froze and turned.

"Here, take my card," he said, handing it to Galen. "Call us if you decide there's anything you'd like to tell us."

Galen took the card and tucked it into his pocket with a nod.

They hurried back to the truck. Galen helped Hope back into the cab where she collapsed, her eyes shut.

He joined her and started the engine. "Do you want me to take you home?"

"I think I want to sleep for a hundred years. I also don't want to drive through the traffic again. Is your couch offer still open?"

"Sure is. And I'm glad – I mean I'd happily take you home, but after tonight, I'm glad I don't have to. I think I'd fall asleep at the wheel if I had to drive myself back across town alone."

"Heh, well, I would've happily offered you our couch, too."

"I can't believe we got away without even giving them our names."

Hope snorted, but nodded, then growled to herself. "Speaking of which, can you give me that detective's card?"

He looked surprised, but dug it out and handed it over.

She studied it and memorised the name. "Detective Steve Grant, ninth precinct". She wound down the window and tossed it out into the night.

Galen eyed her but said nothing... loudly.

"They have an implanted tracking target," she said. "Don't want them showing up on our doorstep."

She quietly watched the traffic bustling along the street. "You might want to do a whirlwind study in medical chimerae. We'll bump into that detective again, and it'd be useful if you could at least pretend to answer his questions without giving away the fact we've been lying through our teeth."

Galen nodded. "That's a sensible plan. Plus, I have a feeling it might come in handy when we find Mr Green. What's the next step for that? I suppose tomorrow we'll try tracking Dodge?"

"Yes probably. Sadly, our one remaining lead is not reliable."

He tipped his head to one side. "Maybe, but I have a feeling that another run-in with Mr Green is inevitable at this point."

She tried to nod in reply, but her eyes were closing of their own accord, and soon she was nodding off.

15 - Sunrise

She woke up disoriented. Curled up on a strange couch with a blanket tucked up to her chin, and her side aching.

As she looked around, her memory clicked back into place. She was back in the room full of armchairs and books.

Her brain clicked forward another notch, and she spun around.

No creepy undead orderly was standing in the adjacent room – at least not that she could see from here. She shuddered at the memory and thanked her stars that the zombie wasn't watching her as she slept – at least not to her knowledge.

Groaning, she sat up and pulled herself into something resembling upright before shuffling off in search of a bathroom.

She passed through a giant room filled with bunk beds. Metal tubes, and green plastic over foam mattresses, all lined up and empty. This must be one of the wards. It seemed so weird to see a deserted hospital. She always knew them as bustling places full of people, all of whom were engaged in a life and death struggle. Either fighting for breath or clawing their way back to health.

She opened the door at the end of the ward and squeaked in surprise.

Mr Creepy was standing in the hallway and looking out the window, as silent as the proverbial grave. She stood still and breathed deeply to slow her pounding heart.

She was debating the merits of sneaking past to investigate the bathroom potential of the doors beyond, when one of them opened, and a sleepy-eyed and tousled Galen appeared.

"Are you okay?" he said, shambling towards her in his own newly-awakened-zombie impression. "I heard a yelp," he said with a smile, then eyed up his orderly before looking back at her. "I swear he won't bite. Doesn't have the teeth."

Hope glared at him, all the while trying to hide her own smile. "Just surprised. I was looking for the bathroom?"

He nodded, then turned and pointed back down the hall. "Third door along."

She moved her weight from foot to foot, eyeing up the zombie.

Galen's face gentled. "He won't touch you, I promise."

Hope's eyes flicked to Galen and back.

"I usually find him here in the mornings. I think he likes to watch the sunrise." He turned to look out the window.

Hope's eyebrows shot up in surprise. She turned to look at the sky. It was hours past dawn now, but the sun was poking out from behind the clouds, sending its rays of light through the dusty air. It was quite beautiful.

"Does it – does *he* have enough of a mind left to appreciate beauty?" she asked, looking back at the orderly in a new light.

"Something remains, though I don't know how much – the brain can get a bit… scrambled during resuscitation. I think that if you do it more gently, it'll have a higher chance of success, but too fast, and… well… it's something I'm most worried about for…" He grimaced.

Hope knew what he was worried about, and she felt for him. But still – raising the dead? What he had planned for his brother wasn't just resuscitation; his brother had been dead for months! And this thing staring out the window? Appreciative of beauty or not, this rotting corpse - it was… well… just wrong!

She hopped from foot to foot. She wanted to say something to Galen about his brother, to be polite. But needs were pressing. She gathered her courage and scampered past the zombie and down the hall.

A few minutes later, feeling refreshed, she re-entered the hallway. Galen had gone. She glared at the zombie, who was still standing staring out the window, ignoring her presence.

The door at the other end of the hallway was open, and delicious smells were wafting in from that direction.

She made her way through an empty mess hall to find a large kitchen, and Galen, just tipping some scrambled eggs on to two plates of toast.

He looked up as she entered. "I hope eggs are okay. I have cereal if they're not, but I figured you could use the protein."

She smiled. "Eggs are great, thank you." She pulled one plate towards herself and inhaled. She might have groaned a little. Her stomach growled in anticipation.

"I've got coffee coming too," he said with a small smile. "This room's draughty, so I usually eat in the staff lounge. You can go by the other door if you want to avoid... ah... unwanted encounters in the hallway." He smirked a little at that, but she ignored the implication that her squeamishness might be a character flaw. It was thoughtful of him to suggest a way around it. Plus, the food looked delicious, and nobody talks back to the person making them coffee.

"The coffee will be a few minutes," he said. "You go ahead – there's cutlery on the coffee table."

"Thanks." She gathered up the plate and took it back with her.

The other door led to yet another ward, after which there were two operating rooms before arriving back at the room full of books. She realised it must've once been the staff break room before serving as Galen's impromptu lounge.

She grabbed a fork and began shovelling eggs in as fast as she could safely swallow them. But the allure of the overflowing bookshelves drew her attention.

When Galen reappeared, balancing his plate and two mugs of steaming coffee on a wooden tray, he found her absorbed in the contents of his book collection – the remnants of her scrambled eggs cooling, forgotten, on a side table. He coughed a laugh.

Startled, she jumped and dropped the books she'd been holding. She scowled, blushing, and scrambled to gather them up.

"I didn't know that the average petty thief was such a bibliophile," he joked, placing a cup of coffee beside her abandoned breakfast.

"Hey, who are you calling average?" She returned to the side table to scoop up the coffee. "And I'm not sure I'd call myself a bibliophile."

Galen smirked. "I heard your stomach growling, and yet you abandoned your food in favour of perusing my collection – *ergo*, bibliophile." He tucked into his own breakfast.

Hope resumed hers as well, but her eyes kept straying back to the bookcase.

"Nothing to be ashamed of. Some of my fondest memories are of losing myself in the university library. I easily spent days there." He went distant, staring back into a happier time.

She finished her toast and sipped at her coffee, eyeing him up, weighing how much she wanted to share. "I have similar memories of hiding out in the community library downtown."

He looked up with interest. "I've been there! A bit pokey, but it has a cosy vibe."

She glared. "Well, I'm sorry it's not up to your standards, Mister University Graduate, but not all of us come from a wealthy background."

Galen's eyebrows shot up. "Wealthy? I'd hardly call us…"

"Wealthy enough to afford university," she interjected; "wealthy enough to buy a hospital." She cast her eyes around.

Galen was glaring now. "Hey, that wasn't me, that was…" he stopped and sighed. "Ah, forget it, it doesn't matter. None of it matters." His face had drooped, and he dropped his fork into his half-finished plate of eggs with a clang. He sighed again. "We didn't get anywhere last night, and we have no more leads." He pushed the plate away and put his head in his hands. "It's all hopeless."

Hope's glower softened. She put her mug down and reached out to touch his arm. "Hey, don't give up yet."

He pulled his hands away from his face and looked at her hand. He put his hand over hers and patted it awkwardly, as if he didn't know what to do with it.

She smiled, picked up her coffee mug again, and said, half to herself, "Let's take stock – what do we know?" She started ticking things off on her fingers. "One: You legit bought a pile of dream steel, but it got caught up in a Customs shakedown at the sky docks. Two: I liberated it from the docks. But then, three: our band of merry thieves stole it out from under me; who, four: doublecrossed you and on-sold it to our mad scientist, Mr Green. Five: the only lead we have of his was the blood we got from his gorilla–dog chimera, who we found dead and rotting in a back alley, with no extra leads."

"A literal dead end," he quipped, "in more ways than one."

She snorted. "Unfortunately, yes. That about sums up where we are right now."

"So, your tracking link with Dodge, is it still active?"

"No. I let that channel drop last night. My magic was running super low. I could barely gather any to defend ourselves with last night." She frowned. That was a failure on her part.

Galen looked down. "Doesn't that mean we have nothing to go on?"

"Hey, don't get downhearted," Hope reassured him. "We still have that sample of his blood, and while it'll have degraded somewhat overnight, it'll be good enough for us to get his general whereabouts. It was the chimera that was going to be hard to track from a degraded signifier." However, she wasn't as confident it'd work after it'd spent so much time sitting in her jacket pocket – especially when she was so short on magic.

"I, ah, hope you don't mind, but I took the liberty of fishing the sample out of your jacket last night. I put it in the freezer. Will that help?"

She looked up in surprise. "You went searching through my pockets?"

"No, I swear I didn't. The sample was already sticking out, so I pulled it out. I promise I didn't look at anything else. I just thought it was important. Sorry – you're right, I shouldn't have touched your stuff, but you were already asleep, and I didn't want to disturb you."

She looked at him searchingly, then her smile grew. "It's okay. Normally, I'd be cross with you for digging in my pockets, but this really will help, so I'll make an exception. It was a good move, and it's saved our arses, so thank you!"

"Well," he responded, smiling shyly at her appreciation, "I don't know much about the ins and outs of tracking, but I do know a bit about biology. I figured it would help preserve the DNA."

"Yes," she agreed, now much more enthusiastic; "it's definitely helpful – that was good thinking!" She began double-checking for damage to the matrix on her arm.

Galen watched her, his face thoughtful. "Why are you helping me with this?"

"Hmmm? You're paying me, aren't you?"

He huffed a half-laugh. "Well, maybe, but surely... Ah, never mind." He looked a little embarrassed.

"What are you asking?"

"Well, from what I've seen so far, your world is full of double-crossing and taking advantage; and judging by the things you've said, I detect a, well, a familiarity with doing so yourself, and yet..."

She raised an eyebrow, but waved her hand for him to go on.

He looked away. "Well, when you asked for the healing potion last night, I thought there was nothing stopping you from taking that blood sample and bolting – finding the dream steel for yourself to sell," he muttered, blushing. "After everything else that's happened to me, being robbed by the person who's supposedly helping me would fit right in."

She stared at him, then blinked. She barked a bitter laugh and blushed as well. "Yeah! I guess most people in my profession wouldn't have thought twice about doing exactly that. From what I overheard yesterday, you've endured enough of that treatment."

She took a deep breath and rearranged her thoughts. "Let's just say I have a complex moral compass – I don't mind taking advantage of people who've done wrong to me or others, but I don't take advantage of just anyone. Also, once I make a bargain, I prefer to keep my word. I don't go back on it, and I don't take kindly to people who do."

She thought for a moment longer, and added, "Because of those two rules, I don't work well with other thieves."

"The only people you take advantage of are the ones who've done wrong?" he asked. "How do you square that with being a thief? Surely you rob from whoever has something valuable."

Hope smiled. "You may not realise this, but I mostly steal from corporations, not individuals. This city's full of shady companies, out to take advantage of gullible punters. I have no problem taking them down a notch or two. They're my bread and butter. The only reason I took on this job is that I was desperate. I overheard you talking about how they were taking advantage of you, though I'll admit that in this case that wasn't my only motivation – and I now have no problem putting one over on *Henry*." She spat out his name like a gob of phlegm.

"However, most of my jobs don't actually involve thieving at all. I'm primarily a tracker. Henry had me tracking down rare magic components, to begin with. I preferred those jobs, but there's only so much money to be made that way, so eventually he had me hunting down other thieves – rivals, or people who owed him money." She grimaced. "It was dangerous work, because they were likely to be armed, and of course they didn't want to be found. But it paid okay, and I socked the money away so I could eventually get out of it and pay for university. My plan was to take my family and go legit somewhere." She looked away, fighting off the grief of a lost dream.

She shook her head. No time for that right now.

"Anyway, I told Henry I wouldn't do that anymore, and I told you I'd help you hunt down your dream steel. Both promises I intend to keep. Besides, you offered me enough money to keep me happy." She smiled. "So, are you ready to get to it?"

Galen nodded, but his eyes lingered on her like he was weighing her words carefully.

16 - Dodge

Thirty minutes later, and Hope wasn't feeling quite as confident.

They pulled up two blocks away from a small medical centre, which her tracker was tugging her towards. They followed the tug through the front door, navigating their way through the usual rabbit warren of halls, stairs and outbuildings.

"What is it with hospitals?" she asked. "Why are they all built like a labyrinth?"

Galen laughed. "How else would we trap the minotaurs? But I don't disagree with you – if I had to guess, it's probably because the buildings are all extensions on extensions, built over a hundred years of enthusiastic infrastructure-expansion committees."

She snorted. "I think I'd prefer the minotaurs. Just around this corner, I think." She stepped into the new corridor but spun around and dragged him back before he could round the corner.

"Did we find one of the minotaurs?" he joked.

She put a finger to her lips to shush him and pushed him back even further.

"What is it?" he whispered next to her ear.

She jumped. Somehow she'd pushed him up against the wall. She huffed and moved back half a step, releasing the hand she'd put on his shoulder.

Galen breathed out. He raised his eyebrows.

"I should've expected this. He has two guards posted at his door." She whispered back, frowning. Then she shook her head in frustration. "They're not going to let two randoms talk to him, regardless of whether they think he's a suspect or a victim."

He looked thoughtful for a moment. "But we're not two randoms."

Hope opened her mouth to object.

"Hear me out!" he added quickly. "The police have already met us at the crime scene – both of them! They already know we have an interest and a way of tracking Dodge; in fact, they'd probably be surprised if we didn't pay a call. After all, who else would have a firsthand account of chimera-on-human violence?"

She blinked. Then stretched her mouth into a wide grin. "I could kiss you."

Galen looked taken aback.

She laughed and grabbed his hand, pulling him out into the hallway again, exclaiming, "I think our target must be around here!"

As they rounded the corner, the two officers stationed by the door snapped their eyes towards them.

Hope took a few steps into the hallway, her gaze fixed on the tracking matrix on her arm. Then she looked up and paused. "Oh! He must be here. They're guarding him. Come on." She strode up to the two officers, who stood straighter as she approached the ward.

"Hello, officers, I was wondering whether we could have a word with the person inside this ward."

"I'm sorry, ma'am," the female officer replied. "We're not allowing any visitors inside. They are a person of interest in an ongoing investigation."

"Oh," Hope said; "that's why we're here."

Galen stepped in. "We're investigating incidents that involve chimera-based violence, and we're hoping to track down the whereabouts of the, ah … owner? … creator? … of the chimera responsible for the violent incident that occurred last night. We found the remains last night, but they were too degraded for analysis."

The officer narrowed her eyes. "You were present at the crime scene last night?"

"Yes," Hope replied. "We spoke with an officer at the first scene. He collected a blood sample for us, that we used as a signifier to track the remains. At that point we had an unfortunate encounter with some locals but were rescued by the detective on the scene, and we duly handed over custody of the remains to him. Unfortunately, they were too degraded, so that means we're still lacking one subject to study. So today we followed the second tracking target here. I'm guessing whoever's behind that door was the victim of the incident. If so, they might be able to help us identify the attackers' original source."

The officer blinked. "You spoke with the detective on scene?"

"Yes a, um, Detective Grant I believe? He gave me his card, but I'm afraid I lost it." She shrugged and smiled, doing her best to look embarrassed about her alleged absent-mindedness.

The officer looked over at her partner. "Can you call it in?"

The partner nodded, stepped away a few paces, and pulled out a police-issue radio. Hope couldn't hear what they were saying. Police scramble-fields made it impossible to overhear the discussion – the aural equivalent of a hideaway. After a brief back and forth, the officer nodded and returned.

The first officer tipped her head on the side, in question.

"Grant says we can let them in to ask questions if we stay in the room." The second officer relayed. "But no touching the suspect." They addressed this last to Hope. "You'll stay well back, all right?"

"Of course, officer," she replied, smiling, but her hopes dipped. Dodge wouldn't talk if the police were present, and to be fair, she didn't want him to either. She didn't want them getting wind of Mr Green's involvement until she and Galen already had the dream steel in hand; after that, they were welcome to him.

She and Galen let themselves be led into the ward.

The officer stopped them barely two steps into the room.

Hope froze upon seeing the bed. Dodge was thickly swaddled in bandages. His neck was in an elaborate brace and his visible skin was a mess of bruises. One half of his face was swollen and a robust shade of purple.

Only one dark eye was open and it widened in surprise as it fell on the two visitors, then it narrowed into a glare. He tried to turn his face away but winced at the attempt. "I told you I won't talk," he mumbled, through swollen lips.

"We're not police," Hope assured him, "just researching the animal that did this. Can we ask you a few questions?"

Dodge barked a laugh. "Why should I stick my neck out for you?" then his mouth widened in a vicious smile. "I don't talk to drone-slaves any more than cops."

She felt Galen stiffen beside her. She turned to find him blank-faced, but his eyes were burning.

That's when she belatedly remembered it'd been Dodge who'd clamped Galen, threatened to sell him to the drone-slavers and taunted him as he'd struggled to break free.

Oh, crap.

She laid a hand on Galen's arm.

He jumped and turned that ferocious look on her.

She gently squeezed the arm and flicked her eyes towards the police officer standing at the door, who was studying the two of them with a mixture of interest and suspicion.

Galen pulled his hand out of her grasp and stepped forward. "What can you tell us about the chimera that attacked you?" he demanded.

Dodge looked between Hope, Galen and the officer, as though confused about what was going on.

To be fair, Hope wasn't sure now, either; she had to trust that Galen wouldn't do anything stupid enough to land them in a jail cell.

"Why do you want to know?" Dodge replied.

"We want to stop this from happening again," Hope replied, jumping in before Galen could steer the conversation into possibly dangerous waters. "We need to know where the chimera came from." She hoped he'd pick up on her unstated assurance that they hadn't told the cops anything about him or the incident.

"Why would I know anything about that?" He sounded peevish and his eyes drifted away.

"Did it just attack you unprovoked?" Galen asked him.

"No." Dodge glared, but added no more.

That line of questioning concerned Hope. She didn't want the reasons *why* aired here, in present company. But it was something their cover personas might've asked.

"Do you know who it belonged to?" she asked. This was the money question.

Suspicious, Dodge narrowed his eyes. Maybe he'd figured out why she was after the information. Was he merely protecting his connections with their clients or hoping that Buzz had another chance at the score? "I've got no idea," he finally answered, "and even if I did, I wouldn't tell you." With that, he firmly closed his eyes and did his best to roll over.

Hope sighed. It was a clear dismissal.

Galen, however, stepped forward again. "Tell us what we need to know!" he demanded, his fists curled. "Or..."

"Or what?" Dodge interjected, glaring at Galen as hard as Galen was glaring at him.

"We're not going to get anything out of him," Hope murmured to Galen. "Come on, let's get out of here." She put her hand on his arm to lead him away, but he yanked it back.

"Let me go!" His eyes were wide, and he rubbed at his neck.

Hope stepped away from him, stung. Her eyebrows drew together and a trickle of fear rolled down her back. This was a bad show in front of the police. "Hey, you're safe here," Hope reassured him, although she did not feel especially safe herself.

Galen blinked rapidly and re-focused his eyes on her.

The police officer had stepped further into the room. "Are we all right in here?"

Galen looked up at the officer, swallowed, then looked down at the floor. "Yes, we're fine. Sorry." He flicked his eyes up at Hope and then to Dodge. He pushed past them all and out of the door.

The officer looked at Hope with raised eyebrows. "Are you okay?"

Hope offered a wan smile. "Yes, thanks. Sorry, he's a bit worked up over this. Two violent incidents in as many days, so he's eager to put a stop to it all."

"So are we." the officer said, and steered her out of the room.

Hope looked back at Dodge, but he was steadfastly looking away from her.

"It seems like your companion might've known the suspect," the officer said. "Is there anything you can tell us?"

Hope looked down the hall. Galen was in the waiting room, drinking from a water fountain. "I honestly don't know anything."

The officer looked sceptical.

"I only met him a few days ago," Hope continued. "I don't know how he's related to your suspect. Something to do with his brother. We found each other on the hunt."

"Then tell me, why are *you* investigating these attacks?"

She smiled sadly. "My sister and her child were injured in the stampede. I'm highly motivated to catch whoever's responsible."

The officer looked her up and down, weighing. "Look, I probably shouldn't say this, but so much crazy shit has been stirred up because of this Conjunction. We're inundated. There's been a string of these incidents recently – more than the usual background noise. We want to find the responsible party, but we're already overloaded. If you've got any information at all, we really want to hear it. We could use the help with the investigation, but leave the arrest up to us, okay?"

Hope held the officer's eyes and nodded. "We will," she lied. She glanced over at Galen, who was perusing the magazine rack. "Right now, though, I have to catch up with my companion and give him a talking-to about proper questioning techniques." She gave a smile and slipped away.

The officer's partner re-joined the first. "All done," they said.

Barely able to restrain her burning anger, Hope followed Galen into the waiting area before whispering to him, loudly, "What the hell was that?"

"I know," he said; "I'm sorry."

"Sorry? You nearly got us arrested!"

"I know. It was stupid. I got angry at him. I'm really sorry." He took hold of her hand.

That surprised Hope. She didn't know what to say, so she gently detached her hand from his, and breathed in and out to calm herself before resuming. "I'm still angry. That was risky, but I know you've just been through your own traumatic experience and that Dodge was central to it, so it's partly my fault, too. I should've remembered and left you outside. Just, please don't do that again – we can't do anything from inside a jail cell."

He nodded, looking chastened.

She steered them out towards the exit. As they were walking back to the truck, her entire body drooped. "All that risk and we didn't even get anything useful!"

"Well," he began as they hopped back into the cab, "I wouldn't exactly say we got nothing." His smirk returned as he handed her a copy of the previous day's newspaper. "I picked this up in the waiting room."

The front page led with a garish headline, *"BLOOD IN THE STREETS"*, and under it was a photo depicting the café's ravaged frontage. The picture shared space with another – an image of the bank that'd been blown up on the same morning, some unusually large spiders visibly crawling up the walls.

Hope could barely believe that both incidents had occurred only the day before.

A byline ran across the bottom of both pictures. *"Increasing crime wreaks havoc on the businesses of our sleepy town."*

She snorted at the word "sleepy". It wasn't like this city was crime free before the impending event. It had only kicked up a notch or two. Nevertheless, she could see no useful information on the front page. "What am I looking at?" she asked him.

Pulling out into the traffic, he replied, "Not that page. Turn to the next one."

She flipped the page over. The next one was all about the parade – before the stampede. In a turnabout from the café story, the reporter praised the skill and knowledge of the local university's Faculty of

Biological Sciences. She snorted at the angle. The editor had milked a photo of violence on the streets while simultaneously maintaining good rapport with one of the paper's main sponsors without damaging their reputation. However, she still wasn't sure what Galen was pointing out. She opened her mouth to ask, then paused. She looked closer at the photos of the faculty members. "Ah!"

"You see it?"

"I do."

In the second row of photos, was none other than their Mr Green, listed as *"Mr Robert Green, postgraduate research student"*.

"So, we have a name now," she said; "but as much as I'd like to pay Mr Green a visit, we still don't know how to find him. I can put feelers out, but it'll take time."

"I think I can help us narrow down the search much quicker."

She looked up. He looked pleased.

"We'll find him at my old alma mater," he explained; "The University of Technology."

She looked back at the picture. Sure enough, the faculty were standing in front of a giant sign that read, *"University of Technology"*. She laughed. "Hah! Good spotting! So, I guess you know how to get there?"

"On our way now."

She sat back and relaxed as he drove into the thickening afternoon traffic, both of them completely unaware of the small, white card tucked into the truck's rear door.

17 - Chimera.edu

They pulled up to the campus to see a flurry of activity. Hundreds of vehicles crammed into the campus parking lot. Catering trucks vied with heavy-duty carriages dragging trailer loads of equipment and massive cages. The shrieks and hoots of disgruntled animals echoed out of the cages, and Hope recognised the menagerie from the parade.

The scene was an anthill of activity as attendants crawled over and around the animals to tend and feed them and muck out the cages and a small army of private security guards kept anyone else at bay. Hope and Galen had to park a respectable distance away to find a free spot.

Hope was still feeling surprised at how little time had passed since the parade. A wave of worry washed over her as she realised she hadn't yet had a chance to check on Sam and Felicity, but it was swept away in a wave of pain when she hopped down from Galen's truck.

Galen spotted her grimacing. "Hey, are you still in pain? Have you taken the tonic yet?" He pulled open the glove compartment and tossed the bottle to her.

She downed it in a couple of gulps, and sighed as the wave of magic rolled over and through her, sweeping away the aches and pains as though they'd never existed. The magic swelled inside her, warming her from within. His magic, she realised with a start, like what she'd felt in the alley the previous night. "You made this?" she asked in surprise.

"Yeah, my own recipe," he replied, a hint of pride in his voice. "I always find it's more effective when it's handmade. The bulk factory-produced brews are okay, but they aren't as potent – they're all churned out at speed and with maximum cost efficiency."

"I'm impressed, and grateful."

He preened a little and smiled to himself as he locked the truck and they walked towards the university buildings.

Personal transport dominated the campus, students on velocipedes or scooters jostling with heavy foot traffic.

Hope saw one altercation in which a pedal-chair knocked down a person carrying an enormous stack of books. She screeched to a halt and hopped out to help but was immediately sideswiped by a velocipede, its occupant shouting imprecations and gesticulating wildly as they teetered, perched high on its front-wheel. By the time Hope looked back, the book stack had already been recovered.

Galen slipped through this crowd as if he were born to it. Hope followed in his wake.

As they strode through the campus, the tide of students thinned out, filtering out through the various lecture halls and libraries. Hope peeked enviously through one hall into a large auditorium. It was stacked to its ceiling with terraces of wooden chairs, each fitted out with a tiny desk and facing a central dais that held a lecturer holding forth. She looked ahead to see Galen watching her with a bemused expression. She blushed and hurried to catch up.

"Biological Sciences is this way," he murmured, keeping his voice low.

They pushed through some glass double doors, crossed a manicured lawn, and entered the atrium of a large building with multiple tiered levels stacked on top like a wedding cake. Inside, they found another hive of activity – people rushing around in all directions, carrying a variety of equipment.

Galen muttered, "this is busier than usual but there's usually somebody in the staff break-room." He led them over to a small office and peeked inside. It was empty.

"Galen!"

They both spun around at the joyful shout. Hope saw a short cannonball of a woman bowling towards them at high speed. She slammed into Galen, and he let out a soft "Oof!" at the impact.

Before he could recover enough to respond, the woman began speaking at top speed. "You're coming tonight? That's fantastic news! I didn't get a reply from you, so I thought you weren't coming, but here you are! And who is this? Is she your plus one? Fantastic!" She ran her eyes down and up Hope's figure appreciatively and waggled a suggestive eyebrow up and down. "Oh, Galen, I like your taste!"

Galen blushed beet red.

The woman grinned, scooted over to Hope, and offered her a

welcoming hand. "My name's Adora. If he doesn't pan out as your date tonight, can I ask you out for a coffee instead?" Then she finally paused, allowing Hope a moment to answer.

Hope looked over at Galen, suddenly curious about his reaction to this proposition.

He was studiously examining his fingernails, but his ears were practically glowing red.

Adora seemed bemused by his reaction, but continued looking at Hope expectantly.

Hope gave her a polite smile. "Thanks for the offer. I'll keep it in mind. But I'm going to say no for now."

For an infinitesimal moment, the woman's smile dropped, but it re-established itself pretty quickly.

Hope continued before Adora started talking again. "However, I'm not actually aware of what's meant to be happening tonight; the place seems pretty busy."

"You!" Adora spun around to face Galen. "You haven't asked her to the Alumni Ball? Oh, Galen, why on earth not? She's so totally your type!"

Galen, who had momentarily regained his normal, honey-coloured complexion, blushed beet red once more, but now he was also glaring at Adora. "I didn't know there was a ball on tonight," he sputtered. "If I received an invitation, I must've missed it. I've been a bit buried in my own... personal projects." He turned away.

Adora looked at him with something approaching horror. "Oh, I'm so sorry, I forgot. Your brother." She paused a moment, then let a sly smile emerge on her face. "Yes, of course I should've realised you'd buried yourself in your work and had forgotten there's an entire world out here." She glared at him and actually kicked him in the shins.

He yelped and looked at her in surprise as she continued. "A world full of your friends who all care about you and just want to make sure you're okay, and want you to have some semblance of your own life – you know, with people, and parties, and things that make life still worth living."

Hope's jaw dropped. Adora was needling a grieving man! But rather than be upset, Galen was actually smiling at her affectionately.

He sighed theatrically. "Okay, you're right, as usual – I have been an awfully lax friend. Tell me why you think I should be dragged, kicking and screaming, to a ball rather than keep working on the important project I'm neck deep in."

Adora smiled beatifically, grabbed his arm and used it to drag him off down the corridor, with Hope trailing helplessly behind.

They stood by the doorway and observed the large hall being fitted out. Numerous people stepped around the three of them, grumbling, while they peeked inside.

"It's the annual Bio-Science Alumni Ball," Adora said. "You know what they're like – lots of schmoozing for the post-docs amongst the well-to-do alumni of years past; a chance for them to secure some much-needed patronage. Anyone who's anyone will be there, of course – which means a plethora of delicate society ladies for me to charm." She smiled like a cat. "But you'd probably prefer the line-up of superstar scientists they've invited to come and stand around and make us look like an actual prestigious university." She nodded her head at the garish, full-size colour poster taking up one wall. It featured a large line-up of heads and names that Hope didn't recognise. "If you came, at least they'd have somebody interesting to talk to. This year's crop of students is a bunch of dullards – all destined to become industrious but mediocre company stooges." She sighed dramatically. "Not a unique or individual idea amongst them."

"Gee, you're really selling it to me, aren't you?" Galen responded drily, "Look, I'm not sure I can spare the time. We're in the thick of something important and time-critical."

"Oh, please come; it won't be the same without you. You've always loved a good ball, and there'll be lots of dancing." Her eyes became full of concern for him. "It'll be good for you to get out of your funk for just one night. Don't forget, you're the one who delegated me the task of pulling you back into the social scene every time you dropped into the depths of despair."

He sighed and brushed his eyes over the line-up featured on the poster. Then he paused. He smiled and turned to Hope, then back to Adora. "You know, I think maybe we'll attend after all."

Adora's face split into a huge grin, which turned just a bit lascivious. "And, of course, you must invite your delectable companion. I'm sure that by the end of the night, I'll have persuaded her to give me just one dance." She raised her eyebrows and cocked her chin at Hope, then furnished her with a big wink and a sly grin at Galen. Finally, she made her goodbyes and returned to supervising the night's preparations.

Hope raised an eyebrow at him questioningly. "Are you positive we want to go to a ball right now?"

He grinned. "I think it's exactly where we need to be," and tapped his hand on a picture on the poster. One of the smaller ones, way below the headliners.

Of course it was Mr Green.

* * * * *

Hope waved Galen off with an admonishment that yes, she did own a cocktail dress and would be dressed, ready and waiting, by no later than 6 pm tonight.

She fumbled for a house key, but the door swung open before she even got it in the hole. So she was standing there, holding her key in surprise, when she was confronted by Felicity, who did not look pleased.

In fact, if she had to say, she looked downright pissed.

"Oh, shit!" Hope said, and tried to pull an ingratiating smile on to her features.

"Seriously? Is that all you have to say?" Felicity's words came out like overheated steam from an engine that was dangerously close to exploding. "You've been gone two days. Two days! With no word from you, right when your family needs you most, and me sick with worry you were off doing something stupid again. And all you have to say is, 'Oh, shit'?"

Hope wilted under the onslaught. "I'm sorry, I meant to get back to you last night, but I got distracted and I haven't had a chance since, because of the job I'm on right now, and…" She trailed off as Felicity's eyes were glowing coals, burning her words away. She tried to make herself very small.

"And what," Felicity bit off, "pray tell, were you doing on this job? I overheard you talking about attending a ball with a man. Explain to me why that was so important you had to leave your newly disabled and distraught nibling without an aunt and your little sister without any support?"

Hope looked down at her feet and mumbled, "something stupid."

"What?" Felicity spat.

Hope looked up at her, then took a long, deep breath. "Something stupid, but something potentially…" She sighed and looked around her at the people walking past. "I think we need to talk inside."

Felicity continued glaring at her, but did not move aside.

"Please, Felicity, you're going to want to hear what I have to say."

18 - Pickup line

A few hours later, Hope was standing in front of the bathroom mirror, double-checking her sparse makeup for flaws.

She was nervous. Sweating even. That wasn't like her.

Was she worried about seeming crass in front of some of the country's smartest people, or were her butterflies for another reason? She squashed the rebel thought down. He was a necromancer, for goodness sake!

Besides, this was still a job – a big one. She didn't have time for *Feelings*, and even if she did, maybe, have *Feelings*, they'd have to wait until after this was all done. Plus, it wasn't like this was an actual date for either of them. Galen hadn't really asked her out; the only reason he'd invited her along was because it was their best chance of finding and cornering Mr Green.

Still, she couldn't help thinking about how much he'd blushed when Adora teased him about her, and how her stomach had fluttered in response.

She shook her head.

Stupid stomach.

It was all giddy schoolgirl stuff. She needed her game face on tonight.

But when the doorbell rang she jumped, and her nerves ratcheted up another notch.

She took a deep breath, wiped her sweaty hands on her dress, and gave herself a last once-over in the mirror.

Then she paused for a moment, waiting. It took her half a second to realise she was expecting to hear the thunder of tiny feet as the little person she loved tumbled out of the back room and down the hall.

Tears welled up as she realised that wasn't going to happen. Sam had locked themself away in the other room, and hadn't come out for anything – even to have a meal; even to see her. They'd withdrawn, Felicity had said, and needed time to adjust to the change in their body.

She shook her head and blinked away the incipient tears.

Hope squared her shoulders. She'd just have to surprise Sam with a solution to that problem, one way or another. Even if her heart was breaking to think about it.

"Enough of that," she whispered, reaching for the door handle.

She heard the front door open and froze, her hand still on the knob.

"Hi, I'm Galen," she heard. "You must be Felicity."

"Oh my," her sister purred. "Hope didn't tell me you were so hot. Come on in and wait in the kitchen. She's still in the bathroom, preening."

His footsteps went past in the hallway.

Felicity knocked on her door. "Come out soon. Before I decide to take your place."

Hope could hear the smile in her voice. She rolled her eyes and slid on a pair of silk elbow-length gloves, which matched her dress – a wine-red corseted frock, with long skirts that swished as she spun around and also hid a surprising number of pockets. Although sadly not as many as her usual heavy jacket or skirt. For tonight she needed a different class of clothing so she could blend in. Her dress would serve well without being too uncomfortable.

She just hoped that Galen would find his own way to fit in; she'd never seen him wearing anything other than loose, comfortable scrubs. Hopefully he'd found something clean and tidy to put on so he could blend in with the other academics.

She eyed her French-twist, prodding a loose hair back in place, then swept out of the bathroom.

Felicity was standing by the fridge, chatting with Galen, who was leaning casually against the bench. But he straightened up, wide eyed, as soon as she entered.

Time stood still, like one of those ridiculous movie moments, and several things rearranged themselves in her head.

Galen wasn't clothed like some absentminded academic, he was dressed to the nines in black, tight-fitting pants and a silky-looking white shirt, and they were clinging to a physique she'd clearly failed to notice was *that* well-toned beneath his scrubs. She couldn't help but notice that the shirt had a ruffled front and was open a few buttons, enough to draw the eye in...

Felicity snorted, breaking her concentration.

Hope shook her head and raised her eyes to see that Galen was smirking back at her while obviously appraising her own clothing choices. She blushed and walked in.

"So, you do own a nice dress," he teased.

"And you scrub up better than I expected," she replied, raising her eyebrow.

His grin broadened. "You look stunning."

She smiled and blushed some more. "Thank you."

Felicity snorted again. "I'll leave you two alone to admire each other." She brushed past them but turned again, a look of concern on her face. "Be careful on your job." Then she addressed Galen. "And you, try to keep her from doing anything stupid."

He raised his eyebrows and gave a half-laugh. "I think you overestimate my abilities."

Felicity laughed, but Hope could see the concern in her sister's eyes.

Hope turned back to Galen.

"Oh, I have something for you, if you'll permit." He held out a spray of tiny red orchids that glittered like rubies. They were exquisite!

He gestured for her to turn and she did so, curious.

He reached forward and tucked the stalk behind her ear, threading it into her hair so the spray of flowers curved over her head and cascaded down the other side.

His hands touched her gently, taking no liberties, but a light, unintentional brush against her neck raised goosebumps on her skin. When he stepped back, she was a little sad that the task was done.

"Perfect," he muttered, admiring his work.

She tried to hide her smile as she turned back to him. She noticed he had a matching pair of orchids pinned to his top pocket. "Are you ready to go?" she asked.

He raised an arm for her, which she took, and he drew her into the hall. She gathered her purse and jacket from the side-table by the door, and once again caught her reflection in the hall mirror. Nestled in her dark-brown hair, the red of the orchids shone like gemstones. She smiled, and they stepped out into the night.

Outside, instead of his usual truck, there was a small carriage pulled by a headless mechanical horse. Hope was delighted. She hopped up the steps and Galen climbed in next to her, closing the little door with a *click*.

She leaned back, enjoying the view of the stars and the sultry breeze. The mechanical horse took off with a smooth, artificial trot, and the carriage ran slick as silk despite the horse's robotic movements.

Hope smiled. "I've always wanted to ride in one of these. Felicity thinks it's a frivolous waste of money. Don't get me wrong, this is a lovely change from your truck, but it must surely have cost a fortune."

Galen looked askance at her. "I may have *borrowed* it from the university pool." He leaned in to whisper, "they aren't likely to miss it for one night."

She laughed, a delightful tingle running down her skin. "Am I rubbing off on you, or are you just opening up enough to show me your true, less-than law-abiding self?"

He smirked, relaxing back into his seat. "A little of both, perhaps. Still, I figured we're heading to a society ball, so it might help if we at least tried to look the part."

19 - Party

When the carriage drew up to the university grounds, Hope found another reason to enjoy it. Honking traffic packed the streets, but their carriage was ushered through a velvet-roped side street and on to a broad and empty carriageway. The cab deposited them at the edge of the same manicured lawn leading to the wedding-cake building.

Galen offered Hope his arm, and she took it with a smile.

Hundreds of tiny candles flickered along the pathway leading inward. Hope eyed up a pair of mechanised spiders patrolling each row, the automatons carefully replacing spent candles for new.

"That's Adora's work," Galen said, pointing at the spiders. "She's an extremely talented tinker."

Hope nodded appreciatively as they drifted towards the double doors.

"She's most famous for her design of the mechanical centipedes," he continued.

"I've seen them around. They're used for parcel post, yes?"

He looked at her, askance. "Yes, the postal service has purchased some. They're effective courier automatons as they can traverse any terrain. Her biggest clients, though, come from the military sector."

She raised her eyebrows as she nodded. "Sounds lucrative."

"Oh yes, very." He gave a half-cough, half-laugh. "It's how she lures in her favourite sexual prey. She's quite the cougar, and it seems the combination of high pay and a brush with danger is irresistible to a certain kind of bored society lady."

Hope's eyebrows shot up even higher, and she opened her mouth to comment.

But Galen, hiding one of his mischievous smirks, had turned to the door. He produced an elaborately calligraphed invitation and presented it to the attendant. "Doctor Galen Moore plus one."

The attendant passed it over a hand-held scanner, then smiled and returned it to Galen. "Right this way, Dr Moore; ma'am. Have a lovely evening." He waved them through before turning to the next pair of guests.

As they walked through the doorway, Hope noticed it was flanked by a pair of very large, very armed, and dangerous looking automatons. She squeezed Galen's arm.

He nodded his head at them. "These are also Adora's work." They drifted over to have a closer look at the large, mechanised humanoids. "They're sentinels – and these are definitely military." The closest one swivelled its head towards Galen. A red light scanned him up and down, then the head returned to observing the incoming party guests.

"She built all these automatons? I thought this was the Biological Sciences division!"

"Oh, it is. Adora's specialty is in cybernetics. Her talent is in studying biological systems and re-combining them with mechanical ones to create highly functional fusions that are – ahem – 'best of breed', she says."

Hope smiled and shook her head. "So, there are animal parts inside of these things?"

"Not necessarily. She patterned some of them on animal neuronal structure. Others have neural interfaces so humans can drive them from sensory tanks. It depends on what the client wants. But I'll admit I don't know all the details; it's all very hush-hush."

She nodded. "Is that why the high security? It seems excessive for a university."

Galen eyed up the sentinels. "Yeah, it's not usually this strong, but protestors have been targeting the menagerie outside ever since the incident at the café. Some animals were attacked – even killed; and threats were made to staff. Adora said the sentinels are here to keep everyone safe."

She nodded absently.

"Incidentally, it's Adora that I'd advise talking to about Sam's prosthetic. It's not technically her specialty, but I think I can persuade her to do a custom job as a favour... unless, of course, you've changed your mind about the *other* option." He said it casually.

Hope ground her teeth and her eyes slid away. "Felicity and I talked about it. She said I should get more information at a more suitable juncture and that she'd trust my decision."

He looked at her sideways.

"I haven't decided yet," she said, primly.

Galen looked a little downhearted, but nodded. "Well, I haven't been idle while I was waiting. Regardless of what you eventually decide, I thought it prudent to keep all options open. I returned to the hospital and acquired the – um – necessary medical item."

Hope's eyes went wide. "You mean you have…"

He nodded, his eyes serious. "As I expected, it was waiting in the deep freeze. It's safe and well stored. Take your time deciding – it'll be ready and waiting."

She sighed deeply. It was pretty creepy that he'd broken into the hospital to steal the discarded, battered, and broken arm of a small child. However, thinking about who it was coming from, it was a thoughtful move of his to keep all her options open. If only it weren't such a high-risk decision. Was she really willing to let him use necromancy to experiment on her precious nibling?

She shivered, then frowned. "I'm sorry. I don't mean any disrespect. You're putting yourself out there to help us, and I'm grateful. I'm not yet sure what I'll decide." She looked up at him.

He seemed to be weighing her words again.

She felt she had to make it clear. "I mean that. It's not just me avoiding the question to get out of giving a negative answer. I have honestly not yet decided. Both options are still on the table, and I'd like to keep it that way until I find out more."

He nodded at this and smiled. "Thanks. I appreciate you saying that, and I recognise that it's a life-altering decision you have to make. And I hope you don't think I'm pressuring you into deciding either way – which is why I wanted to clarify that the alternative is very much available to you. It just won't come as cheap, I'm afraid – Adora never works for free."

"Do I hear my name being taken in vain?" The voice came from behind them.

Hope spun around to see the woman in question rolling towards them, wearing an exquisite, gleaming-white pantsuit and a shirt that was glittering with gemstones. She didn't think they were diamonds, but they sure were pretty.

"My eyes are up here, sweetheart!" Adora said with a chuckle. Then, while Hope was still blushing and trying to re-formulate her words, Adora turned to Galen. "I'm so glad you're here. I've been trying to keep our guests engaged so they don't walk out *en masse*. The post-docs are still farting around setting up, because they can't get their arses in gear on time. I'm informed that Dom's test subjects have escaped again and are crawling around on the ceiling somewhere and dropping on to the guests, scaring them senseless with Dom nowhere to be seen; and I swear Peterson's still writing the paper he's supposed to be basing his display on. Oh, and the usual caveats should apply to Drakey's cabinet, yes?"

Galen smirked at the summary and laughed out loud at the last. "And you wouldn't have anything to do with those test subjects getting loose and causing mayhem, would you?"

Widening her grin, Adora replied, "Why ever would you accuse me of such nefarious actions?"

"Adora is a notorious prankster," he told Hope. "You should ask her about the time she spiked the punch with an experimental nootropic."

"Ha!" Adora exclaimed. "I had the entire department going down experimental rabbit holes for days! But I swear it was responsible for at least seven papers, not to mention two rather fruitful new fields of research."

Galen laughed at the memory.

Adora smiled, but it turned to a scowl as she glanced back over her shoulder into the hall. "Much as I'd like to, I can't reminisce all night. Can I possibly tear you away from your beautiful date for the next ten minutes to help me wrangle the speakers? After that, they'll be too busy trying not to have their ears chewed off by the post-grads. Once we can finally set them loose, they'll make their escape and we'll all be free to party."

He sighed deeply. "I'm just not sure I'll be a scintillating conversational partner tonight. I'm a little too stressed to handle conversing with strangers."

Adora gave him a smile brimming with concern. "I know. I'm sorry to ask. It's just that it's important to me to make a good impression tonight. We've taken a big PR hit, thanks to the recent troubles. Have you seen the news?"

They both nodded.

"You don't have to talk for long, and we've set up an icebreaker that I think will be right up your alley." She drew them forward so they could see the hall.

One side of the room was roped off, with various tables and stands being hurriedly constructed by an untidy mob of nervous-looking grad students. The other side featured an overflowing buffet that had attracted a great crowd of people picking over the food. By far the greatest portion of the room, however, was chock-a-block with dancing couples, who'd been paired up regardless of their gender or age, and all of whom were drifting around in time to some quiet instrumental music.

"We're riffing on the idea of speed dating," Adora explained, "and doing dancing talks. Every one of our guests is up there chatting with each other, and – oops – there goes the music."

The music had paused, and a bright light shone down onto the dance floor. Each couple lined up in rows. They engaged in some parting words, with more than a few business cards being exchanged and tucked away. Then the line of people on one side all moved up by one partner. The person on the end popped off and made a rapid escape to the buffet, to be replaced by a new person herded into place by an usher.

Then the music began again. They all stood for a moment, introducing themselves before moving off again on one of those refined and dignified but downright stuffy slow dances favoured by the upper classes.

Hope found that sort of dance boring – invented by people in dresses too tight to move faster than a slow drift. However, she knew how if she had to – she'd learned a lot from Felicity about the habits of the upper classes. Over the years, several of her jobs had required her to blend in with high society at these kinds of miserable mixer balls, though she'd never attended a ball at this university before now. They had oddly tight security, given how little there was to steal. It had never been worth the effort.

Hope realised she'd been drifting. Galen had asked a question. "I'm sorry. I was off with the fairies. Can you repeat what you said?"

He smiled at her, but then became rueful. "I said, 'Would you consider me a dreadful date if I were to leave you for a while to go entertain some visiting dignitaries?'"

She smiled broadly and scooted in close so Adora could pretend she didn't overhear. "Is this a date? I wasn't sure."

"I…" he began.

Laughing, she added, "I'm kidding. Of course it's okay. I'm sure I'll find something useful to occupy myself with." She raised her eyebrows and glanced over at the student corral, hoping he'd registered what she was hinting at.

He nodded at her.

Did he look... relieved? She wasn't sure, but he turned and let Adora drag him towards the dance floor and neatly insert him into the next round of dancing partners.

Smiling to herself, she drifted over to where the students were setting up. She stood next to the velvet ropes and peered among the maze of tables, posters, and large glass jars of specimens – hunting for Mr Green. She didn't see him amid the scrambling mass, although she spotted a table that bore his nametag and a messy pile of pages spilling over it.

An usher noticed her hovering and approached. "We're not quite ready for visitors. Come back in a few minutes and you'll be able to come in."

"Oh, okay, thanks." She gave him a dazzling smile and drifted off towards the buffet table. As she edged around the dance floor, she cast her eyes in among the couples to see whether she could spot Galen.

She spied him dancing near the centre, with a middle-aged man who was regaling him with what they obviously intended to be a humorous anecdote. Galen was smiling politely and nodding in the right places, but Hope could see the tightness in his shoulders as he moved through the dance steps, his eyes glazed with boredom. The music gave a lilt, and he swept his dance partner in a tight circle, which seemed to quiet the man for a moment as he tried to keep up. However, as soon as he caught his breath again, he resumed his anecdote.

Still, the move was impressive. She'd enjoyed the expert way in which Galen had guided his inexperienced dance partner with his hands. If she hadn't seen how bored he'd looked, she might've thought the guy was his type.

The music stopped and Galen bowed graciously to his partner, pocketing the proffered card before hurrying on. He spotted Hope watching him with a grin, and he grinned back with a roll of his eyes before he met and introduced himself to his next dance partner. A youngish woman with bright eyes and a dazzling smile, she swept up in an explosion of delicate blue lace. Hope snorted. The woman actually blushed as she offered her hand to him. Hope was too far away to see if she also batted her eyes, but she wouldn't have been surprised.

Galen introduced himself to her politely but looked just as bored as with his previous partner, which amused Hope. Clearly, simpering society debutantes weren't his type either.

Hope bumped up against somebody. She spun around, apologising profusely, as did the tall, well-dressed man she'd nearly tripped over.

He leaned against a large stall in front of a table abutting the buffet. The table held an enormous cabinet containing a riot of colourful bottles, various decanters and assorted glassware – each with a tiny name tag in front of it, explaining the ingredients.

"Oops. I'm sorry, ma'am," he said. "I was just stretching my leg and didn't see you coming. Are you hurt?"

"Oh, no," she replied, laughing, "not at all. It was my fault. I wasn't watching where I was going."

"Oh, that's good, I'm glad. I'm a bit accident prone; twisted my ankle again only yesterday. An old injury, never quite healed, and I keep managing to re-injure it." He rolled his eyes. Then smiled at her. "Anyway, you don't want to hear about that. Where are my manners? I'm Drake. Pleased to meet you."

"I'm Hope, and likewise." She shook his hand, an eye wandering to the bottles.

"I don't recall meeting you before. Are you… one of the students? … or perhaps a society guest?"

"Oh, neither, I'm afraid. I'm a plus-one of one of the visiting alumni." Her eyes kept returning to the intriguing array of bottles.

Noticing her fascination, he grinned. "Would you care to try some refreshment?"

"What are they?" She read the tags, each of which had fantastical names, such as 'Metheglin', 'Hydromel' or 'Orange shrub'.

"Oh, well, I love to experiment with brewing and liqueurs and other concoctions." He began selecting a few choice bottles and pouring out a small drop into a line of tiny sipping glasses. "It might seem different from the other students' work, but brewing is a biological science, if you study it right. I'm working on isolating better strains of yeast in order to target specific flavour profiles in my wines." He gave her a wink, and added, "The distilling's just for fun."

"Oh, so they're alcoholic drinks?" She raised her eyebrows.

"Yes, well, mostly. Some are low in alcohol, and the herbal ones were once medicinal remedies. But they're all drinkable – in moderation, of course. That's why they have me over here by the buffet table instead of with the rest of the students. Would you like a try?" He held out a tiny glass that held a thimble-full of a dark-red, almost black liquor.

She took the glass and sniffed. "Oh! Elderberries!"

"Yes! This is my elderberry liqueur with cardamom. Quite popular. The elderberries are delicious. I get most of my produce as an in-kind exchange with the horticultural department, so the quality is topnotch."

Hope took a tiny sip while he spoke. It was sweet and tangy, spicy and full of flavour – and it went down her throat very nicely. She smiled.

"This is amazing. May I try another?" She held her glass up to be refilled.

Drake's eyes lit up, and he began handing her glasses to try. Orange and honey, spices and raspberries, and even the bitter herbs all went down well, one after the other; as she chatted with him and watched the dancers drift and part, rejoin and drift once more.

She may have been checking out one dancer in particular, though she tried to keep her gaze focused on looking out for Mr Green instead.

"I know you said you were here as a plus-one, but were you hoping to meet anyone in particular?" he asked her. "I don't mean to pry; I only ask because you keep watching the students."

"Oh, yes. I saw the parade in town the other day – all those amazing animals. I was hoping to talk to the student responsible... I think he's called Robert Green?"

"Robert?" Drake asked with a thoughtful look. "Yes, I know him, but he doesn't specialise in chimerae – that's what we call the animals. I mean, he does sometimes use them as test subjects, but his specialty is more along the lines of zoological neuro-chemistry and relevant alchemical processes; in fact..."

"Oh, no!" The voice came from behind her.

She tried to spin around, but the floor slipped out from under her. She pitched towards Drake's table, but two firm hands caught her by the arms. They drew her up and gently turned her until she was facing Galen.

He looked pained.

"Why're you sad?" she tried to ask him but was astonished that her tongue suddenly wasn't quite working the way she wanted.

Whoops, that was quick!

"Drakey!" Galen exclaimed. "She's drunk!"

"S'not'roo," Hope tried, then covered her mouth with a hand.

"Is she? Oh dear, I am sorry," Drake replied, looking over his bottles. "There's nothing too potent here, I thought – they're all just liqueurs, but I didn't realise how many…"

"No… S'my fault," Hope slurred. "Kept asking f'more – so damn delick… yummy!"

Drake grinned and shrugged. "I'm sorry, I should've warned you they were high in alcohol and helped you keep count. This stuff can be deceptively strong."

"No, it's my fault," Galen said with a groan. "I got carried off before I had a chance to warn you. Drakey's brews are delicious but notoriously potent."

"Still no' sorry," Hope gave a sloppy smile, her face not quite responding as she wished.

At least I'm not drooling this time.

"Come on, let's see whether we can find Mr Green before you pass out on me. You're not going to throw up, are you?" Galen peered into her face, concerned.

"Nope. 'M'a sleepy drunk, not a pukey drunk. But I wanna dance before we go talk t' Missr Green."

Galen raised a dubious eyebrow. "Are you up to that?"

"Yup!" she said, and waved vaguely towards where Mr Green was being led by Adora onto the dance floor.

"B'size, s'all slow dancing anywayze." She turned. "Bye Drakey. Nice t'meet cha – an' I love ya brews. I'll get s'more some time."

"You too, and any time," he replied as Galen gently and reluctantly led her onto the dance floor.

As a pair, they squeezed in next to Mr Green just as the music began.

Hope stumbled slightly. She could hardly feel her feet! But Galen caught her and deftly steered her through the requisite moves. She was suddenly glad for the slow, boring dance moves now. Maybe they'd invented them to accommodate a high expected level of public inebriation.

Meanwhile, Mr Green had begun an earnest conversation with his female dancing partner, the young lady in blue lace who Galen had previously been dancing with.

Mr Green looked ecstatic. The lady in question looked like she was very much looking forward to the buffet instead. "So, as I was saying, I finally have the last material I need to make it all work. Isn't that amazing, dear?"

"Yes. Amazing," she replied, clearly trying to keep the boredom from drowning her.

"Aren't you happy for me, dear? You always did say you loved my mechanical ideas."

"I'm thrilled for you. But I've asked you before not to call me 'dear' anymore."

"But darling, I always used to call you 'dear', and you loved it ever so much."

The woman pulled back from him and stood glaring at him. "I am not your darling, and I am not your dear. Not any more. We are not together anymore, Robert. Can you understand that?"

"But we're just going through a bit of a rough patch, dear... I mean... Madalyn. I'm sure we can figure things out between us, given time."

"This is not a rough patch. There *is* no 'us', Robert. I've moved on. I'm glad you've finished that machine. Good luck to you – you always were married to that thing more than to me. I wish you many happy returns with it and a good day to you." She spun on her heel and stalked off the dance floor, leaving Mr Green speechless and bewildered.

"Spin me out," Hope whispered quickly to Galen.

"In your state? You'll fall over," he remarked dryly.

"Thass the plan," she replied with a crooked smile and a double-eyebrow flash.

He raised an eyebrow but spun her out towards Mr Green.

On cue, she stumbled on her heel and slammed into him, knocking them both over.

"Get off me, you stupid woman!" he yelled, his face beet red and his eyes bulging.

"Oh, 'm sorry," she slurred, wiggling and rolling off him onto the floor.

"Oh my. I am so sorry," Galen said, helping haul her back to her feet. "My date had a run-in with Drakey's concoctions."

Hope giggled and fell into Galen's arms. "Yah! Had one too many. Ha-ha! One; two; many!" She tried holding up the right number of fingers as she repeated the phrase. "One, two... um... how many fingerses many?"

Galen offered a hand to Mr Green, but he batted it away.

"I do not need your help! Take your inebriated floozy and piss off!" He hauled himself up, stomped off through the gawking couples, and disappeared into the maze of student displays.

"'M'not a floozy!" Hope shouted after him, frowning.

The onlookers tittered. The spat was clearly better entertainment than they'd anticipated on the dance floor.

"I think we might need to get you home," Galen said, reaching out for her.

"Need a bathroom," she replied. "Don' feel so good." She staggered towards the people on the edges of the dance floor.

They fell back hurriedly.

Galen stepped quickly to follow as she wended her way towards the double doors at the back of the hall.

Hope pushed her way through the doors and turned right to head down the corridor. She stopped well beyond visibility and slipped her heels off.

"The bathroom is this way," Galen explained, gently pulling on her arm to turn her towards the other end of the corridor.

"Oh, thanks, but can you tell me where the post-grads have their offices instead?" She straightened up and grinned wickedly at him.

Galen's eyebrows shot up. Then that smile stole across his face again. "Are you even drunk at all?"

She giggled, but it ended in a hiccup. "Truth be told, I am a bit tipsy, but not as drunk as everyone out there thinks. And now we have an excuse to be absent for a while. So come on, let's talk while we're walking." She pulled on his arm.

He broke into motion, leading the way to a flight of stairs going up.

She was walking far more steadily, especially now she had those heels off.

Next time, more sensible dancing shoes!

"So, why did you knock him over?" Galen asked her while he was leading them up the successive layers of the wedding-cake building. "I assume you had a reason."

"I thought you were a student here!" She held up the white key card she'd lifted from Mr Green's pocket. "Every second door in this building seems to be a security door, and all the students were carrying one of these things. I figured if we were going to find anything useful on Mr Green's dream steel, it'd be in his office. They do have offices, don't they?"

Galen looked a little pained. "They do, but they share them – and I doubt Mr Green would keep something as valuable as dream steel in it when it's a shared space."

She felt herself deflate.

Quickly, he added, "But you're right, maybe we'll find where he lives, and that will lead us to where we need to go."

She picked up a bit more after that. "Yeah, that'll help, and you're right, of course. I guess I am a bit drunk – I'm not thinking as clearly as usual. We'll have to find where his lab is instead. If he's building some kind of device, that's where he'll keep the dream steel."

"Device?" he asked.

"Didn't you hear him arguing with his ex? She talked about some kind of machine. I'd bet good money that's what he's got the dream steel for."

He nodded.

They found their way up to the third floor, where he led her out of the stairwell and into a small atrium. The door was locked and had a flat keypad beside it, a solid red light shining from the top.

"Well, here goes nothing," she muttered, and tried the key card.

The light flashed green, and the door clicked open.

They entered a corridor filled with opaque doors and flickering overhead fluorescent lighting.

She sighed in frustration. The doors were numbered, not named. "How are we going to tell which one's his?"

Galen snorted a laugh and took the key card from her. He pressed it to each door. As each one flashed red, he moved on to the next. Finally, one flashed green, and he opened the door with a flourish and a smirk.

She raised an eyebrow, preceding him inside.

It was a small, grey office divided clearly in half. One side was neat and well ordered. The other half was not.

Computer printouts papered the walls, sporting a variety of partial conjuration flows, the rune groupings picked out in various colours. A dozen used coffee mugs decorated the desk, each with a dull-brown residue. The mugs vied for space with a scattering of colourful plastic animal toys, all of which had been chopped into pieces and glued back together in a fantastical variety of forms.

"I guess we found our chimera specialist," Galen said, eyeing the toys.

Hope looked them over but couldn't spot one that looked like the gorilla-dogs she'd seen the other day. She did spot the flying monkey, made of bright-blue plastic. And there at the centre was the elephant-opus, towering over the rest. She tipped it over, toppling several others.

Galen raised an eyebrow, but she ignored it, instead turning back to scan the printouts covering the walls. "What's the bet these matrices correspond to what we saw on those gorilla things?"

"Highly likely. These green ones are variations on common medical systems, and those red ones look like some of the ones I… ah… use in my *other* work. So, now we know whose office this is." He picked carefully at the piles of cascading paper.

"I don't think it is, actually." Hope looked across at the neater side of the office.

"What do you mean? It's all here, isn't it?" He indicated the toys again.

"Something Drakey said to me… or began saying. He said that chimerae weren't Mr Green's specialty at all – something about chemicals? neurons? Plus, as you recall, you said his work was pretty sloppy, even for a student."

Galen looked over the printouts, his eyebrows furrowed.

"Some of these appear to be missing." She pointed to a bare patch on the wall with remnants of tape.

"What's the bet our Mr Green nicked his lab partner's work and tried to do his own dodgy copy?" He fingered a torn corner of paper, still taped to the wall.

"Now that wouldn't surprise me. Still, it can't hurt to go through both – besides, you were going to familiarise yourself with this research in case we needed to bluff the cops again, yeah?" She scanned the neatly stacked contents of the other desk.

He snorted, then sighed and returned to picking through the detritus.

Hope began looking through the ordered stacks of paper on the other side of the room. It was only neater by comparison to the filth of the other half of the office. It still contained the usual piles of printouts and old half-completed assignments. She pulled open a desk drawer to find it crammed full of months of discarded papers and rubbish. She picked through these, hunting for anything useful.

"What are we looking for, exactly?" Galen grimaced as he shifted the grotty mugs to one side.

"Well, in my case, anything that can lead us to where he stashed the dream steel. I guess we'll know it when we see it."

SLAM!

Hope jumped a foot in the air and squeaked as the door crashed against the wall.

"Here they are! The thieves are in my office! Come on, get them!"

20 - The way out

Hope jumped for the door, grabbing Galen. Simultaneously, Mr Green leaped into the room. They collided midway, entangled with each other, and they both toppled to the floor. As they landed, her fist slammed into his nose, causing him to squeak in pain.

She heard footsteps coming quickly up the stairs. Galen pulled her to her feet. They left Mr Green curled in pain and took off down the hall, away from the main staircase and towards a wooden door with a green "EXIT" sign. They dived through the door into a fire stair.

"Up!" yelled Galen, who began bounding up the stairs.

She followed.

"Oi you! Stop!" came a loud voice from below.

"Fat chance!" she yelled back and disappeared around a bend in the stairwell.

They ran and ran, up two flights of stairs; three.

Hope was gasping, her muscles screaming. She was reconsidering her dislike of regular running practice.

The yells and pounding feet were right below them.

"Where," Hope panted, "we going?"

"Roof?" he answered.

They slogged up a last flight, to be confronted with a solid, grey door.

...with the obligatory half a brick, chocking it open.

She spared a breath for a giggle, then burst through it. She kicked the brick away, and the door slammed shut.

"Won't stop them long," Galen panted. "Security has access to all doors."

"Don't need 'em to stop..." *pant* "...just slow 'em." She ran with Galen to the edge of the roof. She looked down the front of the building. People were arriving and departing far below. She took aim and threw the keycard like a skipping stone, to land on top of a departing carriage.

Then she pulled Galen behind the top of the stairwell – a small, square structure, like a lift shaft, sticking out above the roof.

She heard the door slam open and several people run out. Activating her hideaway matrix, she pulled Galen in behind herself to cover them both.

She put a finger to Galen's lips.

The guards' footsteps went all over the roof.

"They got away!" Mr Green yelled.

"Yeah, I don't see them. Must've climbed over the balconies. They're sure not here anymore." It was a deeper voice. Hope assumed a security guard.

"What did they take from you?" asked another.

"All I know is that drunken floozy took my access card, but they were in my office – they could've stolen anything from there!"

"Well, the tracker on your card's departing rapidly. I'm afraid we can't catch them on foot, but we'll send a drone to follow, and we'll be able to retrieve them as soon as they stop."

"That's not enough. Call the police! Send the sentinels after them!" he yelled.

"Ah, yeah, we're not breaking out the sentinels for a petty theft. We'll let the police know. But it would help if we knew what else might've been taken. Come back down with me. We'll check your office for anything missing."

The footsteps stopped at the stairwell door.

"Jonno?"

"Ya?"

"Can you set the drone in motion from here?"

"Sure thing, boss."

The door opened and two sets of footsteps disappeared back down the stairs. The other guard was still scuffling around, and she heard scraping noises, as if he were manoeuvring some kind of equipment.

The noise disappeared to the building's far-distant edge. Far enough that Hope breathed a belated sigh of relief.

She turned around and faced Galen, readjusting her position to make sure all his limbs were either within her perimeter or close enough to fully cover him. They'd need to stay still to avoid drawing attention to themselves, and as ever, it'd be a dead giveaway if anyone looked directly at them.

She relaxed, letting her muscles rest. But then she stiffened again.

The footsteps were coming back.

They approached and then passed the stairwell. She watched as the security guard walked right past them. Heavy headphones covered his ears, and his eyes were fixed on the building across from the wedding cake.

He passed beyond her visual range, but she heard him keep walking to the edge of the building. She didn't dare risk turning her head to look. But those headphones were good to see. Sound was the most likely thing to give them away.

Some kind of radio crackled, then went silent.

Galen was facing the guard, watching him wide eyed. He opened his mouth a fraction, but shut it again and glanced at Hope.

She held up her finger to his lips again.

The look on his face was a mix of terror and exhilaration.

She leaned close to his ear and whispered, "I don't think he can hear us, but we need to stay still until he's gone. We're too exposed. If he sees the movement, it'll draw his eyes. The hideaway won't be enough to cover us."

He nodded and looked at her oddly, weighing again.

Hope's body pressed up against Galen's as she concentrated on keeping the hideaway covering them both. After about two seconds, she became acutely conscious of his nearness; his warmth; his breath brushing across her skin, sending tiny tingles down her spine. She breathed out and turned her head away, trying to regain a modicum of composure.

"Do I disgust you that much?" he whispered.

"What?" she whispered back, blinking in confusion.

"I mean, I know you don't like what I do. You called me *dirty* once, and I feel you never let an opportunity pass to make me feel like it. But you don't need to pull away from me as though my touch revolts you." He turned his head away in shame.

Hope's eyes widened, and a slow smile spread across her face.

She leaned in just a little closer.

Galen looked back at her, his eyes widening in surprise.

Then she saw his eyes change to something warm and hungry that made her stomach flutter.

He opened his mouth, and she brought a finger to his lips to belay the words.

His pupils widened, which made her stomach flip over again. Leaning in closer, she slid her finger across his cheek and down to his jaw. She brought her nose up close, so it was just brushing the tip of his. She heard his breath catch, and his lips parted.

She reached forward with her lips, gently brushing them against his. Soft. Giving. Radiating warmth.

She looked up into his eyes. They were dark with heat.

He closed them languidly, reached forward himself, and this time brushed his lips across hers.

Feather light, but it sent tingles down her body. She closed her eyes and leaned in, brushing her lips gently across his jaw and towards his neck. She breathed in, deep. His cologne was a musky, sweet scent, with an almost buttery undertone. The combination brought to mind fresh croissants and jam. She smiled and lifted her mouth back to his again.

This time, he didn't join her.

She opened her eyes to see him staring at the man who was behind her.

"He's turned halfway towards us," he breathed.

His breath whispered across her skin, and she held back a shiver. His eyes turned, following the security guard as the man moved to the front edge of the rooftop.

The radio crackled to life again.

Galen tensed beneath her.

She laid a hand on his chest, to steady him, to calm him, she hoped. However, when she looked up, he was watching her again with that heat in his eyes. She smiled, but turned her head slowly so she could watch the guard.

"Y'ello?" The guard's voice was loud and paused frequently for responses they couldn't hear. "I haven't seen them either. The drone's nearly caught up with the carriage, though…"

"Just ahead, two minutes or so…"

"You what? *Nothing's* missing?…"

"Ha-ha. Yeah, maybe they broke in to make out. Hold on, we're at the carriage now. There's four occupants, and ah, yeah, I don't think it's them. The bloke'd need an awful lot more titties to blend in with these girls…"

"Yeah, I think they're long gone. I'll send it home on autopilot…"

"Okay, but it's your turn to sweep downstairs; I want to get back to the buffet. I'm starving."

Hope's eyes widened. The guard turned around, looking across the rooftop at a building on one side. "We need to move before the drone flies over us and he spots us. Can you move quietly?" she whispered urgently.

He shook his head, his eyes wide.

She could feel his fingers wriggling again. "Think of it like dancing. On your toes; smooth and easy. The moment he looks away, take us around the side of this block."

Galen's eyes were still wide, but he took one of her hands and placed the other on her waist.

The hands were sweaty, but his fingers were calm, his grip steady. He examined the ground around them and looked up at the security guard, waiting.

The guard was squinting into the distance. He reached up to take his headphones off – that was not good.

"Go!" she whispered.

He nodded once and spun her quickly towards the corner.

His footsteps were perfect as he spun them around the edge, but she cringed as her heel brushed through some loose gravel with a harsh scrape. She pulled him with her against the wall facing the back of the building. Galen was leaning in, tight against her.

She could no longer see the security guard, but she could hear him.

"Hey, I thought I heard something," he said. "I'm gonna take another look."

"Shit," she whispered. She pushed Galen away and peeked around the corner.

The security guard was creeping towards the wall, looking around. He'd pulled out his pistol, pointing it at the ground and advancing on their position. "Come out wherever you are. With your hands up or I will shoot!"

Hope pushed Galen back against the wall beside her, squeezing them both against the bricks to keep them under her hideaway. She peeked around the corner.

The man was walking towards them, holding the radio in his off-hand. "Can't see anything. I'll have eyes up here in a minute." He was nearly abreast of them, his head turning.

There was nothing she could do. She couldn't protect Galen with her hideaway if the guard was looking directly at them both. She could only protect herself!

She looked at Galen, stricken.

"I'm sorry," she mouthed.

Then she took her hand away from him and stepped back.

He was totally exposed.

The guard spun his head towards Galen, now completely visible.

Galen looked hurt, betrayed.

The guard was still turning, raising his gun. He opened his mouth.

Hope ripped off her right glove. She shoved her hand on the man's neck, activating the matrix she'd painted there, releasing a jolt of electricity that caused the guard to spasm. She yelped in pain and stepped back as he fell.

Galen froze. He blinked stupidly.

"Help me check he's okay!" she yelled, shaking her arm in pain. "Then we have to run again!"

Galen's eyes went wide, then he jumped into motion once more, going into professional mode. He checked the fallen man for life signs. "He's okay, just stunned, I think. What was that?"

Hope helped him heave the man into the recovery position. "Something new I've been cooking up. A magical taser, it overloads a person's neural system, and temporarily shuts it down - puts them to sleep. I figured I'd need something non-lethal if we got into a fix." She massaged her hand. "I wasn't expecting it to kick back into me so hard, though, and it took a massive chunk of my magic, but I guess it does the job in a pinch."

"But where's the matrix?" he asked her, his eyebrows drawn together as his glance ran over her empty hands.

Grinning, she raised her bare hand to him, so he could see where she'd painted the silvery matrix across her forearm.

He blinked. Twice. "I really should stop underestimating you."

She just raised an eyebrow and retrieved her fallen glove. "If he's okay, we have to get going. His buddy will come looking for him soon enough, and we don't want those sentinels after us." She looked down at the security guard. "Wait, is he going to recognise you and report you once he wakes?"

Galen looked up at her. "The guard? Unlikely. It's been a couple of years since I graduated, and the guards don't know every alumnus on sight."

She nodded and breathed a sigh of relief. "Good, good. Then let's get out of here." She leaned over the building's front edge and looked down.

"But we didn't get what we came for!"

She grinned back. "Sure we did." She waved her glove. "Right here, on the knuckles."

He looked confused.

"I had a run-in with Mr Green's nose back there. Should be good to track his movements directly now; plus, I grabbed a few papers before we left." She tapped the front of her dress.

He gaped in surprise.

"Dunno if they'll be any good, but hey, I figured it was worth a shot. Right now, though, our priority is to get down the front of this building before security comes back. I can shinny down the drainpipe onto the verandah – how about you?"

Galen turned ashen. "Hmm… now would be a bad time to point out I'm not so good with heights, yes?"

She looked up. "Oh. Um… well… we can try our luck in the stairwell, I guess. We'll probably make it down a couple of floors before the guard catches up to us." She tucked her glove into a pocket and started for the stairs, but Galen grabbed her hand to stop her.

He took a deep breath. "I didn't say I wouldn't do it." He still looked ashen, but he also looked determined. "But you may just need to talk to me over the edge." He nodded at her, his lips a grim line.

She smiled and nodded back, hitching up her skirts.

Hope lowered herself over the edge, feeling her way towards solid hand and footholds. When she had a comfortable grip, she dropped onto the verandah. Then she explained each step in detail to Galen, offering lots of encouragement.

He visibly screwed up his courage and took a deep breath before following in her wake.

"Nice one," she said. "You've got this."

"Just four more levels to go." He gave a shaky laugh.

She smiled encouragingly and began the second climb.

It went better. The balcony rail gave her sturdier handholds, and Galen grew in confidence.

The third went just as well, and Galen was getting the hang of it, only needing minimal coaxing and direction.

But the fourth meant landing on a verandah that wasn't empty.

Hope looked over the edge. Clusters of people were sitting at tables, drinking and chatting. Anywhere they could safely land, they'd be seen. She was just considering whether they could drop behind some ornamental bushes, to avoid being spotted, when a shout above them caught her ear.

They spun around. Mr Green was up there, looking down at them. He looked angry. Then he disappeared back over the edge.

"Time to go," Hope said.

"The guests will see us," Galen whispered.

"Doesn't matter. He'll call the guards. If we stay, they'll be on us in a minute, and now they have a reason to take us in."

"So, we run for it." Galen nodded.

She nodded back. "Yep. Time to go the easiest way." She clambered down over one more balcony edge and stepped onto a table below.

The people seated there jerked up in surprise, scattering their drinks.

"What do you think you're doing?" one of them spluttered.

"Sorry, coming through!" Hope yelled back as she helped Galen follow her down.

"Galen! What's going on?" The question came from behind them. Adora!

"Ah!" he replied, grinning sheepishly. "Hope had a run-in with one of the students, while drunk. We're just trying to get out of here!"

"Over the balconies?" she replied incredulously. "Good lord Galen, you could get yourself killed! I approve wholeheartedly." She grinned as she pulled them both inside.

"We need to avoid security," Hope said, pulling back to resist being dragged inside. "He called them on us, and they believe him, not us."

"Hope had to stun one to get free," Galen added.

Hope looked at him, surprised he'd share that detail. It was pretty incriminating.

Adora raised her eyebrows twice as high, looking bemused. "This one's trouble, Galen. I like her even more now – she'll be good for you."

He smirked and gave a non-committal shrug. "Reminds me of that time we all snuck into the Dean's office."

Adora grinned.

"We left him on the roof," Hope added, glancing between them. "He'll be fine, but it won't last long. Any chance you can help us get out of here?"

"Don't worry, I'll get you out the back way." Adora pulled them back inside but headed down a side corridor away from the stairwell.

No sooner had they turned a corner than they heard a shout coming from behind them. "Miss? Adora? Can I have a word?"

Adora shoved them both through the nearest doorway and closed it behind them.

They stood behind the door, breathless, listening to the other security guard's footsteps approach.

"James," Adora said, "is anything the matter?"

"I've got a small situation in progress. Two suspicious types on foot after they allegedly accosted one of the students. You haven't spotted a man and a woman fleeing through here, have you?" James asked her.

"Not at all James, are you sure they came this way?" Adora's voice sounded unconcerned.

"No idea. They've probably already split. We're just doing a sweep in case they haven't left yet – but if you haven't seen them, I'll let you go. I've got two more floors to check, then I'll join Jonno on break."

"Thanks, James. I'll keep an eye out."

"So," he said casually, "who's in the staffroom?"

Hope chilled. She looked around. This was a staffroom.

She positioned herself by the door with her hand out, drawing in a trickle of magic. She had enough to try her taser again if she had to.

Adora merely chuckled. "Scored with two today. I'll be out in a few minutes."

"Only a few minutes? You're losing your touch!"

Adora chuckled again. "Well, maybe a few more minutes than that."

"Some day I'm gonna ask you to be my wingman!" the guard added.

Adora snorted.

Hope heard footsteps recede back down the hall.

After a few moments, Adora opened the door, joining them, and declared mockingly, "You're staining my reputation!"

Galen snorted. "I'm not sure there's much of a reputation left to stain!"

Adora chuckled to herself and made her way through the staffroom to a door at the back. "Through here." She pointed and waved them on. "There's a fire exit here – hardly used. I'll flag down a cab for you – something suitably concealing." She led them down a dark set of concrete stairs that smelled of damp and pushed through a heavy fire door. It led into the sunken garden that encircled the back of the building.

They followed her to the corner and from there watched her confidently stride out to the carriageway at the front. Cabs still sporadically appeared, disgorging their patrons onto the candle-lit pathway.

Adora waited as a couple of open-top carriages went past, then flagged down the first closed cab to arrive. She gestured to Hope and Galen.

They scampered out of the hiding spot and climbed aboard.

Galen muttered, "thanks, Adora," as he hopped in.

"Any time!" Adora said, nodding, then smiling again. "So, have you kissed her yet?"

He blushed and shuffled himself along the back seat.

"Hah!" Adora exclaimed. "I'll take that as a yes." She looked between them. "It's meant to be my job to make sure your life is more exciting, but I think your girl here is performing admirably."

"Thanks," Hope said, hopping in after Galen.

"I'll see what I can do to smooth things over with security for you," Adora said, closing the carriage door for Hope. "They've gotten used to departmental pranks by now."

Hope smiled gratefully at her.

The cabbie took off down the carriageway and Adora waved them off.

Hope looked out the window as the cab pulled away. She wasn't sure, but she thought she saw a face looking down from over the edge of the top floor. She waved to him as they left.

Unbeknownst to Hope, Mr Green nodded back, a vicious grin on his face. He would've waved back too, but he had to balance the large drone controls instead.

21 - Goodnight

Hope jerked awake at a light touch. The cab was slowing down. "M'awake!" she slurred in sleep-talk. She blinked the blur from her eyes and recognised her own street.

"We're here," Galen murmured to her. "Would you like some help? I did think I might need to carry you in." He was smirking again.

She shook her head, rubbed her eyes, and stretched. "Thanks, but I'll be okay."

"You really are a sleepy drunk," he remarked, grinning. He hopped out of the cab and walked around to her side.

She'd already opened the door but was grateful his hand was there to help heave her upright. The air had turned brisk, a cool wind coming up from the ocean and washing away the late-summer air. It cleared her head a little, but her eyes were still drooping. Fondly visualising her cosy bed, she yawned, rubbed her eyes, and turned to say goodbye.

Galen was standing there, awkwardly, expectantly. But looking as though he was trying not to.

A slow smile spread across her face. "So..."

"I guess I..." he said simultaneously.

Both of them laughed nervously.

She gestured at him. "You first."

"I guess I should get home. I'm afraid I'm running on fumes."

A small part of her heart quivered and burst, deflating inside her. "Oh, of course. We've been pushing things hard lately."

"Unless... Do we need to follow up on Mr Green?" He gestured at the rolled-up glove she was clutching to her chest.

She hastily stuffed it into a pocket. "I might take a leaf out of your book and keep it in the fridge tonight. It'll keep well enough. We can try again tomorrow morning when we're fresh."

He looked relieved and… was that a hint of disappointment? She wasn't sure. It was probably wishful thinking on her part.

"Okay, so tomorrow then… 9 am?" he asked.

"Eight, if you can," she counter-offered. "We should get on this ASAP. The Conjunction is two days away from full strength. We need to be done tracking down the dream steel before then, and we'll only have a day left for the, ah… *retrieval*." She flicked a glance at the waiting cabbie. He was out of earshot, but still…

"Right, right." Galen shifted from one foot to the other. "So, I guess I'll see you tomorrow."

"Yes. Tomorrow," she replied, hovering. She snorted and turned to the door. Then stopped. Galen had taken hold of her hand. She turned back with both eyebrows raised.

He snatched the hand back suddenly. "Sorry, I didn't mean to imply…" Now he began to turn away, but Hope shot out her hand and put it on his shoulder.

He turned back, and she stepped closer. His look of surprise changed to a slow smile. He stepped in and lowered his face to hers, his arms sliding around her waist.

She closed her eyes as his lips met hers.

Soft. Exploratory. Hungry but gentle.

She breathed in, deep and satisfied. Drinking him in.

She pulled away a tiny amount. Holding his head with her hands, she brushed her thumbs down his neck and up again, watching goosebumps rise on his skin. His eyes closed in pleasure. A slow blink like a satisfied cat.

She looked up into those eyes and brushed her lips gently over his mouth one more time.

"Until tomorrow," she whispered.

A smile grew on his face. "Until tomorrow," he whispered back, then he drew away. He waited next to the cab, the door open, while she found her key and successfully unlocked her front door. He gave her a small wave and a departing smirk before hopping back in.

She savoured the grin she had on her face as she crept inside and dropped her jacket on the hook. The flat was dark and quiet. Felicity and Sam usually turned in early.

A soft, tinkling sound made her pause.

Was that glass?

Not hearing anything else, she continued towards her room.

Then came a shriek of fear.

Hope bolted for Felicity's room. She whipped open the door, slamming it against the wall. Then froze in horror.

Felicity and Sam sat upright, still half entangled in their bedsheets and frozen in terror at the creature perched on the bed and hovering above them.

The head of a king cobra swayed before them, cape erect and fangs bared. It hissed menacingly.

It was grafted onto a long, furred but sinuous body – a ferret or a stoat. All four paws were gripping the sheet, tiny claws dug in tight. As she watched, a second such creature dropped through a broken hole in the window and scuttled up onto the bed to join its mate.

Felicity turned her face to Hope. It was white with terror. She opened her mouth to speak.

"Don't move!" came a voice from the window.

Hope spun towards it to see Mr Green looking in through the newly made hole. His eyes sparkled with malicious glee. "I can control them to some extent. I could make them bite the little *girl*, or not, depending on what I wanted. But if you make a sudden move… well… instinct is a powerful thing, and I don't think I could command them to stop fast enough to belay their strike." He sounded smug, satisfied.

Hope had never wanted to smack somebody in the nose as much as she did right now. She gritted her teeth and stayed still. "What do you want?"

He smiled wider. "All I want is for you to leave me alone."

Hope's eyebrows shot up.

"I know what you want from me," he yelled. "You want my precious dream steel!"

The two cobra heads hissed angrily, making Hope nervous. Her palms were greasy with sweat.

"Well, it's mine and you can't have it. So give up on following me or pestering me any further." His eyes narrowed. "Do you have a tracking signifier for me?"

Hope bit her lip but didn't reply. It was all she had left.

"Answer me!" he commanded.

The twin snakes hissed louder, swaying faster.

"Yes!" she yelled back desperately. "Make them back off!"

"Throw it to my pretties. Or I will kill your family now, while you watch."

She scrabbled in a pocket, retrieving the glove. Then hesitated. If she threw it at the snake, it could strike. Instead, she held it carefully and inched it towards the bed.

One cobra swayed towards her. She reached forward with the glove as the cobra approached the edge of the bed. It swayed towards her hand, and she dropped the glove with a squeak of fear. It landed near the creature's tiny feet. The cobra hissed and stooped, struggling to pick it up in its jaws and transfer it to a tiny forepaw.

"Excellent!" Mr Green said. "And now for the important part!"

She looked at him, confused.

Suddenly, the other cobra struck at Sam. Sam shrieked in pain.

"No!" Felicity screamed, yanking them back out of reach.

"No!" Hope echoed. She leaped forward and drew her magic into her fists, ready to throw.

The two cobra-ferrets retreated out of reach. They raised their capes and hissed menacingly, swaying at her.

"Why?" she shrieked.

Mr Green merely tutted. "She won't die – not yet, anyway."

Hope paused in confusion, looking between him, the cobras, and Sam.

"They haven't bitten her. It was just a scratch. For the blood, you see. But I can tell you that if you don't release that magic you're gathering right now, I swear I'll have them bite her – and then she most certainly will die."

One cobra turned to face Sam.

Hope's eyes darted to them, curled in Felicity's arms.

Felicity was hurriedly examining their leg. "It is just a scratch! I see the claw marks." The relief in her voice was palpable.

Hope's breath whooshed out of her and she slowly released the magic from her hands.

The cobra backed off.

"Good!" Mr Green declared. "Now listen closely. I know where your family lives, and I now have the means to track this child, no matter where you hide. I'll be keeping an eye on you and yours. So if you know what's good for you, you'll keep out of my affairs, or I'll send my pretties after your family – and this time, I won't hesitate to have them killed. The little *girl* first."

Hope's face hardened, and her eyes blazed. The fear had given way to a searing rage.

"Do you hear me?" He was yelling so much that flecks of spittle flew out of his mouth and his face was mottled red.

Her eyes burning, Hope nodded. "Oh, I hear you."

The snakes hissed in unison and were slowly advancing on the bed.

Sam cringed and sobbed with shaky breaths.

"I understand. Call them off!" She itched to draw her magic again, but she wouldn't out-draw the cobra strikes, and Mr Green would sense it the moment she began. All she had to offer him were her words. "I swear I won't follow you anymore. I don't care about the dream steel, just leave my family alone – please!" She imbued her voice with as much sincerity as she could muster, desperately hoping he wasn't so unstable as to kill them, regardless of what she said.

But a moment later, he nodded, apparently satisfied. "As I said, I'll be keeping an eye on you. If you come anywhere near me again, I will not be so merciful."

He turned and disappeared into the night. The cobras retreated, slithering back across the bedspread and flowing over the window sill and into the surrounding darkness.

Hope dropped to the floor, her heart racing from the adrenaline still surging through her veins.

Sam turned to Felicity and started crying. Felicity gripped them, white-knuckle tight.

Sam struggled free of both her and the bedclothes and, still crying, threw themself at Hope.

Hope flung her arms around them and cried into their hair. A moment later, she felt Felicity's arms engulf them both.

The front door crashed open, and suddenly Galen was there.

Hope scowled.

*Why is he here **now**? Too late to help with anything. Useless!*

He drew a breath. "What happened? I heard screams from the street." His eyes darted around the room, taking in the crying huddle and the broken glass. He looked down at her cowering on the floor with her family.

Hope's scowl deepened. A surge of irrational rage ran through her.

What right does he have to intrude on our pain?

"You missed him!" she yelled in reply, the last of the adrenaline burning in her words. "He's gone!"

With a shaky voice, Felicity said, "a man threatened us with some kind of hybrid snake."

"Mr Green," Hope spat.

Galen stepped in and reached for all three of them.

"Get off me!" Hope growled.

He jumped back, stung.

Felicity looked between them and raised her eyebrows. Sam pulled away and crawled into Felicity's lap, shying away from Hope.

Hope's heart shrank. She sat back, alone, and wrapped her arms around her knees.

"Can I do anything to help?" Galen asked her gently and reached a hand out to her. "Do you need a place to stay tonight?"

She pulled away. She didn't need help from somebody she'd barely met. "You can go home to your hospital and leave us alone." She dragged her fist across her eyes to clear away the angry tears that were threatening to run down her face.

Looking drawn, he dropped the hand.

Felicity looked up at her again, her eyes wide and her face a blank mask.

Hope dried her hand on her sleeve. Her heart was pumping fast. Heavy feelings swirled inside her. "He took the glove. Our last clue. We're back to nothing, and the Conjunction is in two days! I should've taken the money and run – but no. I stepped in to save you, and now my family's in danger."

Galen recoiled, then dropped his face into his hands as the barrage rolled over him.

Hope was breathing fast. She could see she'd hurt him but couldn't stop the words from boiling out of her. "It's your fault! I don't want any of this. I don't want you. So please, just go."

Still curled over, he murmured into his hands, "You're right." He uncurled and turned to her. "You're right. I'm so sorry I dragged you into all this. You've gone above and beyond for me, and all I do in return is put you and your family in the line of fire."

She blinked. Her self-righteous anger stuttered.

Galen took a deep and shaky breath and stood up, ready to go. "If you need a place to stay, I can still offer you a room at the hospital, but it's up to you. The money's yours, either way. I'll bring it around tomorrow. You've done everything I could ask of you to help." He turned back to her, and his eyes were brimming with unspent tears. "I am truly sorry for putting your family in danger." He dropped his gaze and slunk out.

Hope fell to the floor, the last vestiges of anger disintegrating; to be replaced with guilt. After biting his head off, she'd expected him to bite back. Instead, he'd agreed, and then apologised to her. She didn't deserve that; she deserved to be shouted at!

She wrapped herself in a ball, trying to quash the upwelling of shame.

Felicity's arms wrapped around her, and Sam crawled back into Hope's lap. It gave her the space to push away the spiralling emotions and try to put a lid on her nascent fear. But it was bubbling up again anyway, threatening to boil over. "This is my fault!" she wailed, pressing her face into Sam's hair. "I've endangered us all!"

"Don't be ridiculous. This is not your fault," Felicity responded, calmly stroking her hair. "And it isn't his either. You did this to help save Sam's arm, and that wasn't any of our faults; although judging by the creatures we've just seen, the arsehole outside the window might have something to do with it."

It shocked Hope to hear the burning rage in her sister's words, a rage she hadn't heard from Felicity in a long time. Felicity's teeth were bared in a snarl, and her eyes were glittering. She turned to Hope, and her eyes narrowed. "But I can tell you it's not your new date's fault, either."

"But..."

"No 'buts'! I heard what he said, and I heard what you said. He was just trying to help, and you were grossly unfair to him!"

Hope glared at her. Felicity glared right back.

Hope dropped her eyes to the floor and held Sam closer. "But it *is* his fault. If I hadn't..."

"I don't want to hear it's his fault. You helped him, and that was your decision – and to be honest, I'm glad you did. You've been trying your darndest to pretend you have to be selfish, saying it's all for our sakes."

"What do you mean *pretend*? I have to think about us! It's what we've always had to do to survive on the streets."

"In case you haven't noticed, we don't live on the streets any more. It's been a long time since either of us lived rough or begged for jobs from Henry. I thought we were trying our best to get clear of that way of life!"

Hope looked at her in surprise.

"Well," Felicity continued, "getting clear means more than just not taking jobs from Henry; it means changing your mindset. You don't have to pretend to be a hard-case to keep us alive anymore. We can afford to be kind, to help other people if they're hurting. You don't have to push everyone away."

Hope stared at her in shock, then she felt a bubbling rush pour up her throat and she burst into tears. They ran down her face and into Sam's hair. Sam wriggled in closer.

Felicity let her face soften as she reached over to her nightstand and fetched Hope a handful of tissues.

Hope blew her nose and continued to sob. When all the tears were spent, she was able to summon a watery smile.

"How about I make you a cup of tea," Felicity said.

She hadn't asked. She didn't need to.

In this family, tea meant love. Tea was the calm aftermath of any emotional storm. It was how you showed you still cared. So, Felicity stood up and headed for the kitchen, knowing that Hope would surely follow.

"Thanks," Hope whispered, leaning up against the kitchen table while Felicity pottered around the kitchen, collecting mugs and tea bags.

Sam fetched milk and put bags in cups while Hope stared down at her hands. Sam dragged a chair over to Hope and snuggled up against her. Eventually came the gurgling sound of pouring water, and a warm cup of family love was pressed into her hands.

Felicity sat down on Hope's other side, putting her arm around her shoulders. Hope leaned into her and sighed.

Felicity smiled. "Good, and tomorrow you should go and apologise to your new date."

Hope froze, then frowned. "I don't think I want him to be my date any more."

"Don't be ridiculous." Felicity blew on her tea to cool it.

"I'm not being ridiculous. I just think we're not meant to be together."

Felicity's eyebrows rose and fell again. "Oh, right. You're doing *that* again, are you?"

Hope looked up, confused. "Doing what?"

"Well, he *is* hot."

"What's that got to do with it?"

Felicity raised a single eyebrow and smirked at her. "Why don't you tell me?"

Hope glared at her. "I have no idea what you're talking about!"

Felicity sighed and rolled her eyes so hard it looked like she might have injured herself. "This is what you always do. Push everybody away if they show any interest in hanging around – even friends. You're afraid they'll be too good to be true, so rather than take a chance, you flee. It's excruciating to watch you do it to yourself, over and over. You systematically destroy every chance of happiness that comes your way!"

Hope pushed herself back from the table and wrapped her arms around herself, scowling down at her steaming mug. "What do you want from me? I barely know the guy."

Felicity's voice softened. "Look, I'm not saying you should marry him and have his babies next week. He just seems nice, so it might be worth your while continuing to help him out rather than abandoning him at the first mis-step… and, meanwhile, have a conversation?"

"A 'conversation'," she replied drily.

"Yes, that's all. Just have a talk about what you both want, and then take a chance and give it a go; see whether it goes anywhere."

Hope frowned. "I think I've ruined any chance of having that happen."

"I think you might be pleasantly surprised. But only if you can gird your loins and take a chance. It's time to change your mindset, remember?"

Hope reached out and pulled Felicity and Sam close, her eyes still damp with tears. "Well, regardless, we can't stay here tonight – not with a broken window, when that madman can return and wreak havoc on us."

"What's the alternative?" Felicity asked.

Hope thought for a minute. Was she okay with Galen's offer? Did she know him that well? Staying there by herself was one thing, but Sam and Felicity, too? With a weird, undead orderly and the crazy Mr Green thrown on top? It still seemed the only reasonable option right now, regardless of how personally awkward it felt. She nodded to herself. "I think we can still go to Galen's. He has lots of rooms free, and regardless of what I need to do to make it up to him, I'm sure he won't mind having us stay."

Felicity looked at Sam and then back to Hope. "You were ready to throw him away, and now you trust him with our lives – with Sam's life?"

Hope raised an eyebrow. "Weren't you just trying to persuade me to make it up with him?"

Felicity looked flatly back at her. "Making up with him is one thing; my family's safety is another. Can we trust him?"

Hope thought for a moment. "I can't know for sure. But so far he's been decent, even in the face of defeat – and we need to go somewhere that Mr Green can't easily reach us. Galen's hospital is like a tiny castle. Also, he's a practitioner. We can put wards up and share the watch. And regardless of our differences, he still seems to want to help. I mean, if you're not comfortable putting Sam's life in his hands, we could get a hotel room; but our funds are low, and I'd rather stay with a friend – somewhere I think is relatively safe."

"You don't need to justify it to me. If you think it's okay, it's worth a shot. I wanted to make sure you were comfortable after the disagreement you've had." She released both Hope and Sam. "We need to catch up to him before he goes to bed. I'll start packing an overnight bag." She stood up, slipped her shoes on, and started gathering clothing and jewellery.

Hope kissed the top of Sam's head. "You've been quiet. How're you doing?"

Sam cringed into her arms a moment, then turned a tear-stained face up to her. "I'm sorry," they sobbed.

Hope raised her eyebrows in surprise. "What are you sorry for? I'm the one who's sorry."

"I'm sorry he got my blood. Now he can find us no matter where we go!"

"Don't you dare try to apologise for that! You had nothing to do with what happened – it's one hundred percent not your fault!"

Sam went quiet for a moment, looking up at her through their tears. "I'm sorry I didn't come and say hello straight away when you got back this morning. I was hurt, and so mad at you for being away, and I know that was stupid." They put their head down on Hope's shoulder. "I just wanted somebody to be mad at."

Hope sighed as she realised the truth of the statement – she'd reacted to Galen in exactly the same way. "That's true of everyone, sometimes." She cradled Sam and squeezed them even tighter.

Sam reached around her with their one arm and awkwardly squeezed her back, then let her go.

Hope looked Sam over. She avoided looking directly at the missing arm. "How are you, really?"

Sam lifted the bandaged stump and looked at it. "It doesn't hurt anymore, after the potions; but the doctor said there's still damage inside and it'll take a while to heal completely." They looked up at Hope earnestly. "Mum told me about... about the options." They looked down at the floor. "I don't think I'm ready to decide yet, but I'm glad this isn't forever."

22 - Trouble at the hospital

Barely five minutes later, all three of them were boarding a cab, headed across town to Galen's hospital. The cabbie, sensing the mood, kept up a light stream of patter, while taking them through shortcuts and byways to make good time across the crowded city. By the time the hospital's crenellated roof drew into view, they were joking alongside him.

That all stopped the moment they pulled around to the front of the hospital.

"Keep going," Hope hissed, her face pale. "Around the corner, out of sight."

The cabbie fell silent and obliged.

"What's happening?" Sam asked.

Hope turned around to the back seat. "Nothing good. I think my friend is in deep trouble." She turned to Felicity. "Stay here while I have a closer look." She jumped out but stopped short.

Felicity, leaning out of the cab, had grabbed her arm. "We can't stay here. It isn't safe." After thinking for a moment, she added, "I'll take us to Pam's."

"You can't go there!" Hope said, scandalised. "It's not appropriate for Sam!"

"That's my decision to make, not yours. Besides, we don't have a choice! You've already pointed out that any hotel we can afford wouldn't have enough security. Pam's is safe – you know that – and Sam will be just fine. We'll both be fine. Now go, save your new boyfriend, and come join us when you're done." Felicity's tone brooked no reply. She pulled back into the cab, waving Hope off.

Hope watched it carry her family away, leaving her very alone. They'd be safe enough for the time being. Right now, she had to find

Galen and see whether she had a chance of helping him.

She crept down a narrow alleyway and snuck up to the corner. Peeking around the edge, she tried to make sense of the scene she was confronted with. Tucked behind the hospital's high roof floated the gigantic form of a zeppelin, its engines rumbling, holding it steady. It was one of the regular police patrol ships, not a heavy warship outfitted for battle, but it was imposing, and it meant a full police squad was nearby.

On the ground below, a pair of armed men were poking around Galen's truck, as yet unopened. Another two officers stood over Galen, who was kneeling on the ground facing away from her. He had his hands on his head and was pale and shaking.

Somehow, Mr Green was present and in earnest conversation with one of the officers.

Hope went cold.

How the hell had he gotten here that quickly, and what was he telling them?

She should run, now – while she had the chance.

Whatever Mr Green was saying, it would implicate Galen, and by extension, herself. There was nothing she could do here. She didn't owe Galen anything. She certainly couldn't take on a full squad of police on her own, and this time they would see through her lies and fabrications – Mr Green would make sure of that. She should leave right now to keep her family safe.

But the sight of Galen's pale and shaking hands held her transfixed. She couldn't just leave him here, alone, afraid he might die at any moment. He had no one to rely on – nobody to come save him except her.

Sighing, she pulled the familiar itchy tickle of the hideaway over herself and crept forward to get a better view. A row of decorative trees ran along that side of the road. She hunched along it, staying underneath it to conceal herself from the zeppelin's crew, until she crept close enough to make out what Mr Green was saying.

"Yes, that's him, I swear. He was in my office rifling through my things, and papers are missing! My life's work, and he was in there pillaging it!"

"What did you say your specialty was?" the officer asked him, taking notes.

"Zoological neurochemistry and alchemical nootropics." He folded his arms and narrowed his eyes.

The officer paused a moment to get the information down. "Is that anything to do with building chimerae?"

Mr Green visibly paused. Then he turned a vicious smile on Galen. "No, officer, but my lab partner shares an office with me, and that's his specialty. Why?" he asked, looking innocent. "Is that relevant?"

"It might be," the officer replied non-committal. "Is there anything else you can tell us?"

Mr Green shook his head. "No, that's everything. May I go home now, please? It's been a long day."

"That's all for now. If you've got any more information, please call." The officer handed over the usual small white card, which Mr Green pocketed.

Another officer approached and spoke to his partner. "I think you'll want to take a look at this."

Mr Green lingered, trying to overhear what they were saying, but the officers glared at him and he moved away.

Hope watched the officers approach the truck, one of them holding up a device to take some kind of reading.

"Do we have enough for cause?"

"The readings are above regulation. Could be legit or could be something else."

"Can you get eyes in there somehow?"

"Way ahead of you. And this is what I wanted you to see." They held up something like a small frame – a window for the other officer to see through.

"Holy shit. It's full of matrices – high-grade ones!"

"Yep. And they're all interconnected; this is all one working here."

"Peterson, can you come over here? What do you think of this?"

A clean-cut man wearing a white lab coat joined them and looked through the device. He traced the outlines, moving the frame to view them from various angles. "Don't know for sure – something biological? Could be medical."

"I'm a doctor," Galen, still kneeling nearby, called out to them.

"Most doctors don't have Grade-A conjuration matrices in their personal vehicles, sir."

"I'm also a researcher. An experimental scientist!" He sounded exasperated and scared. "I'm working on some ideas for emergency resuscitation."

The officer raised an eyebrow at Peterson.

Peterson shrugged. "Well, yeah – it could be that."

"'Could be'? Could it be used to make our chimerae?"

"I can't say for sure. It's not my specialty, but... maybe?"

"All right. That's enough cause for me to impound this truck. Take it in, folks, we'll have the scienticians look it over."

Galen visibly deflated. His skin was ashen, and his dark eyes looked longingly at his precious truck.

"All right, I'm gonna call it in and get a search warrant for the truck and for the hospital." He turned to Galen. "Sir, we're taking you in for questioning."

"I haven't done anything!" Galen insisted.

"Then we won't find anything incriminating, will we? Now, you've got two options. We could wait – do the search when I get the warrant, but it'll be easier if you let us have a quick look around right now. Otherwise, we'll be doing a much more thorough investigation, without your co-operation or your presence – up to you." He gave a shrug.

Galen sat up and gritted his teeth. Then he blinked, and flicked his eyes to the hospital and back.

For a moment, Hope could swear they stopped on her. But she knew she was tucked away very well this time. Nobody down here could see through her hideaway... and yet...

"I'll wait for the search warrant first," Galen stated, "and then and only then will I let you in." Then he flicked his eyes towards her and then deliberately up to the window of the second floor.

Hope looked up, and realised who must be standing there, barely visible as more than a small, dark shape. Still looking up at the sky. "Shit!" she whispered, trying to see whether she could spot anything from here. Nothing obvious.

She looked back at Galen, who looked like he was trying his best not to glance in her direction. What did he expect her to do? An entire team of police officers was camped outside his door. Did he expect her to sneak a zombie past them? They'd shoot first and ask questions later. Then who'd support her family?

She looked at him again. He wasn't looking her way, and yet he was no longer the drooping, ashen-faced wreck he'd been a moment before. He wasn't exactly confident, but he looked like... well... like he thought everything would be ok.

Like he trusted her to have his back.

It hit her like a brick in the stomach. That trust.

Tendrils of it worked their way around her heart and drew together, tight.

She knew it was reckless. Her family depended on her. But they were safely tucked away, whereas Galen had nobody but her to depend on.

That did it for her. He'd put his trust in her, and she'd try her best to make sure that trust was well placed.

She quietly withdrew from the scene. She navigated a path along the narrow street, underneath trees and awnings, until she could safely duck across the road and around a corner of the hospital. As she moved, she spotted Mr Green, grinning and sneaking away out of sight, down another side street.

What is he up to? Nothing good, I'll wager.

She shook her head in frustration.

No time to deal with that right now. She had to figure out how to get one undead orderly out of the hospital before an entire squad of cops searched the place.

She crept her way through the greenery, staying under the cover of the hedges until she'd reached the far side of the hospital. She risked a peek out through the branches. Good. The wind had blown the zeppelin a little further away, so the roof was now in between her and any obvious sight lines. Should be safe to make a run for the wall.

A few metres' dash and she stood there, looking up.

There weren't any easy ways in from down here – all the windows were barred. But there was a drainpipe, and the building's corners had decorative ribbed bands in the sandstone that would allow for handholds. She spotted a sash window high up on the third floor. She couldn't be sure, but from this vantage point, it looked like it was open a few inches.

Her lucky night! She'd get to free-climb a building in a cocktail dress. Good thing it wasn't a pencil skirt.

She found a patch of dirt and dried her sweaty palms in the dust. Then she began to climb.

The first storey was easy enough – the bars on the windows were cold but were great handholds. She pulled herself up them and eyed the distance to the decorative edging that was arranged along the bottom of the windows another storey up – a false balcony, too far from her current height to jump to it safely. She could get there by climbing the sandstone ridges, and they were wider on the far side of the corner.

Just as she was reaching around the sandstone for the first good grip, she heard a rustle in the bushes behind her.

She froze and re-adjusted her grip so she could better see below.

Mr Green was back, and he was looking up at her!

No, wait, not at her. At the building. Her hideaway was still in place and, tucked around the corner in the dark, it must be just enough.

His eyes were passing over her, hunting for something. If he'd spotted her, surely he'd be yelling for the police by now. What was he doing?

She watched him while holding very still.

He was bent over something. There was a green flash and a puff of smoke, and suddenly she saw the cobra-ferret thing. It ran towards the building, fast and fluid, and within a heartbeat was up the wall, clambering up the bottom-storey windows.

When it came abreast of her, it stopped.

Hope was transfixed by the sight.

It turned its head from side to side – its tiny, reptilian tongue scenting the air, hunting for her. It turned its beady, black eyes on her and hissed.

She crouched, petrified, hypnotised by those black eyes. She couldn't move; there was nowhere to go. It was too high to jump down.

"Go!" hissed the voice from below. "What are you waiting for? Put the papers inside!"

The cobra turned its head towards the ground to glare at Mr Green, and she saw the creature was carrying something long, white and rolled up. Tucked up against its body with straps.

Its eyes flashed in anger. It turned one last, menacing hiss on her, then continued to climb. She watched as it disappeared up and over the false balcony edge and in through the open sash window she'd spotted.

She breathed in deeply now that the danger had passed.

Mr Green, however, was still below, peering up at the open window. She couldn't move until he left. Her arms ached, and she carefully re-adjusted her grip.

A few moments later, the cobra-ferret returned. It skittered down the building's edge, tail first, and looking back over its shoulder to watch its steps. The papers were gone. It hissed at her as it passed her once again but didn't break stride.

She stuck out a tongue at it, but it ignored her and jumped down the last few feet to the ground.

Mr Green picked it up and crept away into the night.

Hope's fingers were cramping. She took a moment to release one and shake it, then the other. After a moment, she began her arduous ascent once again. Her shaky hands slithered along the sandstone, feeling out the holds. She fitted her body in between the last of the bars and hung off the corner, reaching up to the tiny edge of the false balcony above. Her bare toes barely gripped the narrow decorative ledge, but she pushed herself up.

Just as she got her first real handhold, her feet slipped, and she slammed a hip into the wall. Hanging there by one badly scraped arm, she gritted her teeth and felt around below her for a toehold. There were none, but she put her toes up against the rough sandstone, and pulled against her hand, then swung herself up and grabbed on with the other hand. Her toes slipped again, and her knee jarred against the stone, too.

Ow!

But she had two handholds now.

She heaved herself up over the false balcony's edge and in through the window, falling in a pile on the floor.

"A bathroom again?" she grumbled. "At least this one looks like they washed it this century."

23 - Getting out of trouble

Hope sat for a few moments, catching her breath, rubbing her aching muscles, and inspecting her various scratches and scrapes. But she only gave herself a minute before she hauled herself back upright and began to search.

She looked down the long corridor, eyeing up the number of doors.

How far can a cobra-headed ferret run inside of a minute? It scrambled up the wall pretty fast, so probably quite a distance.

She ducked her head into each of the adjacent rooms.

First, a small laundry – empty except for a washer and dryer. The next was a bedroom with a strange, musty smell, the window and curtains drawn closed. No one had used this room in a long time.

Maybe this was his brother's room?

She hastily retreated, closing the door behind her.

The next open door was a home gym. Free weights and mats, but otherwise empty.

The only other open door was across the hall. She approached hesitantly and peeked through. Some kind of study. The curtains were wide open, and through them she could see the zeppelin floating close by, cameras pointed in all directions.

The rolled-up papers were tucked away on a desk on the far side of the room. Unfortunately, between here and there was empty space. Nothing between her and the piercing eyes of the cameras but a rickety chair and Galen's black leather bag, presumably still full of cash – out of reach, and way too exposed.

She retreated to the doorway. If she rushed through here, she'd be spotted for sure. The windows were enormous. Any movement would attract the watchful eyes floating only ten metres away.

The cameras would have no problem piercing her hideaway.

Is it worth it? What's in those papers? It must be something pretty incriminating. Mr Green threatened my family with death – but is it better or worse than finding an animated corpse?

She huffed in frustration. Then she sighed. She just couldn't risk it. Maybe later the cameras would be more distracted. She eased back down the hall.

First things first: get the orderly hidden away – that's the higher priority. Arrested over dodgy papers was better than shot on sight, right?

Safe from camera view now, she ran down the hall, then the stairs, until she reached the second level. The stairs opened up beside the kitchen and she crept through into the mess hall beyond. The curtains were closed, but the walkway beyond had none. She tiptoed over to a window and twitched the curtain aside to get a peek outside.

The zeppelin was still hovering in place nearby. She slid her arm alongside the window and tested the latch. It clicked open. She nudged it to see whether it'd move. It opened silently a few centimetres before jamming solid. It wasn't much, but it did the job. She heard voices below and the hum of the engines had changed from a distant vibration to a low thrum.

Nothing sounded too alarming yet. She couldn't hear anybody at the doors. They were busy doing something near the truck. There was still a chance to do this the stealthy way.

She crept away from the window, heading for the door. She opened it a crack and looked out.

There it was, at the far end of the hall, staring up at the sky. In the dark. And now she could see why it hadn't been visible to the zeppelin. It had sat down on the floor to look up, all the better to see the stars. The moon had disappeared under the horizon's edge, fast approaching the Conjunction that'd preceded it, but the stars were lovely tonight.

She glanced through the crack at the zeppelin. As long as the orderly didn't move, it'd remain out of view. But if it stood, or moved back even slightly, it might attract somebody's attention. It was only its total quietude that had kept it out of sight so far.

Were she to call to it, it might try to stand. She needed it to stay below the level of the windowsill in order to move without alerting the Imperium to its presence. And she had to act soon. It couldn't be that much longer before they got that warrant. Warrants were pretty quick to come through these days – with emergency fast-tracking in place to cope with the Conjunction crazies.

She tucked her skirt up again, dropped to her hands and knees, and crawled. The floor was hard and scraped on her bruised hands and grazed knee. She grumbled under her breath. "Why am I doing this again?"

She crawled along the floor towards the orderly, keeping well below the line of window sills. It was as still as the proverbial grave and staring up at the sky.

I know nothing about this thing. Will it understand what I say? Will it obey me like it does Galen?

She had a vague memory of hearing Galen talking to it during the surgery, but recalled it hadn't gone well. She crawled up to it as closely as she dared.

It didn't look up.

She looked it over. Its skin was still mottled and grey, and some parts were taking on a greenish tinge.

And the smell! It was definitely worse today.

She turned her head away and breathed deeply. Then she turned back.

"Hey!" she whispered.

No reaction.

She waved her hand in front of its face, trying to break his gaze.

Nothing.

Crap!

She sighed again.

Okay. Time to try dropping the hideaway.

She felt the tingles rush over her and away.

Finally, the orderly noticed her.

It turned what remained of its face towards her. No emotion registered on that gaunt visage, but it did make a sound. A quiet, hissing noise that meant nothing to her, but the subsequent stench increased enough for her to choke out a cough.

She heard a yell. "Hey, I heard something!"

Double crap!

The orderly turned its face back up to the window.

She saw a torch sweeping over the window from below. The orderly followed the beam with its eyes.

"What did you see?"

"Nothing, but I swear I heard someone coughing."

Hope waved her hand at the orderly. "We have to go, now," she whispered. "This way!" She turned back towards the kitchen and waved to the orderly. "Come with me!" She crawled away a few shuffling steps.

The orderly shifted to all fours and took a few halting crawls of its own.

"Can we get a bit more light up there?"

"Sure. Air 42, can you throw some light for us – second-floor windows?"

Hope crawled forward a few more paces.

The orderly followed.

We're getting there, we'll be fine.

Suddenly, the hall filled with light. Bright. Blinding as the sun! It swept the hall from side to side.

She ducked her head and blinked away the glare. Only to see that the orderly had stopped crawling and had hunched over, getting ready to stand!

She didn't think. She leaped. Collided with its legs. Sweeping them out from under it. Landing together in a tangle of limbs.

She gagged at the stench and shuddered at the touch of its awful grey skin. But at least it was below the level of the window. She tried hard to calm her breathing, and the panicky, fluttery feeling that touching its skin had caused in her. She jammed that feeling down tight – no time for a freak-out right now.

The zombie lifted a hand to point at the light.

She grabbed it and pulled it back down. "I know, it's shiny. Like the sun, yes? You like the sun, don't you?" She whispered.

The orderly looked at her, blank-faced. Then nodded!

Good grief! Actual communication with the dead!

She took a wary breath, hesitant to breathe in the smell, and start gagging again. "I know you like the sun, but this is not the sun; it's people. We need to hide from these people to keep Galen safe – do you remember Galen?"

It... *he*... nodded.

Out of curiosity, she asked him, "Do you like Galen?"

To her surprise and satisfaction, he nodded enthusiastically. "Okay, we need to stay out of sight to make Galen happy – okay?"

He paused, but then nodded happily again.

"Can you stay low and follow me?"

He looked blank, confused.

"Crawl on the floor and follow me?"

He nodded.

"Okay. Crawl after me and stay next to this wall." She crawled back along the walkway, the zombie following behind.

When they were both safely inside the mess hall, she gestured for him to stay still while she carefully and quietly closed the door behind them. She paused and sat under the open window to listen in to the conversation below.

"I don't see anybody in there – if there is, they're well hidden."

"Or there just isn't anything."

"Maybe. We'll get a chance to look inside in a few minutes, anyway."

"Is the warrant in?"

"We've got the arbiter drawing it up now – any minute."

She got ready to run. They'd need a hiding spot, but she couldn't think of where they'd be safe. She imagined dozens of torch-wielding officers poking into every nook and cranny.

"I say, officer?"

Hope sat up in shock. That was Mr Green's voice. Again?

"Sir, we've already talked to you, and this is an active scene. Could you please keep back?"

"Oh – certainly, officer, but I thought you should know I managed to have a chat with my lab partner and he told me what went missing from his side of the office."

"Oh yeah? Do tell."

"Well, of course I don't know why, but he stole some kind of plans for a hybrid chimera my partner had been working on. Something to do with monkeys? and dogs? I don't know how that would be something worth stealing, of course; I just thought you'd want to know."

"Thank you. That's helpful – but I need you to clear out of here, now."

"Oh. Of course. Have a good night."

Hope's heart fell. That bastard knew exactly what he was doing. He'd planted those plans to frame Galen for the chimera attack. The police were already suspicious of her and Galen, but this might be enough to push them over the edge. She'd have to rescue the plans or Galen would be in even more trouble. But how to get to them without being spotted by the hovering zeppelin, and then have enough time to hide before the place filled with cops?

Was it worth the risk?

"Say again, Air 42?" A pause. "All right folks. Let's clear an area for the landing rig. The boat's gotta drop to pick up the truck. Then we'll prep for ingress. We'll have the warrant by the time we're done loading up. Okay, people, let's get moving!"

She tuned them out. Without thinking, she grabbed the orderly's hand and started running for the stairs.

He dragged at her as she pulled him through the mess hall.

He was slowing her down!

She stopped and looked around rapidly.

"Here you go, get in here and stay here until I come and get you." She shoved him inside the pantry and closed the door.

She paused a moment to check he wouldn't burst out again and ran back up the stairs. She'd just have to trust the zombie's usual quiescence would keep him from wandering off and getting the both of them into trouble.

Back on the second floor, she again found herself peeking through the window of Galen's study. She could see the zeppelin sedately lowering past the window. A let-down to pick up Galen's truck. The cameras were slowly drifting below the level of the windows. She re-activated her hideaway and waited a moment longer.

The cameras dropped below the windowsills. She looked directly into the windows of the cab that hung below the zeppelin. The windows were tinted, but in this darkness, the lights within let her see shapes moving about inside. If the crew looked over at her, they'd be able to see directly into the room.

But now, they were looking with their eyes instead of the cameras.

Now was her chance!

She ducked as low as she could and ran for the table. She swept everything it had on top over the edge, and into the open bag below: papers and bags, random trinkets, pens, ink bottles and a brush. The items barely fitted on top of the cash. Heart pounding, she ran for the door, clutching the bag tightly, holding it together.

Re-entering the kitchen, the smell again found its way into her nostrils.

Shit. There's no way a police officer would miss that stench.

She opened the pantry door. Her heart stopped.

It was empty. Of course it was.

She looked through the kitchen door to see the orderly shuffling through the mess hall towards the walkway. "No!" she hissed, as loudly as she could, and ran for it. "Stop! Don't open that door."

The zombie wasn't listening to her.

Hideaway – damn!

He was reaching for the door handle.

She leaped for him once again, colliding with his soft, ashy skin, and dragging him to the ground.

He hissed in frustration as she pulled him away from the door and manoeuvred him back towards the kitchen.

"We have to hide!"

The zombie stared around, confused at being unable to move.

She dropped her hideaway once again.

He immediately fixed his gaze on her.

"We have to hide. Remember? To keep Galen safe."

The orderly stared. Then nodded once more and quietened down.

She exhaled, the stench making her gag all over again. She hissed in frustration.

This isn't going to work with that smell!

"All right folks, warrant's in! Everyone get ready to go in."

That was it. No time left. She hauled herself to her feet and pulled the orderly upright. It was time to go – but where?

There were shouts outside. She pulled the orderly back away from the hall door and risked a peek outside the window. Galen's truck was slowly rising against the sky.

Crap, no time. No time! Where can I hide the zombie?

They'd search thoroughly, no matter where she hid away. Wardrobes, cardboard boxes, broom closets – all of them flashed through her mind and were discarded. In each case, she pictured one of the diligent officers turning a bright torch in her direction and blowing her cover.

She stopped. She needed a place they wouldn't bother to search. Somewhere they expected to be empty.

She nodded, grabbed the orderly's dry hand again and turned for the hall on the opposite side to the zeppelin. Could she get there before they came inside?

She had to try.

Even if she used her hideaway, it wouldn't mask the smell! But she had an idea about that too. If only she had the time. She pulled the orderly through the hall and into one of the big wards, the one full of bunk beds.

"Climb up on there and lie down," she told the orderly, who clambered, loose-limbed, up the ladder.

She followed hurriedly after.

The voices were at the front door. There was no time!

She dropped the bagful of random stuff in between the orderly's legs. She pulled out a brush and ink. Then, swallowing her revulsion along with her pride, she straddled the orderly.

She examined the runes painted onto his skin. Something here must work the way she needed.

No, no, not that one… Oh!

She made a few hurried strokes, changing a flow-rate rune here, a directional input there.

The distant front doors were opening.

Scattered torchlight played over the wall.

She leaned down. "Stay still and completely silent until I tell you," she whispered.

She pulled her hideaway back over herself. Then she paused and looked down. She breathed deeply. One long shaky breath. Then she pulled together every ounce of her courage and she lowered herself over him – her head turned away from his hideous face.

She followed her own advice to lie still and silent.

For a wonder, the orderly stayed quiet, and only her own pounding heart and jittery nerves kept her from the terror she felt at lying on top of a very ripe corpse.

The torchlight and voices approached. And now she had two things to be afraid of.

24 - How to hide a corpse

Hope closed her eyes and breathed slowly to calm her nerves. At least the air was not as rank as before. Seemed like her hasty adjustments to the orderly's magic had worked, keeping the air locked inside him.

Six officers entered the room. One pair hurried through to the kitchen. Another moved a little slower, taking the time to look around, acting as backup. The last pair hovered by the door, directing a handcuffed Galen. All three pairs scanned the room but thankfully didn't notice her hiding spot. This room was bare, the bunks visibly empty. Not worth searching very hard.

Which was what she was counting on. Hide in plain sight.

The police who'd moved ahead joined up with others who'd gone around the other way. They were shouting "clear" and banging open the doors and cupboards as they progressed through the rooms beyond.

She couldn't see them, though. Her head faced back towards the entrance. Towards where Galen stood awkwardly, with the detective and one officer standing guard.

Mr Green, thankfully, did not seem to be present.

Galen looked terrified, his hands white-knuckled and gripping each other as if for comfort. He was turning his head, scanning the room. His eyes panned over her and beyond her. She thought she saw him relax, his shoulders lose a little of their tension, his hands loosen their grip. He also seemed to raise an eyebrow and smirk a little. But she couldn't be sure.

Come to think of it, hadn't he seen through her hideaway before? How on earth did that happen? She'd never seen somebody so capable of piercing her strongest conjuration, and she'd thoroughly tested it for flaws, with Felicity, before she'd been willing to rely on it for jobs.

She didn't have the energy to think about it right now, but she filed it away for future reference.

"So, why are you searching my home, detective?" Galen asked.

"I'm sorry to subject you to a search," the detective replied, "but we're under pressure to find the person responsible for this current spate of violence. You're a person of interest in this case. Add the alleged theft and the footage at the university and it's enough to warrant an inspection of your premises. We've got to follow up on every lead."

"I've already told you. I picked up a lost key card. We were just trying to figure out whose office it belonged to so we could give it back," Galen replied, sounding almost bored.

She could still see the tension in his shoulders. This was clearly unsettling for him.

"Yeah, and what about the unconscious security guard upstairs, then?" The detective was scanning the room, watching the officers search.

"Didn't Adora talk to you about that?" Galen asked, and Hope could hear the uncertainty in his tone

"I spoke with Ms Mannon, but I want to hear your version of events."

"I told you, that wasn't me."

"But you know who it was, don't you?" The detective narrowed his eyes.

Galen shut his mouth and looked away.

"Well, we'll find out soon enough. Thankfully, we caught up with you before you got in here, so I can guarantee that your personal effects have not been disturbed since before the university incident. That will help us settle whether we need to arrest you."

"You have no evidence that I've committed any crime!" Some irritation was bleeding through the politeness.

"I guess we'll see," the detective replied, as one of the police officers returned.

"Nothing so far, sir, and we've cleared the bottom level – there's nothing down there but big, empty rooms. This level's got a lounge room full of books, and a stocked kitchen, but otherwise all the rooms are empty too. Sarge is sending us up to the top level now."

The detective nodded, and the police officer returned to the search.

"What can we expect on the top level?" the detective asked Galen.

"Storage, laundry, gym, study..." he ticked off the list. Then seemed to still for a moment.

The detective's eyes narrowed. "Is there something in the study?"

"Nope," Galen replied, equally casual. "It's where I do some of my experimental work, is all. I keep my more sensitive research there." He was now looking a bit nervous. What else was up there? She'd seen nothing out of the ordinary, just the documents Mr Green had planted and trinkets. Had she missed something?

"What's that smell?" the officer guarding him suddenly asked.

Galen jumped. "What smell?"

"Now you mention it, there is something... lingering," the detective said.

Oh no.

She had stopped any new stench from getting out, but there must've been some still hanging around. Not enough for her to smell – her nose had grown habituated – but enough to catch their attention.

The other officer poked around, sending his torchlight into the deep corners. He was looking under beds and drifting ever closer to her hidden self and the rotting individual she was hiding with little more than her own body and a fragile prayer.

She shuddered once again. She had almost managed to forget what she was concealing with her own body, and now she was hyper-aware of it. Dry skin touching her bare arms. The soft, pliable feel of his belly squashed against hers, concealing all kinds of rotting organs...

"Rats," Galen said.

"What?" the detective asked in surprise.

The police officer looked up from the bed next to hers and spun around to face Galen.

"It's just me looking after this whole building," Galen continued, "and I've had a continual battle with the city rats. I put down baits, of course, and have to clean up the occasional corpse, but that just means that every now and then, one goes and dies somewhere inaccessible – usually in the ceiling cavity. I won't even know it's there until it starts to stink."

The officer raised his torch to highlight the suspended ceiling and began making his way back to the detective. "Gods, I hate rats," he muttered. "I had one die like that in the ceiling above our bedroom, once – stank like the *bejaysus*. Had a guy come to remove it, but the missus and I had to clear out to the spare room for days before the air'd cleared enough for us to go back in."

"Yeah, they're revolting." Galen was nodding. "I'd like the name of your guy if you have it."

"I'll ask the missus," the officer replied. "You should get a cat, though – that's what worked for us."

Just then, the half dozen cops crowded back in through the door and stood around in a semicircle, facing the detective.

"Sarge, did you find something?" the detective asked.

The sergeant nodded at one man who stepped forward, carrying an enormous book in his gloved hands. He held it up so they could read the cover.

The detective's eyebrows shot up at the title, and he indicated for it to be opened for him.

Galen looked transfixed by the book.

The detective had the officer flick through a few pages at random. He looked very grave. He spun around on Galen. "Is this yours?"

"Yes, it's mine," he answered, looking perplexed.

The detective spun around to face the sergeant. "Was there anything else?"

"No sir, just this book."

"None of the alleged items? No purloined plans for chimerae?"

"Not that we've found so far. We could look… more aggressively?" he flicked his eyes towards Galen and back.

"Am I under arrest?" Galen asked, a hint of anger in his voice.

The detective turned on him. "That depends. Can you explain why you have a book on necromancy in your possession?"

"Of course. Because it's not illegal to own this one."

"What?" the officer who'd found the book said. "Isn't it?"

"No. In fact, there's a copy available in the public library, if you'd like to go and check."

Looking unconvinced, the detective said, "And yet it's suggestive of a subject that's illegal."

"Not at all. I'm a surgeon. It has surgical techniques in it."

"Unorthodox ones," the detective stated.

"Which are exactly the ones to study if you want to make a name for yourself in this business."

"That's an interesting take. One you can make in the interview room. Officer, take him down to the station."

As the officer started dragging him away, Galen yelled back, "You can't arrest me. You have no evidence of a crime – you said so yourself!"

"I'm not arresting you. I'm holding you for questioning, pending further investigation." The detective turned back to examine the book.

Galen huffed but allowed the officer to direct him back down the hall.

Hope, still holding herself still and quiet, was feeling very exposed and alone in the roomful of edgy cops.

Once Galen had gone, the sergeant turned to the detective. "So, shall we toss the place?"

The detective snorted. Then he hissed out a breath between his teeth. "Believe me, I'd like nothing better, but if he does turn out to be innocent and we've pulled apart all his furniture, they'll have our hides. You know who his family is. Think about the headlines if we destroy their hospital."

"So, what should we do?"

"Do another search. More thorough – take all night if you have to. The doctor's hiding something illegal. He looked suspicious when we said we were heading upstairs, so concentrate your efforts there."

The officer nodded.

"But don't damage *anything*," the detective added.

25 - Processing

GALEN

Galen sat strapped tightly into his seat and tried not to throw up as the world swayed around him. He tried not to think of how only a thin layer of metal-reinforced wood was standing between his body and a solid hundred-metre drop to the city below.

Oh, don't worry, his brain helpfully supplied. *You won't fall through the floor. Even if the floor fell off, the seat strapping will secure you in place. The weak point in this ship is the bracketing holding the cabin to the balloon! If that goes, you'll remain strapped in for the entire ten-second drop to the city below.*

He hated his own brain some days.

"If you puke in here, you'll have to clean it up!" barked a voice to his right.

He risked opening an eyeball to cast a look over the officer who was seated beside him.

"And if you puke on me, you'll regret it." She was glaring at him.

He closed his eyes again and gripped the seat straps tighter. It must've only been a ten-minute flight, but it felt interminable. By the time he felt the clunk and thrum from the anchor slotting into place on top of the Imperial processing centre, his pale, ashen skin had become tacky with cold sweat and his mouth was sticky and dry.

With a scraping crunch, the basket came to rest on the rooftop, and he immediately struggled with the seatbelt clasp.

"Hey, mate! Hey, settle down!" the officer admonished him. "We'll get you out once we're cleared by the ground crew."

"Didn't you say you want me not to puke?" He yanked futilely on the strap.

The officer must've seen how green he was around the gills, and reached over to release his harness and then her own.

He scrambled to his feet, his hands throwing the straps wide. He found the door and rushed out into the main cabin, which was full of seated officers returning from the scene. They looked up, alarmed.

"Let him out or he's gonna puke!" his seat-mate said.

There were groans and grumbles all around, but nobody moved to help.

Galen rushed to the main exit, but the handle wouldn't budge.

A voice outside called, "All clear!"

The officer near the door tapped a keycard to the lock and the door's light flipped from red to green.

Galen shoved the door open.

"Don't go far!" called the voice behind him. He leaped from the basket to the roof below and stumbled forward a few steps. He grabbed hold of the cold, metal railing at the edge of the mooring pad and held on tight, reassuring his lurching stomach that he was on solid ground once again.

The wind up here was cool and whipped his loose hair into his face, but it was also fresh. He drank deep lungfuls of it, trying to regain his lost composure.

"You good?" the officer asked him, after a few moments.

He nodded.

"Good, 'cause we need to clear the roof. There's half-a-dozen other airships waiting for this space."

He looked up in surprise. He hadn't even noticed the noise, but she was right. A variety of engines puttered and thwupped around him. Half the ground crew stood nearby watching him, waiting. The others were wheeling the last boxes of equipment away. He looked back at the officer and nodded once again.

"Okay, let's take you down to processing," she said, somewhat gently.

As they moved out of the area, the ground crew sprang into action, waving up at the patrol ship and shouting, "Clear!" as it lifted away. In the distance, Galen spotted his truck being moved on an enormous dolly that was wheeling its way towards a vertical parking lot.

"What's going to happen to my truck?" he asked, worried.

"Don't worry, we'll take good care of it," the officer replied. "It's just going into Storage and Impound."

That did not reassure him. He watched as his brother and his life's work were shoved unceremoniously into a large container and sucked down into the bowels of the automated impound lot. He sighed, wondering whether he'd ever see them again.

No – that's defeatist thinking. Think positive.

He hadn't been arrested, they could only hold him for twenty-four hours, maximum. He still had time to get out before the Conjunction's totality, early tomorrow evening. After that, all he'd have to do was find the dream steel, for which he had no clues left; somehow get it off Mr Green, avoiding his multiple deadly minions; then set up a grand conjuration, using magical components either missing or in police custody... All before 6 pm tomorrow.

Sure. Easy. No problem.

He was doomed.

He plodded across the roof and followed the officer down into a large, well-lit stairwell that led through a bright hallway. They pushed through a pair of double doors and into a wall of sound.

Galen had only ever seen this level of pandemonium in the ER during a major incident. Dozens of officers were speaking to, controlling, and/or flat-out wrestling with the largest assortment of strange characters he'd ever laid eyes on.

"Bit of a circus in here right now," the officer remarked, leading Galen through to a desk on the far side while he gazed at the action.

In one corner, a woman dressed in a rippling rainbow of silks swayed and hummed to herself, her eyes rolled up into her head so far that only the whites were showing.

A motley selection of folks, dressed in little more than silver paint, had their augmentations plugged into a central figure sitting in a wheelchair and giggling to himself.

People were steering a wide berth around a squad of well-muscled officers who were struggling to re-bind a quartet of feral-looking people – all of whom were dressed in furs and howling at the moon, which they were apparently trying to reach by leaping out of the fourth-floor window.

All around them were similar, strangely dressed and oddly behaved individuals, in various states of being processed.

"Is this... normal?" Galen asked.

"Big events like this always bring out the crazy ones," she replied, eyeing him up. "By comparison, you're a breeze. Shall we?" She gestured towards a free desk and chair over to one side.

"Are they all Conjunction fanatics?" he asked, side-stepping a tiny woman whose eyes were entirely black. She wore an eerie, smoking headdress that held what looked like a pair of live black snakes. Her officer was keeping well back as he asked her basic questions, to very little evident response.

"Yeah, mostly. And the usual suspects are using it as an excuse to go batshit. Half these loons think the world's gonna end tomorrow. The other half think it'll usher in some kind of second coming. Some of them think they *are* the second coming." She gestured at the snake woman. "To be fair, for all I know, they're right. All this week we've been bumping into half-built Doomsday devices, and crackpots who think they can elevate themselves to godhood – all set to go off tomorrow evening."

"So, why arrest me?"

"Why *not* you?" the officer eyed him up. "You've got a van full of Grade-A conjurations – powerful enough for some big and crazy shit. We're obligated to check it out – and that's on top of your known involvement in some prior crime scenes."

The officer trailed off. "Look, it's not my place to make the decision. I'm just here to get you safely processed and stashed in a nice, comfy interrogation room. You can ask the detectives all the questions you need, okay?"

He swept another bewildered look around the room, then nodded.

The officer rummaged through the desk drawers, looking for a pen and the right forms.

At the next desk over, a woman sobbed into a tissue while the officer opposite her was trying to console her. Galen could swear that her skin was faintly blue and was covered in a swirl of tiny, sparkly scales.

"I'm really sorry, ma'am. We don't have any leads, and we don't have enough uniforms free to go looking. Keep an eye out in case your daughter comes back – we'll get on the case after all this madness calms down."

"Ah, here we go!" Galen's own officer shouted triumphantly.

The intake questions were quick and painless, unlike the surrounding noise levels. By the time she led him away, he was grateful to be tucked away in a small, quiet room by himself.

Nine hours later, though, and he wasn't so happy.

HOPE

Two hours after Galen left, Hope was aching from having been lying in the same position for so long. At first, she worried she might fall asleep and her snoring would give her away to the occasional police officer wandering through the room. But her stiff back and aching side-muscles had put paid to that concern.

Now and then, she had the room to herself, and managed to shift her arms and legs carefully and very quietly. But it was still an unnatural position to lie in for so long, and she could only get *so* comfortable lying on top of a rotting corpse.

After what seemed like an eon, the exhausted police officers made their way downstairs and back outside with all the crime-scene investigators in tow.

Some were carrying hard cases of equipment, others carried bags labelled "EVIDENCE" in bright-yellow lettering. Last came the detective, looking grim, an air of determination about him. He was carrying a long, black box with care.

She had no idea what they had found and what it would mean for Galen's future liberty.

Did Galen have a secret dead-raising room she didn't know about? Who knew? For now, all she could do was protect the one thing she knew would be a big negative for him – a 'dead giveaway', as it were – still creeping her out and lying underneath her as quiet as the proverbial grave.

When everyone had finally left, the hospital was still and silent once more. She waited a few extra minutes, to make sure nobody would return for a forgotten phone or hat, before she pulled herself up into a sitting position.

Her bones creaked. She spent a few more minutes stretching herself out and rubbing the circulation back into place. Then a few more minutes trying to wake herself up enough to think.

Is it safe now? Will they come back? Do I need to hustle an undead orderly out of here to somewhere else, in case they toss the place even more thoroughly?

She had no clue as to what they'd found in their last search. Had they found discarded plans or textbooks? Was there another *How to Raise the Undead For Dummies* book in Galen's library? Did he have a diary detailing his research and plans? She hadn't seen one, but who knows what he had stashed away elsewhere – or was sitting on his nightstand?

Huh! That reminded her. She'd grabbed all those documents randomly from his study desk. They'd probably be worth studying before she decided what to do next. She pulled them out of the leather bag she'd had sitting between her legs all evening. Mr Green's rolled-up papers did turn out to be copies of the lab partner's work. One of them even had a torn corner she'd noticed from the missing papers at the university.

The papers outlined several distinct sets of matrices, a couple of which looked like the ones painted onto the gorilla-dog guards. Some others looked very different.

A picture of some enormous spiders had been doodled next to one of them.

Spiders with rat heads. *Ick!*

That sparked a memory, but it stubbornly refused to come to the surface. She pushed it aside for the time being. She set these papers aside and looked at the ones that actually belonged to Galen.

There were only two. Both of the same matrix. One contained a rough sketch that included pencilled-in labels; the other was a carefully scripted proper copy, in silver ink. The parchment had been laid out with a central circle ready for the emplacement of a cylinder of dream steel. Radiating out from this were flow-control lines that looked like they would hook into something else, something much larger. Her thoughts immediately went to Galen's truck. This must be the main control flow for his entire conjuration.

She examined the annotated version. A lot of it was medical terminology, undecipherable to her; however, the more she studied it, the more she became convinced that *this* was what contained the main flow for the resuscitation itself. The actual dead-raising part.

Smart thing to keep this out of the truck, which mainly contained regular medical flows. Perhaps the truck wouldn't incriminate him after all, then. That would be great!

If the police didn't have this, and they didn't have the orderly, and they didn't have Mr Green's planted evidence, did they have anything, apart from Mr Green's say-so? Was it now a "he said – she said" issue? Maybe she could bail him out of the standard holding period and get him back!

She shook her head and rolled up the matrix for safekeeping. There was still one set of documents left to examine. She fished them out of her décolletage and laid them out.

These three documents were all she'd managed to purloin from Mr Green's office before they'd had to leg it.

They were plans – old plans, by the look of it – dated five, four and three months ago. They held some pretty big technical drawings of a large device. Just an overview, unfortunately. Some opaque chemical jargon indicating diagrams of atomic structure, and several notations she couldn't make out at all. There was an overview penned on the back of the oldest diagram, outlining what looked like an elevator pitch for his grant proposal.

"Blah blah blah … device crafted to integrate these pheromones with the known nootropic effects of the dream-steel material. I propose a novel means of controlling the behaviour patterns of animal test-subjects *en masse*, with a particular insight into improved neural-grafted chimerae. I suggest this could have a variety of manufacturing and/or military applications whereby novel body forms with enhanced neural capabilities could be developed to work in hive fashion, with lower production costs than standard automaton or human equivalents … blah blah blah."

He'd doodled another picture, clearly meant to represent himself, of him wearing an electrode-covered hat and surrounded by bright-green cloud shapes that connected him to a small army of the rat-faced spiders, much like the ones in the chimera diagrams.

Shit. Spiders and green mist!

They'd been a few very eventful days, but she could still remember the swarm of spiders scuttling out of the exploded bank. She didn't remember seeing rat heads, but to be fair, she'd been a little busy legging it instead of looking closely.

How much would you bet that was thanks to Mr Green, too? No wonder the cops were eager to find a chimera expert – but why would he rob a bank?

She found the answer scrawled at the bottom of the page in angry red ink. "Grant proposal rejected. Potential investor – need to provide proof of concept."

She idly flipped through the pages to see whether anything else stood out. He'd provided some tables listing the required ingredients and power levels, along with a few rough calculations for determining how much of each was necessary. The quantity of dream steel required was astonishing. She remembered how heavy it had been, rolling around in the toolbox. Just a palm-sized slice no more than 5 millimetres thick had given her enough cash for half a semester of college, and this weighed as much as half a brick.

And after he'd robbed the bank to fund it, the bastard paid off the thieves to rob the dream steel out from underneath both Galen and her.

She paused, looking over the calculations and frowning. That wasn't right.

The numbers were off... Yes. Mr Green had made a mistake. One decimal place out. He had ten times the amount of dream steel he needed, according to his own calculations, and dream steel had its own special internal resonances that meant an exponentially larger effect for every order-of-magnitude increase in size.

*Shit. This thing is going to be significantly more powerful than even **he** expects. What the hells is he going to be capable of, when it hooks into the power of the Conjunction? Will he even be able to control it?*

She read back over the effects he'd listed. Neural control over multiple subjects, the larger or smarter the animal, the fewer the subjects he could control.

She'd already seen him in action, controlling animals both large and small. There'd been an entire army of spiders that first time, and then there'd been the street parade. That comprised more than a dozen larger animals – although he'd lost control over that elephant thing. That must have been stretching his ability. However, that number of animals had been impressive. If he had an exponentially higher power level, how many could he safely control? Could he control people? How many people?

She made a few calculations of her own. Then sat, staring at the number in trepidation.

This did not bode well.

She'd casually joked about Galen commanding an army of the undead, but this seemed much worse. At least she trusted Galen reasonably well. From what she'd seen of him, she thought he'd at least *try* to avoid destroying the city if it came down to it.

But Mr Green? With that kind of power? She didn't trust him further than she could chuck an elephant-opus.

He'd already tried to plant evidence to frame Galen for his own crimes, and he'd straight-up threatened her family. Now he was about to gain the power to threaten her entire city.

And she was the only one who knew about it.

26 - *Losing hope*

GALEN

He sat alone in the interview room. It was cold, and he was tired.
It had been... some time.

He didn't know how long. There weren't any clocks in here.

He'd been waiting, hoping, for hours now. For what, exactly, he wasn't really sure.

Maybe for Hope to solve all his problems for him? That wasn't a reasonable expectation. She shouldn't have to rescue him from the consequences of his own actions. By hiding the orderly for him, she'd given him more than he deserved.

What audacity she'd shown, hiding him practically in plain sight. His heart warmed at the thought.

Then it cooled again. He just had to hope that she'd managed to escape afterward.

And now he was on his own.

He put his head in his hands and let the tears trickle down his face.

His brother's life hung in the balance. Either the police opened up the containment unit and his brother defrosted on some damned coroner's table; or they destroyed his life's work, written on the walls of his truck – all while investigating a crime he didn't commit.

Either way, his brother was as good as dead.

Even if they simply kept him tied up here until the Conjunction came and went. It was two hundred years until the next one, and nothing else was powerful enough for what he needed.

He'd pulled every string, cashed in every favour to get the matrix ready in time.

And it still hadn't been enough.

He put his head back down on the table, and gave in to the fatigue.

HOPE

Hope climbed into the back seat, dragging the orderly in after her. The cabbie cast a sceptical glance at her companion. Hope had swaddled him in scarves and wrapped a shawl around his head.

"Oh, don't mind Aunt Mabel. She's had chickenpox and is ashamed of the marks, is all." Hope gave a nervous laugh. "Not even contagious anymore."

The orderly's pale hand rose to remove the shawl.

Hope grabbed it and held it tight, gritting her teeth and patting it in a mock display of affection.

The cabbie's eyes narrowed. "Just don't cough in here," he said, and turned back to the road. She swore she heard him mutter, "Better than the fish-head freaks from yesterday."

He barely raised an eyebrow when she mentioned the destination.

Pam's Palace was located right next to the central business district, close enough to the centres of power and profit to be accessible to all its usual high class, high-rolling patrons. It was a multi-storey mock castle featuring crenelations, turrets, simulated stone walls, and a working drawbridge over a picturesque moat filled with waterlilies and ducks.

It was the city's most famed attraction – or, more correctly, the high-priced princes and princesses who resided within, courtesans for the wealthiest, most discerning members of the Imperium's upper echelons, all protected by a world-class security system. Nobody messed with Pam's pampered scions, even a part-time princess like Felicity.

Hope had the cabbie drop them off around the back, neatly avoiding the scrutiny they'd invite at the public entrances. However, she also wanted to avoid the multitude of entrances and exits reserved for private members. Instead, she angled for the highly fortified personnel entrance. It had a double layer of reinforced-glass doors, like an airlock, and they were bristling with cameras.

A pair of large bouncers banned her ingress.

"Ma'am?" one asked politely.

"Hi. I'm here to see Felicity Gray. She's a princess here and she'll vouch for us. I'm her sister, plus guest." She tipped her head to indicate her "aunt", and waited, expectant.

The bouncer stepped back and used an intercom system to confer briefly. He leaned forward. "Can you step forward and look into the camera, please?"

She obliged, smirking and waving up at the camera, and put her arm around "Aunt Mabel", giving a thumbs-up.

The bouncer listened in to his headset. He nodded, then stepped forward. "Okay, you're cleared for entry. Please go directly to the third elevator. You want room 472. Have a nice evening, ma'am." The front door buzzed, and he held it open for the pair.

"Thanks," Hope said, and pulled the orderly along with her. They passed into the airlock, and the bouncer buzzed them through the second door. The elevator was open and waiting for them. It smoothly rose through the floors to deposit them deep within the bowels of the building.

The castle theme didn't extend to the employees-only area, so she strolled along a plushly carpeted hall, featuring weird hotel art, and knocked on the relevant door.

She saw the eye-piece darken, and Felicity's voice came through the door. "Is it you?"

"Yep, it's me. Let us in."

"That's not Galen. Who's with you?"

Hope sighed. At least she was being careful. "It's a long story and not one I care to share publicly."

There was a pause.

"Do you need me to prove I am who I say I am?"

"Can you?"

Hope smiled. "On your ninth birthday I couldn't afford to buy you a present, so I spent the day at the botanical gardens gathering caterpillars in a box; thinking I could give you butterflies, but they all turned into moths instead. I was terribly disappointed, but you were delighted."

Felicity laughed, and a moment later, the door opened wide. "They got into everything, though. Ate holes in all our clothes, and mum was so mad." Felicity eyed up the stranger and pulled Hope inside.

As soon as the door was closed, Hope hugged her tight. Then pulled back. "Why are you still up this late?"

"I've just got off shift. I was getting ready for bed when I heard the buzzer – so, will you tell me what happened?"

Hope frowned. "I couldn't save him. They took him away and there was nothing I could do, but I helped the only way I could." She sighed deeply and threw a glare at her companion.

Felicity raised an eyebrow and tried to surreptitiously peek under the shawls. "Hello?"

"Don't bother trying to talk to him." Hope gave a half-smile. "Where's the bathroom?"

Felicity looked confused, but pointed at each of the doors. "Sam's asleep in our bedroom over there, and that one can be your bedroom. The bathroom's down the hall. We don't have a room for your... guest?" She glanced at the orderly once more.

"He'll stay in the bathroom by himself."

"I don't understand." Felicity looked even more confused.

Hope grimaced. "I told you about Galen's... um... side hobby, right?"

Felicity nodded, still looking confused. Then her eyes widened, and she took a large step back. "Please don't tell me that's a... ?"

"I had no other choice! The cops were searching Galen's hospital. I hid him while I was there, but I couldn't leave him there in case they came back. I had to take him somewhere!"

"But why here?" Felicity demanded, incredulously.

Hope cringed. "I'm sorry; I couldn't think of anything else to do."

Felicity hissed in frustration. "Is the thing safe? Do you know anything about it? Is it even house trained? How do they..." She looked the figure up and down.

"I don't know Felicity, why don't you ask Galen when you see him next time?" she replied acerbically, then shook her head. "He seemed pretty harmless at the hospital, and Galen let him wander the halls by himself, so I assume he's at least a little trained. Look, I know it's a lot to ask, but I'm too tired to stay on watch with him all night. First, I'm going to use the bathroom, and then I'm going to lock him in there. I can put up a tripwire, so we know if he tries to leave. If you're worried about him more than that, you can stay up and watch over him, but right now, I'm about ready to pass out."

Felicity looked at her helplessly, her hands opening and closing. "And... Galen?"

Hope sighed and looked down at her hands. "They took him away. They found something while searching, but I don't know what, and there was nothing I could do; all I could do was hide this guy away and hope they didn't find me." She squeezed her eyes shut and balled her hands into fists. "Galen looked so afraid, so alone, and I couldn't do anything to help him." A lone tear spilled over, and she wiped it away angrily.

Felicity's face softened. "You did the best you could, Hope, and I'm sure he won't fault you for that. You got this guy out of the way, at least."

Hope smiled wanly. "Galen seemed so helpless. I don't think he's ever been at the wrong end of the law before." Her face cracked with an enormous yawn. She looked away, embarrassed. "I want to help, but I'm just too tired to think."

"Okay, come on." Felicity bustled Hope out of the doorway. "Get ready for bed. We'll sort it all out after you've had some sleep."

Hope nodded. "Thanks, Felicity." The fatigue she'd been holding at bay washed over her in waves.

She was asleep before her head hit the pillow.

27 - Interrogation

GALEN

He awoke with a jerk. He hadn't fallen deeply asleep. The officers hadn't allowed that. All evening they'd been popping by, one every half hour – just enough to keep him from drifting off too deeply.

This time, however, the door slammed open, and in walked a new detective and her partner.

They pulled out two chairs with a metallic screech and dropped into them.

"Good..." the detective checked her watch "...morning," she said with a forced cheer.

"Morning," he replied.

"Can we start by having you confirm your full name for us, please?"

"Dr Galen Moore," he answered, with a world-weary sigh. "Where's the other detective?"

"He's off shift, lucky man." She smiled.

The two of them looked as exhausted as he felt, but they (unlike him) each had a cup of hot, fragrant coffee in their hands.

He looked longingly at the steaming liquid.

"Would you like some coffee?" she offered.

He had to stop himself from salivating at the thought. "Thank you, yes. That would be lovely." If the two of them were being polite, he should try his best to match them; although he had to use every drop of his remaining energy to keep up the facade of common decency.

The detective glanced at her partner, who hopped up and had a quiet word with the officer standing guard outside the door. "It's been a long day, Dr Moore, and a long night. For all of us." She tapped a pen on the folder in front of her. "Do you know why you're here today?"

"Why don't you tell me?"

The detective smiled. Her partner grimaced. They shared a Look.

"As you may be aware, you've been a person of interest in relation to several incidents involving chimera-related violence." She dropped a pair of large photographic prints in front of him.

There was a lot of blood in one.

Dodge.

The other was a bright and glossy rendition of the half-rotted gorilla-dog corpse in the alley.

He looked them over, then looked back up at the detective with a confused frown. "Why are you showing me these? Am I supposed to know what you want?"

"Is this your work?" the partner barked.

Ah. This must be bad-cop.

He sighed again. He didn't have the energy to deal with this right now. Swallowing his exasperation, he addressed the barky partner. "No. I don't do chimerae. I'm a surgeon with a side gig in experimental resuscitation, not a zoological biologist or whatever."

"At the scene," the detective continued, casually, "you told the officers you were conducting a research study into chimera-based violence – didn't you?"

He froze.

Darn.

The detective raised her eyebrows. "Well, which is it?"

He shrugged. "Is it illegal to have a research project as a hobby?"

The detective and her partner shared another Look.

A knock came at the door, and the partner stood again.

"So," the detective resumed, "shall we talk about your hobbies?"

The partner returned carrying a paper cup filled with steaming ambrosia.

About time.

He accepted the cup gingerly, struggling to hide a yawn. It was too hot to drink, but he held it up to his nose, letting the deliciously scented steam fortify him. "What do you want to know?"

Perhaps if he ad-libbed about chimerae, they wouldn't ask about his more... colourful hobbies.

"What can you tell us about your hobby?" She sat back, watching him.

"I do experimental medical research." He took a careful sip of the hot liquid. It was over-sugared for his taste but went down well and warmed him from the inside. "On a variety of topics." He looked up at them with a half-smile. "I dabble."

"Is that what you call what's in your truck?" the partner asked, his voice cutting across the thin edge of civility. "*Dabbling*?"

"Yes, very much!"

"Can you tell us what it does?"

"As I said to the other detective, it's an experimental resuscitation working."

"Can you be more specific?"

He raised his eyebrows. "Sure. It has matrices for medical stabilisation – blood-pressure, heart-rate, and oxygenation monitors; with automatic adjustment subroutines to bring a patient up to normal, no matter what happened to them. It's state-of-the-art. My masterpiece. I'm hoping to write a paper about it all someday – several papers." He smiled at them.

This isn't going so bad.

"Tell us about the body," the partner said.

"What? What body?"

Had they mentioned a body? Oh!

"Oh, that, you mean in the truck?" He laughed casually.

But they weren't laughing.

He put a hand over his mouth to stifle a giggle. "He's meant to be there. Frozen, don't you know?"

The two cops shared yet another Look.

"It's all above board, I swear. I didn't kill him or anything! Just keeping him frozen and safe!"

I'm waffling, aren't I waffling? Must be tired.

"Caius got freeze-rayed by that freeze-ray guy. Months back now. Couldn't bury him – so frozen he made the ground freeze up. I keep him in the fridge truck. Don't even need to run the fridge 'cause he's all magically frozen! Saves on costs, you know? Not so much money for the petrol."

I'm waffling again, aren't I? Damnit, I'm worse than Adora today. A drunk Adora! Wait-a-minnit, why'm I drunk?

"Did you spike my coffee?" he asked and peered into the mostly empty cup, hoping to see… something.

The detective sighed deeply and looked at her partner. "Can you tell us about the chimerae?" She sounded impatient.

"Oh? Yeah, nasty creatures. Very scary. I ran away."

"You… ran away from the chimerae? Why?" the partner demanded.

"Well, they were trying to hurt me, of course."

"Why would they do that?" the detective asked him, perplexed. "Did you… mistreat them?"

"No! I never!" he replied, indignant. "No, it was Mr Green. He stole my dream steel, and I wanted it back, and he made them attack me!"

The detective's eyebrows were riding high on her forehead. "Mr Green, you said? The same Mr Robert Green who alleges you stole his key card?"

"Yup." He looked into the coffee cup again. It was empty. He was tired and falling asleep again, and there was no more coffee! He huffed and put his head down on his arms.

"Hey-hey!" The partner snapped his fingers in Galen's face. "Stay with us, buddy!"

"He's nearly gone," the detective observed. "Ask him the money question."

The partner rolled his eyes. "Did you create, summon, or control any chimerae in the past fortnight?"

"Nope," he replied, confused. "I've told you, I don't know how." And then he yawned. He could barely keep his eyes open. He put his head down and started drifting off on waves of sleep.

The detective turned to the partner. "You interrogated that Mr Green bloke at the scene, didn't you?"

"Yeah, he alibied out, so we discounted him. So, do you like this doctor for the bank job?"

"I don't think this guy's got anything to do with anything." She huffed with exasperation. "And now they're accusing each other. We've got no evidence to prove it either way. It's 'he-said/she-said', and now he's fallen asleep." She tapped her finger on the table. "Put him in a cell till the serum wears off – maybe we'll turn something up before then, and it'll keep him and his truck off the streets till we get through the backlog. We've got him for the next seventy-two hours, just in case."

That cut through Galen's thoughts just as a wave of exhaustion was receding, and he lifted his head. "No, can't wait that long."

The detective looked surprised. "I thought you were out for the count!"

"Have you got somewhere you have to be?" the partner barked.

"Yes!" he replied.

"Why don't you tell us about that?" the detective suggested.

He fought answering. His mind was swimming. He was beyond tired, but he couldn't remember why he didn't want to say anything. Speaking the truth was always the better path... wasn't it?

His thoughts were fragmenting. "I need to finish it. Bring him. Need the truck for the Conjunction. It's nearly done."

"You mean the conjuration in your truck?" the detective asked him. "What does it do?"

"Revive." He was drifting off to sleep now.

The detective's voice was soothing, persuasive. It brought him floating back to the surface once again. "What will your conjuration matrices revive?"

He blinked, knowing full well what she wanted him to say. It was right there on the tip of his tongue, but a small voice deep inside him thought it wasn't a good idea to let it out.

Why was that? Wasn't he proud of what he could do? He'd studied hard to learn what he needed to do, hadn't he? Dug into old, forgotten archives and hunted down rare and dangerous books. He'd practised on animals. Tried and failed, until he'd made an ugly promise to people he'd rather forget, to get the ultimate piece.

Then, he'd finally tried it out on a human! He remembered the wild joy when his orderly drew the first breath of his second life.

He wanted to share that joy – that pride in his accomplishment!

He opened his mouth to talk...

28 - *Posting bail*

HOPE

The next morning, Hope dragged herself out of bed early enough to see the sun rise. She pulled some half-washed clothes on and headed for the bathroom.

It was a testament to her ongoing exhaustion that it took until she'd completed her morning ablutions before she realised what, or rather who, was missing from it.

She scrambled into the lounge room only to be brought up short by the astonishing sight of the orderly standing by the tiny window, looking up at the dawn; silently accompanied by Sam, who was sitting watching him, fascinated.

Sam lifted their finger to their lips to shush Hope.

She blinked in response.

They crooked a finger to invite her over, so she crept over to their side.

"Mum said you brought him here to hide," Sam whispered to her, eyeing up the orderly.

Hope nodded. "He belongs to Galen. Do you... know what he is?"

Sam rolled their eyes and nodded. "I'm not stupid, you know."

Hope smiled wryly. "Noted."

"So, why's he here?"

"Galen's been arrested. I'm hiding the orderly here until Galen gets free again."

Sam nodded. "What's he doing at the window?"

"He likes to watch the sun rise," she answered, and gave a shrug.

"Oh! That's kinda nice. I thought they were all 'Grrr! Arrrggh!' or something."

"Heh, me too! But Galen's house trained this one." She eyed Sam up.

Sam was cradling their bandaged stump and leaning in to look up at the stitched throat of the zombie.

Hope said nothing, but Sam noticed her scrutiny.

"What?" they asked.

Hope laughed it off. "Nothing. I'm glad you've found a 'friend'." She looked around the apartment. She could hear Felicity's snoring still coming from the bedroom. "I have to go and help Galen. Are you going to be all right here?"

"Of course. I'll keep this guy safe." They smiled.

"Okay, try to keep the mischief to a minimum." She smiled back, then slipped away in search of coffee.

Felicity had left her a note next to the kettle.

"Called the precinct. Couldn't get through. Maybe you could show up in person?"

Hope grimaced. She caffeinated herself and headed out, leaving Sam and the orderly to their silent contemplations.

She hailed a cab and headed across town. A thick wad of potential bail money padded her most secure inside pocket. But it wouldn't be any use if she couldn't actually get to the precinct, and the city seemed determined to make the mission impossible.

There were still twelve hours until the Conjunction this evening, but the entire city had mobilised itself alongside her, and every person in it was conspiring to get in her way. Thousands of chairs, tables, concert stages and port-a-loos were being shipped into the CBD, from every direction, and the entire area had been closed to regular traffic while setup was under way.

On the outskirts, however, nothing blocked the traffic, which meant varying degrees of gridlock, chaos, and generalised mayhem for anyone trying to cut across town.

Hope suddenly felt very small – just one tiny fish trying to swim upstream against a heavy tide. The weight of her exhaustion hit her hard. The last few days had been one mad scramble after another, and she was still reeling.

Could she even make a difference? It felt like an impossible task and she felt very alone.

Then she remembered the look on Galen's face as he was kneeling in front of the hospital – alone and afraid – and how his expression had changed the moment he'd seen her; still afraid perhaps, but no longer alone. He'd trusted her to have his back, and now she was going to do her best to follow through. If only she could get her arse across town to be there for him.

She grumbled to herself as the taxi got caught in another snarl of traffic.

"Yeah, I hear you," the cabbie said. "It's been bad all week, but today, hoo-boy – all the punters've suddenly got to get their arses in gear for tonight."

"Why didn't they set it all up before now? It's not like they didn't know what was coming." She let out a huff.

The cabbie honked at a cargo mech that'd suddenly stopped in front of them, its scaffolding dangerously close to going through their front window. "The dockers' strike put the kibosh on that. Most of these guys have gotten supplies through only yesterday, so everybody's scrambling. At least there's a lotta work going 'round. Every able-bodied person in town has their hands full. Even the air's chockers." He indicated the heavy line of circling airships overhead.

"They'd better clear out in a few hours or they'll block the view of the Conjunction."

"Ha-ha. That's true! I reckon anybody who's in the air after 5 pm's gonna get hauled down – too many businesses will get their noses out of joint, otherwise."

The snarl only grew worse as they approached the precinct. It had already slowed to a crawl. But when the pedestrians were moving faster than the vehicles, Hope finally gave up, paid her cabbie and hopped out to walk the last few blocks.

At the precinct, she found that the gridlock didn't stop at the front door. The station was a madhouse of people coming in and out, all tripping over dozens of people queueing out the door.

As she patiently waited for her turn at the front desk, she saw squads of cops coming and going, some dragging crazed people shouting imprecations about the world ending; others were dressed wildly and clearly suffering the effects of an extended bender.

A squad of shrieking women were handcuffed together, crying out to be allowed back out to frolic with their god. Dionysus would apparently be unhappy if robbed of his brides tonight.

Hope just sighed and stood watching on.

When her turn finally came, she put on her best and most polite smile. The poor woman had clearly had a full day already, and it was barely an hour past dawn. "Hi. I need to do two things. A friend's in for questioning; I need to know his status and whether I can post bail. Second, I have a potential crime to report that may cause extensive danger for the city and everyone who lives here." She gave an apologetic half shrug.

Without batting an eyelid, the officer pulled out two forms for her. "Fill these in, drop them at that window, and take a seat."

She was still debating whether to tell the cops about the dream steel as she dropped off the forms. The only thing she'd really regret about it was that Galen would lose his chance to regain his brother. But was one life worth the city? Would Galen forgive her for making that choice for him? From what she knew of him, he would, although he'd be unhappy about it.

She sighed again. She looked up as she heard her number being called. "Hi," she said to the exhausted-looking desk-jockey waiting for her.

"Hi," he replied with an air of resignation. "Right. I've run a search for your applicant. First, I have to ask, are you family or designated next of kin?"

"Um, no? Just a friend trying to help him out."

"Right. I'm sorry, then; I can't give you details about his case." He started packing up the papers on his desk.

"Wait, that's it?"

"Yes, that's it, I'm afraid." He looked at her impassively.

"But... I came here to bail him out. Regardless of the details, can I at least post bail for him?"

He sighed and looked back through the papers, carefully keeping them out of view. "Sorry, no bail." He replaced them in their folder.

"No bail because he's out or no bail because they won't let him leave?"

"I'm sorry, ma'am. I can't divulge that information to you."

She furrowed her eyebrows and huffed in frustration. She'd have to figure something else out. "What about the tip?"

"Which tip?" His eyes narrowed.

"I gave you notice of a threat to the city. Please, at least tell me you'll be doing something about that!"

"Oh, that. Yes, thanks for the tip; we've added it to the list, and we'll get on it as soon as a unit's available to investigate."

She blinked. "'*As soon as a unit's available*'? That sounds like weasel words for *We aren't going to do shit*." Her patience was wearing thin.

He frowned. "We're pretty busy right now, ma'am, as you can see. All available units are already accounted for."

"But this is serious! I know for certain that Robert Green is going to run a dangerous conjuration to give himself powers he shouldn't use on humans, and he's already shown he's willing to use his magic to harm other people – possibly even murder them."

"And I say again. Thank you, ma'am, for reporting this potential crime; but right now, all available units are busy with actual confirmed crimes. We'll send a unit to investigate as soon as one becomes available."

"Does it help to know he's the one responsible for all the chimera-related violence we've been seeing?"

He raised his eyebrows. "Have you got any evidence for that?"

She sighed. "Only my own testimony."

He returned to looking dismissive. "I'm afraid that's insufficient cause."

"There was a detective. He wanted to know about this – Detective Grant. Gave me a card, and everything. Can you contact him?"

He perked up at that. "Do you have the card?"

"Um, no. I, ah, must've lost it."

He narrowed his eyes again. "Well then, I'll be sure to leave him a message for when he's finished going through his currently overflowing inbox."

"I can't believe you're not taking this more seriously!"

"Please calm down, ma'am. We're all trying our best here."

"Your best? I gave you a credible threat to the people of this city, and you aren't doing squat!"

"Ma'am! Have you seen what it's like out there today? Every madman and his dog's out there right now. I believe you when you say there's a problem, but we just don't have the resources. This isn't the first credible threat we've heard today – damnit, it's not even the first credible threat I've heard this hour, and that's the problem; we're stretched thin, triaging. We'll sort it out tomorrow, after the dust's settled, and that's the earliest I can do anything."

She blinked. Then she frowned and looked again at the chaos all around her. The city was a roiling keg of mayhem. Perhaps Mr Green looked like a big shark to her, but maybe that was only because she was used to swimming in shallow waters.

She took a deep breath, then said, "I'm sorry, you're right. I'm just worried."

"It's okay, ma'am. I know that tensions are high right now. Believe me, I wish we could spare the resources to check out your crime – and all the others on the docket today. But for now, we've got bigger fish to fry, and we need to concentrate our efforts on where we can do the most good. We'll just have to pick up the rest of the pieces over the following days. Now, unless there's something else I can help you with, I need to get on with helping the next customer."

"Is there any way I can find out about my friend? I'm worried about him."

"Have you tried asking his lawyer?" He glanced briefly at the papers once more. "He'll have been assigned a public defender. You can try going across the street and seeing whether you can get some information from the arbiter's office."

She nodded. "Thanks, I'll try that."

He nodded in return.

She stood up and left him to his overflowing pile of folders.

Thankfully, the offices across the way had a far shorter queue. Unfortunately, the news wasn't any more helpful.

"I'm sorry, but your friend's not being represented by a public defender," the woman told her after a brief search online. She was looking concerned. "Looks like one was assigned to him but was turned away."

Hope felt her stomach roll over. "Turned away? Do you mean my friend's totally unrepresented? He's a noob! He could be spilling his guts. He needs representation!"

"I agree. Let me see what I can do for you." She tapped away for a few minutes. "Okay. I've got the lawyer here, and it turns out she'll be free in a few minutes. Please wait over there and I'll send her out."

"Thanks," Hope said, and re-joined the waiting-room crowd. Now she was worried. Just how much trouble was Galen in if his lawyer was turned away?

After the requisite few minutes, a short, stocky woman wearing a bright, fuchsia skirt headed in her direction. "Hope?" she asked expectantly to the room.

Hope stood and waved.

"My name's Sandra Levine, and they've assigned me to Dr Moore's case. Why don't you come with me? We can go across to the station and talk along the way."

Hope shook the manicured hand that was proffered. "Were you the one who was turned away before?"

"Yes, which was extremely unusual. They told me he'd been taken in for questioning but had been released. I insisted on meeting with him, but they told me he'd already left the building. That didn't smell right to me, but there wasn't much I could do. Thanks to your concern, I have another chance to go over there and check things out. See what we can see. What do you think?"

Hope nodded enthusiastically. "They told me they couldn't tell me anything because I wasn't next of kin – but I'm a friend of his, I swear!"

Sandra eyed her searchingly.

Hope felt as if she were having her very soul scrutinised.

"They have a fair point," Sandra said, "but I'll see what I can do. How about this? I'll go in and see what I can find out. If he's there, I'll ask his permission for you to attend."

Hope huffed. It was frustrating she'd have to wait to find out what was going on. "What if he's there, but they say he's not? Would you recognise him if they walked him right past you?"

The woman tipped her head to one side, weighing up her words. "All right. How about this? Do you have any cash on you?"

Hope I blinked. "Yes?"

"All right. You can officially hire me as your lawyer. Give me just a credit in payment for now."

Hope fished out a coin and dropped it in her palm.

"Good. I can now legally call you my client, and we're walking into the station because of an unrelated matter. While we're there, I'll ask after a completely different client of mine, and you'll keep back out of the way and let me know whether you happen to see him. Okay?" She again looked into Hope's soul. "I'm trusting you not to do anything stupid while we're in there. Right?"

Hope nodded, crossed her heart, and said, "Nothing stupid."

Sandra nodded in return, and they entered the station.

Hope, of course, was already plotting just how much 'stupid' she'd be willing to try.

29 - Storm the precinct

Sandra navigated them through the mess of the busy station better than Hope had managed on her own – thanks to the lawyer's credentials, the pair went straight to the front of the queue, and the desk staff barely batted an eyelid when they requested access through the gate. They passed through the doorway beyond and directly into the intake room behind. Once there, they wended their way through a maze of desks and harried officers who were handling incoming suspects.

The two headed for the far door, but that was as far as they got without being stopped.

"Excuse me, miss, ma'am, can I help you?" a young officer asked, stepping away from his desk and into their path.

Sandra turned a brilliant smile on him. "I'm here to meet with my court-appointed client, and this time I won't take no for an answer." She handed him a card that bore Galen's credentials.

"If you'll wait here until I'm done, I'll see whether they're available," he turned back to his desk and the man who was lounging in the chair opposite. The lounger looked like he was barely awake, with a blissed-out smile on his face.

"I'm afraid that simply won't do," Sandra snapped.

The officer flinched and spun towards her, his eyebrows furrowed and his mouth turned down. "We're a bit busy here. You'll have to wait till one of us is free to help."

"I've heard that before, and I no longer believe it. My client's been in here for hours without proper representation, so you're going to look for him right now, and I'm going to accompany you until you locate him."

Warily, he eyed her up. Then he glanced at the lounger in his charge, who seemed to have dozed off. Turning, he shouted to another colleague, "Oi, Lennie! Keep an eye on this one, will you?" He then proceeded to lead them down the next corridor, into a warren of rooms and short halls, full of corners.

All the while, Hope kept an eye out around her, looking for anybody who might be relevant. She noted which direction the other officers were dragging a variety of unsavoury types, all of whom were handcuffed. That corridor must lead to the cells.

After a few moments, they ended up in another room that was full of desks and computers, all as busily in use as the intake room, just with more cops and fewer suspects.

Hope hung back as Sandra and the young officer approached a desk occupied by a tired and grumpy-looking woman.

"Hi Daisy, can you help this lawyer find her client?" the young man asked her.

She glared at him, looked Sandra up and down, and barked, "Name?"

"Sandra Levine," the lawyer replied, nonplussed.

"Client's name." Daisy demanded, her tone both condescending and frustrated. Sandra gave the details as Daisy began a staccato of keystrokes. "That client's being held in a cell, and we haven't got an interview room free at the moment. Come back later."

"No thanks. I'll speak with him in the cell, if need be, but I need to check in on him. That's not up for negotiation."

"No can do, sorry. This place is too busy to allow any room for…"

"Now you look here, Daisy," Sandra interrupted, "your staff have already kept me waiting for hours, and…"

"Don't you talk over me, missy. Can't you see how busy it is?"

"I don't care if this is an active war zone, and if you think…"

Hope backed away from the argument until she could slip back into the corridor. Nobody seemed to care about her. The ongoing argument had transfixed those nearby, and all the other officers were tied up with their own work.

She drew in a trickle of her magic, double-checking for watchers. Nobody was paying her the least notice. With a tingle, she drew her hideaway over her, edged backwards and out of sight. She slunk down the corridor, taking a peek into the nearby rooms as she went.

Each one was indeed full. Police, lawyers, and a variety of suspects and other ne'er-do-wells. Some arguing, some stolidly silent, some weeping softly into their hands. None of them her Galen.

She made her way down the corridor that presumably led to the cells but was brought up short against a barred door. Thankfully, currently unguarded. She looked through the bars, into the cells. They were crammed full of people lounging, brooding, pacing, but none of them were who she was after.

Damnit. How could she find him? She didn't recognise any of these people. This was way outside of her usual stomping ground.

Swallowing her courage, she whispered, "Psst!"

A few heads perked up, looking around; and a man sauntered over as close to the gate as possible without looking her way. "You know there are cameras here, right?" he said idly, addressing the far wall.

"I don't care. I'm looking for a friend – name of Galen Moore, a doctor. Do you know whether he's down here?"

"Can't say I do. Might be able to jog my memory, though…" He rubbed his fingers together as if to show they shouldn't be empty.

She dug into a pocket and ferreted out a few credits. She folded them up and threw them through the bars.

The man deftly caught them, and they disappeared. "I saw a doctor arrive earlier – nearly puked on the way in. Got taken straight to the interview rooms. That was hours ago, and he hasn't ever come back to the cells. That's all I know."

A red light flashed above the door and an alarm blared. The man stepped back and drifted away.

"Damnit. Do you know which room?"

He ignored her.

The alarm was loud, and she heard footsteps rapidly approaching. She hurried back the way she'd come. Hallway doors were opening and people were peering out, hunting for the source of trouble. She looked through each door again.

Hope ran faster.

Not this one, not this one.

"Ignore the alarm and answer my question!" somebody yelled nearby.

She looked in. "Galen!"

He looked up at her, a dopey smile on his face, and his eyes out of focus.

The two officers opposite him leaped up at the yell.

One drew a weapon.

"Unveil yourself or I'll shoot!" he ordered.

"I'm unarmed!" She dropped her hideaway and put her hands in the air. She stayed exactly where she was.

Shit! This was stupid. What was I thinking?

"Stay where you are and don't move!" the man yelled.

"What do you think you're doing?" the woman yelled at her. "Don't you know it's a crime to infiltrate a police station? Jamison, place her under arrest!"

"I don't think so!" came a powerful voice from behind her, and in walked Sandra.

"Who the hell are you?" the man demanded, shifting his weapon to her.

But the woman put a calming hand on his shoulder. They shared a Look, and he dipped his weapon to the floor.

"Sandra Levine, and you are interviewing my client without representation, and you've deliberately lied to me about it – more than once. My… assistant here was simply doing her job in helping me find my client and uncover this crime, and she shall not be held to account for uncovering your…" Sandra paused. She had finally noticed Galen's dopey expression. "What the hell is going on here? Have you *drugged* my client?" She sniffed at the coffee cup beside him, her nose wrinkled in distaste.

The man reached for it, but she yanked it back out of his grasp.

The woman opened and closed her mouth, anger and shame chasing themselves across her face. "We have extenuating circumstances."

"You will release my client immediately," Sandra hissed like a volcano ready to erupt, "along with all his possessions – and you will destroy any conversations you have procured, or I will prosecute this office for falsely gaining a confession from my client when he was under the influence of illicit substances and through intimidation."

"We didn't intimidate him! And I don't think…"

"I don't care what you think, Jodie. This is not legal!"

"You do remember we're acting under emergency measures, don't you? The city is under siege. Lives are in danger, and these are desperate times."

"I read those measures and they do not cover gaining a confession under duress, or… delusional rambling under the influence of a narcotic. Besides, this isn't the first time for you to be pushing the line, Jodie! I don't care how desperate you are; nothing my client has said will stand up in court and you know it!" She glared daggers at the pair.

Hope sidled over to Galen, placed a hand on his shoulder and squeezed it gently.

He smiled up at her with a lopsided grin.

She tried her best to suppress her own grin. Did she look this dopey when she was half-sedated?

Jodie grudgingly relented. "Fine! We'll release your client on bail, pending further investigations."

"An m'truck?" Galen slurred.

"Yes, his truck," Hope added more clearly. "You should release that, too."

"Certainly not," the detective replied. "We're actively prosecuting a legal warrant, and that truck contains Grade-A conjuration matrices and a dead body. We're under no obligation to release it till we've completed our investigations."

Sandra's eyebrows shot up at that, but she continued to stare the two officials down.

"None of those constitute evidence of a crime!" Hope insisted.

"That remains to be seen," the detective retorted, "especially given the other human remains we found at his place of residence!"

Galen's eyes drooped, and Hope looked confused.

"What human remains?" Sandra asked warily, suddenly looking as though she'd rather not have been assigned to this case after all.

The detective looked smug. "Your boyfriend here didn't tell you he had body parts in the freezer, hey? Maybe you're wondering whether you should be defending him after all."

"You shouldn't answer that, Hope," Sandra cautioned.

"Wait," Hope said, "by 'body parts', do you happen to mean a small human arm – child size?"

Sandra sighed. "What part of not answering don't you understand?"

The detective looked as if all her Christmases had come at once. "So, you admit you know about it! Jamison, arrest her! The charge will be accessory to a crime."

"I don't think so," Hope replied, placing her hands on her hips. "As I told you, there's been no crime here. That arm belongs to my sister's child, and you'd better have kept it well-preserved and unsullied, or I will have your heads!"

"What?" the detective and Sandra asked simultaneously.

Hope looked between the two incredulously. "Galen is a microsurgeon. Surely you have that on record somewhere," Hope replied slowly, as though to somebody who was very stupid. "He is pioneering research to restore my nibling's lost and damaged arm back to full function – after it was amputated in the wake of the chimera attack last Sunday. That's what the truck's matrices are for."

Sandra and the detective stared at her, dumbstruck.

Galen was grinning up at her rather adoringly.

"The... body...?" the detective began.

"My brother," Galen mumbled. "Frozen a year ago. Can't bury 'im; he keeps freezing up the ground."

Sandra nodded once and held out her hand. "Don't say anything else, Dr Moore." She turned to the detective. "Seems to all be in order here – no crime to prosecute."

The detective glowered. "I'll release the truck. The body and the other remains will stay in our morgue, where they'll be well looked after." She glared in Hope's direction. "Until we can confirm their provenance. If they are as you say they are, we'll release them back into your custody."

Sandra nodded, but Hope's eyes flitted nervously between Galen and the detective. "How long will that take?"

"Well, not today, that's for sure. We're pretty busy, unless you haven't noticed. We've got bigger things on our hands right now." She gestured at the door as more strangely dressed folks were being herded back and forth in the corridor beyond. "We'll get to it as soon as this backlog's taken care of. Now go, before I change my mind."

Sandra glared at her tone. "We're not done, Jodie." However, she turned anyway and hurried Hope and Galen out the door.

Hope held Galen upright as he stumbled down the hall. She propped him up through the outgoing processes, collecting his effects, including the keys to the truck, and she watched as he sloppily signed the release papers that Sandra held out for him.

Soon, they were back on the street, waiting by the loading bay for Galen's truck.

Sandra swapped contact details with her and gave the two of them instructions about how and when they should reappear. She also gave reassurances she would contact them the moment the Imperium officially cleared the body for release.

"Is there anything we could feasibly do to get it cleared today?" Hope asked.

"The way things are in there, I'd be surprised if anyone's free for weeks," Sandra replied with an exasperated huff.

Hope glanced nervously at Galen. "If, hypothetically, there were some financial means, would we be able to fund some kind of fast-track process?" she hinted, trying to keep some hope alive.

Sandra eyed her speculatively. "That's an interesting hypothetical. As your lawyer, I can only strongly advise against any speculation along those lines. If the wrong person got wind of that kind of attempt, it would undermine any goodwill that might've been built up already. In fact, it might cement in their minds the idea that said person (and any associate thereof) was not trustworthy and/or law-abiding. Such people might be subjected to an emergency hold again. This time without bail or hope of reprieve."

Hope nodded, forlorn. "Thanks anyway. That's probably good advice."

"I assure you it's the best possible advice, under the current circumstances," Sandra affirmed.

At that moment, a large roller door buzzed to life, revealing a massive, trundling automaton on treads. It chugged slowly forward, dragging the dolly containing Galen's truck. "Please step back outside the yellow zone," it rumbled in a monotone and waited until the visitors did as requested. Then, using a pair of huge, pincer-ended cranes, it lifted the truck off the dolly and slowly lowered it to the surface of the car park.

Galen winced as the truck dropped the last few inches, but all it did was rock on its tyres.

"Thank you. Please wait until I have safely retreated before you board your vehicle," the automaton recommended, while retreating into the unloading bay.

As soon as the roller door had closed, Galen sprinted for the back of the truck.

"Thanks, Sandra," Hope said to her. "You've been more than helpful."

"It's been… interesting to meet you both," Sandra replied. "Perhaps you could stop by and fill me in on more of the details before we move on to the next stage of the process? It would help me argue your case better if I actually knew what was going on."

"It'll be at least a day or so before we can get to that. After the Conjunction." Hope heard a sound of despair emanating from inside the truck. "I have to go."

Sandra nodded. "You have my details. I'll have an invoice ready for you, the next time we meet."

"Fair enough," Hope replied, and watched Sandra head back across the street.

She then ran around the truck to see what was going on. Galen was sitting on the floor of the truck, his head in his hands. The large box, which she'd used as a seat last time, was open and distinctly empty. She hopped up beside him and put an arm around his shoulders, which were shaking gently. She held him and waited until he was ready to speak.

He turned a tear-streaked face to her. "It's all useless. All this work!" He glanced around himself, at the matrices. "There are too many pieces to this puzzle, and now they're all scattered, and there's no time left to find them again. Even if we can get the pieces for the matrix, and the dream steel, we won't have my brother!"

Hope drew him in tight. She breathed in deeply and let it out in a whoosh. "It's not over yet," she told him, hoping her tone was convincingly fearless. "There's still time before this afternoon's main event. We'll find some way of getting it all together, including your brother."

He swiped away his tears and looked balefully at the empty casket beside them. "You heard them. Even the lawyer said there was no way."

Hope drew her lips into a grim smile. "Not exactly."

He looked up at her in surprise.

"She merely said that it'd be risky if we tried to bribe our way in, because we don't know who to bribe without getting caught. That would get us in hot water. Thankfully, though, I happen to know a guy."

Galen's face transformed. Like the sun rising, she could see hope bloom in his eyes.

A genuine smile spread across her face as she said, "Now, let's get out of here. You need some sleep, or something to eat, or both, while I go see what I can do about your brother's body – and I know just the place."

She got him settled in the front seat. This time, it was his turn to fall into a drunken stupor while she drove him to Pam's. Soon after, he was gently snoring beside her, but she kept the smile on her face, even if only to hide the growing anxiety over what she would have to do next.

30 - In favour

Hope eyed the alley with the greasy café. She'd half hoped she'd never have to see this dank dive again.

She debated her options, but again came up short. The truth was, she *had* begun to care about Galen. She still wasn't sure whether she *cared* cared, but either way he was a friend indeed, and that meant she was willing to help him get what he needed.

Still, did it mean she was prepared to do *this*?

She scowled and kicked a rock. Then she huffed out a breath and started walking before she could talk herself out of it. She was through the door and ducking through the usual overhanging detritus before she started getting nervous again, by which time it was too late to back out.

The door to Henry's office was already open, and he looked up and spotted her. He sat back in his chair, one eyebrow raised.

She stood there awkwardly in the doorway as he scrutinised her.

After a few moments, he nodded and waved her in. "Close the door behind you, love." He waited, watching her as she sat before him. "This'd better be important. I've got a million balls in the air right now."

She snorted. "I wouldn't be here if it wasn't important, believe me." She breathed deeply, to steel herself. "I need a favour. The kind only you can provide. I've come prepared to pay."

Henry raised an eyebrow at that. "And what makes you think I'll grant it? Word on the street is you said we were quits. Plus, you doublecrossed me on the dream-steel job."

Hope raised her own eyebrow at that. "I distinctly recall your own doublecross on that deal. Plus, I technically never took your job, so I technically didn't doublecross you. I'm very careful about that kind of thing."

He snorted. "Now we're quibbling over technicalities. You knowingly took on a job of mine, on your own, outside of my auspices. You took what was mine, and nobody would object to my taking its price out of your hide. Especially given how goody-goody you are about working alone because of how people have supposedly betrayed you."

She hissed in frustration. "You knew I'd overhear that deal. Besides, I was going to bring the dream steel to you to fence. I didn't know you'd sent another team after it, and I'll remind you they did doublecross you. They on-sold it to a third party."

He nodded and mulled this over for a moment. "Even so," he acceded. "All right, love, what brings you here, then?"

"The third party your terrible trio sold the dream steel to. He has plans for some kind of mind-control device. He'll be powering up the main conjuration for it during the Conjunction tonight and using our dream steel to do it."

"And? What do you want me to do about it? I say good on him. Sounds like an interesting initiative. Are you planning to nick it from him? If so, it sounds like something I might aim to acquire."

She rolled her eyes and pulled out a sheet of paper – the plans she'd purloined from Mr Green. "He made a mistake in his calculations. This thing is way overpowered. It won't control only a few people; it'll control hundreds. And that's just to start; you know as well as I do there's a resonance factor involved when you use dream steel."

Henry frowned at that. "What difference will that make?"

She looked up, surprised. But she explained anyway. "Every connected person lends a small boost from their own energy, meaning one more person to control, and so on, and so on. Dozens of people could become hundreds, which could become thousands, or more. It's possible that by this time tomorrow, the entire city could be trapped, under his control. Couple this with the fact I've noticed he's considerably unhinged, and I don't think he's going to politely relinquish control of us all with an apology and a cup of tea."

His self-interest visibly piqued, he was now intently studying the rough plans. "You know it'll happen for certain, or is it just a guess?" He examined her face, looking for tells.

She sighed. "I've made an educated hypothesis based on the available data."

He snorted. "Right. A guess then. So, apart from maybe getting out of town for the evening, which I had already planned on doing given the high concentration of morons likely to blow themselves up this evening – what exactly are you hoping I'll do for you? Surely you're not expecting heroics on behalf of the city. Even you should know that's not my style."

She rolled her eyes again. "Of course not."

Hope took a deep breath. This was it. She'd figured out what she needed to say to him. It was loosely based on the truth. He'd just have to cope with that. Given that *'loosely based on the truth'* was his usual MO, she didn't feel guilty about using it on him. She just hoped she could get away with it. It was hard to con a professional swindler. "I have a plan. But it involves getting help from a new acquaintance of mine, and he's asked a favour of me in exchange. If I don't get it for him, he doesn't help me. And for this favour I need your help."

"What kind of favour?" he purred, his eyes flashing.

She paused and looked away. "There's a body in the lockup at the local precinct. I need you to liberate it and get it to me before the Conjunction."

He was silent, watching. "By 'body', you don't mean a living person, do you?"

"Does it matter?"

"It matters how I'd break it out. Plus, I want to understand what I'm getting involved in before I stick my neck out. So, is it?"

"Well, yes, and no." She half-shrugged.

He narrowed his eyes.

"He's in the morgue, frozen solid. Some kind of bullshit freeze-ray from the last round of mad scientists. He's not dead, and my acquaintance can unfreeze him during the Conjunction as long as he's busted out in time – but not if he's in the morgue."

He eyed her suspiciously. "That sounds like bullshit to me."

She snorted. "Weirdly, it's still true."

He searched her face again. "I actually believe you. Though that's not all of it, is it?"

She sat up straight. "That's everything relevant. You don't need to know the rest. Get the body out, safe and sound, and get it to us in time for the Conjunction. That's the favour, and I'll pay you whatever it's worth. If you can do it."

"And you'll take care of the mind-control machine, is that it?"

She nodded.

He tipped his head to one side. "That's a hard ask in this timeframe, love, and you know it."

"I know. That's why I came to see you."

He folded his arms and sat back. "And I'm still not sure why I should lift a finger for you. You left me high and dry. I'm not exactly inclined to help you out."

Hope's heart fell. But she steeled herself to reply. "Look, I know you'd just as happily see me curl up and die as help me out, but I also know you give a damn about this city. Even if it's only so you can continue using it as your own personal money-making scheme. And I'm telling you that if you don't help me out, the city is going to be in thrall to a completely different self-serving megalomaniac than yourself – by 6 pm tonight. And all you need to do to stop it is send some goons to help me out. Probably won't even need more than a couple of phone calls. You can leave the rest up to me to fix."

Henry sighed. "You've never really understood why I do things, have you?" he muttered. Then he went silent for a while, scrutinising her closely. "If I do this for you, you'll owe me a favour. One last job, and you can't say no," he replied quietly, with a predatory smile.

Hope's lips pressed together in a thin, grey line, and her eyes blazed. "I'd rather pay you."

The smile widened. "I'm sure you would."

She paused, waiting to see if he'd say more, but he just narrowed his eyes and waited. "Fine!" she bit out. "One favour, but I won't do anything that puts me or mine in danger. You explain the job and I get to decide on that. I get to say no if I think it's a suicide mission, too."

"Fair enough. In exchange, I'll get you your body."

"Before the Conjunction and in perfect nick, or the deal's off."

"Pristine, by 6 pm tonight." He nodded and held out his hand.

She glared at him, then stuck out hers too.

They shook hard, just the once.

She continued to glare at him.

He raised an eyebrow at her.

She put her hands on her hips and waited.

He snorted and made a shooing gesture. "Off you fuck. I'm not revealing my sources to you."

She sneered at him, spun around, and slammed out through the door. She stomped over to the opposite side of the alley and sat down to wait.

It wasn't long.

Henry appeared at the doorway. "It's done."

"Where do I go to get it?"

"By 'done', I mean the process has begun. It will take non-zero time to complete, so be patient."

"I have places I need to be," she replied. "I can't wait around here for however long it takes."

"So give me something of yours I can track," he replied with a smile, "and I'll send it right to you, wherever you are."

That had Hope on edge. She sure didn't want Henry to have any part of herself. "Have you got a standard target?"

He snorted out a laugh and handed over a small but heavy card.

Hope glared at it, then at Henry. "You use this only to send me the item," she warned. "I'll ditch it the moment it changes hands." But she duly pocketed it and stomped off down the alley to find herself a cab.

31 - How to hunt a scoundrel

The bouncers let her into the building with little fuss. Sam was at the coffee table with a roll of paper and a pile of scattered crayons. They were struggling to draw with their off-hand. The paper kept moving, and Sam was huffing at it.

Hope grabbed a mug and popped it on the corner of the paper.

They glared at it. "It's too hard!"

She smiled in sympathy. "It was hard when you first started, too. You'll get there."

Sam nodded, setting their mouth in a grim line and picking up the crayons once again.

"Is Felicity working?" she asked.

They nodded. "Should be back in a few minutes."

"Where's Galen?" She looked around, even though he obviously wasn't in the tiny room.

"He's crashed out. Mum put him in your room because you weren't here." Sam eyed her curiously. "Have you two made up yet?"

She huffed out a breath. "And why's that any business of yours?"

They just smirked and raised their own eyebrows expectantly.

She shook her head. "We've barely had time to think, let alone talk, and there isn't time now. The Conjunction is only a few hours away. We have to find Mr Green and stop him before something terrible happens."

"Can't we let the cops deal with him?"

Hope paused to think about that. She wished she could hand this task over to somebody else. She wasn't exactly a big fish in this pond. For so long she'd been content to remain a little fish, schooling with the others or swimming away from danger. To take on this predator, she'd have to swim out past the safety of the reef, find her teeth, and strike

249

back. She wasn't sure she was ready, but she didn't have much choice.

"I wish we *could* leave it up to them. I asked, but they're overwhelmed with everything else going on tonight. Plus, we need to find him ourselves so we can get that dream steel – for Galen's brother."

Sam looked confused.

"So," came a rough voice behind Hope, "you really are going to help me with that?"

She turned.

Galen was standing in the doorway, bleary-eyed and dressed in sparkly pink sweats, which had a huge, palatial logo across the front.

She smiled. "Been shopping in the gift shop?"

"Closest shop with clothes," he muttered, the ghost of his usual smirk brushing his lips, "and I didn't want to go home just yet."

"You look like you could do with some coffee," she said, eyeing him up.

He groaned in pleasure. "Oh, so very much!"

"We only have instant. Anything better will take a while to go fetch."

"Any caffeine will be a godsend," he remarked, yawning and rubbing sleep out of his eyes.

She walked over to the kitchenette and dug out the jar of instant. Sam helped by fetching the mugs, which saved her from scrabbling randomly to find them. They were always in the least-expected cupboard.

"So, where's the orderly?" Hope asked, glancing around the room again. He wasn't standing by the usual window.

"He has a name, you know," Sam said.

Hope looked up from spooning the coffee. "Does he?"

Sam nodded. "Galen told me he's called Phillip."

Galen nodded, handing over a carton of milk he'd retrieved from the tiny mini-fridge. "And he's locked in the bathroom to keep him out of mischief."

"You didn't have to do that!" Sam exclaimed. "I liked having him here, keeping me company." They disappeared off towards the bathroom door.

Galen raised an eyebrow at the departure, throwing a curious look at Hope, who just shrugged. His expression grew sombre and then wary. He opened his mouth...

The kettle beeped and clicked off. He shook his head and closed his mouth again, staring into the steam.

Hope smiled to herself as she poured the boiling water and tipped a swoosh of milk into the mugs. She handed one over. "It's not a proper espresso, but it's hot, and it's here," she said, cradling her own.

He sighed deeply and sipped with his eyes closed. "A coffee in the hand is worth two in the street. Thanks." He tipped his head from side to side, as though debating a voice in his head. "Did you manage to..." he cut himself off.

She looked up at him.

His shoulders were tense again.

"I've got somebody on it. I'm assured that he'll be with us before it all goes down tonight."

He smiled at her through the steam, his eyes glistening.

She smiled back. "I can't guarantee they'll be reliable, but it's the best I can do."

Galen nodded. "Thank you. It's more than I could have asked for."

She shrugged it off, but smiled down into her coffee. "Oh, I also brought your bag from home. Did you find it?" She glanced sideways at Sam, who had rejoined them and was unashamedly listening in.

They grinned and raised an eyebrow. "You mean the big ole bag of dodgy cash in the corner?"

Hope's eyes opened wide. "You didn't go poking around in somebody else's things, did you?"

"I would never!" they protested, but with a cheeky grin. "But you can't blame me for taking a peek in the top!"

Hope narrowed her eyes at her nibling.

Galen drifted over to poke around inside the bag.

She dug into her jacket pocket and pulled out a large wad of cash that she held out to him. "I took this for bail money, but it turned out to be unnecessary."

He looked up at her in surprise and laughed it off. "Don't be silly. I already told you the money belongs to you. No, what I wanted was... Ah, the control flow! You got it out!" The relief in his voice was palpable. He clutched the manuscript to his chest.

Hope smiled. "Yeah, I just dumped everything from your desk into the bag. I didn't have time to pick and choose. Did you know that Mr Green tried to use one of those ferret things to plant evidence in your room?"

"You got *everything* from the desk?" he exclaimed, smiling even wider. He rummaged through the bag even more intensely, pulling out a heavy, grey pouch that was about a hand-span wide.

"What's that?" Sam asked.

He looked shifty. "Ah, better you don't know – your mother might not be happy with me..."

Hope immediately became suspicious of the tone, but decided not to grill him about it in front of Sam.

"Just something I'm exceedingly grateful to have back, instead of in somebody else's hands." He tucked it away in the front pocket of his sweats.

At that moment, the door opened and in swept Felicity wearing a glittering, sapphire-coloured Cinderella costume, complete with crystal-clear, sparkling 'glass' slippers, which she tossed to the side with a satisfied sigh.

"Oh, you're back." She gave Hope a quick hug. Her eyes caressed the coffee her sister was clutching. "Can you make one of those for me while I change into something more comfy?"

"Sure thing, Cinders," Hope replied with a smile.

Felicity rolled her eyes, tossing a mock glare over her shoulder as she retrieved the slippers and disappeared into the bedroom.

"Your sister's a princess?" Galen was staring after Felicity.

Hope raised her eyebrows. "Yeah. Why else do you think we're staying here? Is that a problem?"

"No problem at all. You said she worked here, but I didn't realise she had one of the top jobs." He closed his eyes, savouring his coffee.

"Yeah. Doesn't pay as well as you'd think, especially part-time, but she gets to rub elbows with all the high-society mucky-mucks." Hope refilled the kettle and started another cup of coffee.

"Even Imperial family?" He looked askance at her.

"Rarely," Felicity answered, reappearing in comfortable shorts and a T-shirt, "but yes, sometimes we even entertain the royalty. So, what's the plan?" She accepted a steaming mug from Hope.

Hope peered into her own mug, as if there were answers hiding in its murky depths. "Honestly, I don't know. Henry is sending someone to... ah..." She eyed Sam warily. "...fetch the item out of lockup, but we still have to find Mr Green inside of the next few hours in order to have any chance of stopping his badly planned experiment, or of getting Galen's dream steel back."

She looked up at him.

She'd expected him to be looking dubious, but he was looking at her expectantly, as if everything was under control and would magically fall in line.

His trust in her was so badly mis-placed. She frowned into her coffee again. "I don't have a signifier anymore," she muttered.

"So, how can we track him down without one?" Galen asked.

Hope deflated, her frown deepening. "I don't know."

Sam stepped up beside her. "Aunty Hope? He took my blood."

Hope looked at Sam bleakly. "I know, honey. I swear I won't let him hurt you with it."

"No. I mean thanks, but that's not what I meant. Can you use my blood to track that blood?"

Hope looked at Sam quizzically, then her mind started to tick over. Could she use Sam's blood to track the scratch that Mr Green had taken? She shook her head. "The blood sample he has is tiny. It'd get lost among all the places you've been in the rest of the city. Plus, I think your presence would overwhelm any tracking signal that small. I'm good at sorting through multiple signals, but you're like a shining beacon. It'd be like trying to see a star in the daytime – the sun outshines it."

"But you *can* see stars during the day sometimes," Sam said.

Hope raised an eyebrow.

Sam rolled their eyes and pointed out the window at the sky, to where the Conjunction would be in just a few scant hours. "During an eclipse."

Felicity smiled sadly. "It's a lovely idea, Sam, but Hope was using a metaphor. It doesn't really work the same way."

But Hope tapped her fingers on her chin as her mind continued to spin. "Unless," She looked up at Felicity. "Unless I use Sam *as* the signifier. Then they wouldn't be a potential target. The tracker magic would eclipse their signal."

Felicity's face went white. "No."

"It's the only way…"

"No! You are not putting Sam in danger!"

"They are already in danger. We all are. If we don't find Mr Green before the Conjunction, the city will be under his control. Sam included."

"I don't care. This is Sam we're talking about, and I will not let you use them like this."

"Mum?" Sam said, tentatively.

"No!" Felicity insisted.

Sam put their hand on Felicity's shoulder. "Mum, don't I get a vote?"

Felicity's shoulders drooped.

Standing firm, Sam said, "I don't want anybody to die just because I was too afraid to help."

32 - Body re-snatchers

"Okay, are you comfortable?" Felicity asked.

"Not even a little bit," Hope grumbled.

"I wasn't asking you," Felicity said.

Sam giggled. "I'm fine, Mum."

"Could you just..." Hope pushed Sam a little to the left. "I need my arm free."

Sam turned around in Hope's lap, then shuffled over to sit with their back to the truck's door. They rested their bandaged stump on Hope's shoulder and lay their legs across her knees.

"Oh, that's much better, thanks!" she said in relief, and pulled the seatbelt across the pair of them.

"That's not safe for driving!" Felicity said from the window.

"Don't worry so much, Mum," Sam complained.

Watching, bemused, from the driver's seat, Galen said, "Yeah. Don't worry, I'll go slow."

"It's not about you, there are other drivers on the road," she replied.

"I doubt anybody will go fast, even they wanted to," Hope grumbled. "Haven't you seen the traffic today? We'll be lucky if we go faster than a crawl. Besides, there's no other way we can fit in here and navigate the tracker."

Felicity reluctantly nodded.

"Can you hop in back? We've got to get moving," Hope told her.

Felicity huffed but turned and climbed into the back of the truck.

Once the door had slammed down into place, Galen started the engine but kept it idling.

Hope activated the re-painted tracking matrix on her arm, then grabbed Sam's wrist and put it in place on top, intertwining their fingers. She felt the familiar wave of magic wash out of her, rippling out across the city. Before it returned, she muttered, "A little help?"

Galen took the large, soft ribbon he had ready and used it to tie Sam's wrist firmly in place on top of Hope's. The signifier had to remain in contact with her matrix, otherwise she'd lose contact with the target. Their clasped hands would help, but the ribbon ensured they stayed secure.

The ripples returned to her, and she closed her eyes to sift through them. There were eight strong enough to use.

"Okay," she began; "there's a bunch of potential targets. I'm going to assume that the two biggest ones are Sam's arm, still in lockup, and our apartment. One of the smaller ones is the room at Pam's. We can eliminate all three of them, for sure, when we triangulate. That leaves five. Sam, can you think of anywhere you've been recently where you left something of yourself behind?"

Sam thought. "Only the café where I got hurt."

Hope nodded. "Of course. That leaves four. Anywhere else?"

Sam shook their head.

"They scraped a knee at the park last week!" Felicity called out.

"Oh, yeah," Sam exclaimed. "I forgot."

"Yeah, you've been busy since then. Good. That leaves just three. We'll give them all a closer look."

Galen took them out into the city traffic, beginning with a swing around the ring road to give Hope a chance at a rough triangulation. They used that to confirm and eliminate all the known locations. The hospital lined up with one of the three remaining targets. That was another easy elimination – probably medical waste from the operation in a dumpster somewhere.

The next target wasn't very far away – inside the industrial zone. It took twenty minutes of crawling through traffic before they finally came upon it: a pathology lab. Galen said it was most likely one of the blood samples taken during the operation. Which left only one location, and it was close to the suburb in which they'd found the second crime-scene – the gorilla-dog remains.

The problem? The district was crawling with temp workers returning from the CBD, all of them flush with cash and half-drunk, ready for a fight. Not a safe place to bring a kid.

Hope had Galen drive around the outskirts to scope the location. It was an industrial estate, gated and fenced, and looked quite a maze, which meant it was hard to pin down a target from the outside.

They cruised past the only entrance to the estate and noted several figures lounging by the gate, each with a suspicious-looking bulge in their jacket.

"Can you narrow it down any more?" Galen asked quietly.

Hope pointed with her free hand. "It's in that zone, right in the middle. But unless we go in, we're going to be hunting through dozens of workshops."

"So why don't we go in?" Sam asked.

"Too unsafe," Hope answered. "Those guys at the boom gate aren't just hanging out. They're lookouts. This is some kind of gang territory, and I don't know whose." She eyed the guards worriedly as they drove away and turned to Galen. "We shouldn't drive by again. They've already clocked us." She turned back to Sam. "We had a run-in with some gang-bangers out here a few days ago. It didn't go well."

Galen looked concerned. "You mean the guys at the crime-scene? Who the cops scared off?"

She nodded. "I bet they're from this gang, and I'd rather avoid them if we can."

"I agree, but do we have a choice?"

She grimaced. "Unlikely. Still, I don't want to bring Sam or Felicity into a confrontation."

Galen nodded. He pulled the truck over a few streets back from the estate. "We're running out of time," he muttered to himself, eyeing up the approaching sunset; "and... I'm worried about..." He didn't finish what he said, but Hope knew he was concerned about his absent brother.

They'd spent the afternoon prepping a few matrices for quick use and waiting to hear back from Henry, but it was mid-afternoon and they still had no word. So they'd hit the road, hoping Henry would catch up to them. But now it was rapidly approaching evening, and she was starting to worry.

"Can you call him?" Galen asked.

"I can," she replied, biting her lip, "but he doesn't normally pick up. I guess it can't hurt. You guys stay quiet while I call." She listened to the empty dial tone.

She was about to hang up when, surprisingly, Henry picked up on the fourth ring. "Where the gods-damn hell are you? I've had my folks driving 'round chasing you for the past hour! You're all over the city!"

Hope's eyebrows rose. "I told you we'd be on the move."

"You didn't tell me you'd literally not stop for two hours."

She huffed. "We've been triangulating the tracker! We've stopped now, in the east sector, past the industrial zone, in the sticks."

"What are you doing over there?"

"Hunting down our only lead!" she replied, exasperated.

"You know that's Biter territory, right? Nasty fuckers, they are, and pretty territorial. Watch yourself or you'll end up getting killed."

"Thanks. So I take it you can't help us get in, then?"

Henry just laughed. "You said you'd take care of it. I'll be busy skipping town instead."

"Gee, thanks for your support. I sure hope there's a town for you to come back to."

He audibly sighed. "Why don't you ask Tink for help when she gets there? She used to run with the Biters."

"Tink? You put the unreliable trio in charge of bringing our body? They'll on-sell it to the first body snatcher they can get cash out of!"

"Calm down, love. I explained to them that this is their one and only ticket back into my good graces. If they fuck this up, I'll be sending the Cutters after them. Besides, beggars can't be choosers. Don't forget this was your last-minute request and we're a tad short staffed at the moment."

Hope grumbled under her breath. "Well, fine. Thanks, I guess."

"Don't thank me. You owe me a favour, and I'll call on you after all this is done. That's all the thanks I need."

"You can't collect if I don't live through the afternoon," she replied, then hung up on him. That felt good.

She turned to Galen, who had been unashamedly eavesdropping on the conversation. "The package is incoming. We need to go somewhere we can accept a body and have a quiet chat without being interrupted."

He nodded. "I spotted an empty carpark a few blocks back – looked a bit more private than this. Should do the trick." He pulled out into the traffic again and drove them there.

Hope scanned the area. It would do. "Sam, I need you to hop in the back to stay safe. We can't be sure these people will be friendly."

"Nuh-uh, I'm not hiding. I want to see," Sam replied, holding up their intertwined hands, "and you'll have to do your magic again, anyway."

"I can do that again, but I won't see you hurt."

They lifted a foot and kicked the tiny window leading into the back of the truck. "Mum, can I stay with Hope?"

Felicity hopped out and leaned through the window to respond. "I don't want you in danger, Sam." Sam's face fell. "But you're right. If Hope reactivates her tracker, she'll use up a lot of energy, and she'll need that in reserve. I want you to be safe too, Hope. You two stay in the truck. Galen can talk to the people who come, and I'll be in the driver's seat, ready to drive at the first sign of trouble."

Galen raised an eyebrow at this, but nodded his assent.

Hope was dubious. She remembered how badly the conversation with Dodge had gone. "I'll keep the door open so I can hop out if Galen needs help."

They didn't have to wait long. A black hearse with tinted rear windows slowly rolled into the parking lot, driven by Buzz. He scowled as he looked them over, then ignored them.

The hearse lifted a good few inches as Tink unfolded herself from the passenger seat. She scowled as well, but sauntered over to them.

Hope couldn't see Dodge. That was a good sign.

Galen stood next to the truck, arms folded, and glaring right back. "Do you have my brother?"

Tink's scowl dropped for a moment. "Your brother? We've only got a body!"

Galen's glare grew and, surprisingly, Tink's face softened a little.

"Sorry, man, I didn't know. Yeah, we've got him, but the boss's instructions're clear. The only one we can hand him over to's Hope."

"I'm here, just stuck." Hope piped up from the passenger seat.

Tink eyeballed her, sitting with Sam on her lap, but said nothing.

"You can help Galen put the body into the truck," Hope said.

Tink side eyed Galen, and returned to the hearse.

Galen opened the back of the truck, then joined her.

She pulled out the rolling platform the body was lying on. "He's frozen solid, you know?" She found a grip on the heavy-fabric bag.

"Wait, let me check him over," Galen replied, unzipping the bag as Tink stepped back.

Sam gasped as it revealed a familiar face, but Hope put a finger to their lips to keep them quiet. Tink wasn't owed any of Galen's private information and she could answer Sam's questions later.

Un-zipping further revealed a long, black box resting on his brother's chest.

Hope's heart soared. She'd already guessed what the box contained. It was just the right size to hold a small, child-sized arm.

Tink eyed the box. "Didn't know what that was, but it was tucked in with the body – figured you'd want it."

Galen took it out and set it aside. He looked up at Hope and nodded solemnly. "It's still sealed. Should be secure inside."

She nodded gratefully.

He gave his brother a thorough check-up as Tink grew increasingly agitated.

"Are you done?" she burst out.

"I'm making sure my brother is intact," he replied.

"Why, have you got places to be?" Hope called out to her.

"What's it to you?" Tink snapped back, stepping closer.

"Henry said I should ask you for help getting into the Biters' turf without ticking them off."

"Boss didn't say nothing about that."

"Well, you'd better call him and confirm, because I just got off the phone with him five minutes ago."

Tink looked down at the ground.

"What's the matter? He not taking your calls right now?" Hope teased.

"I don't have to help you with anything," Tink snarled, her hands fisted.

Hope raised her eyebrows and put her free hand on her hip. "Henry said you'd help me with this. You don't want to disappoint him, do you?"

"We've done what he said! Got this body out of a fucking Imperium police morgue, brought it to you intact and on time. We don't owe him anything more!"

Hope snorted. "Are you kidding? Do you think that's all you'll have to do? You doublecrossed Henry, for fuck's sake! You're lucky to be alive right now. Even the Cutters would think twice before going up against him. You'll be paying him back for that little slip-up for a long, long time."

Tink scowled, but Hope could see she'd gotten through to her in the resigned slump of her shoulders. She growled to herself for a minute, then drew her shoulders up. "Why d'you want to go messing with the Biter gang, anyway? They're bad news!"

"Didn't *you* used to run with them?"

"Yeah. Emphasis on 'used to'. There's a reason I got out. Only some kinds of women are willing to hang around them."

"I'm surprised you'd be afraid of them, given..." Hope indicated Tink's heavily augmented frame.

"I wasn't always this strong," Tink muttered. "Those slimeballs'll chew you up and spit you out – and that goes double for your little lap mate there." She pointed to Sam and then Felicity. "As for the courtesan, they'll take their time with her."

"I've already had a run-in with them. I'm acquainted with how delightful they are," Hope replied dryly.

"Then why are you going in there? Are you stupid?"

Hope's eyes flashed. "I'm going in because if I don't, the crazy dude you sold the dream steel to, is going mind-fuck half the city! We're going in there to stop him."

Tink's eyes went wide, and her jaw went slack. "What?"

"Tink!" Buzz yelled from the car.

"Just a minute," Tink yelled back at him.

"Get that weirdo out of this car and let's get this over with so we can get outta here!"

Tink cast a look at Galen, who was carefully checking for damage to his brother's toes. "Doc's not done yet." She turned back to Hope.

The dismissal clearly angered Buzz, but he didn't argue back. Looked like the power dynamic had shifted there.

"What's that about mind-fucking? I thought the crazy hat-guy was just doing freaky-animal shit."

"That's what he'd originally planned, but his freaky-animal shit involves using some kind of mega-powerful device to control their minds. I've seen his blueprints, and the device has at least one mistake. It's going to be ridiculously over-powered for a small army of animals. Did you see how much dream steel he ordered?"

"Yeah, it was a lot – that's why it was such a good score."

"Yeah, well, from what I can tell, it's enough to spark a chain reaction. We'll all be under his control, like a bunch of robots." She hastily added, "no offence intended."

"I'm not a robot!" Tink spat, scowling. "I'm augmented. I've still got my own brain!"

Hope raised an eyebrow but decided not to make the obvious joke. Tink looked to be turning this over in her head, and Hope really needed some help getting inside while keeping Sam and Felicity safe.

"All right," Tink announced, nodding once. "I'll help."

Hope raised her eyebrows.

Tink scowled back. "That crazy arsehole put Dodge in the hospital. I can't attack him. Henry's orders are for us to get the hell out and leave you to it, but I sure as hell will help you get one past him." She turned to Galen. "You done yet?"

He eyed her speculatively, then nodded, zipping up his brother.

Tink pulled on a pair of heavy leather biker gloves and lifted the body overhead, easily. It was as stiff as a board, and she carried it away from her body. Frost covered the fabric. "Tell me where you want 'im."

Galen directed her into the back of the truck.

Hope felt the truck's bed lurch and groan as Tink climbed in.

A few moments later, Tink returned to the hearse.

Hope was about to object, but saw she walked to the driver-side window rather than the passenger seat.

"Wait while I get these people into the compound?" Tink asked.

Buzz was already shaking his head. "No way I'm waiting another five minutes, Tink. It'll take enough time to get back across town to the party." He glanced up at the setting sun. "Get in and come now, or I'll leave you here and you can find your own way back."

Tink's face fell, but she quickly hid it and anger blazed across her features. "Well, fine, fuck off then! I don't want to see you again any more anyway – we're done!" She slammed her hand against the hearse's roof, leaving a sizeable dent, and spun around. She stomped back towards the truck, leaving Buzz looking shocked.

His own face filled with anger. He jammed his foot on the accelerator and spun the car, tyres squealing as he peeled out of the car park, leaving her behind.

"Arsehole," Tink muttered. "Right, you coming or what?"

Hope just looked at her. "We need to get the truck in there, too."

"What, seriously? Shit!" Tink rubbed her hand across her face, eyeing up the buildings. "All right." She walked around to the driver's side of the cab. "Shove over, I'm driving."

Felicity cast a questioning look at Hope. Hope shrugged. So Felicity shoved over. Then shoved over even more as Tink actually hopped in.

Hope was squashed against the door. Lucky they were all family as they were getting up close and very personal.

"So, what's the plan?" Hope grunted as Tink pulled out of the parking lot and headed for the front gate.

"No plan," she growled in reply. "I just got here, yeah? Just keep your mouth shut and go along with whatever I say. That goes especially for you, kid."

"Aye-aye, captain," Sam joked, saluting.

Tink snorted. It might have even been a laugh.

33 - Getting inside

As Tink pulled up to the boom gate, Hope saw that the number of loungers had doubled. Most were relaxing with a drink and shooting the breeze. One of them, however, carried some kind of walkie-talkie and was vigilantly observing everyone who went by. They were speaking into it as Tink pulled up.

Four of his colleagues stood as the truck approached, and another pair appeared from a nearby building, walking casually and keeping an eye out for other vehicles.

Tink leaned out as the one with the walkie-talkie and his mate, sauntered over to the driver-side window. "Hey up, Booza. Long time no see," she drawled.

"Hey up, Tinkerbell," he replied. "Long time. Why're you here?"

Tink scowled even harder at the nickname. "I got some party supplies to deliver."

"Boss never told us to expect any party supplies."

She smiled. "Not for you lot, doofus. For..." She turned to Hope with raised eyebrows.

"Mr Green," Hope supplied.

"Mr Green," Tink repeated. "He works out of one of the workshops here."

Booza looked them over, then flicked a look at his walkie-talkie buddy, who had another quiet word on the device.

"Boss says let 'em in, but they gotta pay an entry fee," he relayed.

"What kinda fee?" Tink asked warily.

"What kinda supplies you carrying?" Booza asked.

"Not the kind we can share," Hope piped up sternly.

"Well, them's the rules; ya share or ya don't come inside."

Hope looked at Tink, who shrugged.

"What if I could make it worth it to you?" Hope asked.

"Well, that'd be nice, 'n' all, but the boss'll have my hide if I don't come up with some goods. What're ya shipping, anyway?"

Tink opened her mouth to reply, but Hope jumped in again. "Dead animals."

"What the...?" he said. "What kinda party supplies is that?"

"Haven't you seen what Mr Green's up to?" Hope asked him. "He uses them in his medical experiments. Do you still want some?"

"Sheeeet. Haven't ya got anything else?"

"Not really."

One of the others leered in through Hope's window. "What about some of your time, sweetheart?"

"Not gonna happen," Tink answered.

"Oh, little Tinkerbell, ya used to be up for a good time."

Tink flexed her steel muscles and scowled harder.

"Well, if you're not gonna put out..." Booza shrugged and casually glanced at his mates. Two of them fingered the suspicious bulges under their jackets.

"You don't want to start anything today," Tink threatened.

"Rules are rules, Tink, and you should know the boss is a stickler. Outta my hands."

A heavy knocking sound emanated from inside the truck, and Galen yelled, "Glove compartment!"

The jumpy dudes with bulges suddenly became less subtle about their weapons. Most of them had their hands on the holster, but two had drawn them, holding their weapon low and ready.

"Who's that?" Booza demanded.

"Hold your fire!" Hope called out. "I'm getting you your entry fee." She moved slowly and carefully.

Booza stepped around to the window to watch her moves more clearly.

Hope opened the glove compartment. The lid fell open only an inch before it bumped against Sam's side. Sam gave a small grunt and squeezed back against Hope to give the lid more room.

Hope reached in and pulled out a zippered container. She unzipped it to reveal a small rack of stoppered vials, each containing a labelled healing potion.

"Oh yes," Booza said, gesturing to her. "These'll do nicely. Hand 'em over!"

"I'm gonna keep these and give you a couple."

"Nope, not today, you're not!" He grabbed at the rack.

Hope scrabbled with it, but he yanked it out of her hands. She was left holding only two vials, which she quickly hid in her hand as he made off with the rest of the container. She pocketed the pair and glared at their grinning hosts.

They whooped in delight at their unexpected score and Hope worried they'd lost their bargaining chip. But the boom gate rose and the other loungers stepped back as Tink drove the truck through.

"That seemed a bit too easy," Hope muttered.

"Yep," Tink said. "The trick will be getting back out again."

They made their way into the industrial estate, Hope directing Tink through the labyrinth of roads, side alleys, and workshops.

Most of the latter were closed up tight, but plenty of folks had clearly come to their workplaces to take advantage of the roof spaces as viewing platforms. Various groups of spectators sat on sun lounges, beanbags or milk crates, sunnies firmly in place; chatting or dancing and waiting for the show to begin at sunset – most of them inebriated in one way or another.

At least one group looked like it was holding a wedding.

Music of all genres was pumping from every direction, the only common denominator being that it was *loud*. The sound was helpfully covering their engine noise. After all, they weren't sneaking up that quietly.

It was the smell that gave it away first. Not quite as whiffy as a piggery, but still with that overwhelming, *eau-de-manure* stench of a zoo. Like walking into the fertiliser section of a nursery.

Felicity was holding her nose. "Ugh! Guess we're close."

Sam buried their head in Hope's shoulder and made gagging noises.

"Guess manure beats B.O. then," Hope joked.

The smell was emanating from a small cluster of workshops that was surrounded by an empty car park. Nobody was moving around on these rooftops, but one had an extremely large parabolic reflector set up on top.

Hope turned serious. "All right, this is where you two get out and go home," she told Felicity and Sam. "I'm pretty sure we can find it from here."

"You can't walk outta here on your own!" Tink exclaimed, scandalised.

"Why not?" Felicity demanded.

"Well, firstly, 'cause you just got here, and the guys at the gate might become suspicious if you leave on your own so soon. Secondly, Booza didn't buy our story about animal parts – he thinks that *you* are the party supplies." She poked a finger at Felicity. "Finally, forgive me for saying it, but from their perspective, you're both classed as prey. I used to run with these guys. Trust me when I say you're exactly their type, and they don't play clean."

Hope and Felicity shared a Look.

"We can't go in," Felicity announced, frowning and looking at the buildings. "I don't want Sam to be in danger."

Hope nodded. "I know, neither do I. But you won't be any safer sitting in the truck."

Sam looked up at their mother. "I don't want to be left behind."

"You don't get a say in this," Felicity snapped.

Cutting through the burgeoning argument, Tink declared, "I'll take you both out."

They all turned and looked at her.

"I know a back way out. On foot only. I was gonna use it myself. I'll get you two out safely."

Hope smiled warily.

"Thanks," Felicity breathed.

"Yeah, whatever," Tink said, looking a bit embarrassed. "I need to scout the place first; make sure it's not being watched." She hopped out of the cab. "But I'll be quick."

Felicity nodded. She shuffled towards the open door and Hope sighed with relief as the pressure on her reduced.

"Should we untie our hands?" Sam asked her.

"Give me a few moments to double-check the tracking location," she replied. "Then we're good."

She helped Sam awkwardly climb down from the cab. Sam was still fighting the instinct to use their missing arm, but they managed by leaning on their elbow and sliding down on their butt.

Hope led them around the perimeter of the carpark. Following her tracker's internal tug, she walked them over to a nearby building. Across a wide swathe of empty parking spots lay the building that housed their target.

There were three workshops side-by-side, each with a huge roller door at the front and a small shopfront adjacent. The two workshops on the left had their external shop door chained and padlocked shut, but the one on the far right was unchained.

"Is it in there?" Sam asked quietly.

"Yeah. The target's up high, on the far left. They must all be connected somehow."

"And the animal guy?"

"Can't be sure, but that giant dish is a big clue he's there, too; if not, we're bang out of luck."

"Well, I hope he's in there." Sam glared at the building. "And I hope you get him."

Hope smiled. "Me too." Then she turned serious. "It's time for me to let go of you now. It'll feel a bit weird."

Sam nodded, and Hope untied their arms, releasing her tracking spell. As ever, she felt a sudden rush of exhaustion as the magic stopped flowing through her. That energy had been sustaining her today. She was still operating on only a few hours' sleep.

"Ugh!" Sam grumbled. "I feel tired!"

"A nap would be a good idea once you're safely out of here. Plus something to eat. Let's see whether Tink's back yet."

They both turned back to the truck.

Felicity was watching them like a hawk, and Galen was in the back, doing some last-minute tinkering and touching-up.

Which meant that neither of them had spotted the approach of two members of the uncomfortably familiar trio of shady teens they'd met before.

Hope scowled and pushed Sam behind her.

"Well, looky who's here?" Dig mocked. "Aren't you the sweet thing we missed out on a couple of nights ago? Come ta have another go, eh?"

"And looks like she brought a friend," Theo added, eyeing up Sam.

"*Two* friends," Dig corrected, eyeballing a scowling Felicity. "And this one's pretty – I bags this one." He eyed Felicity up and down, slowly. "You'd look prettier if you smiled. Don't worry, sweetheart, you'll smile for *me*."

Felicity hissed, her eyes blazing. "Don't you dare lay a hand on me!"

"Or what, princess?" He reached for her.

Felicity looked back towards Hope, and said, through gritted teeth, "Funny you should call me that. Pam will be particularly unhappy with you if you touch me."

On hearing the name "Pam", the two thugs jerked, and looked Felicity up and down a little more. "You're not one of Pam's!" Dig sneered.

"She *is*!" Hope said, keeping Sam behind her.

The thugs scowled, and Theo yelled, "Well, you're not! And neither's that little cheesecake behind you."

"Sweet," Dig added, lasciviously, "and ripe for the plucking!"

"Pam can't do nothing if we touch her," Theo agreed.

Hope could feel Sam tensing behind her and laid a hand on their shoulder to reassure. She didn't know exactly where Galen was, but had been feeling him draw on his magic since the two first appeared. She drew on her own magic but found it sluggish, temporarily drained by her exhaustion and the long-term tracker usage.

Felicity stepped out in front, putting herself in between the pair and her child. "You'll have to go through me first if you want them."

Dig smirked. "Nope, I don't." He dug a hand into his jacket and pulled out a gun.

He didn't get a chance to point it, however, as Galen leaped from the truck bed, landing heavily on Dig's back and releasing half his pent-up magic into it. The gun fell to the ground with a clatter, by which time Galen – one hand blazing with a deep, blood-red glow – had turned on Theo.

Theo looked between Galen and Hope. Her hands now also glowing with energy, hers a deep sea-green.

Felicity stepped forward, picked up the gun from the ground and pointed it at him.

That's when he decided it was safer to split.

This was the moment Tink reappeared. "Hmmm. Guess you didn't need my help after all," she muttered, watching the departing thug with a grin. "I see you've met Dig and Theo." She approached the prone form and kicked him in the nuts. Hard.

Galen winced but Hope just raised an eyebrow.

"You've met him before too, I see." Hope said wryly, watching as Tink put another sharp-toed foot into his abdomen.

"This shitstain's why I left the Biters." She smiled down at him and kicked him once more. "That's satisfying. All right, time to get out of here – before his mates bring backup."

Felicity collected Sam, then turned to Hope and handed her the gun. "Here, take this and stay safe."

Hope knew little about guns. She could see it was a small revolver of some kind. She knew they didn't hold many bullets, and she knew which end to point at the other person, but that was about all.

She pocketed it anyway. It was better than nothing.

Felicity took Sam's hand and turned towards Tink, but Sam pulled their hand away and ran over to Galen.

Sam took a deep breath and spoke all at once. "I want you to do it. Put my arm back on."

Galen raised a quizzical eyebrow. "Are you sure?" He looked at Felicity for confirmation.

Sam nodded, then turned to Felicity and glared.

Felicity let her look of uncertainty fade into a smile. She nodded at Galen.

Galen's face lit up. "Okay, then. You need to heal fully first, but I'll make sure it's ready when you are, when this is all over."

Sam grinned. "When this is over." Then turned back to Felicity, taking her hand again.

Hope hugged them both one last time, and watched them follow Tink across the carpark and down an alleyway, and then they were gone.

"You ready?" Galen asked Hope gently. He'd opened a huge, mirrored umbrella shape and fixed it to the top of the truck, connecting the focal point via cables to the control-flow setup inside.

Hope raised her eyebrows and nodded in appreciation. It was ready to take on the Conjunction. If only they had the dream steel. That was still the last required part, connecting the flow and the cables coming from the parabolic mirror on top of the truck.

She turned towards Galen with a wry smile. "No. But we'll go, anyway."

He snorted.

She turned back to the workshops. "I should scout the place first. There's a chance he'll be watching on monitors, but on the off-chance he isn't, I'll try to be sneaky. I'll find some viable signal to let you know you can safely approach."

"What kind of signal?"

She shrugged. "Maybe throw a rock?"

He smirked at her. "No need for that; just wave."

She paused, then looked at him through narrowed eyes. "You can see me through my hideaway, can't you?"

He smirked again and shrugged. "Yeah."

"That shouldn't be possible!" She approached him with an eyebrow raised.

He didn't reply, but he widened his eyes in feigned innocence.

"Okay, so *how* are you seeing through my hideaways?"

He looked away. He seemed embarrassed by the question. At first she didn't think he'd answer, but then…

"My eye," he said, hesitant, gesturing vaguely at his right eye.

Her eyebrows went up. "Oh, don't tell me it's…"

He sighed and blushed. "Yes, it's an augmentation – a good one. Adora's work, which is why I know that her work is exceptional. But it's still… fake."

"So cool!" Hope exclaimed simultaneously. Galen flinched as she launched herself at him. She grabbed his cheeks and held him steady while she inspected the eye.

It looked just like the other one. If she hadn't been told, she'd never have spotted it. She gazed into it deeply. There was something odd about how the pupil reacted to the light, and its shape and colour were a bit too uniform.

It widened now, as she watched. She moved back a smidge to see that Galen was watching her with an indulgent smile.

When he noticed he had her attention, he leaned in and kissed her softly.

She smiled under his lips and held herself still, enjoying the gentle touch that was all too brief. He pulled back from her and she ran a finger across his cheek. "When all this is done, we should probably… talk."

"Yeah, yeah, of course." He shrugged her off and turned away.

She frowned. That did not sound like a positive reaction. Well, now was not the time. There'd be plenty of time later.

He hopped back into the truck and hung out the window. "I'll be waiting for your signal – just don't take too long." He nodded up at the on-rushing sunset, and the moon that was edging across the last narrowing patch of sky, the sun moving ever closer.

"All right. I'll wave you in if it's all okay."

"What if it's not?"

"You'll see me running away. Try to keep up!"

34 - The lab partner

Hope pulled the familiar tingle of her hideaway over herself and snuck over to the nearest buildings. She couldn't see any obvious movement inside, and there weren't any external security cameras. That was a blessing.

The three workshops were all two-storey buildings lined up side-by-side. Each had a big roller door, firmly closed, and a shopfront area with a human-size door and a few windows surrounding a small front desk. The two workshops on the left had heavy shades behind the windows, but the right-hand side had nothing, not even curtains.

She still couldn't see any movement inside, though she could hear some noise coming from that direction. It was a faint, rumbling sound, like some kind of party going on. It sounded like a fair few people talking to each other. That was going to be a problem.

She sauntered towards the building, hands in pockets, as though she was meant to be there.

Nobody stopped her, and nobody came out to greet her either. That seemed unusual. If there was a party full of people, why wasn't anybody looking out?

Creeping up to the shopfront, she looked in through the windows. It was relatively bare – just a countertop with a register. Behind it, some shelves bearing various boxes and packets and what looked like a fridge beside them.

The voices were louder, and it became clear they weren't human. A sign on the door declared this was "Bob's World of Pets". The noise from inside was some mix of yipping and whining. Animals in distress.

She tried the door handle. It was unlocked!

She quietly opened it and poked her head inside.

Nobody.

She shrugged, looked back at Galen, and waved him over.

He put the truck in gear and rolled it silently up to the building. They'd need to have it on hand if they got the dream steel out.

If they made it out.

She put her finger to her lips. "Stay here," she mouthed to him, still in the front seat, and pointed to the wall beside the door.

She crept back inside to look around more thoroughly. On the left were some windows and an internal door, both of which led into the showroom behind the roller door. It was a large open space filled with displays for worming tablets and pet tags, and shelves stacked with boxes of animal feed.

She could hear the noises much more clearly now. That, coupled with the now almost overpowering stench, led her to believe that there must be a lot of animals in there, and they weren't happy about their current situation.

Galen approached the outer door.

She gestured for him to come in and hide against the inner wall beside the door. She snuck forward and stepped onto the shop floor. Beyond the already visible wall of boxes were rows of shelves. They stacked against the walls up to a mezzanine level, which had its own stacks of boxes towering overhead.

She didn't see any way up to the next level. There must be stairs hidden somewhere in the warren of box piles that stretched into the deep, dark underbelly of the lower level.

Standing against the right-hand wall were rows of shelves packed floor to ceiling with cages. Many were empty, but plenty were still housing a variety of unhappy small animals – mostly dogs, cats or rabbits but also a few tanks of reptiles.

But what had her staring lay in the middle of the room. The cardboard displays had been shoved aside to encompass an enormous work table with a scruffy and exhausted-looking man shackled to it. The chains clanked and grated as he looked around himself.

"Hello? Is anyone there?" he asked in a croaky voice.

She was just debating whether to unveil herself, when he shut his eyes and continued, "Don't answer that! I'm going to assume nobody is here, because if there was somebody, I'd be forced to kill you."

Hope froze.

"That said, if there *is* somebody here, I'd be ever so much obliged if you'd kill me – please?"

She blinked.

"I've been trapped here for I don't know how long. Starving and sitting in my own shit." His voice cracked. "No better than these poor animals in their cages. I can't control what I'm doing; I can't even try to escape – he won't let me." He drew in a shuddering breath. "Please, just kill me so it can end."

She slipped down the side of the cages, edging towards him, and peered over his worktable. A small lamp shone down on the desk, pushing back the darkness.

Sedated and bound before him was a small dog. He seemed to have been painting runes on its body. Next to it was an old lanyard with a university key card. The name "Dominic Purcell" had been printed below a picture of him looking both younger and happier, even despite the usual bad ID photography.

Dominic sighed deeply and took his hands away from his face. "I'm finally going mad. Talking to myself; wishing for invisible rescuers." He frowned down at the dog. "You don't deserve this, but I can't... I have to prepare you for surgery. At least he can't force me to make this permanent. You'll be at peace inside a few days."

He stroked the animal's belly. Four little paws twitched as if the dog was running. He smiled sadly and picked up his brush again.

A sound made him look up, followed by some under-breath cursing in Galen's voice.

Dominic whimpered. "Hello? I heard you this time. Please stay back."

Galen stumbled through the door into the room, blinking in surprise when he saw the man.

Hope gestured at him to go back out through the door.

"No, you have to go!" yelled Dominic, and he raised his hand, hesitating above a giant red button in the middle of the worktable.

Galen glanced between the two, stepping back.

But it was too late.

"I'm so, so, sorry." Dominic slammed his hand on the button.

A buzzer blared, making the animals around them leap and chitter in agitation at its continual, abrasive sound. Them with a grating clunk, all the cage doors unlocked.

Hope did not feel ready to take on a pet shop full of angry animals, even with Galen's help, but what could they do?

They both drew on their magic as the animals pushed open the doors and took their first steps outside.

The awful thing about it was how wretched and starveling the poor things were. Dozens of tired, bony little creatures leaping their way down to the cold floor and shivering. And yet each one growled, yelled or hissed, baring their teeth. Even the rabbits and guinea pigs rolled their eyes and squealed menacingly.

Galen stood looking in shock at the small army of furry creatures.

"I don't want to do this," Hope whispered, but the first dog barked in her direction. She stepped back, and a cat yowled and scratched at Galen's ankles.

"Ow!" he yelled, and dozens of tiny eyes turned towards him.

"They won't stop," Dominic said, and he sounded genuinely miserable. "That bastard's left an unbreakable compulsion in each of them to attack an intruder when the siren goes off. Just like he programmed me to set it off. I couldn't fight it." He put his head in his hands. "I've tried."

And then the horde attacked.

Hope kicked each animal away from Galen, who was getting swamped.

He retreated into the boxed section, away from the cages.

Some dogs and cats were coming after her, despite being invisible. She wasn't un-scentable, it seemed.

She leaped up as a dachshund puppy worried at her ankle, its tiny teeth unable to break through her boot leather.

Behind her, Galen yelped and leaped up on top of a pile of boxes. The dogs and rabbits couldn't reach him there, though a pair of lanky cats clambered up after him. He kicked them back down to the ground. Then he started throwing things at them – boxes, bags, and bales flung far over their heads.

At first, Hope thought he had poor aim, because he kept missing them, but then she realised he was throwing food for them. Bags of kibble; a bale of hay. He was tearing into them, so they'd scatter across the floor.

The food briefly distracted some of the animals – they hastily grabbed bites, but they all reluctantly drew away from the food to growl and yip and bite and claw once more.

Hope pushed back a larger puppy, and it broke her heart to hear it yelp. A cat leaped onto her back and clawed its way up her spine. Hope swore and banged herself against a nearby railing to dislodge the attacker. It grabbed hold of her arm, dug in with teeth and claws, and raked several nasty gashes across her arm before she threw it off.

She cast about. Surely there was some way to make them stop without killing them? These poor, wretched creatures were the victims here. Still, she didn't want to be nibbled to death by cats!

What did the chained-up guy say? They attack while the siren was blaring.

That gave her an idea.

She scrambled up a stack of boxes and into the mezzanine level. The siren was loudest up here. Coming from somewhere up among the rafters. Turning her head from side to side, she hunted for the sound and tried her best to ignore the yelps and sounds of pain coming from below her.

There!

Two speakers either side and above the big open shop floor, attached to the beams.

Climbing up a tottering pile of crates and boxes, she jumped the last half a metre to the nearest beam. She winced in pain from her clawed hand, but she pushed that pain to the side and dragged herself up to sit on the beam.

She edged herself along it.

"I hope you have a plan!" Galen yelled up at her.

She grimaced. "I'm trying something. Keep them busy for me!"

He grunted something back, but she couldn't hear it.

She crept forward, out over the big, empty drop. She could see down to where Galen was standing up on the boxes, trying to barricade himself with stacks of tinned food and bags of cat litter. Most of the creatures below were too tired and hungry to jump up to where he was. They surrounded him on the floor and yelped, howled and hissed at him. Some gnawed or clawed at the boxes on the bottom level, but they weren't progressing quickly.

She reached the first of the two speakers. She yanked the wires trailing from the back of it and it was silenced.

She looked down at the animals below.

They paused for a moment; some running for the food and grabbing a bite to eat, before once again reluctantly turning to yelp ineffectually at the stack of boxes with Galen perched on top.

Hope turned. Now came the hard part. She had to cross to the other side of the ceiling. The second speaker was hanging right over the middle of the empty warehouse floor, above where the door led into the little shop. It was at least a six metre drop to the floor below.

The beam she was on was solid but ran perpendicular to the roller door, leading to the back of the warehouse, not across the floor. She could crawl all the way back along the beam and around to the next one, parallel to the far wall, or she could head across a narrower-looking cross-brace. The latter option would be quicker, but she wasn't sure the cross-brace looked solid enough to take her weight.

"I had hoped I'd seen the last of climbing around stacks of boxes in warehouses," she muttered to herself.

Galen yelped below her. The edges of his hastily built fort had tilted slightly. The animals had made some headway in chewing their way through the first row of supporting boxes and bags, spilling their contents out in a cascade. He leaned backwards into the boxes. "Can you hurry it up a bit?"

She decided to risk the cross-brace.

Halfway across, and predictably, she began to deeply regret that decision. It creaked and groaned portentously.

Then, on cue for her regular bad luck, she heard a noise behind her that sent a shiver down her spine.

An ominous hiss.

Risking a look over her shoulder, she saw one of the ferret-cobras creeping along the main beam. It was working slowly, scenting the air with its tiny, forked tongue, trying to figure out where she was. It kept turning its head towards the creaking, trying to figure out what exactly was going on in that direction.

She sped up her crawling little steps a bit more, readying herself to jump. The creaking grew into a groan, and then CRACK. It dipped, bowing under her weight.

She leaped, grappling for the next beam. The extra push sent the pieces of cross-brace clattering down to the warehouse floor.

"Hope!" Galen yelled.

The cuts in her hand opened up and screamed at her as she swung from the beam, trying to bring her movements back under control.

"Ow!" she whimpered.

She looked back at the ferret. It had reached the point where the cross-brace had met the original beam, and was contemplating leaping the distance towards her.

She struggled and pulled herself up onto the new beam, this one running down the centre of the roof. The next cross-brace looked just as flimsy.

She looked back. The ferret had given up the debate and was making its way back down the first beam to come up this one. She couldn't go back along the beam now.

She had to risk it again.

The creaking came quicker as she crawled in double time. She looked back; the ferret had nearly caught up to her. The cross-brace made a loud warning crack and sank an inch. She was too far from the final beam. Even if she jumped, she wouldn't make it. She looked up and leaped anyway.

The leap broke the final shred of wood holding the brace up, and it clattered to the floor to join the rest. At the top of her arc, she scrabbled near the ceiling, swinging her hands in the air for the random assortment of wires and pipes she could barely reach. Her fingers connected with a metal pipe high against the ceiling.

One end of the pipe broke out of the ceiling as her weight slammed onto it, water spraying in a fountain from the broken end and drenching her. The pipe arced down with her weight and she swung her legs up towards the far beam.

At the end of the swing, she kicked forwards. Her foot connected with the speaker. It went dead, and she hooked that leg over the beam, just as the other end of the pipe came loose and fell with a great clattering to the floor below.

Water spilled in a fountain from the broken pipe. Good thing the speaker was dead, or she'd electrocute herself up here. The ferret sat on the middle beam, hissing angrily through the spray.

"Hope?" Galen yelled again. "Are you all right?" He leaped from the broken remains of his box fort, the animals now scattering from his approach and re-forming around the pile of food.

He ran, grabbing the chair out from under the table, and jamming it up beneath her.

"Stay back!" she yelled. "There's a cobra-ferret here!"

He paused, looking up.

The creature had again disappeared down the middle beam and was zipping around the U-shape of the next cross-brace and heading her way. This time, there was nowhere for her to retreat to. The warehouse floor was too far down to jump.

She grappled in her pocket, searching for the gun Felicity had given her.

It was coming so fast! She had the gun, but how did she hold it swinging upside down from the rafters like a bat?

Too late!

It hissed as it leaped for her.

THWUCK

It tumbled down to the boxes below, then scrambled to its feet again.

Galen swung at the creature again, with the length of broken pipe. He smacked it again and this time it stayed where it landed, shaking its head, stunned – which left it vulnerable to one last, decisive hit.

Its flared head flew off its furry body and landed among the other animals. They instinctively dodged it before resuming their feeding.

The room had gone quiet. At least relatively so. Only the sounds of animals eating their fill and the pained sounds of sobbing from the shackled man below.

Galen filled her vision, upside down.

"Are you hurt? Did it bite you?" He hurriedly checked her arms for wounds.

She yelped as he looked her arm over. "Just cat scratches. Help me down?"

Galen supported her shoulders as she flipped down from the beam and onto the boxes.

The animals scattered around the two of them as she walked up to the still weeping man. "I'm sure we can get you out of these shackles," she offered.

"No!" he yelled, looking frightened. "No. Please, just leave me alone."

She huffed in frustration and confusion. "You don't want to be free?"

"I won't be free, even if you unchain me. I haven't been free in a long, long time. If you free me, I'll be forced to fight you, and that means I'll get hurt, and then die." He looked up at her, his eyes pleading. "You're still in danger. Please just go – run from here before it's too late!"

"We can't leave," Galen said, quietly. "There's something we still have to do."

"What can you tell us about what else is here?" Hope asked Dominic.

But before he could answer, she heard a new sound. A low, menacing growl.

"It's too late. They're already here!" Dominic climbed underneath the desk and cradled his head in his arms, his shoulders quaking in fear.

Hope and Galen drew together, facing the shadowy depths of the warehouse beyond.

35 - Pack attack

Hope could see a short distance into the long stacks of cardboard boxes on the mezzanine, but the sunlight from the shop windows didn't penetrate all the way to the back.

Deep in the shadows, she saw the flash of a pair of red eyes. Then they were gone.

Galen stepped up beside her, hoisting his new metal pole onto his shoulder.

She drew the gun and hastily checked it. The revolving thingy seemed to have several metal circles inside it.

They're bullets, yeah? And is there a safety?

She turned the pistol over in her hands, looking for a likely switch. "Do you know anything about guns?"

He shook his head. "I'm sworn to heal, not take lives. Aren't *you* the criminal?" She could hear the smirk in his voice.

She rolled her eyes. "I've not really had a call for it either. I'm not a hired gun. Do you reckon these things have a safety, or is that only the automatic ones? Do I have to cock it?"

"Beats me," he replied with a shrug. Then she felt him tense. "We've got company." He nodded up and to the far side.

Something large, with gleaming eyes, was crawling through the boxes piled up on the mezzanine. Something else was growling up and to their right.

"Two creatures are up there, trying to flank us. And something's hiding deep in the stacks." She turned to the man cowering under the table. "Dominic!"

He flinched but looked up in surprise.

"What are they?" she asked him, continuing to scan the deep shelves.

Dominic whimpered, and Hope thought he wouldn't reply, but then a faint voice drifted up. "These aren't mine. Mine were mostly harmless – a camel with a leopard's head; an intelligent ape on the body of a horse; an octopus-faced elephant – but these? My lab partner stole all the leftover pieces and used the smartest of the caged animals here to make them. They work together as a team. I don't know what else he stole from the menagerie to make his animals, but they're all terrible." He fell silent as the pair of creatures crept forward and became visible – rottweiler heads on leopard bodies.

They growled deep within their throats, the sound a strange combination of the noise from both types of beast. They were looking for a safe way down to their prey.

Hope swung the gun from one creature to the other, waiting for the first to charge. But it was the third creature who began the fray – the one deep in shadow with angry eyes.

Those eyes glared and burned as it bounded forwards on all fours, a terrifying mountain of muscle, hair and flying spittle. The last of the gorilla-dogs.

It charged straight at them.

She fired and fired again. Bullets struck its body. They left tiny, red wounds, dripping rivulets of blood. It flinched as each bullet hit, but they didn't slow it down, just made it angrier. It hurled itself down onto the cages below, falling the last metre to the floor with a thump.

She heard an incoming snarl from the left and ducked as the first leopard bounded down the stacked boxes to the lower level. Galen stepped forward, and she left him to it. She didn't dare take her eyes off the hairy mountain in front of her.

It rolled back onto its feet and paused behind the desk, growling and sniffing the air, hunting for the source of its pain.

She felt a rush of wind as Galen swung out with his pole. Heard a loud crunch as it smacked the leopard across the nose. She flinched and saw it spin and fall; landing in a clatter and tumble up against Galen's former box fort.

Its partner was pacing around the mezzanine, its ears perked as it searched for a way to enter the battle.

But she didn't have time to see more. The gorilla-dog reared up in front of her, just beyond the heavy desk. It beat its chest and howled a challenge. Then it brought its great fists down.

She leaped backwards as the fists smashed through the table. The top shattered into fragments, the man beneath screaming and scrambling out of the way.

The gorilla-dog raised its arms again. Galen smacked it on the side of its head, and it swung towards him.

Hope shot it one more time, this time in the neck.

It yelped, then coughed on blood, and one arm hung limp. But it still didn't go down. It lurched sideways and swung its remaining fist in Hope's direction. It smacked her against the wall with a backhand like a freight train.

The gun clattered out of her hand, out of reach, and her head swam as she fought to refocus her eyes. She felt the tingle of her hideaway falling away.

The leopard on the mezzanine swung its head, fixing her with its blazing eyes.

Galen was smacking the gorilla in the neck repeatedly. Both its arms now hung limp, although its dog head growled at him and snapped its teeth.

Beyond, Hope could see the first leopard getting back on its feet and shaking its head, saliva dripping from its loose jowls. It readied itself for another pounce.

"Behind you!" she yelled, and Galen swung towards her.

The leopard sprang onto Galen's back and knocked him to the floor. He shrieked in pain as it ripped its clawed feet across his back, and the rottweiler head sunk its teeth into his shoulder.

She scrambled back to her own feet, intending to do something. But now the second leopard sprang down, its eyes fixed upon her.

It landed on the remains of the box fort. The boxes gave way beneath the weight, and the creature tumbled heavily to the floor. Undeterred, it scrabbled to its feet and turned on her, growling, and its eyes flashing, promising violence.

Galen shrieked again as he struggled to free himself.

But she could do nothing! The second leopard sprang at her, and she fell backwards. She pulled her legs in, used both her feet to kick out at it, striking it in the chest.

Thrown back, it smacked into the other leopard, knocking it off Galen's back. The other leopard snarled and spun around, batting it away. They snapped at each other, momentarily distracted.

Hope grabbed Galen under his armpits and dragged him out of reach.

She retreated towards the door, hoping to escape, but the movement drew their attention once more. The pair turned and split up to stalk their prey from either side.

Meanwhile, Hope could see the gorilla-dog lifting itself off the floor. It howled in heart-breaking pain as it raised its head up with its arms. Rivers of blood were running from its deep neck wound. Galen had partially severed the stitches holding the head in place. But its muscles still rippled under hairy skin, and its eyes burned with incandescent rage. It opened a mouth full of sharp teeth and growled – a deep, threatening rumble.

Hope grabbed Galen and pulled him behind her. He whimpered, and struggled to pull himself towards the door, inches at a time.

She drew her magic into her hands. It was the only thing left to defend them with, but it required touching the leopards to do it, which risked their teeth and claws. There were three of them and only one of her. But she'd die fighting, and she'd take at least one of them down with her.

The gorilla-dog began a stumbling, three-limbed run, and the pair of leopards crouched to leap.

Two things happened at once. An ear-shattering bang half deafened her, and the door behind her burst open.

The door threw her forward to land on the pile of shattered table legs. She heard a yowl and a thump and saw the body of one leopard land in a crumpled pile in front of her, while the other growled and then whimpered.

She looked up to see it wrapped around a heavily augmented arm, all shiny steel musculature.

Tink!

The head was biting and the body clawing, to no avail. Tink flexed her arm and tore the head from its body. The two parts landed with a wet thump to either side.

A moment later, several hundred kilograms of silverback barrelled into Tink, throwing her backwards into the doorway. She struggled as its arms pulled and gouged and the dog head lunged for her face, but she shoved her fist inside its mouth and pushed the head back, keeping it from biting her still-human face.

Hope leaped forward and pushed her gathered magic into her taser matrix. She released it into the back of the dog-head, but the magic went wild. It skittered across the head and down its neck as a stream of wild-magic backlash whooshed back into her own arm.

She was thrown backwards into the boxes, her arm glowing with pain. She blinked rapidly, gasping and trying to make her lungs work again. The ache subsided, and she looked down to see that her taser matrix had been half destroyed by the cat scratches. It was a miracle the magic had worked at all. Still, it had distracted the gorilla-dog enough for Tink to get an arm free and tear the stitching from its neck, ripping the head free. The head swiftly joined that of the other leopard.

Hope grinned up at her.

Tink grinned fiercely back. "You started the party without me!" she mock complained.

Hope snorted. "You're late!"

"Well, better late than never." Tink reached down to help her up.

"I didn't think you'd come back," Hope confessed.

Tink just laughed and hauled Hope to her feet. "Like I said, this guy put Dodge in the hospital. I was hoping to return the favour."

Now that the noise had calmed down a little, Hope could hear a strange clicking sound, coupled with the lab partner's crying and whispering, "I'm sorry, I'm so sorry!"

She turned to him. He had the gun! It must be out of bullets, but he was pointing it at them and dry firing over and over.

She felt confused for a moment, and then horror spilled over her as she spun around to look at Galen.

He'd collapsed against the boxes – and he was pale. So pale!

36 - Nooooo

Hope ran to his side. "No, no, no! Don't you die on me!"

Blood pooled beneath him, running from the gashes in his back. His skin was grey from blood loss. But what worried her most was the single bullet hole through his upper chest.

She checked for his pulse.

She couldn't find it. And he wasn't breathing.

"No, please don't be dead!" She pulled him down to lie on his back.

Tink, looking drawn, came over and sat down opposite her.

Hope fumbled in her pockets, hunting for the healing potions she'd stolen earlier. She pulled out one of the pair and pulled at the stopper.

Tink grabbed her hand. "Don't waste it on him. He's already gone."

Hope snatched her hand back. "It's mine to waste!"

Tink sighed and sat back as Hope unstoppered the vial. She opened Galen's mouth and poured it inside, keeping his head tipped back so the liquid would go down his throat. She dripped the last few drops into the wound, just in case.

Then she began what little CPR she half-remembered from seeing it on TV. She pumped on his chest, pushing hard and fast between his ribs. Blood oozed from the wound.

Tears coursed down her cheeks.

She stopped to breathe into his mouth, tasting the sickly sweet of the healing potion mixed with the tang of blood.

"Hey," Tink said gently, as Hope continued to work. "Look, I can see he means a lot to you, but they shot him in the chest. He's not breathing. He's dead and there's not much time left. I'm sure he would've wanted you to let him go, finish the job you guys were trying to do instead."

Hope stopped for a moment and looked down at Galen's face. It looked calm and content; peaceful. Would he have wanted that? For her to abandon him and try to finish the job? Save his brother instead of himself? Maybe he was gone and she should stop.

She tried to pull her fear-scrambled thoughts together and think it through. What was it he'd told her? These days we could resuscitate people who, in the past, we would've considered long dead. It was only a matter of keeping the brain protected.

Galen wasn't gone. Not yet. Not while she could still get oxygen to his brain.

"I'm not giving up yet," she growled, and got back to work.

Tink sighed again and settled down with her back against the boxes to wait.

Hope kept trying, but as every minute passed, her heart dropped. And she was getting tired. This was hard work. Her muscles ached and sweat ran dripping down her face. She could hardly see. Should she do something more? Should she *shock* his heart? Would that damage it more?

She heard Tink gasp and felt a hand grab hers.

"No!" She shook it away.

But it wasn't Tink's!

She wiped away the sweat and tears, and looked down into Galen's grey eyes. His smirk had never looked more beautiful.

"Oh, good!" he rasped. "I'm glad you stopped. I think you broke my ribs." He winced and touched them gently.

She laughed out loud. It might have been a little hysterical. "You can put it on my tab." She looked him over. His tiny chest wound was rapidly closing up, and he was breathing easier with each blessed breath he was taking in.

She collapsed to the floor beside him and called her own breath back. Her triceps ached, and a wave of exhaustion rolled over her.

"So, what next?" Tink asked them.

"Dunno. Hey you!" She called over to the shackled man. "What's your name again?"

"Dominic," he replied.

"Hi, Dominic! Can you tell us who else is here?"

"Just Morty and Robert." He spat that last name.

"No more animals?" Tink asked.

"Oh, yeah, there are probably more of them."

Hope hissed in frustration. "What other animals are left?"

"I don't know. I've been shackled here for days."

"Okay," Tink said, "so who's Morty?"

"Oh, I don't know his real name. He's the mortician who worked next door. He's been sewing the animals together for Robert ever since I refused, but we've never actually spoken to each other."

"Is he like you?" Hope asked.

"Nah. He's way more mind-fucked than I am. Robert gassed him every day, getting him under control and doing what he wanted. I was Robert's first human subject. I didn't know it, but he'd been working on me for a long time, slowly adding layers of minor commands." He frowned and looked down at himself. He was haggard and very, very dirty.

"Gassed?" Tink asked.

"Yeah, he uses that green gas. Some combo of sedatives and pheromones to make you more open to his commands. Don't breathe that shit in."

Tink shook her head. "How do we not breathe it in?"

Hope pulled herself back to her feet. "You'll have to hold your breath and hang back. We've got that covered. I'll do a little more scouting before we all go in."

Tink frowned but nodded.

Hope turned to Galen, who was still curled up on the floor. "Are you going to be okay?"

He scowled in pain, but managed a nod. "It'll take a few more minutes for the potion to knit my skin back together and pop the ribs back in place enough so it won't hurt when I walk, but I'll be ready by the time you get back."

"Here, take this." Hope held out the last potion.

"It's too soon for me to take a second one, but thanks. I'll hold it in reserve."

She smiled at him and stood, pulling her familiar tingle over herself.

Tink raised her eyebrows and blinked rapidly, as if to dislodge a blur in her eyes.

Hope took a step and then paused, looking back at Galen.

He was looking right at her again.

"It's still weird you can see me," she said.

Galen just smirked. "Be careful."

She winked at him and turned to go.

Near the back of the warehouse, she found the stairs up to the mezzanine. At the top was a gaping hole in the wall surrounded by scattered bricks. It looked like something had smashed its way through from the other side. She stepped carefully over the shattered bricks and dust. This must be the way the animals had come through, and how Mr Green was going in and out without opening up the shopfront for the far workshop.

On the other side of the hole was a similar mezzanine, but the warehouse floor was very different. It led into a white-panelled room blazing with light. It stank of disinfectant with an underlying copper tang she didn't want to think about. The room was cooler than the pet store, and her breath clouded in the air, despite the lighting. The rumble of massive air conditioners filtered up from below.

The dazzling down lights lit up a row of six stainless-steel tables. Two were empty, but the rest bore huge, lumpy piles draped in surgical-green sheets.

At one of these tables stood a glassy-eyed man. He was methodically sewing something red and glistening, with a large bodkin and slick, black thread.

This must be the mortician that Dominic had mentioned.

She looked beyond him. The entire back wall was a morgue, bearing row upon row of stainless-steel doors. Were there bodies in there? She had no way of knowing, and it didn't matter either way.

To her left were the stairs to the floor below. Following the mezzanine balcony, to her right, was a small office and a door with a bathroom sign. Past that was another hole in the wall, leading into the third workshop.

She tiptoed along the raised walkway, ignoring the man working so mindlessly below her, and peeked through the hole.

"No, it's not possible!" she whispered to herself as she gazed at the scene beyond.

For all the noise they had made – the blaring siren, the animals, the gunshot – and there was Mr Green, pottering around on the floor below... with giant earmuffs on.

He hadn't heard a thing! He seemed to be... singing to himself.

He was working on the painted matrices that surrounded a central dais, laying out some pre-made parchment and touching up the edges where the flow lines met.

The control matrices circled an enormous machine that was topped with some kind of glass bulb. It looked like he'd up-ended a fishbowl or flower vase on it. It was half-filled with dark-green, swirling vapour that gave off the occasional glitter. It sloshed around more like water than cloud.

Mr Green was tinkering with the devices that were supporting and feeding into the glowing tank. Every time he tweaked it, she could feel... something.

There was magic down there, that's for sure, but it hadn't fully engaged yet. The energy was constrained within the central control flows and the machine itself. And yet she could feel a gentle buzzing – something pressing down on her. Like the soft but persistent brush of an impending migraine.

She blinked for a moment. Then she shook her head, bringing herself back to the here and now, and looked around to search the room for any extra defences.

She froze. In the far corner stood a sentinel – silent and scanning the room. She recognised it as the same type that stood guard at the university. Mr Green must have stolen it to guard his inner sanctum.

She ducked back around the edge of the wall, listening hard for any sounds of pursuit. Had it spotted her? It would have artificial vision, wouldn't it? Hadn't it seen through her hideaway?

Galen had mentioned they were part biological. So maybe, just maybe, her luck ran that way.

Either way, it was time to head back.

Galen and Tink were both waiting on the mezzanine for her, beside the hole in the wall. She was pleased to see a good bit of colour had returned to Galen's cheeks.

"What's in there?" he asked, his forehead creased with worry.

"Morty's busy with his work next door – and as for Mr Green..." She shook her head in disbelief. "He has earmuffs on. I don't think he even heard anything."

"What?" Galen said, deadpan.

Hope smirked. "Seriously."

Tink stood up straighter. "Is that all?"

"No. There's a university sentinel in there with him."

Galen sat up straight. "What? How'd he steal one of those?"

Hope shook her head. "I don't know, but I'm assuming it's bad news."

He furrowed his brow in thought. "I doubt he managed to override the defence settings. It won't be programmed to attack."

Hope raised an eyebrow. "Do you want to risk that?"

Galen frowned.

"How about I go in hard?" Tink smacked a fist into her palm, "Grab

Mr Green before he knows what hit 'im?"

Hope turned to her. "Can you get to him faster than a sentinel can get to you?"

Tink frowned. "Maybe?"

"I'm not really liking that idea. I could sneak in and grab Morty first – see if we can get any information out of him about any remaining defences. Hopefully, he won't yell and set off another alarm. I doubt that Mr Green'd miss that twice."

Galen pulled the grey pouch out of his front pocket. "I guess this is the time to share my little side project."

Hope raised her eyebrows at him. "I was wondering what that was."

He dug inside the pouch and pulled out one slightly dented neural clamp.

Tink gasped. "Hey! Is that our…"

He glared at her. "It's mine now!"

She threw her hands up. "Hey, it was never my idea – that one was all Buzz's stupid plan."

He squinted at her, then turned back to Hope.

Hope looked at the clamp's bent metal clasps. "It's broken though, right? When I slammed the toolbox on it?"

"Yep. I've been tinkering with it. I'd planned to use it on Dodge if I ever got my hands on him again." He gave Tink another glare, but she just pressed her lips together. "But this is a better use for it."

"Hah! No wonder you were worried the cops might search through your stuff!" Hope smiled and took it off his hands. "Now, normally if I found out a guy had one of these, I'd give them a very wide berth, but I think I might just forgive you – just this once."

"Your support is appreciated," he said drily. Then he grimaced. "Can you feel…" he trailed off, as though listening to a distant noise, "some kind of buzzing?"

She nodded. "Yeah – and I'd put good money on it being from that mind-control device he's tinkering with. It got stronger in there. It'll get harder to ignore the closer we are to the device."

He nodded. "And the closer we are to the Conjunction."

"How much time have we got left?"

"Not long," Tink said. "About five, ten minutes before the moon moves into place. I assume you need to get done before the eclipse begins?"

Galen shook his head. "We have until the totality, which'll be roughly ten more minutes after the eclipse starts. We need to get the dream steel into the truck before the totality, or..." He screwed up his face.

"Or you've lost your chance," Hope stated, her eyes full of concern.

He nodded, his face solemn.

Tink clapped her hands together. "So, what are we waiting for?"

Hope grimaced. "A safe moment to strike. We need Mr Green to be distracted, so he doesn't try anything else on us. If he hits us with that gas of his, the device will be much harder to ignore."

Galen was nodding. "Should we activate the air bubbles, then?"

Hope shook her head. "Not yet. You said they only last a couple of minutes. We'll need them for when we start the direct confrontation with Mr Green – he'll be using the stuff in earnest then."

He looked even more worried, but gave a nod.

Tink raised an eyebrow. "Air bubbles?"

Hope nodded. "Yeah, to counteract the effects of the gas."

Tink straightened. "Have you got one for me too?"

Galen shrugged. "We don't have half an hour to paint one on you – sorry."

Tink frowned, turning away. "It's okay. I can hold my breath for quite a while, anyway. It'll have to do."

Hope nodded. She stepped back and drew her hideaway over herself again. Then headed back into danger.

37 - Fight!

Hope descended into the mortician's workshop, the clamp in her hands.

Morty was completely occupied by his work. She crept around one table, sparing it a glance. Half covered with a sheet was the second cobra-ferret, all splayed out. It looked like it might be dead or at least heavily sedated; either way, it looked pretty beat up. Its head was damaged, and it had been de-fanged.

Morty had been working at a second table, his hands operating beneath a sheet that obscured his work, along with the enormous pile of something. Every now and then, it gave a twitch.

That one *wasn't* dead.

She crept around the table, staying below the level of the counter until she was behind him, hoping to peek at his work. But as she stretched her neck up, he threw the edge of the sheet over whatever it was, and turned away to wash his hands in the basin. All she got from the brief glimpse was that it was something scaly – another snake or large reptile. A big one, and likely now outfitted with the pair of cobra fangs.

She nervously glanced up at the mezzanine level. She couldn't see either of her friends through the hole in the wall, and the hole leading to the third workshop remained blessedly sentinel-free for now.

Morty had collected his tools and was filling the basin with soapy water – blankly staring into the swirling suds. Hoping he'd stay still, she crept further forward, reaching out and lifting the clamp above her head.

At the last minute, he turned. She lunged, clamping his neck and latching it shut.

He gasped, and his body turned to jelly, dropping through her arms. His head slammed against the side of the basin, and she struggled to stop him from landing on the floor.

He lay limp and heavy in her arms. She checked him for vitals. He was breathing – thank goodness! But his eyes were glazed and open. Had she just knocked him unconscious? Gah! How was she going to get him up the stairs now?

Halfway through dragging his heavy body backwards across the floor, his eyelids fluttered open. He gasped like a fish and waved his arms in the air, doing a great impression of a struggling octopus. It made it impossible to lift him onto the stairway.

She was trying to shove her hands under his armpits and heave him up the first step, when she heard a voice echoing from the neighbouring room.

"Mr Dunn? Is it ready yet?"

Hope froze. It was Mr Green. There was nowhere to hide here! The lights were too bright and there weren't even any shadows she could melt into.

She heard footsteps approaching.

Galen poked his head around the corner and she waved him away.

She ducked down behind one of the steel tables, pulling the mortician with her. She put her hand over his mouth.

He looked up at her, dazed and confused.

"Mr Dunn! I asked you…" The voice stopped at the hole in the wall. "Mr Dunn?"

The mortician twisted and flailed in her hands and kicked the nearest table, causing a loud clunk.

"Is someone there?" Mr Green demanded in a voice that registered a little fear.

Hope peeked out.

"Yes!" Tink yelled above her, drawing his attention. "I'm here, and you'd better get ready for an arse kicking!" She stalked across the mezzanine towards him, but he stepped back. He smirked and activated a switch on his weird helmet, pulling a clear mask over his mouth and nose.

Green smoke began pouring out of something on his back, cloaking him in choking clouds. They dispersed rapidly across the room, bringing with them a strange, bitter smell.

The buzzing in the back of Hope's head weighed on her mind, pressing into her consciousness. Hope hurriedly activated her air-bubble matrix.

Tink reeled backward, her mouth squeezed shut in a grey line.

Mr Green stepped back to the wall. "Sentinel! Get up here!"

Tink lunged towards Mr Green, but he sidestepped and Tink slammed headfirst into a huge and immobile metal form that filled the hole in the wall. She gasped in shock and immediately began coughing.

"Attack them!" Mr Green yelled.

"Negative," the robot replied in a monotone. "You are not authorised for offensive capabilities."

"But she hit you; it's self-defence! Fight back at once!"

"Negative," the robot repeated. "You are not authorised for defensive capabilities."

Mr Green hissed in frustration. "What good are you, then?"

"My capabilities are…"

"Shut up! Fine! Stand right here in this doorway and don't move." He stepped back through the doorway.

"Affirmative." It moved to fill the gap.

"Attack them!" Mr Green yelled again, shouting past the robot's legs.

"Negative. You are not authorised…"

"Shut up! I wasn't talking to you, anyway. I said, attack them! Now!"

Hope groaned as the weight of his enhanced magic pressed down upon her mind, but it failed to gain a hold. She looked up at Tink and saw her standing stock still. Her face showed she was struggling hard, but she was not attacking. At least not yet.

Morty had fallen again and lay silent on the floor, his eyes rolled back into his head. Gassed one too many times, probably.

"Look out, Hope!" Galen yelled down at her.

She looked up in confusion, then registered movement all around her. The tables held piles of shapes covered in thin sheets, and the piles were wriggling.

She grabbed the clamp from Morty's neck, stood and ran for the steps a moment before a veritable flood of massive spiders wiggled and clambered out from under the surrounding sheets. They dropped onto the floor, one after the other, with fat, plopping noises.

From the other table, coils of scaly body were sliding loose with a rasping hiss.

She ran up the steps, two by two, sparing one last glance behind her. The sheet flung away from the larger table, and an enormous snake reared up, hissing in anger.

She reached the mezzanine level, yelling, "Tink!" But the woman had frozen in place, fighting for control of her mind.

Hope grabbed hold of Tink's hand and pulled, but Tink was as solid as a mountain.

"No!" Tink bit out. "Leave me!"

Spiders rushed up the stairs, flowing up around Tink's ankles. They crawled over her, but didn't stop, rushing *en masse* towards Hope.

Hope leaped through the doorway, joining Galen.

He was crushing spiders as they arrived, but there were too many. They kept slipping through and crawling up his legs, where he smacked them off with a shudder.

Hope gathered her magic into her hands, building it up for... something. She wasn't sure what she could do. They were too small and too fast to zap individually.

Galen swung his pole around wildly, reducing their numbers, but nearly hitting Hope.

She looked past them to see Tink turn to face them. "At last!" she said, reaching for Tink to help her through the hole. But then she saw Tink's face.

Tears were coursing down her cheeks as Tink took one heavy step after another. "Run! I can't stop this!"

Hope's heart fell. Tink was still fighting off the effects of the compulsion, but she was losing.

Hope spun around. "Galen, let's go!"

They ran down the stairs ahead of Tink, swiftly followed by the oncoming swarm of giant spiders. One leaped onto her departing back and bit her shoulder.

She shrieked and threw it off her, yelling at Galen. "Are they venomous?"

"How would I know? I'm not a spider expert!" he yelled back, as they landed at the bottom and splashed through the now flooded floor.

They ran down the narrow aisle filled with cages, sloshing through puddles and scattering the few remaining animals, who fled in terror before them, making a beeline out the open shop door.

Galen followed them, but before Hope could reach the pack's gruesome remains, a hand grabbed the back of her jacket and brought her up short.

She struggled out of the jacket and leaped forward, but Tink side-stepped and put herself between Hope and the door – blocking off the only viable exit.

Tink stood still a moment, a grimace belying her internal struggle. But she slowly stomped towards Hope, backing her up towards the shattered remnants of the wooden table.

She stepped into the stream of water, that was still fountaining from above, and paused. The shock of the cold made her stop and blink.

It gave Hope an idea.

"Get on the countertop!" she yelled at Galen and climbed onto the table's shattered remains.

"What? Why?" he yelled, but he was doing it!

Tink paused, breathing heavily. Her hands fisted so tight that Hope could see a tiny rivulet of blood joining the water, running from where her fingernails had dug into her palm.

Beyond her, the swarm of spiders rolled towards them in a dirty brown wave, pouring off the edge of the mezzanine and dropping to the floor below with tiny splashes.

Leaning forward, Hope drew on the magic that'd been building in her. She only hoped it would be enough for what she wanted to do.

The shard of wooden tabletop wobbled, teetering and threatening to over-balance, tipping her into a sea of water and soggy spiders. But she kicked a leg out behind her to hold her balance; watching Tink, who pulled her head up and took one more step towards her.

Hope thrust her hand down into the puddle and unleashed all her pent-up magic through the taser matrix.

It rushed through the water and surged up Tink's legs.

Tink fell to the ground, her body rigid.

It continued outward, in a growing ring, washing over the spiders like a wave. Each one it touched contracted, pulling its legs into its body, then going still.

Searing pain backwashed over Hope and she collapsed, her arm seizing up and her thoughts going fuzzy. She fell into the water and the shock of cold made her gasp and shiver.

A splash and Galen was running.

Tink lay still.

Galen held his pole cocked and ready to swing, but she showed no signs of getting up. Instead, he swung it at the remaining few spiders that dropped from the mezzanine. The taser pulse had knocked most of their kind out, and they lay crumpled like huge, misfolded paperclips in the water. The rest were swiftly dispatched.

Hope was cold and in pain. Between the spider bites and the

backlash, she was feeling very unwell. Her breath was freezing and coming quick. Her heartbeat, rapid and irregular, rushed through her ears.

Am I dying? Is this what the spider poison does? How long will it take for the venom to reach my heart?

Galen rushed to her side. "Hope! Are you okay?" He ran his hands lightly over her body, checking for damage.

"Spider bite!" she squeaked, in between rapid breaths. "I feel like I'm passing out!"

"Calm your breathing." He checked the bite she'd indicated.

"Can't," she whimpered. "Think I'm dying!"

"You're not dying," came a loud voice behind them.

"What would you know?" Galen yelled back at him in a panic.

"They're tarantulas," Dominic replied. "They're not venomous. Their bite can hurt, but it won't kill you."

Galen looked stunned. Then he smiled at her.

"Mr Green," she panted, "makes things deadly!"

Galen cradled her face between his hands. "I think it's going to be okay." His voice was much calmer than Hope expected.

"I'm not okay!" she squeaked and tears ran down her face. Her hands were numb and tingly, and she fumbled, trying to wipe away the tears.

My hands aren't even working properly any more! Is this paralysis setting in? Everything's going dark!

Galen took her in his arms and held her close, breathing deep and slow. "It's going to be okay," he murmured in her ear. He held her against his chest, his warmth radiating into her.

Gradually, her breaths slowed down. She felt way less woozy now, and sensation returned to her fingers. She put her arms around him and pressed her face into his chest.

"Are you good?" he asked her.

"I think so." She looked up at him, a little ashamed. "A panic attack, yes?"

He nodded, and she looked away.

Then her eyes widened. "Shit! Tink!"

Galen released her, and she hopped down off the tabletop and splashed over to Tink.

Tink was lying in the puddle, struggling to calm her own breath but looking very much alive – and furious.

"Are you yourself?" Hope asked her.

"I fucking hope so!" She pushed her hands underneath herself. "I'm gonna strangle that arsehole!"

"We've got bigger problems!" Galen yelled, pointing up at the rafters.

Both Tink and Hope looked up to where the most massive snake Hope had ever laid eyes on was, even now, uncoiling to stretch down towards them.

Tink stood up and yelled at it, "Come and get me!"

It hissed and slithered along the full length of the central beam, lying stretched out far above them.

"It's an anaconda!" Dominic yelled in shock. "Watch out, they crush their prey."

"I can cope with strong muscles," Tink replied, looking up at the massive beast.

The anaconda hissed and struck towards Tink. She grabbed for it, but it retreated out of reach, its head swaying back and forth.

"That's not normal!" Dominic shouted, clearly frightened.

"It's had cobra fangs added to it!" Hope yelled to Tink. "Be careful of its bite, this one *is* venomous."

"Huh?" Tink looked back at her, and the snake struck again. She ducked sideways, but she was slow, still getting used to commanding her own body movements again. When it zipped around and struck from the other side, it caught her, grabbing her by the neck, and lifting her off the ground.

She shrieked and grabbed it around the neck, pulling at it.

Galen ran over and tried to hit it with his pole, but it was too far out of reach. He ran for the stairs.

The anaconda coiled itself tightly around Tink's body, lifting her higher into the rafters. Her legs kicked viciously at its body and it hissed in pain, releasing her neck and wrapping her in its body again and again.

Tink wriggled, trapped within the enveloping mass. She pushed at the coils with her arms and legs but struggled to get leverage on its slick sides.

The snake spun her upside down, and she got her legs free. She braced them against the beam and pushed. The beam groaned in protest and the great snake spasmed, coiling more tightly.

She pushed outward with her arms, her steel muscles creaking. She pushed harder, yelling in pain and effort.

Hope heard some awful tearing sounds, but Tink had finally shifted one of the coils. As she pulled one arm free, its head struck at her once again.

She plunged her arm deep into its throat as it buried its fangs into her arm. It tried to draw its head back, but was caught fast by its own fangs.

"I've got you now!" Tink screamed at it, spittle flying from her mouth. She shoved her arm deeper into the snake's maw. She pushed her legs harder into the beam, which creaked and groaned under the twisting weight and her powerful thrust.

Every loop of its body began releasing, unwinding and wriggling in spasms of pain and fear as it realised it was choking on Tink's massive tree trunk of an arm.

Hope could see its mouth biting and biting, great gobs of venom dropping onto her arm.

Tink shrieked in pain. Her body went rigid, shoving her arms and legs harder. Her arm twisted deep inside, then she grabbed hold of something. She tore her arm free of the beast, tearing out vital innards as she went.

The snake spasmed one last time, spewing blood instead of venom. It came loose all at once, slipping off the beam. It plunged to the floor, with Tink still tangled in its coils.

She kicked and wriggled but couldn't free herself in time.

Hope shrieked in fear and heard a sickening crunch as Tink landed head first on the cold concrete floor, several coils of loose, snaky body landing on top of her.

Hope ran for Tink.

"Bring the potion!" she shouted, pulling limbs free of the muscled ropes, hoping to find Tink still conscious underneath. She saw the limbs spasm, then fall still.

"No, no!" she yelled as Tink's face became visible, her eyes sightlessly staring into the void, frothy spittle dripping from her mouth.

Her neck was mottled with bruises and bent at an unnatural angle. But the worst part was her chest – some part of her augmentation must have broken loose and had torn out of her, opening her chest up from the inside.

Hope grabbed at Galen. "The potion. Can we still use the potion?"

Galen examined Tink gently, but then he sat back on his heels and looked at Hope, his eyes full of sorrow. "It's too much." He shook his head.

"But it worked for you!" She fumbled around Tink's chest, trying to find a decent place to start the CPR. But how did you do CPR when you could stare right into the chest cavity and see her heart torn to shreds?

He put a hand on her back. "There's too much damage to heal. We can't keep her alive long enough for the chest wound to knit together."

"No!" she sobbed, but she could see that it was true. Tink had died so quickly. So irreversibly.

Hope drew in a deep breath, then let it out. Then she pushed the feelings down inside, swatted away her tears, and reached forward to close Tink's eyes. "At least she died fighting. Valiant to the last breath."

Galen nodded.

She brushed Tink's blonde hair from her face, then sat back to look up at the mess of the surrounding room. "We can't just leave her here. We don't know how long she'll be lying around." She swiped at her tears.

"She's too heavy for either of us to carry."

She stared at Tink desolately. It was true. They had to leave her in the frigid water, floating with dirt and worse from the cages, and surrounded by dead and dying spiders. "She doesn't deserve this."

"We'll come back for her afterwards."

Hope glared. She stood and turned to the mezzanine level. "Time to find Mr Green." Her voice was full of quiet rage.

38 - Dealing with Mr Green

The sentinel still barred the way into the final workshop. When Galen looked in at it from their side, it spun its head and its red eyes zeroed in on him. But true to what it had told Mr Green, it didn't go after him, only stood there, looking.

It ignored Hope when she popped her hideaway-covered head around the corner.

Back inside the first workshop, she and Galen shared a Look. Then he nodded at her and slipped away. She watched him disappear out the shop's open door.

He was gone. She was on her own now.

Looking back through the hole, she saw again that a small corner of the banister was between her and the sentinel. It wasn't much, but enough for her to squeeze around to the steps without being in full-view.

The sentinel's eyes stayed fixed on the spot where it'd seen Galen. She breathed a sigh of relief. That was one foe she did not want to tangle with alone.

Morty lay slumped on the ground at the bottom of the stairs. Still breathing, at least – either fast asleep or passed out. Either way, he didn't look like he'd be a problem any time soon.

She touched the lump of the neural clamp in her pocket, confirming it was still secure.

On the far side of the mezzanine, the other hole gave a partly obstructed view of the banister leading down the stairs inside the far workshop. As long as she stayed down, she'd remain out of Mr Green's view, assuming he was on the floor below. She just had to get past the sentinel.

A wave of sadness washed over her as she remembered Tink

fearlessly charging in only a few minutes earlier. She wasn't exactly friends with Tink, and there was unresolved business they never got to clear up, but she hadn't deserved to die like that.

Hope selfishly wished Tink were still around to stand by her side, no matter that it had been a somewhat uneasy alliance. But no use dwelling on the impossible.

She crept down to the floor and slunk around the now abandoned tables.

She had to get herself up and behind that sentinel, and didn't think that walking right towards it on the mezzanine would go as unnoticed as her slinking around the corners. If its sight worked the same as humans', then as long as she wasn't in direct view, she'd get by.

Thankfully, the doors on the wall of body fridges weren't flush with each other. The gaps between them would serve almost as well as a ladder. She climbed them, hanging off their handles and hoping they were strong enough to hold the doors closed against her weight. She slowed her breath and calmed herself. Any sound might give her away.

Holding her breath, she climbed up and over the railing, coming over and hugging the wall beside the sentinel. She had to hope that its peripheral vision was oblique enough to give her hideaway the boost it needed.

The sentinel maintained its steady gaze. It stood as still as a giant wall of steel, but nothing more.

Up close like this, she realised it was giving off a faint hum that reminded her of a fridge. She struggled to suppress an incongruous giggle.

Its upper body filled the hole from side to side, but its legs, while solid, were narrower. Her only option was the thirty-centimetre gap between its ankles. She reckoned she could get through it if she was careful… and it didn't move.

Hope squeezed herself down as tight as she could.

Please don't move and crush me!

She took a slow and quiet breath, then shimmied through the gap into the room beyond. It didn't move a metal muscle.

As she pulled her feet through, she heard a noise from above. She froze, looking up, her heart racing. It was looking down between its legs.

Had it seen her?

She held her breath.

After a moment, it lifted its head back up to the hole in the far wall and she allowed herself a quiet exhale.

She crawled along this new mezzanine to give herself some distance, before looking out over the scene beyond. This time around, she had time to get a better look at everything.

Unlike the previous two workshops, this one was open to the sky and was flooded with natural light. Much of its roof and back wall were missing, and she looked right up to the dish in place on the roof. It was angled towards the horizon, directly into the burgeoning sunset. The three planets in their familiar, bright triangle were difficult to see without a great deal of squinting against the blazing brightness of the setting sun. Even the disc of the moon was almost invisible, but she knew it was close.

All the pieces were rolling into place.

She turned her gaze away and looked around the room. The remaining walls were covered in sprawling rune flows. Nothing so elegant as Galen's tight bindings – these were large and disparate, painted and re-painted many times. They covered every surface, including up the wall she was standing beside.

The floor was littered with piles of broken and empty cages, bloody sheets, and other detritus cast aside from next door's chimeric work. Strung haphazardly over the mess were multiple snaking cables, all connecting the disparate conjuration matrices to a central tangle falling down from the great collector above. One large bundle led towards a raised central stage that held a giant structure made of wheels and cogs and glistening steel. At its top was something like a large, inverted glass bowl, now full of roiling green energy that pulsed and grew in intensity with every passing second. Attached to this, by more wires, was Mr Green's glistening copper helmet. Unlike the mess surrounding it, this whole assembly had been cleaned and polished to a glittering sheen.

And there, in the middle of the steel structure, was Mr Green, tinkering and calibrating, adding a dash of clear oil from a tiny can and polishing it off again, lightly turning a cog or adjusting a dial.

Flowing out across the dais were the set of runes she recognised as his control matrix. Most of the trailing cables connected to this and led off towards the other rune flows on the walls. Most of those flows were still dark, waiting for sufficient power to activate. But the central runes were already faintly glowing a radiant blue.

She couldn't spot the dream steel from this angle, but now she was close enough to feel it as a soft hiss and swirl in the back of her mind – a lurch in the bottom of her stomach – a sensation that was distinct from the heavy pressure of the device below.

It was above her.

Hope crept further along the remains of the upper walkway. Ahead, a rickety ladder was lashed from the banister of the mezzanine up onto the roof. She crawled up to it, looking upwards until she could see straight into the dish of the reflector. It was right there.

She kept her eyes away from the dream steel by force of will alone. If she let herself be drawn in by that distraction, she'd be lost to it and miss her chance to do anything. However, she noted where it was, for later.

Mr Green had secured the dream steel into the focus of the parabolic reflector. The power of the Conjunction would hit that reflector and direct it all straight into the dream steel, where it would be amplified a thousand-fold and would then pour down the cables, feeding the control flow laid out below, out into the surrounding conjuration flows and then back into whatever contraption he'd built on that dais.

Even now she felt the weight of magic building. The totality hadn't begun yet, but a portion of the transmuted solar wind was already making its way through space towards them. And yet it was still only a bare minimum compared with what was to happen next. The rising crescendo would begin in earnest the moment the moon's disc swept in front of the sun. All that solar energy pouring full-power into the lunar matrices – headed their way. That energy raised her hackles, both figuratively and literally.

She slunk back along the mezzanine, snuck past the sentinel, and made her way down the stairs. The buzzing grew worse as she crept ever closer to the glowing control matrix and that strange, pulsating glass globe.

Mr Green had finished with whatever adjustments he'd been making and was now grinning up at the slowly approaching eclipse through a solar viewing lens. He lifted the wire-covered helmet off the large device and set it upon his head. He fiddled with the straps under his chin, adjusting them to fit, and tipping his head back and forth to ensure the helmet wasn't slipping.

Hope crept forward, holding the neural clamp loose and ready. She edged past the piles of cages, inch by inch, keeping some of the detritus between her and him, until she could go no further. The last space was the empty dais, wide and clear of everything but painted runes and cabling snaking across the floor. She had no hope of remaining unspotted if she crossed it. If she wanted to clamp him unawares, she had to wait until he was focused elsewhere. Right now he was puttering around too much to miss the sudden appearance of a new person, and she was wary of the holster she'd spotted strapped to his hip.

If she missed him, he would try to fight her off. She was a wiry woman. He was a large man, and he only had to get one hand free. She'd rather the odds were more in her favour.

She needed a distraction.

It was Galen's turn.

She readied herself.

As the moment stretched on, she listened for any sound of his approach. The moon silently slid ever closer to the sun.

Off in the distance, a crackle and pop drew her attention, and that of Mr Green. But she recognised them for what they were – early fireworks, set off too soon.

Mr Green shook his head and returned to his duties, and Hope sat back on her heels to wait a bit longer.

Then she heard it. The rev of the engine, the building roar as it approached.

Mr Green looked up, suspicious, as the noise grew louder. His eyes widened.

There was a screeching *CRASH* as the truck smashed rear-first into the roller door, caving in the bottom half. It ploughed inward for a few metres; the metal shrieking in protest and spinning away in shards, then came to a crunching halt on a pile of discarded crates.

Frozen in shock, his jaw open, Mr Green watched Galen clamber out, unharmed but looking a little knocked about.

Mr Green turned on him in a rage. "You again! You won't stop me now – it's too late. It's already begun!" He waved at the machine behind him. Its whirling green had increased in intensity. "In just a moment, you'll see how well I've done my work – and I won't let you take my success away from me!"

Behind him, the moon had almost touched the edge of the sun, and energy was already racing down those cables into the blazing matrices around him.

Hope used his distraction to creep forward, coming up behind him.

But he spun his gaze around the room, and she was forced to drop back again.

"What you're doing is dangerous!" Galen yelled, waving his arms to keep Mr Green's attention. "Don't you know it'll affect everyone around you? Not just your twisted pets."

Mr Green put his hands on his hips. "I'm counting on it! Especially a particular wedding party nearby."

Galen looked shocked. "You already know? Do you know that the resonance of this quantity of dream steel could affect the entire city?"

It was Mr Green's turn to look surprised, casting his gaze up towards the dream steel. Then he grinned. "Really? Well, won't that be a bonus!" He flicked a switch on his helmet, setting off the diffuser that began spraying green mist.

Hope held her breath. The matrix around her neck should hold the air bubble a few minutes more, but she had no idea exactly how much longer.

Galen, likewise, flinched, but he lifted the metal pole he'd brought with him and approached warily, keeping Mr Green's attention.

Hope readied herself to move.

"I know that your partner is here too!" Mr Green began glancing around, trying to spot her.

She ducked back behind a pile of empty packing crates.

"I can feel her mind here somewhere."

Hope's eyes went wide. He was already sensing their minds? The effects of that device must already be spooling up. She felt the weight of his mind pushing against her defences, hunting for her, trying to grab hold of her.

But he hadn't spotted her yet, even if he knew she was here. She crept forward again while he had his head turned away. There was no more time to wait. She had to get close enough to him to throw the clamp around his neck.

Galen strode forward, holding his length of pole over his shoulder like a batter, ready to strike.

"Stay there!" Mr Green grimaced, facing Galen. "Why aren't you obeying me?"

Galen grinned in response.

Mr Green adjusted the green-mist sprayer, making it spew more of the choking clouds.

Hope readied herself for a last burst. The full strength of the Conjunction was arriving. The weight of Mr Green's mind control leaned down, heavier and heavier. Soon, he'd be able to command them without resorting to the soporific mist.

Galen nodded once, then leaped forward, swinging for Mr Green.

She leaped as well, timing her jump for just after Galen's arrival.

Galen swung his pole, hard.

Mr Green ducked, spinning as the pipe swung over his head. He was grabbing at his holster.

Hope leaped forward and jammed the clamp roughly around his neck as a gunshot rang out.

She flinched at the ear-splitting noise and let go of the clamp for a split second.

Mr Green slumped in her hands. As he slipped out of her grasp, the clamp unfastened itself, dropping to the floor with a clang.

Beyond him, Galen was falling too, his face white with shock.

"Guh!" he grunted.

Hope yelped and leaped forward. She put her hands on him and pushed hard as the blood oozed from his stomach. "Don't die on me again!" she yelled.

Mr Green was stirring beside her, but she ignored him.

"I'm okay! I'm not dying just yet, but I wish people would stop shooting me. Get back to him!"

Hope breathed a sigh of relief, ready to turn back. But her in-breath drew an acrid smell into her nostrils. Then her body went rigid.

What was happening?

She let go of Galen, and the blood oozed out of his stomach once more.

They both stood, Galen groaning in pain. They turned to face Mr Green, his face twisted with rage.

Galen was breathing in short, sharp breaths beside her, and she heard the steady drip, drip of blood hitting the floor unimpeded.

He was already low on blood. How much more could he stand to lose?

But she couldn't help. She was powerless!

"Yes! Finally, enough power to get through to your pathetic little minds." Mr Green waved the gun in the air as he gesticulated. "I've had enough of you two meddling fools. Can't you see what I'm trying to create here? I'm trying to build a better world for humanity, free of the need for labouring, and you two just keep getting in my way. Well, no more! You two have hounded me for too long – I can't let you hold me back any longer!"

Hope fought desperately, grappling with whatever was holding her mind at a standstill, to free herself once more. But the grip on her mind was iron clad. Her mental fingers were scrabbling against it. Her will kept slipping away from her, but she had to keep trying!

"You, doctor. You will kill your annoying girlfriend. Hit her with your pole."

Hope's heart pounded in shock.

No! Not this!

Galen whimpered, and she saw the mental struggle conveyed in his contorted muscles, but he obediently lifted the pole in his hand.

He choked out, "No!" as he swung the pole at her.

It struck a glancing blow on her shoulder.

She was free for one glorious moment and she wrenched herself to the side – enough to avoid the second backhand strike that swiftly followed.

Mr Green's hold bore down on her once again.

As the movement pulled his stomach, Galen gasped in pain. He dropped the pole to the ground, kicking it away.

"Stay still and die, you wench!" Mr Green yelled at her. "Here, clamp your girlfriend and try again." He leaned down to pick up the neural clamp and thrust it at Galen.

It banged into Galen's stomach. His eyes glazed with pain, and he hunched forward, only to stop short again and stretch up to full height.

Pain! That seemed to clarify her mind. But only for a second – not long enough! And with every passing second, she felt his control gaining in strength.

Galen lifted the clamp. If he got it around her neck, she'd be out cold, and then Mr Green would make him kill her. She needed more time, a longer period of freedom, but the strength of his control only grew.

Galen stood in front of her now, the clamp held out towards her. His face was twisted with the effort of fighting, his teeth gritted. She saw in his eyes how hard he was trying to throw off the command. He, too, knew what was coming.

Mr Green stood over them. He was laughing as the clamp's glittering runes moved inexorably towards her neck.

Fighting with every ounce of her will, she lifted her hands a few centimetres in front of her – but it wasn't enough. She couldn't make them push the clamp away.

She took a deep breath and dug her fingernails into her hands. It bought her the space to lift her hands up to touch the clamp, but the pain receded. She held on to herself for only a second before the strength in her hands slipped away, the clamp relentlessly closing in. Her limp, powerless fingers touched the cold steel, unresisting as it zeroed in on her neck.

Mr Green laughed even harder at her moment of disobedience – at her submission.

Galen took one more step forwards. And she let him.

She would stand there and let him kill her, too. There was nothing she could do about it. She fought with every ounce of her strength, but it wasn't enough. She was too small, too powerless.

Looking at the gleaming metal of the clamp, she knew it would seal her mind and then her demise…

…and then she saw what she had to do.

She looked into Galen's anguished eyes, trying to convey a message of hope.

She bit down on her tongue, hard, and in her split second of control, her fingers reached for the clamp once more, scraping at it with her fingernails.

Mr Green gasped in surprise, but then laughed in delight as his control reasserted itself with a final, heavy weight.

Her hands dropped away. She would not slip past his control again.

Galen stepped forward one final time, and the clamp fastened around her neck. He flicked the latch closed with a click.

Hope collapsed to the floor, her mind reeling.

Mr Green laughed in delight.

She couldn't see Galen but could feel hot, wet drops on her skin. Whether they were tears or blood, she did not know.

"Right. Now doctor, take this gun." He held it out to Galen, and for just a moment he looked away from her.

She surged to her feet.

He spun around in surprise, trying to bring the weapon back to bear on her, but Galen had already taken hold of the gun, as per his instructions. And he wasn't letting go.

Hope whipped her body around as fast as she could, and slammed the end of Galen's pole up into the back of Mr Green's helmet, which was conveniently positioned directly above her.

Something broke and magical feedback rolled through the thing like a wave, rippling outwards across the whole room.

Mr Green's eyes rolled up into his head and he fell, convulsing, to the floor.

Galen collapsed beside her and she once more jumped to his side and pushed down on the river of blood that'd been flowing out of him.

"What happened?" he croaked.

She smiled. "Destroyed a flow-control rune you'd added to the clamp. It must've reversed it. A neural clamp is just another form of mind control, after all. It gave me a bit more wiggle room to fight off his compulsion."

Galen opened his mouth to reply, but the machine beside them exploded outward, showering them with detritus.

Hope crouched over Galen as the sentinel stalked towards them, one arm full of the central glassy part of the machine, still whirling with green energy.

The robot had leaped down from the mezzanine level, into the heart of the machine. It stood looming over the cowering pair and assessing the room, its glowing eyes fixed upon Mr Green's unconscious form.

"Subject is incapacitated," it boomed.

"Commence retrieval," came a tinny voice from within it.

"Acknowledged," the sentinel boomed in reply. It reached down and grabbed Mr Green's limp form in its other arm.

His eyes shot open, and he squirmed and squawked in protest, "Unhand me, you stupid metal oaf!"

He was roundly ignored.

The sentinel spun around, facing Hope and Galen, and levelled a shoulder gun at the pair.

Hope froze in terror. Whoever was commanding the robot now *did* have the authority to access offensive capabilities.

Galen held up a fragile hand, leaning over and putting his body between Hope and the sentinel. That wouldn't make any difference, but she appreciated the intent.

"Shall I neutralise the intruders?" the sentinel boomed.

There was a pause, after which the tinny voice responded, "Not at this time. Retreat to safety with the subject."

"Acknowledged."

The gun retracted with a click.

The automaton leaped down off the dais and disappeared through the gaping hole in the roller door.

Hope let out a breath that might have been a sob.

"What the hell was *that*?" came a voice from above them.

She spun. It was the mortician! "That doesn't matter right now. Can you help Galen?"

He made his way down the stairs. "Who are you? What happened here?"

"All excellent questions and I swear I'll answer them after this crisis is over, but my friend is hurt. Will you help?"

"All right." He nodded and picked his way across the floor to join them.

"I can diagnose myself," Galen squawked, in protest at his rough examination. However, his movements were becoming slow, and his face was disturbingly grey again. He'd already lost so much blood, and a healing potion could only do so much.

"We can take him to the hospital," Hope said as she helped the mortician fold up a semi-clean sheet to use as padding to push against Galen's stomach.

Galen's attention was fixed on Hope. "Please! My brother!" He looked over her shoulder, then slumped in fatigue.

Looking in that direction, she saw the sun's light was fading rapidly as the totality approached. The magic was still pouring down the cables, but half of the surrounding matrices were dark, now that the ruined machine had disrupted the control flows.

There wasn't much time to get the dream steel to Galen's matrix, but she had to try. "Can you keep him stable for a few minutes?" she asked the mortician.

Looking perplexed, he nodded. "Where are you going? We still need to get him to a hospital!"

Hope ran for the truck. "There's something I have to do first!"

39 - Caius

Hope ran upstairs, heading for the ladder and the dream steel. She spared a glance above her, squinting up through the hole in the roof to see the moon was already taking a large bite into the sun's glowing disc. It was a thick crescent now, a huge Cheshire-Cat-like grin, slowly thinning.

Soon, the last rays would shine like a diamond ring, and then would be the totality.

She had no time!

How could she get this dream steel extracted, carted downstairs, and reseated into the new matrix in time?

It wouldn't work!

She couldn't fail this!

Then she paused. She took a deep breath and allowed herself the space to think.

It didn't have to be reseated. She just needed the power to get to Galen's matrix, and the cables were right over there. But they weren't within reach of the truck. She needed to bring it closer.

Running for the cab, she was absurdly grateful to find that Galen had left the keys in the ignition and the engine idling.

She hopped in and revved it. She only needed to back it up a few metres, but there were huge piles of broken masonry, remnants of the roller doors, and scattered parts from the destroyed machine in between. She revved the engine again and rolled forward a little. Then she jammed it in reverse and shoved her foot hard on the pedal. With a squeal of tyres, the truck lurched backwards and rammed its way over and through the piles of flotsam.

She heard the gurney bouncing around inside and hoped the tyres wouldn't burst and that the complex matrices painted inside would still be intact when she was done.

The engine whined as she climbed the hill of detritus.

Then it stalled.

Thankfully, she'd already crested the hill, and it rolled *towards* the dais, not away. The truck slid backwards until it thumped up against the raised edge and came to a sudden halt. It was sitting at a jaunty angle, but it was there.

That's it. That was as close as she'd get it. She had to hope it was close enough.

She leaped out and ran back around. The matrix in the truck was about a metre from the tangle of cables spilling down to the control-flow column. The cables were glowing with energy, and little crackles lit up the surrounding air. Nearby runes glowed faintly from the overflow, even though they were disconnected from the main control channels. The Conjunction's energy had fed into the dream steel in torrents. With nowhere left for the energy to go, it built and built. The weight of it pressed against her mind like the ceiling of an unstable cave, waiting to fall and crush her.

Galen's parabolic mirror had broken, but the central receptor was still intact, and that would be enough.

She grabbed hold of the receiver embedded in the mirror's focal point and activated her magic. A small vestige of her own magic trickled through into Galen's control matrix – not enough to power the full array, but enough to wake up the starter flows. She felt them sitting there, waiting for more power, waiting for her to do what she needed to do next.

Then she paused.

This next part was going to hurt. A lot.

She gritted her teeth and grabbed hold of the control column. The energy that had built up in the dream steel cascaded into her in a raging deluge. The swelling chaos flooded her mind with power and she struggled to hold on to it – to direct it through her body and into the receiver.

She pushed the first trickle of energy into the truck, and the central control flow grabbed hold of it. That's when it bit down. It drew the magic from her, sucking it out like a hungry babe at the teat – drinking it in as fast as she could channel it. The torrent roared through her like a tidal wave, like a thundering waterfall, like nothing she'd ever experienced before.

Something inside her swelled and pulled tight, like a balloon, filling and stretching beyond her ability to hold it all. She felt the moment it went *POP* – like a membrane giving way. Her mind was floating loose, tumbling around without her control as the power raged within her.

There was yelling nearby, but her ears couldn't process the noise into words. She struggled to keep a grip on her sense of self, her sanity – anything at all. There was nothing but the magic flowing through her. Her mind was slipping, but her body was rigid, taut with the strain.

Inside, her grip was shredding, her mental fingers loosening their hold, and beyond that, she realised that she sensed... something. Several somethings. Other minds around her, faint, growing in strength, full of surprise, joy, fear, hope.

Her own mind was fading. Her personal magic reserves had been low before, but now they were guttering, as was her consciousness.

Hold on!

A voice in her head cut through the noise. Was it her own voice? She didn't know, but it didn't feel like it.

Stay focused!

Nope, definitely not her.

It gave her something to grasp – a branch to hang onto, to resist the pull of the riptide, the downward suck of the raging magic filling her, flowing through her, pulling her under.

She held on.

She'd been holding on for an eternity.

How much longer?

Just a little more!

The voice was calm, reassuring.

And she could feel it! The torrent, still turbid, had reduced its flow. No longer a tidal wave, but an undertow. Then a strong ocean current. It ebbed. The current became a river, now just a stream, and finally, a distant, leaking trickle.

As it receded, she felt herself deflating like an overstretched balloon, discarded and tangled in reeds by the side of a floodplain.

Gasping in relief, she sank to the floor. She let herself rest and revel in the sensation. It had drained everything from her, leaving her so empty she had no energy left to open her eyes.

She was sinking.

But a noise above her made her curious.

She drew a long, slow breath and pulled the pieces of herself back together, like gathering up the shredded remains of a tattered curtain.

She pulled her eyes open to see a face peering down at her – a familiar one.

"Galen?" she rasped, her throat torn and bloody. Had she been screaming? She hadn't noticed.

Galen blinked. He was a welcome sight. But wasn't he on the floor, hurt?

Speaking of hurt, her body was insisting on sending her a message, one that hadn't been able to get through before, but was now becoming harder to ignore.

Her hands! Her arms! They ached, they screamed, they were on fire!

She bit back a scream, managing a slow, drawn-out groan instead. Her torn throat was just as painful.

Galen had moved away but returned holding a small vial – the last healing potion!

He pressed it to her lips.

It took an effort to suppress her need to moan against the pain and drink down the liquid.

Cool, healing magic washed over her and through her, bringing blessed relief to her poor burnt arms. Galen's familiar magic was washing away the pain.

Her head cleared a little, enough to look more carefully at Galen.

But it wasn't Galen. The hair, the way he held himself.

It was the other one!

It had worked!

He stood there, looking at her curiously.

But that meant… "Galen!"

The brother shook his head, pointing at himself.

Struggling to lift herself off the ground, she pointed behind him. "No, not you. He's hurt. Go! Help Galen!"

The man looked at her, shocked. Then he screwed up his face in a snarl and moved out of her view.

All she could do was lie there, resting, panting, listening to shuffling sounds and a few scattered words being uttered in a raspy voice.

Eventually, she gathered enough energy to roll over, and she looked.

She saw Galen, still collapsed on the floor where she'd left him, with his brother and the mortician standing over him.

As she watched, Galen's eyes fluttered open. It was only brief, but she saw the moment he spotted his brother. His face lit up with a delighted smile. He looked over at Hope, still smiling, and mouthed,

"Thank you." Then he closed his eyes and drifted away into a well-deserved slumber.

Galen's brother smiled and returned to fussing over his sibling's wound. Having found some bandages, he was binding a heavy pad around Galen's stomach, and the mortician was holding it in place.

However, neither of the men was the source of the noises she'd heard. She looked around in surprise. There was a small group of people standing nearby and looking bewildered.

"Hello?" one rasped, his voice dry and croaky. "Where are we?"

The mortician looked up at them, and his face was a study of emotion – confusion, followed by fear, mixed with curiosity. "You!" he stammered, pointing at the man.

The man looked over at him. "Who are you?"

"Hah. I worked on you yesterday!" The mortician's voice was full of awe.

"Worked on me?" The man frowned in confusion.

The mortician's mouth worked soundlessly for a moment. "Your funeral's tomorrow." A mix of awe and fear coloured his voice. He turned to another man. "And you're Bob – the pet guy from next door! I watched one of Mr Green's monsters kill you a week ago. That horrid little cobra-thing bit you, and you died!" He turned to Hope. "How is this possible?"

Hope's heart filled with dread.

Crap. Galen's brother wasn't the only one – the matrix had revived all the other bodies in the morgue!

A wild hope bloomed as she looked over the small collection of people.

Searching...

Yes!

There was Tink, standing at the back, her neck still mottled with bruises and disturbingly misshapen, but her chest was closed.

The mortician's eyes were flicking from person to person in growing horror. "How did this happen?"

"It must've been a side effect of the magic mixing," she croaked, improvising what she hoped would be a plausible lie. "Galen's matrix was intended for resuscitation of his brother, who was alive but frozen in stasis. Mr Green's was about animating the hybrid animals. The mixture must've done... this." She waved her hand at the people.

The mortician was thoughtful but nodded along as though it all made sense. "This is dangerous magic. If the Imperium finds out... If they think we did it on purpose, we'll all be killed. They might even kill us if they think we did it by accident."

Hope raised an eyebrow. "Well, I won't tell them if you won't."

He looked at all the people milling around. "What do we do with them? They can't stay here. This place will be crawling with Imperium before long."

She looked up in surprise, and then she heard it.

The low *thwup thwup thwup* in the distance.

She didn't know whether they were coming here, but it was likely. They would've sensed that torrent of half-wild magic across the entire city. Typical that they finally sent out a unit to investigate, now it was all over.

She looked at the re-animated people around her. Some of them were naked and sporting clearly visible Y-shaped scars. "Do you have anything for these people to cover up with? Some spare clothes?"

The mortician shook his head. "There's some spare sheets in the cupboard. But that won't deter the officers for long."

"It'll do for now." She turned to the others. "Go on. Get covered up and then come back."

The naked people snapped out of their fugue state and began climbing the staircase to the other workshop.

Galen's brother looked up at her. "I've done what I can for now. Looks like I gave you the only healing potion – I didn't know it was the last one."

She nodded. "He said he couldn't have it. He's already taken one today."

The brother frowned. "Then he'll need a hospital soon, in order to safely recover."

Hope dragged herself upright by hanging on to the back of the truck. "Okay, can you drive? I mean, are you well enough to?"

He thought about it a moment and nodded.

"All right, you take the truck, then. Get him to the hospital. I'll leave some other way."

He nodded again and eyed her up in a strangely familiar way. It reminded Hope of how Galen weighed her with his eyes.

"I can't lift him yet. I'm still too weak."

Hope looked around. "Tink?"

Tink hadn't left with the others, being already clothed. She looked a little dazed but looked up at the call of her name.

"Tink, help him lift Galen into the truck."

Tink blinked, and screwed her face up in a resentful frown, but she went to help.

Hope turned to Galen's brother. "Tell me. What's your name?"

He glared at her. "Caius."

She raised her eyebrows. He'd clearly woken up on the wrong side of the casket. Couldn't blame him, though. It'd been a bit of an ordeal – for all of them. Still, no time for social niceties right now. The airship engines were headed their way.

"All right, Caius. We need to get these people out of here, for all our sakes. Can you take them all in the truck and stash them at Galen's hospital? Keep them safe until we have time to figure out how to help them?"

Caius huffed in response, but he nodded. He hopped up into the bed of the truck and helped Tink settle Galen securely on the gurney.

Afterwards, Tink hopped out and pushed the truck back down the pile of rubble, onto flatter ground.

Hope turned to the small crowd returning from the staircase. "You guys go with Caius; he'll keep you safe until we can figure out how to help you find your own lives again, okay?"

There were confused scowls all around, but they obediently climbed up and settled in next to Galen.

She took one last look at the unconscious Galen before Caius closed up the back door, and implored him, "keep them safe."

He eyed her, nodded one final time and headed for the cab, without a goodbye.

As the truck moved away, the mortician breathed a sigh of relief. He idly kicked at the pile of remaining detritus. "Right!" he said with false cheer. "So, what are we gonna tell the cops?"

Hope looked out the broken windows at the incoming airship. It was nearly here.

"The truth. Just leave out the last five minutes."

40- Not so little anymore

The incoming aircraft was not just a patrol ship, it was a fully decked-out warship. Hope stepped out through the remains of the roller door to watch its final approach.

She was amused to watch the remaining lounging thugs first come to attention, then turn into a mad scramble, scattering party supplies. They disappeared rapidly, fading into the surrounding buildings like tiny reef fish fleeing the shadow of an approaching shark.

The ship's heavy engines throbbed deep within her soul. The sound struck fear into the hearts of any small-time crook born under Imperium rule, and she hastily checked whether there was anything they could book her with, despite knowing, rationally, she hadn't done anything illegal – at least this time.

She strode forward into the carpark and stood in full view as the airship made its final approach. The crew threw down heavy sandbags to serve as makeshift anchors and tethers for the zip lines.

Half-a-dozen black-clad folks, sporting heavy weaponry, zipped down to ground level. Hope raised her hands in the air and stood still as they fanned out and checked the surrounding landscape.

They approached her cautiously.

"Stay where you are, and keep your hands where I can see them," one yelled at her.

She raised an eyebrow and flicked her eyes to her already raised hands and back again. But she kept her mouth shut. No use getting snarky with the folks holding guns.

The man approached and stood near her while his colleagues filed past. "Ma'am, can you tell us what we'll find inside?" he asked her. His words were clipped and careful, professional mode on.

"Mostly just a big mess and some dead animals. You got here after it was all over."

He nodded, ignoring the minor dig, and angled his weapon away.

"Oh! There's a guy shackled up in the pet shop. He didn't want us to set him free."

The man looked back at her in surprise.

"I think he's been rendered harmless, but he might still be under a compulsion to attack intruders. He's unarmed."

The man nodded and pulled out his radio. "Possible hostile, unarmed and last seen shackled in the pet store. Proceed with caution."

"It's not his fault. He was under duress. Please be gentle with him – he's going to need a therapist, not a cell."

"Acknowledged," he responded, and relayed something in a cryptic police code through the radio. He turned back to her. "All right. Can you please identify yourself, ma'am?"

"Hope Gray, amateur practitioner. I'm the one who warned you this would all happen," she gestured to the building behind her, "and then dealt with it for you." She paused a moment. "You're welcome."

That elicited an eyebrow raise. He relayed the new data, nodding at the reply. "Do you have any ID on you?"

"In my front pocket." She pointed but made no move to reach inside it.

He gestured at her to take the ID card out, and she carefully reached in and retrieved it for him.

Behind him, a portable passenger lift slid down the ropes, lowering a small team of lab techs with their equipment and Detective Grant. The techs filed past her into the building, and the detective joined the officer beside her.

"Thanks Brady; I can take it from here."

The officer nodded at him, returned Hope's ID to her, and went to join his mates in the workshop.

"Ms Gray, can you step over here and chat while we let the team do its job?"

Hope followed the detective across the car park. "Good to see you eventually got your arse in gear," she said with a smirk. She felt safe enough sassing the detective now the guns were no longer trained on her.

He rounded on her with flashing eyes, but checked himself when he spotted her smile. "Yes, well." He gestured vaguely around him. "We've been a bit busy over the past hour."

Looking out over the city, for the first time since the Conjunction had begun; she saw that more than a few small fires were sending pillars of smoke into the air and plenty of Imperium airships were busy rushing across the sky.

"We've had our hands full, and some communication wires have gotten crossed. I didn't even get wind of your incident report till after we'd left the station."

"So, how did you find us?"

"We got a tip-off from a high-profile source – including a detailed report about how a certain Robert Green had allegedly pulled off the recent bank robbery and was allegedly preparing a potential city-altering incident. The source also provided us with a tracking signifier. I'm surprised it led us right here, though."

Hope raised her eyebrows, then scowled. Reaching into her jacket, she pulled out a heavy white card that was embossed with the letter H. "Is this the target you're tracking?" She handed it over to him.

The other man raised an eyebrow. "Could be."

"Bloody Henry," she muttered. He probably thought this was *helping* her. She shook her head. No, he'd probably sent them after her because there was a chance she'd fail and he wanted to cover his bases. Well, he wasn't wrong.

Detective Grant listened to something on his radio that elicited a scowl. Then he drew himself up and faced her. "I have to ask you, do you know the present whereabouts of Mr Robert Green? Is he hiding in the facility?"

She shook her head. "No – he was here for the action, but one of the university sentinels he'd stolen whisked him out of there, just as the totality started. I didn't see which way they went."

Detective Grant looked surprised when she mentioned the sentinel, but then crestfallen when she revealed his suspect had absconded. He began making rapid notes into a hand-held notebook.

Hope waited for a few moments, watching him. "So... am I under arrest or something?"

He looked up suddenly, as though surprised she was still there. "Not at all, ma'am. Mr Purcell is talking. He's informed us that Mr Green had been holding him prisoner... and how you rescued him, before confronting Mr Green. He's on record claiming that Mr Green's the individual who's allegedly responsible for the chimera attacks, having stolen his matrices."

"Mr Purcell?"

"Mr Green's lab partner. The man shackled in the pet shop?"

"Oh. Dominic!"

"Yes, he says he's quite grateful for all your help, you and your friends." He paused. "You wouldn't happen to know where *they* are at present, would you?"

"Why? Are they in trouble too?" She eyed him up.

"No. In fact, I was hoping to inform Dr Moore that all charges against him have been dropped, pending completion of our investigations here."

"I'll pass that along next time I see him."

"Yes, right. You do that."

She raised her eyebrows again.

He waited, evidently hoping she'd add something more, but she kept her mouth shut.

He eventually went on. "So, why did you put your report in at the front desk? Why didn't you get in touch with me directly? I gave you my card, and you knew I was already interested."

"Are you kidding? Your office was dead keen on stitching up my friend for the job instead of going after the real party. Doesn't exactly encourage folks to be forthcoming."

He nodded. "Fair enough. I'll keep that in mind for the next time we meet."

Hope raised an eyebrow. "Next time?"

"You think I didn't look you up in the system?" He had a smirk of his own.

Hope went cold. She pressed her lips together until they went white.

"Just because we haven't managed to pin anything on you doesn't mean you haven't come to our notice from time to time." The detective was looking serious. "You're firmly on my radar now."

She scowled and looked away. "Just perfect."

"Well, it's not all bad. You did good work here, Ms Gray, even if you had to take things into your own hands. Stay on my good side and we won't have a problem. But from now on, leave the policing to us?"

Hope raised an eyebrow and a smirk. "Do the policing next time and I won't have to."

One of the lab techs called out to the detective by name.

He held up a finger, indicating to wait a moment. He presented Hope with a new business card. "Call me directly next time, okay?"

"I hope there won't be a next time," she replied, scowling at the card.

"Even so." The detective smiled. "This one doesn't have a tracker in it, in case you're wondering. No need to 'lose' it this time."

She raised an eyebrow again, but he just smiled and slipped away to rejoin his colleagues.

Hope watched from a distance as the police began the clean-up operation. It was a big mess, but thankfully not her problem any more.

Instead, she needed to get back to the palace to check in on her family, then decide what to do about Galen, and all of his new zombies.

Perhaps she could just leave them all to his new brother. He and Galen would get along just fine without her.

That was probably for the best. Galen hadn't reacted well when she'd suggested they should talk some more. She should just take that hint and leave well enough alone.

She frowned. It was a pity, but that's the way it went sometimes.

Still, it wouldn't hurt to check in on him at some point, to make sure he was recovering okay – she owed him that much, at least; plus, there was Sam's arm to organise.

She glanced at the workshops one more time. The setting sun had turned the sky into a riot of colour, staining the buildings red. The police swarmed around the workshops, like a school of fish cleaning the meat off a newly made corpse. She didn't envy them the clean-up job, but she'd done her bit and now it was time for them to do theirs. She had her own part to play.

She smiled to herself and turned to head out. As she snuck away to rejoin her family, she held her hand against her jacket to stop the heavy weight of the dream steel within it from banging against her thigh.

Epilogue

Robert Green woke up some time later.

It was dark, and he didn't know how long he'd been out. The room was chilly and lit with a single, green glow that he realised he recognised.

He sat up. The sight of the familiar glass contraption, full to the brim with pulsating green swirls, filled his heart with joy.

He stumbled over random items in the dark in his excitement to check the device; and only felt better when he came to touch the faint, nearly invisible runes inscribed onto the glass.

More than anything, this was the culmination of his life's work, and he didn't begrudge a few tears as they slipped loose and ran down his cheeks.

It was here. It was safe. It was complete!

Despite everything…

A noise!

The door opened and brightness blinded him.

He spun, hissing, and covering his eyes from the painful light coming from everywhere.

Two pairs of footsteps entered the room, one heavy, the other light.

He scowled through squinting eyes. "Who's there?"

"Who do you think?"

"Oh, hi. Well, thanks for getting me out of there; I was…"

"Did the process complete?" the voice cut him off. "Is it working, or was it all an enormous waste of my time, energy, and investment dollars?"

"It finished." He gazed into the swirling green depths of the globe.

"Are you certain, or are you just guessing?"

"I wouldn't guess about this! This is my life's work – my greatest creation! You can see it's full of energy. It was all still in place when the totality commenced. And I felt it take hold of the minds of the unfortunates who tried to take it away from me, before they..."

"They succeeded in their efforts?" sneered the voice.

"Yes. Well." He huffed. "Well, it's safe now."

"No thanks to you. You jeopardised it all, using this tech for your own purposes; wasting your time copying Dominic's work and killing people at random. It was because of your sloppiness that the Imperium got involved, and we don't need that kind of scrutiny! And I hear you went flitting around the city on some kind of personal vendetta."

"But they were going to..."

"I don't care what you think they were going to do. I certainly didn't put all this money into your project for you to waste your time this way. You should've been on site doing the work I paid for instead of wasting it on your personal issues."

"I got it done, didn't I?"

The voice went silent a moment. "Barely. Your work is sloppy, your attention to detail sloppier. However, I suppose you came through in the end."

"Excellent. Then I'm free to move on to the next stage of my plan." He smiled and reached for the device.

"*Your* plan?"

He froze at the icy tone. "Well, yes. I need to use it on my fiancée. I did mention that was why I was doing this, didn't I?"

"That was not part of the original agreement."

"But... you knew I wanted it for this. I won't need it for long, and it's not as if using it will interfere with your own plans. You still have to..."

"That was *not* part of the agreement." The voice was heavy with finality.

"In that case, I'm making a new agreement!" He leaped for the globe.

Heavy footsteps.

A hand grabbed his neck from behind... hard... yanking him back. His fingers brushed the shiny globe. It wobbled briefly, then settled back into place.

"Let go of me!" he screeched as he reached up and grabbed hold of the cold metal hand. An irritable comeback died on his lips as another hand reached around and grabbed him by the throat and squeezed.

"I don't appreciate it when somebody reneges on an agreement," the voice behind him said lightly. "But at least it makes my choice of the next step very easy to decide."

Robert kicked feebly, and he scrabbled at the iron grip.

"Goodbye, Robert."

The light footsteps left the room while Robert's life hung in the balance.

A few moments later, his lifeless body hit the floor, and the heavy footsteps left the way they came in.

The beautiful green light played over his skin, like dappled sunlight on rippling water.

But there was no one alive left to see it.

Glossary

arbiter (profession) — a person who adjudicates matters of law.

augmentation — a magically imbued prosthetic device.

augmented — a person with *augmentations.*

automaton — an autonomous or semi-autonomous mechanical device, often partly powered by magic.

chimera (pl: chimerae) — a hybrid animal created by taking and joining parts of other animals into a single creature. Requires ongoing magical support to maintain the health of the resulting beast.

conjuration — a "spell", usually requiring a combination of a written *matrix* and some verbal components.

control matrix (AKA control flow) — the central, controlling *rune flow* of a *matrix* that directs the flow of magic through the rest of the *matrix*.

Customs and Excise — Governmental department in charge of collecting taxes on goods imported and/or manufactured.

dream steel — a valuable magical material used as a filter for some kinds of *workings*. It dramatically amplifies certain kinds of magical energies.

drone-slavers — drone-slavery is one of those ancient traditions much frowned upon, but too essential to discard. If you find yourself in too much debt, you can work it off by selling yourself into drone-slavery for a time. Of course, rumours persist of people being kidnapped and sold to drone-slavers illegally.

hideaway — a magical *working* that imbues the practitioner with a field of semi-invisibility - making them harder to detect by the eyes of living beings.

Imperium — the system of government of this nation, also used to refer to the armed forces, both internal and external.

matrix — a written set of runes for a *conjuration*, usually written in silver-inked calligraphy.

necromancy — a forbidden branch of *thaumaturgy* in which a *practitioner* attempts to raise and command the dead

practitioner — a person with magical abilities that actually uses them.

rune flow — a sub-set of connected runes in a *matrix*, usually with a specific purpose.

scientician — a scientist that studies one of the many branches of *thaumaturgy*.

sky docks — docks for zeppelins.

spell-scribe (profession) — a person who makes their living copying matrices for other practitioners. Requires no actual magic ability, but a deft hand with a pen.

starter flows — a set of initial *rune flows* in the *control matrix* that act as a boot-process to wake up the rest of the *conjuration*.

tinker (profession) — a magical mechanic - whose specialty could be in *automatons* or *augmentation*.

thaumaturgy — the research field encompassing all the branches of magic, both applied and theoretical.

werelight — a tiny spark of raw magic, which glows at the level of a lit candle.

working — a *conjuration* put together for a specific purpose, to be invoked at a particular time. Often used interchangeably with *conjuration*, but technically a sub-set thereof.

When a favour comes due, horror awaits beyond the wall. Will she risk everything to save the innocent?

The Conjunction left Hope owing Henry one last favour, and it's time to collect. She's headed across the wall into the war-torn coastal zone after a missing shipment. But there's a floating-city on the horizon making the roving military patrols jumpy.

When her mission goes south the only way out might be right through the Dead Zone. And is Galen somehow involved? He's been ignoring her ever since the Conjunction. Will he help her escape?

Stay tuned to read the next action-packed adventure for Hope and Galen.

taryneastwrites.com/books/king-tide

Be the first to know when I have a new book coming out by signing up for my monthly newsletter. No spam, just updates on what I'm doing, sneak peeks for upcoming releases and other special content.

taryneastwrites.com/newsletter-subscribe